D

Once more with feeling

Emma Lever

Thorogood Publishing Ltd
10-12 Rivington Street
London EC2A 3DU
Telephone: 020 7749 4748
Fax: 020 7729 6110
Email: info@thorogoodpublishing.co.uk
Web: www.thorogoodpublishing.co.uk

A CIP catalogue record for this book is available from the British Library.

ISBN 978-185418364-4

Cover and book designed and typeset by Falconbury

Printed in the UK by Ashford Colour Press

Once more with feeling

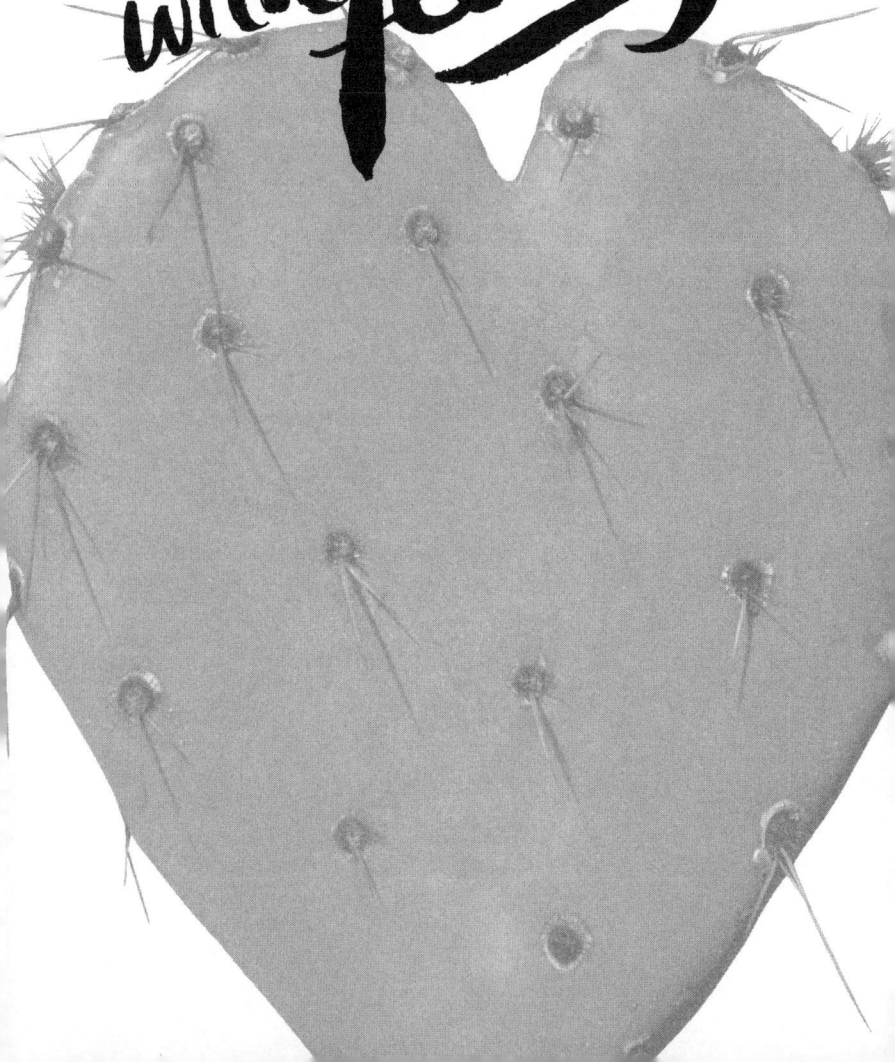

For Liberty & H

In memory of Emma Waddell
1968 – 2006

Chapter 1

Beca took a drag on her cigarette and looked at her watch. It was three o'clock near enough. Discounting the time she would spend asleep that night, there were just another 16 hours of this self-imposed child immersion therapy to survive. From her hiding place she could see the glass of wine she'd left behind. It was turning syrupy warm and undrinkable in the summer sun.

These were strange times indeed. They had to be, for why else was she spending the weekend in the countryside with a passel of kids? Her plan had called for nothing less than total exposure to the wiles and vagaries of her friends' children. This was the last challenge, the final test which would, if she survived, shape the rest of her life. This weekend was the shit-or-get-off-the-pot finale to what had become an all-consuming obsession: to have a baby, or not.

Abi, Sally and Claire, her closest friends, were on the terrace knotted together at one end of the long table which was now a post-lunch bombsite. Sally was the centre of the group, or more specifically her new baby was and Beca couldn't keep her eyes off the bald, mewling child.

The pro-baby camp that had pitched its colours somewhere near her heart wanted to be there with them lapping up every word, but she had been dismissed with a request from Claire 'to be a poppet' and entertain the children. After all, what possible interest could she have in a new born baby? None. Evidently the other two had agreed because neither had jumped up to stop her, which was why she found herself hiding behind a bush playing hide and bloody seek with their off-spring. Boring, but nonetheless a crucial part of the therapy. Much more time spent with this whiny, unfathomable bunch and she'd be cured; she could send her hormones packing and get on with her very child-free life.

Beca's eyes kept wandering back to the tiny bundle in Sally's arms as time and again the now familiar visceral urges kept overruling her well-educated brain. Looking at the baby was as compulsive, and annoying, as reading and re-reading adverts on the Tube. She didn't want to do it, but she couldn't stop herself. Why not though? She wasn't interested in babies any more than she was in cheap international phone rates. She couldn't be, it was so out of character, and it was important to keep reminding herself of that fact. If she could get her hands on her drink, she'd be fine. A whole bottle would be better still, maybe then the frightening mumsy feelings would go away.

'Fifteen, sixteen, seventeen.' Harriet, Claire's eldest, rolled each syllable around in her mouth like a multi-layered gob-stopper before spitting it out and trying another. The other children began to wander off before she had even reached twenty. Dulcie skipped away wafting the petal-shaped skirt on her fairy dress while the boys beat the long grass with sticks sending clouds of seed and chaff into the air.

While this baby obsession had been wreaking havoc with her ordered life, Beca had not remained idle. Ever the pro-active completer, she'd drawn up a business plan, along with mission statement, conception strategy and long-term schedule and budget. It was all worked out, in the ghastly event that she decided to go ahead. Or was that joyful? It rather depended on which part of her rapidly emerging split-personality had the floor. God, she needed that wine.

'Fiffffftty.' Peals of laughter and screams erupted as the children charged off towards the orchard, in exactly the wrong direction. Beca darted out from the bush, stuck two fingers in her mouth and whistled.

'Hey! That's cheating,' Abi shouted. 'Get back.' The children hadn't noticed anyway.

Beca was close enough to see the smile on Abi's face. She also noticed the full glass of wine in her hand, so at least she wasn't going to die of thirst any time soon. Beca watched as Abi rejoined the other two still cooing over the baby. What were they talking about now? Why did she care so much? Something had gone dreadfully wrong. A year ago she would have had no interest in the mind-numbing details of swaddling a baby. The dummy, good or bad debate would have left her yawning. And as for the taxing issue of weaning, she hadn't cared, at all.

'Here darling,' she heard Claire say as Sally breastfed her baby in an old rattan chair. 'You've got to keep your milk supply up. It's *sans gas* of course. Have to be careful of those bubbles. You do know that bubbles give babies the most frightful wind, don't you?' Sally's trance had been broken. She looked up and pushing a straw-coloured lock from her face she smiled.

Bloody Claire. Thick-set bossy Claire. From school friend to mother, she had always had an unerring ability to transform her loudly delivered opinion into bona fide fact. Still, it was worth remembering about those bubbles.

'If there's anything you'd like to know. Anything you're not sure about, you will ask won't you,' Claire continued.

'I've got to admit it's all a bit of a shock,' Beca heard Sally say.

'Don't worry, that's just your hormones. Are you still bleeding?' Claire asked.

Sally nodded and reddened slightly.

'Course you are,' Claire continued. 'It's only, what, three weeks? I always bleed for ages after labour.'

Yes, being a bloody drama queen you would. Beca was still cross at being cold-shouldered by her friends. It was all very well sweeping Sally and her baby into their collective embrace, but hadn't it occurred to Claire or Abi that she might want to join in? No, of course not. She'd done a very good life-time's job of being entirely uninterested in breeding. Sally held her baby up on her chest and began to pat her back. As Beca watched, the gooey, light-headed feeling swept over her again.

'Here we go,' she said and waited for the cloying, candy-floss pink moment to pass.

'Who are you talking to?'

Abi's appearance made Beca jump. 'No one, nothing. I'm just driving myself insane. Where did you come from?'

'Thought I'd keep you company. Claire's doing her perfect mother routine. Here,' she added proffering a glass of wine.

'Thank God.' Beca guzzled. 'I heard her.'

'Are you alright?' Abi asked folding her arms across her chest.

'Never better.' Aside from the full-on war raging within.

'You look anxious.' Her best friend had a better-in-than-out look on her face, but then she always had been alarmingly in touch with her feelings. It was tempting to blurt it all out; to share the news that hard-nosed, career girl Beca had finally seen the light. Then again, perhaps it would be better to wait awhile; she might have gone off the whole idea by tomorrow. Who was she kidding?

'What's wrong?' Abi asked when she got no answer.

'Nothing.'

'Trouble at work?'

'Exactly.' Beca drank her wine. 'Sally's baby is lovely, isn't she?' she said testing the water.

The look of surprise on Abi's face was as predictable as it was easy to read.

'I can't imagine why they named her after a cat,' Beca continued. 'Tabitha? How daft is that?'

'Don't be so heartless. It's sweet.'

'If she had a tail.'

Off in the distance Beca could hear Harriet and the others shouting out for her. She leant against the springy branches of the rhododendron and looked at Abi. 'Tell me something, why am I never included?'

'In what?'

'In the conversations you three have all the time about children and baby stuff.' Beca was aware she sounded peevish, but she was never going to attain Abi's level of maturity so what was the point of trying?

'You always look so bored.'

'People change,' Beca muttered into her glass. 'It would be nice to join in, sometimes.'

Abi smiled and put an arm around her waist. 'Come on. I think Claire's working up to a theory on vaginal tears.'

Beca halted in her tracks. 'Perhaps I could show the kids how to blow up frogs.'

'No, no. I insist. It will be educational.' Abi's arm tightened around her and together they strolled back towards the old Norfolk manor house.

As they reached the terrace, Beca saw Eddie coming out through the French windows, pretending to swing a cricket bat. Tom and Dan followed him into the sunshine. The men were looking rather downcast.

Abi laughed at them. 'That'll be England all out then.'

'Narrow escape,' Beca said, playfully pulling away from Abi's grasp.

'What? You think the presence of men will stop Claire?'

'Is it my imagination or as soon as you have a baby, your body and every nasty thing that happens to it becomes the subject of open debate?'

'Absolutely. You must be pleased to have sworn off breeding.'

'That was the plan,' Beca mumbled to herself.

'Where were you?' demanded Harriet as Beca and Abi returned to the table. 'We looked for you everywhere.'

'I evaporated in a puff of smoke. Now, off. Leave me alone.' Beca pulled her sunglasses down from her forehead and sitting back in a chair closed her eyes.

'But – '

'Go and play with Claire. I heard your mother say she was going to let you cut her hair.'

Eddie finished playing air cricket with a great flourish and flung himself down into the chair next to her. Beca had always found it alarming that he and Claire looked so alike. In-breeding amongst the minor aristocracy, most likely. A theory which did much to explain why, although lovely people, they were incredibly dim. It was one of those gender iniquities that while both were broad-in-the-beam, Eddie was cuddly like great uncle Percy's teddy bear, while Claire looked like she'd been let out of her harness after dragging a plough all day.

'So how's work?' he asked.

Beca sighed. 'Great. Just marvellous. Nothing more pleasurable than a chat about work at the weekend.'

Eddie guffawed. 'Any tips? Pointers? You know, what's going up and down?'

'Strictly speaking telling you could land me in jail. But seeing as it's you.' She gave him a cheesy thumbs-up and watched as he went off to play aeroplanes with his two sons.

Tom sniffed extravagantly as a means, she supposed, of catching her attention. She obliged him with an arched eyebrow. 'Hay fever?' she asked.

He looked away, sneering perceptibly. Odious man. What did Abi see in him? It was such a waste. Beca studied his haughty profile until Tabitha's screaming broke in on her uncharitable musings.

'Here, let me.' Claire swooped in and scooped the baby up in her arms. As an unfamiliar hand started pounding her on the back she howled even more. Sally flushed but didn't protest. Her delicate thoroughbred sensibilities didn't stand a chance up against Claire's draught horse.

Abi muttered darkly.

'What?' Beca needed enlightenment.

'She's got to let Sally do it herself. They can't bond if every time Tabitha squawks Claire steals her away.'

Beca was impressed at the importance Abi attached to a bit of winding. 'Claire, why don't you give Sally her baby back? You're interfering.'

'What would you know?' Claire asked.

'Absolutely nothing,' Beca replied with mock contrition. 'But any idiot, even a childless one, can see you're not helping.'

'Give Tabitha back,' Eddie said. 'You've got three of your own.'

'I'm only trying to help.' Claire's mouth shaped up like a cat's arse. The child was duly restored to her mother and immediately fell silent.

Sally beamed with delight. 'I'd best go and change her nappy. Perhaps that's what's bothering her.' She bent down to retrieve the elephant print nappy bag.

'Can I come?' Damn, how had that slipped out? Beca tried to brave the astonished looks with a toothy laugh. None of her friends were decent enough to play along so she snatched up the change bag, swung it over her shoulder and strutted nonchalantly into the house with Sally and Tabitha following in her wake.

The astonishing news that the children needed feeding again so soon after lunch was further ammunition for the no-baby camp. Beca found herself in Claire's kitchen blunting a bread knife on a breeze-block sized loaf. She was using the table rather than the worktop because it was lower and she hoped the extra weight she could apply would help in the task. The knife was as ancient as the kitchen and Beca's game of pretending to be Ruby from *Upstairs, Downstairs* had worn off half a loaf ago.

'Sally looks amazing,' she said to Dan through gritted teeth. He was busy jockeying fish fingers around a vast cast-iron frying pan.

'Doesn't she. Look,' he said taking the knife away from her. 'If you hack at it like that it's bound to end up in pieces.'

'Bloody home-made bread.'

'I heard that.' Claire was laying the table with an assortment of brightly coloured plates and cups emblazoned with the latest must-have children's characters.

'There. Done,' Dan said with satisfaction. 'Now, if you butter them first before you cut the crusts off it's easier.'

'How do you know all this stuff? You've only been a father for three weeks.'

He shrugged. 'Spend any time in the kitchen and you'll learn. Claire's kids aren't slow in letting you know what they want. Oscar told me this morning he and Charlie like theirs cut into soldiers while Harriet insists on triangles.'

'You couldn't have a word with Tom, could you?' Abi blew a wisp of hair out of her eyes as she sorted out spoons and forks. 'He seems to think parental responsibility ends after the moment of conception.'

'Let's face it. If you'd wanted Modern Man you shouldn't have got hitched to that entirely unreconstructed chauvinist,' Beca said. 'He's a 1950s throwback. Does Dulcie have any specific bread pattern preferences?'

'She eats it as it comes, but if someone else gets the Barbie plate there'll be hysterics,' Abi replied.

A pack of pit ponies thundered down the stairs. All conversation stopped until they were seated around the kitchen table and the business of getting food into hungry mouths brought the decibel levels down.

'So, got a new man in your sights?' Dan grinned over his shoulder as he started on the washing up.

Beca grabbed a tea towel off the front of the Aga and twisting it into a tight cord she flicked the back of his legs. 'It's unusual for you to be so interested in my s-e-x life.'

'She said "sex",' Harriet pounced. 'S-e-x spells sex. That's a naughty word isn't it, mummy?'

'Where did you learn that?' Claire was aghast.

'Sex, sex, sex.' Oscar jumped down from his chair and ran around the room. 'Sex, sex, sex.'

'He's stupid. He doesn't even know what sex is,' Harriet stated with big sister superiority.

Claire for once was speechless.

'What's sex, mummy?' Dulcie asked through a mouthful of fish fingers.

'It's nothing to worry about,' Abi replied.

'Why's it nothing, mummy?'

'I'd better see how Sally's doing,' Dan said drying his hands on his chinos.

'And I've got a nicotine habit to feed.'

Beca breezed out into the hall, past the line of wellington boots and old dog baskets and out into the beckoning sunshine of late afternoon. She could smell cigar smoke coming from the terrace and giving Tom and Eddie a wide berth she crossed the lawn, went through the door in the old garden wall and escaped into the orchard. The sun was beginning to go down, but it was still warm and the air felt balmy and comforting. Beca found a secluded spot under a peach tree and sat down, squashing the long grass around her into a springy blanket. She pulled a flattened cigarette packet out of the waistband of her Capri pants. Tabitha's pink polka-dot socks were wedged on top. She spread them out on her thigh, then pulled them over her fingers like puppets. She sniffed them and instantly that gooey, squidgy feeling smothered her again. Oh dear God, it was ludicrous, insane. She didn't want a baby. Didn't, didn't, didn't. Having one would destroy her body, not to mention her career. She did not want a baby. Beca pulled hard on her cigarette as if the habit of smoking somehow proved her point.

What was the use of pretending? Fags or not, she wanted a child of her own. She wanted one so much that her throat tightened just at the thought that she might not. This had to stop. She shook her head, furious at the unseemly urges that kept attacking her from within. So much for her clever idea of spending the weekend immersed in the triviality of babydom. By Sunday night she was supposed to run screaming towards the nearest sterilisation clinic. Not even Tabitha's shitty arse had put her off. It looked so sweet when pooey. She was envious of Sally's engorged breasts. For Christ's sake, she even wanted to sit on a valley cushion and complain about her stitches, although she wasn't entirely sure what the cushion or the stitches involved. She had it bad; really very bad indeed.

For months she had done everything she could think of to talk herself out of this ridiculous predicament, but her hormones were raising the victory flag over her beleaguered body. Assisted by every television commercial and fly-on-the-wall baby documentary, they had won. It was Cave Mothers 1, Beca Morley 0. With a bitter laugh Beca finally admitted defeat and surrendered. The pro-baby camp had done it. She would have a baby. And why not? She'd spent enough time and money researching the subject, and surely it had to be less effort than this continuous tussle with her feelings. But if she could barely explain why she felt so strongly about it to herself, how the hell was she going to tell the others?

She took a last drag on her cigarette and waited for retaliation from her brain; a stroke perhaps. Nothing happened. Feeling peculiarly at ease with herself she adeptly flicked her cigarette butt away with a thumb nail and watched it smoulder on the dry ground. Knowing Claire and Eddie would take a dim view of her burning the place down she jumped up and ground it carefully out, and then spat on it to be sure.

A sense of calm after the storm had settled on the sitting room. With the children bedded down, their parents had at last collapsed into the dog hair-covered sofas. A full supper sat heavily in their stomachs and there was little thought of doing anything more than stretching out and waiting for the digestive juices to start working.

Beca sat on her own, her legs flung over the arm of a chair whose only sign of former glory was the square of bright chrysanthemum print that had for generations been protected by an antimacassar. One of Eddie's cocker spaniels rested his head on Beca's thigh, his soft brown eyes pleading to be stroked. She gave his ear a scratch and before she knew it the dog had leaped up and settled awkwardly on her lap. She was grateful for the company. It was only in the evenings when the couples reconnected with some simple gesture of affection that Beca felt self-consciously single. The rest of the time she delighted in her single status. She knew her friends loved her as much as she loved them, with the obvious exception of Tom, but naturally they loved their partners more. It was a different kind of love, one Beca had little experience of. It placed the recipient way up there beyond the others. She watched as Eddie topped up Claire's glass before filling anyone else's. Tom rubbed Abi's feet as she stretched out her legs across his lap, and Dan and Sally gazed at each other and their daughter, silently congratulating themselves on their brilliance. Beca was resolutely commitment-free, but even she could appreciate that on occasions a smelly dog made a poor substitute.

'I say, Beca. There's something different about you. Can't put my finger on it. It's been bothering me all day. Have you done something to your hair?'

'Very observant of you, Eddie. I've had it cut.'

'Knew it was something like that. You look like that actress, Aubrey someone.'

'Audrey Hepburn?' Abi offered.

'She looks like a boy,' Tom said.

Eddie chuckled. 'Not with those tits she doesn't.'

'I don't think it's appropriate to talk about another woman's breasts,' Claire said in a huff. 'Even Beca's.'

'You don't mind do you? You're one of the lads. God you haven't gone all lesbo on us, have you? That would be a turn up.'

'Oh do shut up, Eddie,' Abi said.

Beca's mind was elsewhere. 'Can I hold her?' she asked, cutting the conversation dead.

It took a moment for Sally to realise Beca was talking to her. She looked up and smiled. 'Of course.'

Ignoring the silence she had created, Beca squeezed onto the sofa and took Tabitha in her arms. The sleeping baby fretted in her inexperienced grasp, but settled once she was nestled against Beca's chest. The warmth of her tiny body passed through the layers of clothes between them. Beca cradled her head in her hand, kissed her soft downy hair and breathed in her sweet babyish smell.

'She's perfect,' Beca choked.

Sally beamed with pride.

Oh Christ. Beca coughed to clear the lump in her throat. 'I'd so much like to have my own.'

'Own what?'

'Baby. I've decided to have one,' she confided in a whisper.

'Have?' Sally asked.

For God's sake. 'A baby. I'm going to have a baby.' How obtuse could the woman be?

'You're not pregnant are you?' Abi asked with alarm.

'No. Not yet.'

'Aren't what?' Claire demanded.

'Beca's going to have a baby.' Sally leant over to fill her in.

'Good show.' Eddie toasted her with his glass. 'All women should have babies. Keeps them happy.'

'You don't do us blokes any favours,' Dan said.

Eddie shrugged. 'It's what Claire says.'

'I hadn't meant to tell you yet, but there we go,' Beca said. 'I've been thinking about it for months.'

'I suppose even cats make good mothers.' Tom was such a bastard.

Claire howled with laughter. Sally joined in and Abi made no attempt to hold back. Tabitha woke up and began to cry as Beca's body tensed up. The child was swiftly reclaimed by her mother. Beca returned to her own chair and sent her awaiting companion scurrying away to his basket with just one glare. She was furious at her friends' reaction. Had she said something absurdly funny? She hadn't reckoned the idea of becoming a mother would provoke such uncontrolled mirth.

'Precisely what is so bloody hilarious about me having a child?'

'It's just not one of your core competencies.' How nice that Tom found it all so amusing.

'What?' Sally asked.

'It's not something she's very good at,' Dan translated.

'Really, it's not that funny,' Abi said. 'But you've always disliked them.'

'So did you once.' Beca turned a packet of cigarettes over in her hands.

'I know, but we were much younger then.'

'Well? It's just taken me a bit longer to come around to the idea.' She was desperate for a fag.

'You're the most baby-phobic woman I've ever come across.' Tom made no attempt to cover his amusement.

Beca looked at him with loathing. 'Piss off, Tom.'

'I'm sorry, I don't want to sound rude, but you're just not the sort.' Claire's tone reminded her of a snippy French teacher they'd had at school.

Beca pressed back in her chair. 'What sort?' she asked. 'I'm a woman, I've got all the right bits. Assuming they're working I could easily have a child.' Anger made her voice quaver.

'Yes, but you're not the sort to be a mother, not a good one anyway.' Claire's words trailed off and hung heavily in the silence.

Beca was crushed. Her eyes prickled with tears. She hadn't cried for years. Not even the most outrageously rude bastard at the bank could make her cry. She gritted her teeth.

'At last, something Beca's not good at.' Tom raised a glass to her.

'Shut up,' Abi snapped. 'That's a terrible thing to say,' she said turning on Claire. Eddie exchanged an anxious glance with Dan and in unison they got up and left. Tom held out until a collective glare drove him from the room.

'I didn't mean it like that exactly,' Claire said. 'It's just she's so focussed on her career.'

'And that's a crime?' Beca wished she'd kept her stupid mouth shut about wanting a baby.

'You've said so yourself,' Claire said ignoring her.

'I absolutely have not,' Abi replied.

'So I'm selfish?'

'No, of course not. But it would involve a lot of changes. I'm sure you'd be a very good mother, it's just,' Abi tried to find the right words.

'You don't have the nurturing instinct.' Claire triumphantly folded her arms across her ample chest as if to emphasise her point.

Sally gasped and held Tabitha closer.

'Bullshit. Outrageous bullshit,' Abi said. 'She's brilliant with Dulcie and Billy. You didn't mind her running around after your lot today.'

'But that's completely different. She only sees them occasionally. I'm not trying to be horrid, but I don't think she has the first idea about motherhood.'

'I think it's a lovely idea,' Sally chipped in.

'Well you would. Your hormones are still all over the place.' Claire's firm put down had Sally in retreat.

Beca sat and watched them arguing, their faces red and shiny with too much wine and heated debate. It hardly seemed to matter if she was there in the room with them or not. Abi and Claire battled it out as they always had, with Sally quivering on the sidelines unsure which way the argument would turn. It was like being back at school again, except now they weren't shouting about boyfriends and copies of *Blue Jeans*, but her life. She was in serious danger of crying.

'I had no idea you had such a low opinion of me.'

'We don't.' Abi squeezed herself into Beca's chair and put an arm around her.

'Then why is it open season? My feelings are no less important than yours. I'm always there for you lot. I do my damnedest to be a good friend, which isn't always easy considering what massive pains in the arse you are. You're right, I never have wanted babies, but I've changed my mind. People do.

It happens from time to time. I thought you might be pleased for me.'

The others looked at her sheepishly.

'I'm not as robust as you all seem to think. Just because I don't work in some clappy-happy, touchy-feely, care-in-the-community, hugs-before-bedtime job, doesn't mean I'm an insensitive, heartless bitch.'

Claire looked contrite. 'I'm sure if you want a baby you'll make a good mother, after your own fashion. But forgive me for pointing out the obvious. Don't you need a husband first?'

'Me and Dan aren't married,' Sally said.

'Yes, but that's different.' Claire rolled her eyes with exasperation. 'Beca doesn't even have a boyfriend.'

It was so galling when the screaming bloody obvious was presented as brilliant insight.

'I'm not a complete idiot,' Beca replied with scorn. 'This isn't some flash-in-the-pan idea, I've been planning for months. Believe me, the lack of a boyfriend is a minor detail.' Strictly speaking that wasn't entirely true but she was in no mood to share such news with her friends. Instead, she got up and left the room without bothering to say goodnight. Of course there was a plan. She had a rolling schedule based on six potential conception dates worked out. What remained to be decided was precisely who was going to do the honours. A tricky one to resolve considering her track record with men.

Chapter 2

'**W**hat bit of "Sell the stock," did you not understand?' Beca glared at the hapless trader standing in front of her desk. She didn't need this hassle first thing Monday morning, not on top of the six tortuous hours it had taken to get back from Norfolk the night before. Besides, there were more pressing concerns weighing down on her, like choosing a man to father her child. The trader looked nervous, which was never going to be attractive in her eyes. His neck had gone red, particularly the pimply bit where he shaved, and when he swallowed hard the flesh wobbled and chafed against his collar. Was this pathetic specimen of manhood a likely candidate? She scoffed at the thought and made a mental note to rule out all the men at work.

'Spare me the excuses.' Beca leant across her desk towards him. 'If you can't do your job, get out of here, because I'm not having some half-witted arsehole like you screwing up my bonus. Get it?' The trader nodded. 'Good, now fuck off.' He tried again to defend himself but Beca dismissed him with a flick of her hand.

She sat back in her over-sized, black leather chair and smiled ruefully. One bollocking and the week had only just begun. Perhaps she had been a little harsh, but she needed to vent her rage after the weekend's abuse from her friends. She was going to be a brilliant mother and anyone who didn't agree could just sod off.

She chewed a fraying cuticle and looked out at the vast expanse of trading floor spread out before her. It was slick chrome and black. Banks of computer screens divided the room into rows and within each row were men – and it was mainly men – pacing around in a heightened state. It looked like a modern day lunatic asylum with the inmates gesticulating wildly to themselves, some laughing, some shouting, each engaged in heated, urgent global business. Many of the traders barked into hands-free telephone headsets, thus leaving both arms to drum their message home. Others preferred the old-fashioned version and so looked doubly strange with one shoulder hunched high to keep the receiver close to their ear. Millions of pounds were being traded by these lunatics and it made Beca laugh to think that she was one of the turnkeys.

There were three computer screens built into her desk and with eyebrows fused in concentration she stared at the middle screen. She hit a button on her telephone. 'Liz. You remember the night we went to Charlie's bar and drank all that champagne?'

'Yes.' Her secretary's voice came back at her with a giggle.

'What was the name of that bloke; the one I got off with?'

'The really tall one?'

'That's him.'

'David, something, wasn't it?'

'Lennon, that's right. David Lennon. Thanks.' Beca scrolled down a column of names, inserted 'David Lennon' and clicked 'save.' He wasn't well placed on her list, ranking only 25th, but he was worth having as a fall-back in case some of her prime candidates were unavailable. Deep in thought she softly tapped her fingers on the keyboard, then swiftly hit another button on the telephone.

'Hi, it's me,' she said picking up the receiver when her call was answered. 'I thought I'd catch you before you take Dulcie to school.'

'Thanks,' Abi replied.

'You don't sound too great.'

'Billy had me up all night. I think he's got an ear infection. I'm taking him to the doctor's.'

'Poor little bugger. Does it hurt?'

'Like crazy. He hasn't stopped crying.'

'Give him a hug from me. Do you mind if I pop around tonight? Tom will be out won't he?'

'Yes, but I don't know. I'm really tired. It took us hours to get back last night.'

'Me too, but don't worry, I'll be out of here by 8:30 at the latest. I want to go over my plan with you. Hang on a minute.' Another call cut in which Beca dealt with. 'Sorry about that, Abi.'

'What plan?'

'To get pregnant.'

'Christ, you're not still on about that are you?'

'Absolutely am.'

'I don't want to stay up late.'

'I'll cheer you up.'

'OK, but I'm throwing you out at 10:30.'

Beca hung up and immediately the telephone buzzed. She hit the speaker button again. 'What is it, Liz?'

'Your 8am with Sir Conrad?'

'Shit, what time is it?' Beca looked at her watch. 7:58. Two minutes. Shit, shit, shit. She fumbled under the desk for her shoes and straightening her suit she headed for the lift. Other women at the bank chose to imitate their male colleagues by wearing sludge grey and pin-stripe. Not so Beca. Her tastes were retro but undoubtedly chic, and if a pale blue Jackie O suit made her stand out in a crowd, what of it? As she passed her secretary's desk, her faithful ally held out a lipstick.

'You'll need this,' Liz said.

While she waited for the lift Beca preened herself in the chrome outer doors and then tossed back the lipstick with a grin.

'Good luck,' Liz called as the doors closed behind her. Beca held her stomach as the lift whizzed her to the top floor for her meeting with the chairman of the bank. When the doors opened she was propelled back a hundred years from the loud, fast, technology-driven world of the trading floor to the stillness of a gentleman's club with wood panelling and bucolic oil paintings. The air conditioning was working full tilt to counter the effects of the fire roaring away in the fireplace. Beca hated the contradiction and as her heels caught in the thick pile carpet she couldn't help but wonder if Mickey Mouse was about to come out and greet her.

'He's expecting you, Ms Morley. Go straight in.' The executive secretary's face was a perfect mix of frosty respect and disdain, and she continued to watch sourly as Beca waded through the carpet to Sir Conrad's door. She knocked loudly and after taking a deep breath, went straight in.

'You're late,' her boss grumbled without looking up from his huge walnut veneered desk.

Beca's insides quaked but she set her jaw in what she hoped was a brash, arrogant City manner and strode forward. 'Apologies, Sir Conrad. I had a disciplinary matter to deal with.' Her voice came from deep down in her throat. Sir Conrad looked up at her quizzically. Perhaps she had overdone it.

'I heard. Get rid of him.' This man didn't need a black hat to show he was a baddie.

'I will if you want.' Beca shrugged. 'But it seems to me he's worth another chance.'

'Forget him. Sit down.'

Beca sank into one of a pair of deep, low, leather chairs and tried hard to keep her skirt from riding up to her waist. She crossed her legs elaborately and perched on the edge, clinging to the left arm of the chair to stop herself being swallowed up. Sir Conrad looked over the rim of his glasses at her. Dirty sod. She smiled back at him.

'Know why you're here?' he asked.

'There are rumours going about,' she started.

Sir Conrad raised an eyebrow encouraging her to continue.

'That you're going to dump Andrew Conway and put me in his place.'

'Indeed,' he said with a malevolent half smile. 'Can you remind me why you might be the right man for the job?'

'Because I'm the best you've got, and you know it?'

Sir Conrad slapped down his pen, threw his head back and barked like a walrus. His pitted nose and dangling jowls reminded Beca of a David Attenborough film she'd seen once, and she was hugely grateful that he made no attempt to pin her down with his tusks and start mounting her.

'Wouldn't let any of your male colleagues speak to me like that, you know,' he guffawed.

'That doesn't stop you promoting me though.' Beca was sailing close to the wind.

He let out a final bark, wiped his mouth with the back of his hand and looked directly at her. 'No. I keep promoting you because you're the best analyst this bank's had since I came upstairs. You've got what it takes. Never thought I'd live to see the day when a female got as far as you have. Your people are loyal to you. You've got a nose for the market and you're not afraid to take risks, big ones sometimes. You're charm itself, but ruthless and completely without compunction.'

Crikey, don't overdo it. 'That's very kind of you, Sir Conrad. I'll take that as a compliment.'

'Do so, but be careful. You're only as good as your last deal. Let me down, and you're out.'

Beca could picture being frog-marched out by security with her Rubik's cube and shaking Elvis desk ornament. Her chuckle was less all-knowing and more a simper. She berated herself for it. 'And the remuneration?'

'50% up on your basic. Bonus according to performance.'

'Nothing less than four times,' her heart was going like the clappers.

'Nothing more than two and a half.'

'Three.'

'Done. Haven't you got work to get on with?'

'Absolutely, Sir Conrad. Thank you.' She was about to say, 'Very much,' and perhaps kiss his feet but thought better of it. She swiftly exited before she changed her mind. As she closed the door behind her she heard the intercom on the secretary's desk click and wondered how long it would take her to work out what fifty percent of her salary was. She turned back as she entered the lift and smiled. 'Just pea-green with envy.' Beca did a really good Scarlett O'Hara.

An aeroplane thundered overhead just as a train shot along the railway track that ran through Kew into Richmond. Abi's house was not more than 50 yards from the line and directly under the flight path so the meeting of these two great machines brought conversation to a complete halt in the little back garden. Rain fell in big blobs hitting the golf umbrella that Abi and Beca were sheltering under with a steady repetitive thwack. They had borrowed Dulcie's painting smock to cover the garden bench, but Beca could still feel the dampness seeping up to her bottom. Abi huddled next to her, her auburn hair curling about her face, making even the faded jeans and food-spattered catalogue fleece she was wearing look attractive. She was the antithesis of Beca whose neat dark hair and suit marked her out as the career woman. Abi's slim hand emerged from her sleeve and she held out two fingers for Beca's cigarette.

'Why don't you just have one of your own?' Beca asked.

'I couldn't. That would be like smoking properly.'

'And bumming mine isn't?'

'No.'

'But you make the filter soggy. It doesn't taste the same after you've slobbered all over it.'

'Please.'

'Dry your lips first.'

'Just give the bloody thing to me or I'll leave you out here on your own.' Beca reluctantly handed over her cigarette. Abi took a tentative puff and as the smoke hit the back of her inexperienced throat she coughed.

'Give it back to me,' Beca joked, trying to extricate the cigarette from between Abi's fingers.

'No, I want another go.'

A blob of ash fell on Beca's damp suit where it promptly dissolved into a nasty stain.

'Arse.'

Abi giggled. 'Don't worry, you can afford another one.'

'You're not going to tell Tom about my promotion, are you?'

'Absolutely not. I can do without him sulking around the house.'

'I don't know why he always takes it so personally.'

'He just doesn't like you, I'm afraid. You have a corrupting influence over the mother of his children. Look at this,' she said holding out the cigarette.

'Did I force you?'

'Ah, but you're here tempting me with your loose, immoderate behaviour.' Abi took another puff, more confidently this time and leant back to blow the smoke out. She smiled. 'God, I love cigarettes.'

'Buy your own.'

'Tight arse. You earn enough to fund my habit.'

'More wine?' Beca poured but the bottle was empty. 'It was full a minute ago.'

Both women laughed until Abi shushed them. 'Don't wake the kids up. I'll get another bottle. Give me the brolly.'

'No. Tom will be cross.'

'Fuck Tom. We can have another bottle if we want. Give me the brolly.'

'No. Run.'

'Cow.'

'Where is he tonight, anyway?' Beca shouted behind her as Abi ran in through the back door.

'Working, poor bastard.' Abi returned with fresh supplies.

'He works late a lot, doesn't he?'

'You can talk,' she said wresting the cork from the bottle. 'Anyway, tell me about your plan.'

With half a bottle of wine in her stomach, Beca was eager to explain. 'I'm going to have a baby. I've got it all scheduled out. If I conceive on my next ovulation date then I'll go on maternity leave after bonus month next year.'

'So?'

'It's never good to be away from the office when they're handing out cash. It's far too easy to be overlooked.'

'I had no idea. But why the rush? You're only 36, that hardly makes you menopausal.' Abi refilled both their glasses.

'Not far off though.'

'There's still plenty of time to meet a nice man.'

Beca sipped her wine and studied the tree next to the back fence. 'But I don't want to.'

'What?' Abi looked astonished.

Beca continued staring at the tree knowing it would be better to avoid eye contact at the moment; Abi's looks could be ferocious. 'I haven't changed my mind on that score. I'm not interested in a life partner. I want a baby.'

'But, I just assumed. Jesus, Beca, I thought you'd changed your mind.'

Beca mutely shook her head.

'Not all men are like your father.'

Beca turned and looked at her friend. 'What? Cheating, philandering, self-obsessed bastards? No, you're right. But from my limited experience I'd say quite a lot of them are.'

'You never give them a chance to prove otherwise, do you?'

'Of course not. It's how I've managed to stay single all my life. Men are great fun,'

Abi interrupted. 'Until they fall in love with you.'

'And then it's off with their heads.' Beca ran a manicured fingernail across her throat.

'I'm being serious.'

'I'm not.'

'Well try. You can't spend your whole life being afraid of men.'

Abi's words stabbed at Beca's softest, most vulnerable flesh. She automatically reached for another cigarette as if the nicotine would offer some support. 'That's a ridiculous thing to say. What's there to be scared of?'

'You tell me.'

'I'm not afraid, I just don't want to be like my mother. You were there, you saw the way he humiliated her.'

'She let it happen. You're nothing like her.'

'Indeed not. I've worked hard at it.' She drew on her cigarette. The evening wasn't turning out to be as much fun as she'd hoped.

'And so you're going to swear off men forever?'

Beca shrugged.

'I think it's sad. You make light of it. You treat relationships as if they're a big joke, a game for mugs, but you're throwing away any chance of happiness with both hands.'

'Not if I have a child.'

'And what kind of example will you be setting for it, if you're afraid to make a commitment of any kind?' Abi could be so bloody self-righteous sometimes. She had a way of making Beca petulant and even though her arguments were sound, there was no way she was going to agree with her and do something about it. If she suggested therapy again, she would probably brain her. Beca hadn't bothered being a sulky teenager, her mother would have been too drunk to notice if she had. Perhaps she was making up for it now.

'I would love my baby more than anything else in the world. Don't dare suggest I wouldn't.'

'Of course you would. But why now?'

'The urge to get pregnant? God knows. It's been eating away at me for ages. I didn't exactly invite the idea in, I've tried everything I can think of to make it go away, but nothing's worked. I've become the lunatic woman that smiles and talks to other people's babies in the street. You should see the anxious looks I get from some mothers, as if I'm going to abduct their child.'

'I remember how desperate we were when I couldn't get pregnant. It took nearly two years. I was frantic thinking I couldn't have a child.'

'Then you know how I feel.'

Abi searched Beca's face, then nodded to herself. 'So what's the plan?'

'I've drawn up a list of potential candidates.' Beca pulled out a neatly folded sheet of paper from her jacket pocket and smoothed it out on her lap. 'I've ruled out all the married men I know.'

'That's good of you.'

'It would be too messy, like shagging your best friend's dad. Colleagues are out. I don't fancy the idea of spotting similarities between my child and some half-brain in pin-stripe from work.'

'How about a stranger off the street?' Abi asked sarcastically.

'Shabby, meaningless, and I wouldn't know about any genetic defects,' Beca replied side-stepping the barbs. 'Have you got any crisps? I'm starving.'

'When did you last eat?'

'Lunchtime.'

'I could do you an omelette.'

Beca shook her head. 'Thanks, but I'll have something when I get home.'

'Tom's had all the kettle chips. Will these do?' Abi asked returning from the kitchen a moment later. 'They're Dulcie's. She doesn't even like them that much, it's just the bag's pink.'

Beca took the brightly coloured packet and opened it. The unnatural taste of prawn cocktail fizzled on her tongue. They were foul but addictive.

'There is a more conventional, tried and tested method,' Abi suggested.

'Artificial insemination? I looked into it. I found a very useful website for a sperm bank. They send out frozen vials all over the world. Only problem I could see was that it was for horses.'

Abi curled up her nose.

'And if I did go through the internet route how would I know what I was getting? Besides, the chances of conceiving aren't great, compared with the natural way – I'm talking people here, not horses. As for a clinic, you don't just turn up one morning and get squirted with a turkey baster. They do all sorts of blood tests and examinations. And if there's anything even slightly amiss I'll be put on hormone pills and injections. Can you imagine? Me sticking a needle in myself? I'd faint. You remember that time you talked me into giving blood.'

Abi laughed. 'You threw up over one of the nurses.'

'Exactly. And anyway, there'd be just far too much poking and prodding around the nether regions.' Beca shuddered inwardly.

'You'd better avoid childbirth.'

'That's different. It's natural for a start. Besides, this way, I get to stay in charge. I won't be at the mercy of a bunch of white coats.'

'So who's left?'

'Ex-boyfriends.'

'There are enough of those.' Abi laughed. 'But are any of them still speaking to you?'

'The list is in order of preference,' Beca replied ignoring Abi's drunken sniggers.

'Why ex-boyfriends though?' she asked dipping a hand into Beca's packet of crisps.

'Because it cuts out all the small talk. Besides, there's something comfortable and familiar about an ex-boyfriend, they're a bit like old slippers.'

'You're talking about husbands.'

'No. You have to take them seriously, or at least pretend to. If I get bored with my slippers, I can just throw them out.'

Abi shook her head with despair. 'Give me a cigarette.'

'A whole one?'

'I need one. Let's have it then.' Abi took the list from Beca. 'What's with all the crossed off names?'

'Those are the ones I called this afternoon. I've had to rule them out. Three are married, one's doing time for embezzlement and the other two hung up on me. And no I'm not being paranoid because when I called back they did exactly the same thing.'

Abi laughed. 'You're not renowned for your sensitivity. Perhaps they're still reeling from their encounter with you.'

'Wimps.'

'Who's next?' Abi ran her finger down past the blacked out names. 'Hal Carson,' she said slowly as though searching her mind. The bottle of wine swilling around her insides wasn't helping her cognitive processes. 'I remember him, he was nice. I shouldn't have thought he'd speak to you again.'

'Why not?'

'Because you were queen bitch to him,' she said flicking ash with the deliberate actions of a pissed novice.

'Was not.'

'Oh yes you very definitely were. I liked Hal. He was a really decent bloke. He was so in love with you, and you,' she said pointing an accusing finger in Beca's face, 'you broke his heart. It makes me very cross just thinking about what you did to him.'

'I didn't do anything.'

'Exactly. You didn't love him, not enough anyway.'

'Come off it. We were completely incompatible.'

'I've never seen you laugh as much since you split up.'

'Don't be silly,'

'It's true. He really brought you out of yourself. You were relaxed. Frivolous almost. Laid back, dare I say it.'

'Stoned mostly. He was lovely, but he was so not together about his career. He could have been a really great artist, but he was too easy-going. He was forever giving his pictures away. It used to drive me crazy. I'll bet anything he's still in that bedsit scratching out a living with his drawing.'

'You didn't give him a chance. Anyway, he's too nice for you. Leave him alone.'

'But he's next on my list.'

'Then scratch him off too. There's no way he'll sleep with you.'

'He might.'

'Find someone else.'

'I don't want to. He's the best of the rest.'

'Shows your poor taste in men then, doesn't it?'

'Their genetic qualities weren't uppermost in my mind when I went out with them.'

'I still think you should leave Hal alone.'

'No.'

'Why?'

'Because our combined gene pools will make a good baby. He's gorgeous, kind, generous, does all that touchy feely stuff I'm no good at. He's creative. Great with his hands.'

'It's a shame you didn't think of that before you binned him.'

'You didn't used to be so bloody sanctimonious. Just because you've got children doesn't mean you're absolved from your past. You were just as bad as me.'

'But I loved every single one of them,' Abi replied with a wild flourish of her hand.

'Should I be worried by this conversation?'

Both women jumped at this unexpected intrusion. Tom was standing inside the back door, swaying somewhat and dripping wet. Abi fumbled her cigarette into Beca's hand, then batted away the plume of smoke that engulfed her. Beca wasn't convinced Tom would believe she'd taken to smoking two cigarettes at the same time.

'Had a good evening, Tom?' she asked with a mocking tone.

'Splendid, if you consider working late to be fun.'

'You look the worse for wear.'

'I went for a quick one with the boys. Don't you have a home to go to?'

'I'll get going,' she said to Abi. 'Thanks for the chat.' She kissed her on the cheek and left her friend to explain the two empty bottles of wine.

'God-forsaken, back-arse of bloody nowhere,' Beca ranted as she finally found a cab to take her home. The rain eased off as she arrived back in Notting Hill and while she paid the driver, the neighbour's cat came out of the shadows to see what was going on.

'Evening, Rhett.'

The black cat swaggered over to her and wrapped himself around her legs. The porch light clicked on automatically as she looked for her keys and when she opened the huge front door of the grand Victorian stucco house, the cat shot inside. His owner lived on the ground floor and while Beca sifted through the post – junk mail and a Visa bill – Rhett sat on her doormat and watched. When Beca climbed the stairs he bounded past her and was waiting to greet her when she reached the first floor landing.

Beca was always struck by how empty the flat felt when she got home, particularly if it was late. On the other hand, if it was anything other than empty she would have been straight onto the police. As it was she turned off the burglar alarm, kicked off her high-heels, padded past the answering machine – no messages – and went into the kitchen. Rhett was already there sitting in front of the fridge. Beca had the drunk munchies badly, but the fridge was empty and again she wondered why she was surprised. Who on earth else was going to fill it if not her? She settled for a bowl of cereal and UHT and made a mental note to get to the shops some day soon.

She stood at the counter which divided the kitchen area from the living room, and leant an elbow next to her bowl. She couldn't be bothered to take her meagre supper to the dining room, nor indeed the few feet to one of the sofas in front of her. Rhett jumped up onto the worktop and looked longingly at her bowl. After a brief stand-off she pushed it towards him. Spots of milk flew onto his whiskers and face as he lapped it up and when Beca scratched his ears he purred.

She ran a hand along his bony back and looked around the flat wondering what it would be like to have a baby living there. Would the sound of its voice change the essence of the place? Certainly on a practical level the off-white sofas might need to go. She didn't have to move much to take in the whole first floor of her flat. It was open plan, the ceilings trimmed with cornicing rising high above her. The tall sash windows were elegant but would be a nightmare with a baby crawling around as would the cast iron spiral staircase. Beca had visions of her child squeezing its way between the banister uprights and getting stuck, or worse.

The kitchen would be safe enough. All she ever used was the toaster and the coffee maker. The architect had insisted on putting in a state-of-the-art extractor fan over the stove. She would need it, apparently, when grilling tuna fish steaks. It had seemed pointless embarrassing herself with a confession about her culinary inadequacies. The kitchen reminded her of the home corner in her infant's school classroom. Not because she cooked with play-dough but because the glass tile walls barely reached half the height of the whole room. It was an open-top kitchen pod filled with chrome gadgets plonked down in the middle to separate the living space from the rarely used dining room.

'So what do you reckon to having a baby about the place?' The cat looked up at her then continued drinking. 'You can still come and visit me. There'll be plenty of room.' She could fit a full-sized climbing frame in the living room and still have room for her Eames lounge chair and precious film collection.

'We could turn the spare bedroom at the front into the nursery, the nanny can have the one at the back. It's going to be just perfect.' God, she was doing it again, talking to the cat. She'd be featuring in adverts for the Samaritans next if she wasn't careful. Self-consciously she found herself looking around for a smirking hidden audience, then shook back her shoulders to show she didn't care.

The cat drained the bowl of milk and then tried the bran flakes. They weren't to his liking and he shook his head to get the soggy mass of rabbit food out of his mouth. He looked at Beca as if it was her fault and then set about cleaning himself. Her mouth remained shut for the briefest moment; the need to talk far outweighed the humiliation.

'I know the others think I'm mad, but there's nothing wrong with being a single parent. Lots of women do it all the time. Perhaps not intentionally from the outset, but at least I'm not kidding myself.' Rhett stretched towards her and pushed his head against her chest. She indulged him in a good scratch along his cheeks and around his ears. 'It must be so nice being a cat,' she said watching him purr himself into ecstasy. 'You know, you're the only male I have any genuine feelings for. Isn't that ridiculous? And you're not even my cat. God, I can't even commit to owning a pet. I have to lure an old lady's mog into my home, while no doubt she's downstairs worrying where you are. Come on, let's take you back.' She scooped the cat up in her arms, took him downstairs and using the spare key Mrs Butler had entrusted to her, she opened her door a few inches, pushed him in and silently closed it behind him.

It was late. Beca was due to get up at 5:30 but her head was filled with too many thoughts for sleep. She made herself a cup of tea and curled up in her pyjamas on the sofa. She flicked the remote control and the video recorder whirred into action midway through *Heaven Knows Mr Allison*. Robert Mitchum, at his best in grubby Marine fatigues, had just wiped out some Japs. Deborah Kerr was sick in a cave. She was naked on account of the fever, and only an old blanket lay between her and immodesty. He loved her, she loved him, but she was a nun. Smouldering, thwarted passion, Beca's favourite. She reached for the Kleenex and settled down wishing Robert Mitchum would come and rescue her. Now there was a man.

Chapter **3**

The rest of the week had been tough at work and Beca had felt richly deserving of the 'quick one' on Friday night with Liz. However, like most trips to the bar with her secretary, it had turned into a marathon drinking session. On this occasion, that had suited Beca's plans just fine. If she hadn't been so hideously drunk she wouldn't have got any sleep that night. As it was she'd fallen out of a taxi, stumbled upstairs at three in the morning and collapsed onto her bed still fully dressed. It was a tried and tested method to quieten the nerves. The reason for her current troubles? Today the search for Hal Carson began and time was tight. According to her conception schedule there were just three short weeks until Big 'O' Day 1.

The one drawback of obliterating all intelligent thought with alcohol was the gruesome hangover that greeted her now. Beca lay prostrate across her bed groaning, her mouth fixed open; her tongue and teeth bone-dry. She could feel a slick of crusted saliva that had meandered down her cheek to her ear. She tried summoning up some moisture in her mouth but failed. With each waking moment the memories came flooding back thus beginning the inevitable sweaty waves of self-loathing. Her eyes felt as if glass had been ground into them and night-time gunk and mascara had sealed them shut. Gingerly she attempted to open one eye. Her eyelashes resisted until with a final meaty pop they were ripped from their moorings and Beca's left eye slowly opened. And instantly shut again. As brilliant sunlight scorched a hole on her retina she screeched, rolled over and played dead.

Two hours later Beca woke up again, light-headed, sick, but not blind. She dragged her aching body to the shower and subjected it to a cold water assault. It was when the cognitive processes began working that the low-level tremor she'd been fighting all week escalated into border-line panic. What if she couldn't find him? What if he'd moved abroad, become celibate, or died? Beca's empty stomach twisted and back flipped in a nasty bilious mess. Supposing he said no? Her mood was dark. Her sense of humour disappeared down the plug hole. She needed a cigarette and some coffee.

Screwing up the Post-It that said 'Buy More Coffee,' Beca poked around yesterday's soggy coffee grounds in the cappuccino machine and then blasted them with a stream of boiling water. The results were barely palatable but helped wash down the first cigarette of the day. With the familiar feeling of ants crawling across her scalp, the caffeine kicked in and Beca knew that this was the best she was going to feel that morning. She headed for the nearest coffee shop before the effects wore off. Two double espressos left her jittery, hyper and paranoid. A perfect combination for sitting in grid-locked traffic.

Three driver-only double-decker buses, engaged in a to-the-death race back to the bus garage, had managed to block the entire four lanes of Camden High Street at the bus stop in front of M&S. The would-be passengers, already irate with each other for the breakdown of order at the stop, scattered into the road as the buses opened their doors. The elderly and infirm were left to fend for themselves. Beca watched with dismay as they struggled into the road with their trolleys and shopping bags, waving pointlessly at the drivers who were too busy winding each other up to notice their passengers. The motorists behind seethed and began barracking the passengers for being so slow. Why didn't anyone have a go at the bus drivers?

Beca felt tempted but street brawls had never really been her thing. Instead she directed her caffeine-fuelled fury at the nation as a whole, particularly Londoners, and more specifically arsehole bus drivers with shit for brains. She tried imagining the same scene set in Geneva or Zurich. It would of course be done with impeccable manners. Perhaps it was time to emigrate. But then if she was in Switzerland, she'd have to drive a battery-powered eco car, not her 1963 powder blue Mercedes convertible. Beca drummed her fingers on the white leather upholstery and, thankful for small mercies, waited until the bus drivers thundered off up the road leaving half their potential passengers reeling in a cloud of diesel fumes. London. It was a special place.

Finding a parking space was no less grating on the nerves and in the end Beca abandoned her car in a council estate up near Chalk Farm. She began her descent south down Camden High Street and got as far as the railway bridge before being sucked into the vortex of trendy youth. It was a mistake going there on a Saturday. Camden Market hadn't changed. People might have grown up and found better things to do with their time but the place remained the same. It was a magnet for every would-be rebel; its grubby, down-at-heel tawdriness a perfect stomping ground for disaffected teenagers to snarl and sneer at one another. Beca chuckled at the neo-neo punks and Goths with unconvincing weekend-only dyed hair, and girls staggering leaden-footed in Frankenstein-inspired stack heels. She'd been lucky to survive her youth without any body art. Now it seemed compulsory to have at least one tattoo and several body piercings. She was beginning to sound like a crotchety pensioner, but then there was nothing like the follies of youth to leave the observer feeling old.

The traffic was bumper to bumper but moving fast and Beca found herself trapped on a traffic island with a large teenage girl displaying unpleasant amounts of flabby midriff which poured over the sides of her hipster trousers; her belly button mutilated with a bull-horn piercing. She was big, as in six feet of Scandinavian blonde, and unashamedly broad with it. Beca leant against her in a hostile bid to secure some more personal space. The Pride of Spitzbergen didn't take the hint. The girl's mouth was slightly open revealing a tongue quivering in salivary juices like a wet and fleshy oyster. Pearl-like in the middle of this mass was a heart-shaped bolt. Was she trying to be alluring? Beca shuddered. Thank God her teenage years were over and done with, being young was such a nightmare. Then, on reflection, it was a breeze compared to what she was about to take on. She was minutes away from asking a man she hadn't seen in eight years to have sex with her. There was a Goth-free wine bar across the road. Beca went straight in and ordered a double G&T.

She sat up at the bar rolling a smoking cigarette between a finger and thumb, and sipped her drink. She'd been so wrapped up with the logistics of finding Hal that she hadn't once thought through what she was going to say to him. The last time she had seen him he'd been on the point of crying. Even now, Beca didn't feel too proud of that moment. She had then and still had a three month rule which avoided anyone getting too emotional and awkward when it came time to split up. Only she'd gone and broken it with Hal. They were together for six months, a record-breaker by her standards. Hal had been getting serious and she'd known it was time to get out before he went all out and said 'I love you.' Only she left it too late. He did say 'I love you.' It had been in a bar, not unlike this one. He'd been smiling, happy to see her.

Beca stirred her drink and tried to blank out the look on his face when she'd told him it was over. She'd been honest, if too direct when she'd said she didn't love him. He'd laughed at first, thinking she was joking, that she was being enigmatic, a tease. She'd muttered something crass about being afraid of commitment, then something even more stupid about how her womanizing father had put her off men. He'd said they could work it through together, but she wasn't interested. It was far easier to make a break and run. He'd persisted until in the end she got the bank to transfer her to New York. That had done the trick.

Abi was right. Trying to find Hal was grossly insensitive, but she hadn't been joking – he was the only man she wanted to be the father of her child. None of the others left on her list came close. Beca knocked back the rest of her drink and ground her cigarette out in the thick glass ashtray. Anyway, the chances of him actually living in the same place were close to zero. It had been eight years after all. Her courage bolstered by gin and a half disguised hope that she'd fail, Beca followed the route imprinted in her memory towards Hal's place.

The record shop was still there but had been renamed One Eyed Jack's. It had a new black and yellow paint job and a new flesh-to-liquid loud sound system. Despite the changes Beca could detect the same weirdo obsessiveness of the staff and the border-line autistic behaviour of the male clientele as they ferreted through racks of albums. This was a specialist record shop, an independent that catered for the most extreme and esoteric of tastes.

'Does Hal still live upstairs?' Beca waited for the black-clad youth who passed as staff to reply. He peered at her through a curtain of thick seaweed-like, bottle-black hair. His head nodded. Beca smiled. His head continued nodding, rocking like a caged-up bear in rhythm to the wall of noise that surrounded them.

'Does Hal still live upstairs?' she tried again, adding sign language in her attempt to communicate. The rocking continued. Was Seaweed Boy brain damaged?

'Hal? Yeah, he's up there.'

Beca was stunned. She'd scored a bull's eye first time, although her elation didn't last long. Fear of a hostile reception gripped her once more as she headed for the back of the shop. The door was barely distinguishable from the rest of the wall, both being entirely covered with gig flyers, but Beca knew where to look. She knocked loudly, and waited. She would have loved to retreat but she made herself try again. Nothing.

'He's not answering,' she said, parting Seaweed Boy's hair to get near his ear. She was surprised it wasn't bleeding.

'He's not in,' he replied.

'But you just told me,' Beca's voice trailed off. 'Never mind. Can I get his phone number off you?'

The youth shook his head.

'Why not?'

'He hasn't got one?'

'What?' She couldn't shout much louder.

The music suddenly stopped, Seaweed Boy carried on rocking while Beca reeled back, unsteadied by the silence.

'He doesn't have a phone, man.'

'Still? You're kidding me.' Times must be tough if even eight years later he couldn't afford a telephone.

'Uses our one.' The music started up again, his head pounding slotted straight in, no beat missed.

'Can you give him this.' Beca got out a business card. The shaking speakers made her handwriting scratch across the card as she wrote, 'I've got a proposition for you. Call me,' and added her home and mobile numbers as well. The youth took it, looked at it and nodded. Beca had serious doubts.

Shuddering at the thought of so much youth pressing its flesh against her, Beca zigzagged up side streets until she eventually found her car. With her ears ringing and an involuntary lurching movement gripping her body like a Salem virgin she drove home.

Beca was quietly confident that Hal would call her. He would get back from wherever he'd been, Seaweed Boy would give him her card and he would call immediately. It was that simple. Only he didn't. On Sunday morning Beca did some rescripting: Hal hadn't come home at all on Saturday, leastways not until the small hours, and fighting the urge to call her straightaway for fear of disturbing her, he had fallen asleep clasping her card in his hand. On Sunday she waited in for his call, but it didn't come and Beca found herself making excuses for him: he must be hung-over, in need of a fry-up first; he was too ashamed to call her.

It did not occur to her that the best part of a week would come and go without so much as a peep from him, but as she eased herself past cool, foamy bubbles and into the bath on Thursday evening, that was the unflattering scenario that presented itself to her. Beca liked baths scalding hot, so when her body had adjusted to the moderate temperature, she ran the hot tap again and slowly boiled herself. She stuck out her feet on either side of the elaborate Victorian taps to cool them down and as the smell of tea rose filled her bathroom she closed her eyes and her troubles lifted away. The moment of pleasure was fleeting, no sooner had she blacked out the images of the day than Hal popped up in the grainy home movie that played on a continuous loop inside her head.

Now of course she regretted ever having given her card to Seaweed Boy. She had no control over the situation. Supposing he'd lost it or forgotten to give it to Hal? What if Hal had lost it, or didn't recognise her name? She thought once again about calling One Eyed Jack's, just like she had every hour since Sunday. Stretching a steaming arm out over the roll-top edge of the bath she held two wet fingers against the white tiled wall. If the left drop got to the bottom before the other, she'd call first thing tomorrow. She watched as both drops streamed down towards the skirting board. The right-hand one won by a neck. Maybe not first thing tomorrow, maybe after lunch. Beca hated the dithering and uncertainty. She'd put the ball into Hal's court and that had been a massive error. She couldn't see over the net and for all she knew, while she was blindly hopping around on the base line waiting for him to return the ball, he'd sloped off home with it.

The water had raised Beca's body temperature to an unhealthy high. Unable to stand the heat any longer, she climbed out of the bath feeling dizzy. She wrapped her lobster skin in a towel, sat on the bath mat and dried her feet.

Perhaps Hal was on holiday. She laughed at herself. Idiot. Why didn't she think of that before? Of course, he was away, that was why he hadn't called. It was the perfect explanation and feeling cheered with this acceptable scenario Beca pulled on a vest and pyjama bottoms and went downstairs. The hot bath had punched out any appetite she had so she filled a bowl with Twiglets and made herself a gin and tonic. She looked at her supper with guilt, even someone as unhealth conscious as her knew it by-passed most of the important food groups. Did the juniper berries in the gin count towards the five portions of fruit and veg a day the government wanted everyone to eat? Unlikely. The fact that she wasn't improving her chances of conception either was a moot point given that a more vital asset was missing, namely Hal's sperm. There was an old bottle of multi-vitamins in the cupboard next to the detox supplements she'd never got around to taking. She swallowed three.

Beca loaded the DVD and curling her feet up underneath her she settled down to watch *Mildred Pierce*. Joan Crawford took to her role as the eponymous heroine with gusto, but after only a few minutes of struggle and hardship, Beca's thoughts wandered back to Hal again. She had a strong picture of him in her mind, but she wasn't sure if the Adonis-like face she'd painted him with had any bearing on reality any more. Perhaps the broad-shouldered hulk she imagined was mere fantasy. Even if he had been so well proportioned in the past, it didn't mean that he still was; eight years was a long time, and he had always been partial to his beer. Over the past week she'd built him up to mythical proportions which was why it hurt even more that he hadn't called. There was a police line-up of likely candidates in her mind all of whom, except Hal, were thin and weaselly. Just one look at them and she could tell their progeny would be weak and degenerate. On the other hand Hal epitomised manhood, he reeked of it. He had become more virile than the Cerne Abbas Giant. He would deliver the goods, even if he was incapable of using a telephone.

Beca crunched a mouthful of Twiglets then washed them down with a swig of her drink. As soon as she'd swallowed the gin her taste buds shrieked out for more Twiglets. Both tastes were addictive and she kept up the routine until the bowl and glass were empty. She suspected there was a boffin working away somewhere coming up with the most compulsive flavour combinations. Admitting he was doing a good job, she went off to the kitchen for refills. When she came back Joan Crawford was looking tragic but defiant. She was a perfect role model for today's ambitious woman, but would eyebrows the size of mouse pelts ever catch on again? Mildred Pierce had done it all and in the Dark Ages before women were allowed to think. She had that chain of restaurants and the kid. If she could do it and find time to wear so much make-up then surely Beca had a chance. But did she? Was Claire right? Was she incapable of maternal love? Did she lack that crucial nurturing gene? Besides the kid turned out bad in the end.

She bridled at the thought of a compulsory pre-conception test, but doing one might set her mind at ease. A quick multiple-choice examination at the local town hall might prove if she was mother material or not. Mostly 'A' answers would mean she was a natural, a majority of 'Ds' would put her in the same camp as Snow White's stepmother. If she was borderline, she could then plead her case further in a 250 word essay on 'Being a Good Mother.'

Without a test she had to rely on instinct, and that was telling her to have a baby. But knowing that she wanted a child and thinking that she would make a good mother was not evidence on its own. It wasn't much of a case against the litany of defects that Claire had presented to her in Norfolk. It seemed the only way to prove her critics wrong was to go ahead, have a baby and be brilliant at bringing it up. Beca liked the challenge, besides, the future without a child was too bleak to consider. She had two plans, two futures. Plan A involved a child. With this plan came nice, comforting images of playing in the park, building sandcastles at the seaside, making play-dough cats and dogs in the kitchen, and getting excited about Christmas again. Plan B on the other hand came with despondent images of Twiglet and gin binges and an early death. Beca sighed. To her the child she wanted was a real person already, with a future; to not create that person was close to infanticide. She was fed up with her heart constantly racing, her stomach plummeting like a stone every time she thought of Plan B. She was getting things out of proportion she knew, but how the hell could she tell her heart to slow down? How could she rationalise what was so impossible to explain? Logic didn't come into it, as she was rapidly discovering was always the case where children were concerned.

The next day at the bank was bruising. Someone in the aviation division managed to sell 500,000 shares in an aeronautical company for $1.20 each instead of $120. Understandably there was some shouting and finger pointing. Sir Conrad became apoplectic with rage and, although she wasn't directly involved, Beca had felt the sharp side of his tongue. No one was spared and more than a few innocent people went home without jobs, along with the complete incompetents who caused the ruckus in the first place. No doubt the HR department would have a busy weekend sorting out the mess.

Beca was not in the mood for the obligatory Friday night drink with her colleagues from work. Hal was out there somewhere, and she needed to find him, or else go back to her list. She picked at the edge of a beer mat, tearing off strips and piling them into an ashtray. She hadn't expected that finding a candidate would be so difficult. What was it with men these days? The soles of her shoes kept sticking to the beer-stained floorboards as she waited to get served. Truth was she was taking her time. She couldn't muster the will to get pushy and flash a smile at one of the barmen who were busy spinning bottles for a group of female fans, and she was in no rush to get back to Liz and the others. A puddle of beer was growing on the bar in front of her which she managed to stem with the tattered beer mat. She channelled it past her and on towards a man who was leaning against the bar with his back to her. With just an inch between him and a soaked elbow she relented and redirected the beer off the edge and onto the floor.

Eventually she got served. With a drink in both hands and a fresh cigarette hanging out of her mouth she edged her way back to the table. The dark, cellar wine bar was packed with Friday night drinkers. The low ceilings reverberated with noise, and cigar smoke hung in a thick fog. Voices were loud, watches were chunky, talk was about money – making it and spending it; the usual after work scene in the City. The bar was a fair trek from Beca's office but usually worth the effort. It was an old stomping ground and many conquests had been made there with Liz.

Tonight she was sick of it. For once she could see the irony of rich people slumming it in such a run-down dive.

Liz took her drink. 'Heavin' innit,' she shouted above the throng.

Beca shrugged.

'Come on girl, drink.' Her friend laughed as she clinked glasses, but gin on an empty stomach just fuelled Beca's irritation. Everyone looked ugly and too eager tonight.

'What about them?' Liz nudged Beca's side and gestured towards a couple of likely lads, square jawed and keen.

She shook her head. 'Sorry, Liz. I'm not interested.'

Tapping a number into her mobile, she darted outside in time to hear, 'We're shut,' shouted above the ear-melting decibels of One Eyed Jack's record shop.

'Well if you're shut, why did you answer the phone?' The line went dead. 'Fuck!' Beca redialled and waited. 'Don't hang up again, please,' she added. 'I want to speak to Hal. Is he there?'

'No.'

'Did you give him my card?'

'What?'

What did this bloke use for a brain? 'I was in your shop last Saturday, I gave you my card to give him.'

'Oh, it's you.'

Eureka. 'Did you give it to him?'

'Yeah?'

'And?'

Nothing. Beca could almost hear the neurones connecting in his head.

'Where is he?' she asked.

'I dunno. Look, do you want to see Demented, tonight?'

'What?'

'Demented Are Go. Do you want to see them with me?' Seaweed Boy sounded exasperated at having to explain. Beca was staggered. He was at least 15 years younger than her. Could she bring herself to sleep with him? He would be easy enough to seduce. It would be a lot less complicated than re-engaging with Hal, but no, she couldn't love a child with seaweed for hair.

'Any other time I'd love to,' she said trying to keep the sarcasm out of her voice. 'But I really need to find Hal. Could you hazard a guess?' There was another pause.

'He said something about going to the cinema. An all-nighter.'

'Where?' Beca willed him on. 'At the Prince of Wales?'

'Yeah, that knackered place behind all the big cinemas.'

Beca hung up and went back in. Liz had lassoed the two men and was working hard on both of them.

'Which one do you fancy?' she asked as Beca returned.

'Neither. I'm going to shoot, this place is doing my head in.'

Liz pouted, then broke into a broad grin. 'More for me then.'

Beca smiled. It had been three months since Liz's boyfriend had gone off with someone else and she was still tarting around trying to convince herself that being single was more fun. Beca knew for a fact that the bride magazines were still in her bottom drawer at work. She also knew that Liz would be going home alone tonight; try as she might she was never going to be one-night-stand material.

Beca gave her hug. 'Why don't you come too?'

If Liz answered, she didn't hear. She was suddenly deaf and blind to everything except the nightmare that had come alive at the bar. She took an unsteady step back and her friend turned to see what had drained the colour from her face.

'What is it?'

Beca put a hand over her open mouth and continued to stare at the distorted characters playing in slow motion before her.

'Jesus, you're freaking me out. What's wrong?' Liz asked.

A triple dose of adrenaline snapped Beca back from her dazed state. Her fingers trembled as she held her glass to her mouth. It was empty. She took Liz's and drained it.

'Over there, at the bar. That man.'

'What, groping the woman with the spray-on dress? Do you know him?'

'His name's Tom Goodall. I was a bridesmaid at his wedding.' Beca's stomach shifted dangerously.

Liz looked at her with horror. 'Blimey, he's not your mate Abi's husband, is he?'

'Was last time I checked.'

'Looks like he's forgotten. Supposing someone saw him?'

'Someone has.' Beca slammed Liz's empty glass down on the table.

'Hey slow down, let's not jump to conclusions. Maybe –'

'Maybe what?'

'Doesn't look good, does it?' Liz admitted.

'I'm going to have a word.' Beca's hands clenched into fists.

'No, wait, listen to me,' Liz said grabbing her arm. 'Just wait.' Beca tried shaking her off. 'I know what I'm talking about. Don't go diving in. You need to be certain.'

'I can't be much more certain than that,' Beca said pointing towards the bar. People could sense trouble and moved away; the two men Liz had picked up disappeared.

Liz pulled Beca behind a pillar out of sight of the bar. 'He'll deny everything. You need more evidence. Trust me.' Beca searched Liz's face. She had the sad-eyed look of a woman who'd been there before. 'There's no point you sticking around here getting worked up. It'll just be messy,' she continued. 'I'll put the word out, someone's bound to know who she is. If it's more than a one-off, I'll find out about it. Leave it to me. Go on, go home.'

Beca unclenched her fingers and took a deep breath. Gradually she began to feel calmer, the urge to start a punch-up was strong, but futile; Liz was right. She gave her friend another hug. It was a relief to get away but she felt like a coward for sneaking out without hitting him once. Even though she hated Tom, she'd never once questioned his love for Abi, yet there he was groping another woman, and so publicly. Didn't he care if he was spotted? Perhaps that was part of the fun. Or maybe a code of silence operated amongst pricks in the City. Unlucky for him then that she wasn't a signed-up member of that particular club. She'd have his balls before she was finished with him.

The warm evening air did little to clear her head and she felt sick as she looked for a taxi. Even though it was clear beyond doubt what Tom had been doing, she kept hoping that she'd misread the scene. Perhaps it had been a matey hug; he could have been congratulating that woman on some great success. Beca was deluding herself, but reality was a little too horrible to deal with at the moment.

It was after 11 o'clock by the time she got to the Prince of Wales. Knots of people hung out in the foyer chatting and drinking beer that was on sale at the kiosk along with flapjacks and tar-like coffee. It was an independent with a slate of films that catered to any film buff's most exacting whim. Tonight was an all-nighter feast of kitsch musicals. Beca got herself a cup of coffee and lit a cigarette. Her hands were still shaking and the image of Tom all over that tart was seared into her brain.

The Prince of Wales was a place where people went to be seen and the foyer was heaving with leggy girls in glittery go-go pants and their super-trendy boyfriends killing time before the Club scene kicked in. Then there were the serious filmos dressed in regulation black from neck to toe with logoed crew jackets and film festival over-the-shoulder courier bags. One guy even had a can of film under his arm. Trustafarian film students, Beca guessed, most with a strong whiff of ambition – they were going to Hollywood, they were going to be big. One particular group caught her attention, they were having a loud debate – for the benefit of others – about the place of voice-over narration in film. Was the director's cut of *Blade Runner* without the voice-over better than the studio version? Life and death stuff, Beca thought acidly. She had more weighty matters on her mind, like what the hell was she going to tell Abi? If indeed she was going to say anything at all. 'Oh, by the way, I saw your husband wrestling with some floozie.' Or, 'I didn't know you and Tom had an open marriage. You don't? Well it can't have been him performing tonsillectomies after work then.' The coffee did little to settle her stomach.

Deanna Durbin was warbling cutely on screen, combining white ankle socks and little high-heels in a way that was probably illegal now. She could really hit the high notes, not that anyone cared. Angry shouts for silence from a solitary fan were laughed down. Beca stood at the back of the cinema, her eyes adjusting to the dark, and watched the middle-aged man trying to defend Miss Durbin's honour. He was the type who'd blow a fuse one day and shoot everyone.

Mercifully Deanna was on the point of living happily ever after. A moment or two later the ancient curtains shunted unsteadily across the screen rendering the end credits unreadable against faded pink velvet. Then the first foot stomps began. The house lights came up. There were whistles and heckling from the audience. A blizzard of polystyrene cups hurtled towards the screen, those that fell short into the front rows were thrown back. Before Beca could begin her search, the lights dimmed and the curtains creaked open. The ensuing noise was deafening as *The Sound of Music* began. That explained the troupe of transvestites dressed as nuns. The auditorium fizzled in anticipation as the camera swooped through the mountains of Austria. At last Miss Andrews was sighted on a hill top and as the camera panned towards her, she flung open her arms and sang *The Hills Are Alive*. The nuns were in ecstasy. The atmosphere reminded Beca of the kids' Saturday morning cinema club she'd gone to when she was young. Every week she would sit like all the other children, perched on the top of her pull-down seat, eating her Curly-Wurly and watch Flash Gordon and Tarzan films. Would her child ever get to kick the seat in front and throw popcorn? Not if she didn't find a father first.

A herd of wildebeest stampeded through her stomach as she remembered her mission. She was so much more nervous than when she went to Camden. Would she recognise him? Would he recognise her? Would he be pleased to see her? It was like being sixteen again and going through the traumas of a blind date with a friend's boyfriend's best mate. She set off down the central aisle peering at the rows of faces flickering with Technicolor shadows.

'Sit down,' someone shouted. Beca hunched down an inch or two by way of compromise, but frankly she couldn't have cared less if she was cast in silhouette on the screen. She saw someone, a likely Hal candidate.

'Hal,' she called. The person in question made no response. 'Excuse me, sorry,' she whispered. A disgruntled row stood while she shoved her way closer to her target. 'Hal.' Finally the man looked at her. 'Oh. Sorry.' Another wave of half-felt apologies followed as she pushed her way out again. She carried on down the aisle aware of growing unrest behind her. She was getting fed up.

'Hal, are you there?' she said with hands on hips.

'Shush,' said most of the audience.

'Sod off.'

'Oooooo,' came a chorus from the camp nunnery taking up the back six rows.

'Oh, very mature.' Beca was getting increasingly pissed off.

'Look, could you just fuck off.'

She suspected one of the over-privileged film students.

Where the bloody hell was Hal? She reached the front of the cinema and aware that all eyes were boring into her, she turned on her heels in a flouncy carefree manner and shook her hair back like a girl in a shampoo commercial, forgetting it was now quite short. She tripped and fell so quickly that she had no time to break her fall. The auditorium erupted with cheers, cat-calls and applause. Beca picked herself up, bowed and limped back up the aisle with her dignity in tatters.

Seething, her cheeks burning red with embarrassment she stood at the back of the cinema beneath the projector box and reconsidered her tactics. She was not going to be beaten by this mob. An usher stood nearby leaning against the same wall. He was thin and weedy, his hollow chest looked likely to collapse in on him. It was no contest, Beca had his torch off him in seconds.

She turned the beam on her tormentors.

'Hey, do you mind,' another posh-from-Chelsea voice shouted.

'Frightfully sorry.' Beca continued to pick out faces and the occasional furtive fumbling in the dark.

'Sit down,' someone shouted.

Beca swung her torch on them.

'I'm trying to find someone.'

'Aren't we all,' said Mother Superior.

'What's his name?' came another voice from the opposite side of the cinema.

'Hal. His name is Hal. He's about 6'2 and blonde.' A rumble of approval emanated from the nuns.

'Cooeeee Hal! Oh, Hal!' they shouted. Nothing.

One of the film students stood up. 'Hal, if you're out there, mate. Can you sort your woman out?'

'He's stood you up, love,' said the Reverend Mother.

'No he hasn't, he just can't speak at the moment,' said another nun.

'Saucy!' she-he replied. 'That'll be ten Hail Marys and five how's your father.'

'What's going on?' From his expression and general demeanour Beca reckoned this newcomer must be the manager.

'I'm looking for a friend.'

'Can you leave, please, you're spoiling the film for everyone.' His opinion was endorsed by the audience.

'No. I need to find him.'

'Well do so somewhere else. I'm going to have to insist you leave.' A bony hand gripped her elbow.

'Get off.' Beca shook herself free and glowered.

'I'll call the police if you don't leave now.'

'Don't be such an arsehole,' Beca retorted as she stomped out into the foyer. 'You're so out of order. I could understand if it was an Ingmar Bergman night, but Julie Andrews? No one minded.'

'Can you leave?' The manager remained humourless and stony-faced.

'Look, I'm sorry,' Beca back-pedalled. 'It's really important I find him. I'll just wait here, you won't hear another peep.' The manager's face didn't crack. 'Please.'

'Any more trouble and you're out,' he said and walked off just as Julie Andrews and the entire audience burst into song again.

Beca lit a cigarette, scrunched up her empty packet and got another cup of coffee. Plan B? What was plan B? She only had two weeks to find someone. It would be back to the list and another round of rejections from her ex-boyfriends. Damn Hal. Why wasn't he there? It was so bloody typical of him. She paced around sucking hard on her cigarette. OK, so they hadn't actually arranged to meet. But that wasn't the point. She sat on a beaten up art deco chair and drowned her cigarette butt in the dregs of her coffee.

Time passed. Beca waited, not because she held out any hope of seeing Hal, but because she couldn't bring herself to admit defeat and go home. The film ended, another girl was going to live happily ever after and moments later the auditorium doors burst open and spilled out people. Then a tall figure sidled out towards a side exit. He ran a hand through his hair before putting on a motorbike helmet. Beca's heart lurched, she nearly yelped with glee. It was Hal, instantly recognisable and unmistakably beautiful.

'Hal,' she shouted. All eyes were on her, except his. He kept moving, faster now. 'Hey, Hal,' she called high-pitched with excitement. She gave chase and caught up with him at the exit, breathless and laughing. 'Have you gone deaf?' she asked, tugging at his sleeve.

He stopped, trapped. 'What?' he asked shaking her off. 'What the fuck do you want?'

Beca gasped and stepped back horrified by the malevolence on his face. 'I. Nothing. I just wanted to have a word. It doesn't matter.'

'Good.' The door flew open as he rammed it with his shoulder and disappeared leaving Beca reeling and on the point of tears.

Chapter **4**

Beca ran a pen through another name on her sperm donor list, then went back over it again until it was completely obliterated by black ink. It was the 15th name to receive such savaging. Why didn't any of them want to talk to her? She wasn't that much of a bitch, was she? She swept the thought from her mind. It was hardly her fault they were all feeble half-wits. It might show poor judgement on her part for having gone out with them in the first place but she wasn't responsible for their moral character.

A week had passed since her unpleasant encounter with Hal, sufficient time to get spitting mad with him. At first she'd just wanted to lick her wounds, by mid-week she'd recovered enough to be really cross with him. Was it totally unreasonable to have expected him to be polite? By today she was furious with both him and herself for ever having considered such a second rate loser, and she apologised to her future child for nearly tainting it with such unworthy genes.

But Beca's ire wasn't total. There was a niggling, irritating thought that kept coming back. It was the look on his face when he'd seen her. That split second moment before his defences had gone up. She'd replayed it over and over again and knew she was right. There had been a fleeting, almost imperceptible look of pain. Was he still hurting? No, even Beca's ego struggled with such a notion.

She pretended to get on with her work. Up on one of her computer screens was a highly detailed chart. At a distance it could have passed for a sales projection for one of the big retailers she tracked, but if Sir Conrad took an impromptu walk of the trading floor she'd be facing unemployment. It was her ovulation chart. Beca had weighed up the need for absolute detail versus the likely humiliation that would follow if the information contained in this computer file fell into the wrong hands. If one of her male colleagues discovered the unsavoury method for checking her fertility and announced it to the world she would probably have to kill herself. Until then, she was ready to take the risk. She needed detail. She needed to be on top of the facts. Most of these came in the shape of unpronounceable words and as she rolled a few over her tongue she marvelled that anyone ever got born at all. There were so many different elements. It was like perfectly choreographed dancing. As she sat there a Busby Berkeley number was being tap danced out by her hormones. They were building up for the finale. Any moment now the prima donna of this month's review was going to appear, ready to be wafted by chiffon-waving dancers into the arms of her waiting hero. Only he wasn't waiting, he was nowhere in sight.

Beca looked at another computer screen which showed an analysis of her body temperature taken first thing, on the days that she remembered, for the last three months. With this information she was able to confirm that Big 'O' Day 1 was less than one week away. Where the bloody hell was her hero?

'Are you alright?' Liz crashed in on Beca's thoughts.

'Fine.' Beca hit the 'esc' button and the screens went black. 'Just life stuff.'

'Anything I can do?'

'Say something funny.'

Liz looked nonplussed. 'Maybe I should come back later.'

'What is it?'

Liz's eyes looked bright with intrigue, she leant towards Beca and spoke in a rasping whisper. 'I've found out about your friend's husband, the two-timing toe rag we caught with his hands…'

'Not here,' Beca interrupted. She looked around but no one seemed to have noticed her secretary's theatrics. She slid out of her chair and went to the ladies' loos. She could hear Liz's heels clicking behind her.

The cloakroom was vast and so tasteless that Beca often wondered if Ivana Trump had been invited to give a helping hand with the designers' mood boards. Still, she wasn't beyond pinching the occasional super soft loo roll, even if it was peach coloured, like everything else in the room. By the time Liz arrived Beca had begun checking the cubicles. They were unusually wide, presumably designed to accommodate the shoulder pads that had been *de rigeur* back when the building was put up.

'So tell me. Tom's her mentor, full of paternal affection and nothing else,' Beca said as she checked the last one. She turned when Liz made no reply. 'It's not going to be like that?'

'No. Sorry.'

'Let's have it then.' Beca folded her arms over her chest and braced herself. She'd been dreading this moment for a week, keeping up the futile hope that she'd misinterpreted what she'd seen.

'You wouldn't believe the trouble I've had,' Liz began.

Beca leant against the washbasin unit; this wasn't going to be the edited version.

'I've used up all the favours owed me, but it turns out I've got a knack for this detective business.' That explained why Liz was looking so pleased despite the attempt at a serious face.

'How did you get on?'

'I reckoned the woman we were looking for worked at the same bank as your friend's husband so that's where I started. There's a girl here in personnel who I chat to every morning in the queue at the coffee shop. Turns out she's friendly with one of the secretaries in the personnel department over at Redwig Morgan, and she introduced us. We went to that new sushi bar near the station. Have you tried it?'

Beca shook her head and hoped an arched eyebrow would help get Liz to the point.

'I asked Trudie, that's her name, if she knew the woman we were after. I gave her a full description and everything, but nothing clicked. So then I asked if she'd let me take a sneak at the personnel files.'

'She could get fired for doing that.'

'That's what she said, which is why I told her you'd find her a job here?'

'Me?'

'Yeah.'

'If she gets fired?'

'Well, actually, I had to promise you'd get her a new job anyway. The pay's better here. It's alright, isn't it? I'll be in deep do-doos if it's not.'

Beca shrugged. 'We'll sort something out. What happened next?'

'I went over yesterday afternoon to start looking through the files and guess who I saw.'

'I don't know.'

'Go on, guess.'

It was a toss-up between being cruel or being patient. Beca suppressed the snarl. 'Trudie?'

'No. Her.'

'Who?'

'The one your mate's husband was with.'

'Jesus.'

'Exactly.'

'Did you say anything to her?'

'No chance. But after that, it was a doddle. The security bloke on reception knew who she was, and it turns out so does Trudie, by reputation, if not personally.'

'What does that mean?' The frustration was evident in Beca's voice.

Liz drew breath to answer then stopped as one of the few female traders at the bank walked in, and after a cursory exchange locked herself in a cubicle. Liz might have looked a smidgen more guilty if she'd whistled an aimless tune and stared at the ceiling.

Beca turned to look at herself in the mirror. Irritation and anxiety were written across her face in deep lines that refused to budge when she tried smoothing them out with a finger. She checked her make-up. This didn't take long, coming as she did from the 'less is more' school of beauty. She then helped herself to a lipstick from Liz's make-up bag. It was pearlised and made her mouth look as subtle as the front end of a red 4 x 4. She pulled a paper towel out of the dispenser and rubbed it off. The colour worked on Liz, but then a bowl of fruit worked for Carmen Miranda.

The trader showed no signs of quitting the cubicle. Beca picked at a speck of fluff on her repro Dior shift dress and smoothed the material down over her hips. The black suede stilettos which had seemed like a good idea that morning were a bugger on her feet. She pulled herself up onto the washbasin counter, loosened the straps and let the shoes swing away from her red heels. The sound of a fight with a loo roll holder was followed by some rearranging of clothes, and a flush. Eventually the cubicle door opened, the woman washed her hands and left.

At the sound of the door shutting, Liz let out a great gasp of air. She leant closer towards Beca. 'Her name's Melissa Cartwright. Very posh and very stuck up with it. None of the secretaries like her.'

'What does she do?' Beca fiddled with the sensor-activated taps and splashed her dress. She swore and tried brushing off the drops of water before they soaked into the fabric.

'She's a junior researcher. Only graduated last year. Struts around like she owns the place, according to Trudie.'

'Can't imagine why. They're two-a-penny. What department is she in?' She turned on the hand dryer and held her dress as close to it as she could.

'Petrochemicals,' Liz shouted above the whirr.

'Tom's in legal, which means they don't work together,' Beca shouted back.

'That makes it worse?'

'Makes it less of an accident, like brushing shoulders over the Power Point slides. Most sectors don't even say hello at the Christmas party. He must have gone after her; devious bastard.' Beca tried getting the dryer to stop; hitting it didn't work either.

'Most likely she went after him.'

That was hard to believe. Why would anyone want to pursue Tom? He was so dull. At last the dryer ran its cycle and stopped. 'How old is she?'

'22.'

'Bloody hell, is that all? He's old enough to be her father. Does she even know he's married? Shit, supposing he's stringing her along. She could be completely innocent in all this.'

Liz shook her head. 'She had a fling with a VP last year, practically the same week she started working there.'

'Was he married?'

Liz nodded. 'With three kids. Although according to Trudie it wasn't his first affair.'

'So this Melissa Cartwright makes a habit of having affairs with married men. Maybe Tom was just a passing fancy, though God knows why.'

'I'm afraid not. The bad news is they've been seen together since the beginning of the year.'

'Six months. Poor bloody Abi.'

'So what are you going to do now?'

Beca began to shred a paper towel in her lap. The spotlight was on her. She'd wanted evidence and now she had it. It was just the tricky issue of what to do with it. 'I can't keep dodging her calls. She's got to be told, but I don't know what to say. Are you sure you're right? Perhaps Trudie made a mistake.'

Liz quashed her hopes with one look.

Beca sifted through the shredded paper in her lap. 'What would you do?'

Liz's lips thinned. 'She's got a right to know.'

'Abi and Tom are supposed to be the perfect couple. He's a knob-head, but they really love each other, at least they did. Why did he have to go and spoil everything? It's so selfish.'

'Men are,' Liz said with weary savvy.

'God Almighty, what am I going to tell her? She's been in love with Tom for years. I just can't do it. Not without more proof.'

'What more do you need?'

'I don't know, but something. I'll have to think about it when my head's not hurting so bloody much.' She slid off the washbasin counter and brushed bits of paper towel off her dress.

'Men.' Liz spat out the word like it was a hair stuck to her tongue.

Poor Liz. Did her ex-boyfriend have any idea how much damage he'd done? Beca caught sight of her own strained expression in the mirror. How to Break Your Best Friend's Heart had just gone in at number one on the week's to-do-list.

Beca sat on the Tube home and stared at her shoes. Her feet were screaming to be released but not even the pain could blank out her thoughts. Abi's problems had pushed How to Find A Man out of pole position, but nonetheless it kept up a good job of harrying for the top spot in Beca's stress-riven mind. As the train lurched its way along the track, images of Tom installing Melissa into Abi's beautiful home jostled for brain space with Hal rigged out like Ivan the Terrible gripping his sides with sadistic laughter as she threw herself prostrate at his feet begging him to have sex with her.

At least tomorrow was Saturday.

Beca burst through the front door, threw the newspapers on the floor and grabbed the edge of the kitchen worktop with trembling hands. Every muscle was screaming at her, the tar in her lungs had been blasted to the furthest extremities of her bronchial passages and her chest cavity felt like it was going to explode, which wouldn't matter much because her heart had migrated to her ears and was busy bursting her ear drums. Even her cheeks were throbbing. Beca hung her head between her outstretched arms and groaned. Sweat had pooled in her cleavage, it ran down under her cropped top, over her quivering stomach and was slowly absorbed by the waistband of her shorts. She could feel more sweat running down the back of her long legs. Her whole body shimmered and tingled with the effort of exercise. Perhaps she had overdone things a little.

Eventually her heart-rate returned to something approaching normal and she began to uncurl. The pain as she stretched her hamstrings was excruciating but in a nice sort of way and soon the glow of thermal explosion was replaced by one of satisfaction. Five miles. Not bad for an old bird with a twenty-a-day habit. Beca pulled off her trainers and left them on the floor. She peeled off her clothes and cast them aside as she padded upstairs to the bathroom for a shower.

The smell of freshly ground coffee filled the flat as Beca finished off making her cappuccino with a dusting of chocolate. She gave the chrome container another shake until the milky foam pressed over the sides of her cup under the weight of chocolate powder. She deserved it. Had she not just beaten her own PB? With a newspaper and some magazines wedged under one arm, she picked up her coffee and a banana smoothie. She crossed the living room, climbed out through the sash window and onto the terrace. She sat in a chair and put her feet on the balustrade. The terrace stood above the front porch and gave Beca a great view up and down the elegant Victorian street. At moments like this she knew life was good. She sipped her coffee and flicked through a mint copy of Wallpaper* magazine. The smell of wisteria surrounded her and down below life buzzed in a clever, chichi Notting Hill way. She had a day of utter indulgence planned beginning shortly with a haircut and manicure, followed by lunch and a leisurely afternoon of shopping.

The sound of the telephone ringing shattered the moment. She listened hoping it would go away, but its lure proved too much. She got up and answered it.

'Beca. Hi, it's me.'

Oh God. 'Abi, hi. How are you?'

'Fine. Have you been avoiding me?' she joked.

Beca's mind raced from zero to sonic boom in milliseconds. Her stomach bowled along not far behind. She coughed and hemmed which bought a little time. What the hell was she going to say? 'Of course not. I've just been very busy.' She sounded high-pitched, strained. Her voice had changed. Could Abi sense her unease? Could she tell Beca was lying to her?

'Are you alright?'

She could tell. Beca panicked, she tried laughing. 'I've been for a run.'

'You sound like you're in pain.'

'I overdid it a bit, that's all.'

'I was phoning to see if you want to come for a walk this afternoon. We're going to Kensington Gardens.'

'Is Tom?' she sounded like a bell tolling before an execution. 'Is Tom coming?' Now she sounded Mickey Mouse cheerful, which was better.

'Of course. He's got some work to finish off at the office this morning but he'll be back after lunch. So shall we meet you at the Diana playground?'

Abi had no idea. She hadn't got the first, faintest clue. Tom wasn't working, he was with that woman. Beca lit a cigarette and counted to five.

'Actually, Abi, thinking about it, I'd probably better not.'

'Dulcie would love to see you. She's been asking for you.'

Beca now felt as guilty as Abi had probably intended, but she held firm. On no account whatsoever did she want to see Tom. 'I'm still ploughing my way through my list.'

'How's all that going?'

A change of subject. Thank God. 'Bad, really bad. I've only got one week to go and I'm getting desperate. I had no idea so many men hated me.'

'I'm sure they don't.'

'Alistair Kelman practically screamed when I called.'

Abi laughed. 'You do have a habit of chewing them up. Isn't there a bird that eats her mate after copulation?'

'No, it's a spider. A black widow spider – white spinster spider in my case.'

'Don't you have to be a virgin to be a spinster?'

'Don't quibble.' Beca went back onto the terrace to retrieve her coffee.

'So what are you going to do?' Abi asked.

'I'm tempted to shag anybody,' she said leaning over the balustrade. The milkman was working his way slowly up the street and she weighed up his potential. There was a long silence and she could hear Abi drawing her breath. Never a good sign.

'I don't know how to say this, but.'

'But?'

'I was talking to Claire last night about your idea to get pregnant.'

'And?' Beca began to feel defensive.

'Oh dear this isn't very easy.'

'Just say it, Abi, for Christ's sake. Is anyone dying?'

'No. Of course not.'

'Then it can't be that bad. Just tell me.'

'OK. I think you're making a big mistake having a baby without a partner. It's really hard bringing up a child even with a husband, I just don't think you know what you're getting yourself into.' Abi rattled out her speech. 'There. I've said it now.'

'Oh.'

'I've upset you, haven't I? I'm sorry, Beca. It's just it seems a shame to rush into things. You're only 36. Why don't you try finding a decent man? Claire was telling me there are all sorts of dating agencies, and places on the internet where you can meet people and chat.'

Beca's temperature was beginning to rise again.

'You could meet a really nice man and then think about having children.' Beca could feel Abi's enthusiasm pinging down the telephone. She imagined her smiling, the phone wedged up to her ear as she got lunch ready for her children. No doubt the sun was shining in through the window bathing her in an aura of motherly perfection not dissimilar to the Madonna. 'Wouldn't you be happier if you were in a relationship first?'

'If I was, do you think I'd be trying to get pregnant this way?'

'You're cross. I'm sorry. It's just Tom and I are so happy. I want you to be too.'

Beca bit her tongue. She would sooner swallow it than upset her friend. She put her hand over the receiver and banished the Furies with a scream.

'Are you alright?'

'Fine,' Beca replied through gritted teeth. 'I'll speak to you later.' She hung up the phone and screamed again. She needed to take a happy pill, relax and have some nice thoughts. But it was too much. It was bad enough having to put up with Abi's 'no woman is happy without a man' prattle, but coming from one whose own perfect husband was screwing around was just too much.

Beca went around the flat banging things but stopped when the phone rang again. She glared at it, then marched over and answered it.

'What?' she shouted into the receiver.

'Your telephone manner hasn't improved much.'

'Who is this?'

'Hal Carson.'

Beca's heart went off at a gallop again. 'Have you phoned up to abuse me as well?' She tried laughing in a sing-song carefree manner, like this call wasn't the most important one of her life.

'You said you had a proposition.' His voice was flat and humourless which threw Beca and she stumbled to find the right words to reply.

'Yes, I did. I was hoping you might,' she hesitated. 'Look, I can't do this on the telephone. Can we meet up?'

'Is that necessary?' He wasn't making things easy for her.

'I'd prefer it. Unless of course you're going to be unbelievably rude again, in which case I'd rather forget it.' Hal didn't respond. 'OK, you can be a bit rude. Are you free tonight?'

'No, I'm out. Monday is the earliest I can make it.'

'OK. Do you know Neptune's in Soho?' Beca asked.

'Yes. 7 o'clock.'

'It'll have to be later. I've got a meeting that won't finish until 8:30.'

'Cancel it. I've got plans for later.'

'I'm not sure I can.'

Again, Hal was silent.

'OK, OK. I'll cancel.'

He hung up without saying goodbye. Beca stared at the telephone. She felt like she'd been run over by a freight train. It had never occurred to her that Hal might have changed from the sensitive man she'd once known into a complete arsehole.

Chapter 5

Beca slipped out of the ladies' cloakroom and checked in both directions. Liz was at the far end of the empty corridor looking anxious as she kept the lift doors from closing.

'Come on,' she said.

Beca's spike heels clattered on the marble floor and echoed like small arms fire as she dashed towards her. Liz took her finger off the button and ducked out of the lift. 'I hope it's worth it,' she said as the doors closed.

Beca grinned to herself. She had the same feeling of excitement that she used to get when bunking off school, playing truant to meet a boyfriend or to share cigarettes with Abi, Claire and Sally in the Co-op café when they were supposed to be in double biology. But Beca had left her wayward, delinquent years well behind her. If anything she was the school swot now. Diligent and conscientious, she hadn't taken a day off sick since she'd been with the bank, which was coming up for fifteen years. Never in all that time had she cancelled a meeting with Sir Conrad, but Hal had left her little choice. It was 7pm or not at all.

Quite possibly nobody had ever cancelled a meeting with Sir Conrad before because he had got on the phone to her himself to find out why. Beca had pleaded a family crisis.

'Well I hope it's a matter of life and death,' he'd said.

'It is, in a manner of speaking.'

Sir Conrad had been less than satisfied and after telling her she'd blotted her copybook he'd hung up.

'Overbearing bully,' Beca muttered as she watched the floor numbers descend to ground floor level. It wasn't as though she was taking the whole afternoon off. Thin end of the wedge, Sir Conrad had said. What wedge? Was she threatening him with the European Courts for making her work obscenely long hours? No. Had she ever complained that she worked double the national average week? Exactly.

The lift doors opened on the ground floor and Beca shot out, clicking her way through the foyer. She had stretched the bank's dress code to breaking point today, but the average business suit lacked the 'come fuck me' factor that she needed for tonight. A quick change of jackets in the ladies' cloakroom and a fresh layer of makeup was enough to do the trick. It did feel odd leaving work with a goodly portion of her cleavage on display, but it worked magic on the doorman who opened the main door in an unusual gesture of gallantry. Beca flashed him a smile and walked straight into Sir Conrad who was coming the other way. She let out an involuntary screech which startled him even more, then left him reeling in a vapour trail of Issey Miyake as she fled down the street.

Shit, shit, shit. Shit. That was dumb. Utterly brainless. Why hadn't she just said hello and carried on walking as if nothing was wrong? God, she was in so much trouble. How was she going to explain the dress? And her Manolos? Maybe he hadn't noticed them. Of course he hadn't, he'd been concentrating on her lack of clothes. What the hell was she going to say tomorrow morning?

The Underground platform was more than usually crowded. It didn't bode well and anticipating a scrum to get on the next train, Beca jostled her way to the platform edge and maintained a close watch on her space, repelling newcomers with fearsome looks and a sharp elbow.

Stuff Sir Conrad. Beca had more pressing concerns. She had spent the whole of Sunday trying to imagine her meeting with Hal. She'd fast forwarded through endless films for inspiration and then practised in front of the mirror. But no matter who she'd tried to be, the principal problem remained the same: how was she going to broach the subject with Hal? The more she went over the options, the more it came across like some erotic chat-up line. 'Would you like to have sex with me?' 'Like to sow your seeds in me, big boy?' Still, perhaps writing porno screenplays could be her new career, now that she'd messed up at the bank. How exactly was she going to switch from general pleasantries to the crux of the matter? While drunk was the only answer that she had come up with so far. It wasn't brilliant but it might have to substitute for anything sensible.

At last a train pulled up alongside the platform. As it finally juddered to a halt Beca realised she had misjudged her place; the doors opened a few feet from her. Her hard fought for prime position was suddenly relegated to back-of-beyond no hoper's spot. There was little doubt in Beca's mind that she was going to get on that train. It was vital. Her entire future happiness, the shape of her life, the existence of another human being hung in the balance. What did it matter if someone else got home late? She had an important mission. Beca pushed and shoved her way forward. That she left a trail of seething and bruised people behind her was of no account. She was on.

The train didn't manage to get past more than two stops before it ground to a halt in a tunnel. The lights in the carriage flickered and then failed. Groans and anxious laughs were drowned out by the engines as the driver tried to coax some life out of his train. The lights came on then went out completely.

Time dragged. It had been stupid to assume the decrepit tube system would be quicker in the rush hour than a taxi. Very stupid. At best she had twenty minutes to get to Neptune's. She didn't have to be there precisely on the dot, but she didn't suppose Hal would be hanging around long if she was late. Why hadn't she booked a taxi from the office?

She was trapped, a victim of the vagaries of public transport. It seemed unreasonable to start swearing when she had some poor woman pressed to the side of the carriage, but the sense of panic, the importance she placed on getting to the bar on time were chewing up her insides. She tried breathing deeply and twisted her fingers while making offerings to the god of trains. If the train started moving, she'd live a more virtuous life. If it moved and kept moving, she'd even give up smoking.

Nothing happened. Then after several minutes a weary sounding driver announced with no sense of irony that the train had broken down. It was starting to get very stuffy. Beca pulled down the window in the connecting door. The air in the tunnel was dirty and foul smelling but held enough oxygen to support life.

Just when her thoughts had turned from a failed childless future to no future at all, the train began to move. Or rather it jerked its way forward and as she and all the other passengers willed it on, it finally pulled into the next station.

The train doors opened and all who had suffered the sardine experience fought to get out. This was a great opportunity to take charge and be a hero, but Beca instinctively knew the George Cross would never be hers when she abandoned the less able bodied to the crowds and fought her way out above ground into the relative fresh air of Holborn. She had five minutes to get to Piccadilly Circus. She scoured the streets for a taxi. Nothing, not even a dubious looking minicab. There wasn't much else for it but to run.

Black satin shoes with four inch clear plastic heels would never have been her preferred choice of footwear for running two miles across London, not least because they cost a fortune. The same went for a figure-hugging dress that clamped her knees together and didn't afford the freedom her limbs needed to jump a box of matches. She covered very little ground in a series of frantic, staccato steps, her bottom swinging sideways and her arms pumping like a long-distance walker.

It was ridiculous. Beca stopped, looped the straps of her handbag over her shoulder, bent down, pulled her dress up to her hips and took off her shoes. With a Manolo in each hand she streaked down High Holborn and then into Shaftesbury Avenue. By the time she reached Cambridge Circus her feet were stinging and the smile she had affected for curious on-lookers had worn off. She checked her watch. She was now three minutes late. A taxi with its 'for hire' light on swung into view, she threw herself at it leaving the driver little choice but to stop.

'Neptune's Bar,' she said as she jumped into the back of the cab.

'It's just round the bloody corner.'

'I'll pay you double. You miserable bastard,' Beca added under her breath.

'What was that?'

Beca ignored him. She was gasping and trembling from the exertion and now that she had stopped running, sweat began to erupt bead-like on her forehead. She could feel her armpits prickling. Alluring? She thought not. Then she noticed her tights had disintegrated. What had probably started as a series of small tears had expanded and joined to form two gaping holes, a bare and blackened foot stuck out of each one. Beca hiked her skirt up to her waist and yanked her tights down just as the taxi pulled up in front of Neptune's. With milliseconds to spare she smoothed down her dress and was ready to step out as a bouncer opened the door.

The exterior of the bar was designed to frighten off all but the super confident and even Beca's heart trembled just a little as she approached the sentry guard of four shed-sized bouncers. Perhaps she should have chosen somewhere a little more low key. A place she'd been to before might have been a good start, instead of the most fashionable night spot in London.

Beca looked at the vast night club laid out below her, then climbed down the grand staircase that only Fred Astaire could have tackled with any style. What had she been thinking? The club was huge, it was packed with Soho's super-trendy and it felt like every one of them was watching her. The style was Gaultier meets Esther Williams, post-modern camp rubbing shoulders with 1940s kitsch. Beca congratulated herself on reaching the bottom step without falling, but found it difficult to be nonchalant about the perfectly formed man swinging from a trapeze above her head. He appeared to be wearing nothing but a broad smile and a large conch shell. She wasn't too sure just whose modesty the shell was protecting. Beca headed for the safety of the loos.

She caught the reflected looks of a couple of women as they preened themselves in the mirror set above a row of washbasins. She claimed a space between them, slipped off her shoes and turned on the taps. With her skirt pulled up, she washed first one, then the other foot in the sink. The bar was posh enough to have linen hand towels which she used to rub off the worst that London's pavements had to offer. Ignoring the frosty vibes, she looked at herself in the mirror. Her cheeks were more pink than vivid red now but her eyes had a startled appearance. She looked nervous. Ten minutes later she still looked nervous only now she had too much make-up on. Beca lit a cigarette and forced her face into a smile. It was closer to a grimace, but as near to seductive as she was going to get. It would have to do.

The bar was a raised circular affair in the middle of the room. It meant combating more steps but Beca was thirsty. She caught a barman's eye and he obliged her with a gin and tonic. She took a swig, life instantly got better. She took another and her frozen features thawed into a more natural arrangement. Calmer, decidedly cooler now, she leant back against the bar and took in her surroundings. She'd really excelled herself this time. In an effort to impress Hal with her finger-on-the-pulse trendiness, she had chosen of all places, a pick-up joint to meet him. Brilliant.

Another reason for choosing the check-in lounge at Terminal 4 above this place was its layout. Fanning out in all directions from the bar were the usual arrangement of tables and chairs, but every now and then there was a cluster of pink satin, scallop-shaped booths. The backs were so high that their occupants were hidden from view to all but the most persistent investigators. Beca presumed, as she did a first tour of the room that Hal wouldn't be stupid enough to have chosen a booth. She'd never be able to find him; surely he'd have figured that out. Still, she found herself back at the bar without having spotted him. She ordered another drink. Emboldened by more gin she set off on a second circuit, this time taking in the booths. Plenty of trysting couples but no Hal.

She reminded herself why she was doing all this. Hal wasn't the end goal, he was the means to the end. So what if she made an idiot of herself?

If she found him, then next weekend they could be making a baby. Beca nodded to herself by way of encouragement and lit another cigarette. Smoke peeled off from the end and went straight in her eye. She squinted and swore as a tear trickled down her cheek. She turned around to head back to the ladies' loos and there he was, about twenty feet away, leaning against a giant pink scallop with a knowing half smile on his face; that disarming, infuriatingly smug smile. If it was designed to make her feel awkward then he almost succeeded, but Beca managed to maintain dignity and eye contact as she walked towards him wiping mascara from her cheek.

He made no attempt to meet her halfway and her heart lurched off ahead of her as a whole new crop of worries sprang up. Should she kiss him hello? God, he was so good looking. Or maybe just shake his hand? What was best? Beca smiled and shifted her drink into her left hand in case he wanted to shake her right. Her eyes ran over his face scrutinising every slight change. He could slice bread with those cheek bones. Age had only improved him, the creases and lines added character – a depth she fully planned to spend a fortune trying to avoid.

Perhaps Hal wasn't as well versed in social mores as Beca because when she turned a cheek and puckered up, he looked blankly at her, said hello and then slipped into the booth. Beca suspected he'd done it on purpose. She followed, edging her way around the leather table and then hung there, uncertain whether to run away screaming or sit down.

'Oh,' she said lamely. She remembered to shut her mouth after a while but remained half sitting, holding onto the table edge wondering if there was any point completing the action. In the end her thigh muscles decided the point for her. She sat down.

'This is my wife.' Hal said resting his arm possessively around a stunning woman's shoulders.

'Oh,' Beca said again. A full-on code red emergency klaxon exploded into life somewhere behind her left ear.

'Sopphieee,' the woman purred with a French accent. Her quivering porn-star mouth formed a damp, round 'O'. She was stylish yet slutty. Beca hated her.

'Beca,' she replied. Her name didn't resonate in quite the same way. She held out her hand which Sophie limply shook. Her touch left an itch in the palm of Beca's hand that she rubbed on her hip. 'I didn't realise you were married.' This was just dreadful. Why hadn't he said anything about a bloody wife? What a complete waste of time, not to mention the utter humiliation.

Sophie cast a surprised, hurt look at her husband. 'We've been married for five months.' She squeezed Hal's thigh a little too high for polite company.

'But we've been together for years, haven't we,' Hal managed to add before licking out the inside of her mouth. Beca recoiled from the sexual heat burning off them. Her brain was doing backward somersaults. Too much gin, too much shock.

They both looked at her expectantly. Exactly how the fuck was she going to get out of this one? Panic of elephantine proportions pummelled her. The klaxon got louder and she got ready to evacuate. She needed to think, and quickly. But thinking was going to be difficult with Sophie sitting opposite her. She was wearing one of those spaghetti strap dresses that clung to the sticky-out bits and skimmed past the slim, toned, lithe parts. Beca could feel her mouth shaping up for a sulk. There was no evidence of underwear, no ugly knicker line or hint of white M&S beneath and nothing propping up her breasts which were, undeniably, as pert as a 16 year old's. She probably was 16, which made Hal a virtual paedophile.

'You said you had something you wanted to ask me.' That smile was back on his face. Beca could swear he was reading her mind. 'A proposition.'

Beca weighed up her chances. Ice cubes and red-hot infernos came to mind. She was wasting her time here. Not once in the zillion different scenarios that she had played through in her mind had a wife popped up to spoil everything. It was time to admit defeat and go home.

'I did, you're absolutely right, but under the present circumstances I can see how it might not work.'

'Couldn't you have figured that out before dragging us down here?'

That rankled. Beca tried to remain polite. 'Let's just say I didn't have all the facts. Now that I do, well, trust me.'

Hal shrugged. 'Come on, babe, let's get out of here.'

'But I have another drink coming,' Sophie replied.

'Leave it.'

'I don't want to.' She clearly wasn't budging. Hal sat back down again and looked at Beca. Was he expecting her to get up and leave? She had another drink coming too, so bollocks to that. There was a long silence. It extended past the excruciating point and Hal started drumming his fingers on the table. This would have been the perfect time for Beca to go, if she hadn't been so pigheaded.

'If you'd told me you were married, none of us would be here,' she said to Hal. 'I wouldn't have called you if I'd known you had a wife.'

Sophie looked indignant, Hal leant back in his scallop and smiled.

Beca's eyes widened. 'God, no, it's not what you're thinking. I don't fancy you or anything like that.' She laughed. 'I wasn't trying to get back with you. What I wanted was your sperm. I'm going to have a baby, only I need someone's sperm.'

Hal stared at her in stunned silence. She thought perhaps his jaw dropped slightly but she wasn't sure. At that precise moment she was more worried about what his wife might say, or more to the point, do. But she didn't do or say anything. They stared at her. Beca lit a cigarette and exhaled a huge plume of smoke. She really needed to learn to keep her mouth shut.

Sophie shrugged. 'He is beautiful, no?'

There was no need to gloat.

'I can see why you would choose him.' Sophie ran her hand through his hair. Beca stayed stony faced. No way was she encouraging this preening. 'I see the way women look at him. But you know, I am not upset that you have said this. I think it is a great honour to be asked such a thing.'

'Are you mad?' Hal asked, and Beca was glad he did, for she would have otherwise. 'You do know what "sperm" means, don't you?'

'Of course. Do you think I'm an idiot? I don't see why you Englishmen are so cold about these things. Me, I gave my sister some of my eggs. She didn't have any, so I gave her mine. It was no big deal to me, but it meant everything to her. I was happy to help.'

'I'm amazed at your reaction,' Beca said.

'You're not the only one,' Hal added.

'I'm very liberated. We're all adults, are we not? I think you should agree.'

It was Beca's turn to be stunned.

'No, absolutely not. I can't think of any reason why I should do her a favour. There's no way I'm sitting in some cubicle with a wank magazine. Go and find someone else.'

Beca took a long drag on her cigarette. Her brain said stop, but her mouth just kept moving. 'For your information, artificial insemination wasn't what I had in mind. The success rate is higher the natural way.'

Hal stared at her momentarily and then began to laugh.

'I don't understand. What is she saying?' Sophie laughed, taking her cue from Hal.

'She wants me to have sex with her.' Hal could hardly contain his humour.

Sophie stopped tittering and looked at her husband. 'But this is outrageous. Why are you laughing?'

'Because it's hilarious.'

'No, no, no,' Sophie shrieked. 'I will not have you two swapping jokes, playing games I do not understand. This is my man, *comprenez*? That means he screws me and no one else.'

Hal shook with laughter and wiped his eyes.

'I haven't asked him to,' Beca said. 'I just wanted to set the record straight. I thought he might have been up for it, that's why I wanted to meet him. It was your sperm I wanted, not you,' she said looking at Hal.

Hal laughed even harder. 'You know you really are the most insensitive, self-obsessed person I have ever met.'

'I'm telling you so you don't go away thinking I'm carrying a torch for you or something stupid.'

'So we're clear, even if I wasn't married, nothing would induce me to climb into bed with you. Do you think I'd want my child being reared by an emotional retard like you?'

Beca ground her cigarette out in the ashtray. 'My mistake. I had no idea you felt like that about me.'

'What do you expect? You turn up after eight years and think I'm going to help you out. Why would I?'

'Don't sulk. I thought you'd be game on for it. I thought you were one of those tree-hugging, free-loving, child-in-man's-body types.'

'But I don't even like you.'

'Fine. Forget I ever called. I'd have paid you, by the way. I wasn't expecting you to do it for nothing. No doubt a struggling artist like you could have done with the cash.'

Hal's face hardened and Beca was pleased; she'd hit a sore spot.

'How much?' Sophie's voice hung in the air.

'What?' Beca was confused.

'How much would you pay him? Us?'

She had heard right the first time. 'Well, I hadn't thought of a specific figure.' This woman was barmy.

Hal pulled his wife to her feet. 'I just wanted to know how much she would have paid you?' she protested. 'I'm curious. There's no harm in that.'

'Drop it.'

Sophie shrugged with Gallic indifference as Hal took her by the elbow and guided her away. At last the drinks arrived along with the bill.

'Have they been here all day?' Beca asked the waitress as she checked the long column of figures. Just fantastic. Insulted, abused and now she got to pay for the privilege. It had been a set-up. She should have known he'd go out of his way to get his own back at her. True, he'd had no idea what she was going to ask him, but it wouldn't have cost him anything to mention the small matter of being married. Not unless he'd wanted to rub her nose in it. Perhaps she hadn't treated him as well as she could have eight years back, but who'd ever heard of bearing a grudge for that long? It was pathetic.

The fact that she'd set her cap at him would always be a mark against her character. The distance of time had fogged her reason. It should have been obvious from the start he'd be petty-minded. Anyone who still poked out an existence above a record shop was bound to be bitter.

She toasted her lucky escape. Where the hell did he get off criticising her? The fact they'd shared a bed for a while years ago did not give him carte blanche to be rude. She put her glass back on the table and stared at the bubbles collecting under the slice of lemon. Who was he to call her an emotional retard? Since when was he so bloody well informed about the developmental state of her emotions? He'd drawn a whole set of conclusions, based on what? Knowledge that was years out of date. Showed how narrow-minded he was.

She drained her glass, lit another cigarette and reached over for Sophie's untouched drink. As she sipped the vodka she fidgeted with her lighter, tapping it on the table top, opening and shutting the lid and working herself up into a strop.

For another thing, what business did he have saying he didn't like her? She, as it happened, hadn't thought much of his wife, or him for that matter, but had she mentioned it? Was she ill-mannered enough to point it out? No, because that would have been rude. At least one of them there had managed to stay civil.

Mentioning his need for money had pissed him off. It was a minor victory, just a scratch compared to the battle scars she was carrying. She emptied Sophie's glass and sat back in her scallop seat. Three weeks of dogged hard work and she had nothing to show for it except a large drinks bill and a battered ego. And who said getting pregnant was the easy part?

Chapter 6

After a night of calm reflection Beca was still foaming at the mouth with indignation. She'd woken up with an almighty headache and had spent the morning brutalising her team. Hopefully her behaviour was out of character enough to be shrugged off. Then again, she didn't give a crap if they were all weeping into their coffee. Hal's smug face haunted her. He had been insufferable, arrogant and opinionated. She hated herself for ever having got in touch with him. Self-loathing swept over her every time she thought of last night. What had happened to her good judgement? She used to pride herself on how selective she was. Not any more. She was angry because he'd been so rude to her, but she was doubly cross because his curt manner had really got to her. It needled that he'd managed to wind her up so successfully. A few simple twists of the key in her back and she was off, whizzing around like a manic clockwork toy.

How dare he question her suitability to bring up a child? The weight of his knowledge on the subject was less than that of an ant. Smaller than an ant's turd, in fact, which was clearly what he was using for brains these days because why else would he have married that lunatic. It just went to show what an emotional retard he was, if he placed self-supporting tits above intelligence.

Sir Conrad's usual morning tour of the trading floor had failed to materialise. If she hadn't been so pissed off with life this piece of news might have brought relief. As it was, she had no fear of the inevitable drubbing she'd get when he finally did appear. Bumping into him the afternoon before in full trollop regalia was too good a chance for such a sadistic man to miss, but since last night she had become hardened; his insults would bounce off her.

Beca took the sandwich and bottle of water Liz had ordered for her and went out. She wrestled through the throng of people in the lobby, shouldered open the glass door and swept outside. The quick application of a pair of sunglasses saved her sleep-deprived eyes from the blinding sun. It seemed everyone else in the City had got the same idea to converge in the amphitheatre-shaped piazza at the front of the bank and spread out in the sun. What they were all looking so bloody pleased about was a mystery. It was sunny. Big deal.

She picked her way through the office workers stripped of their jackets and ties and searched for Abi's number on her mobile. The secret of Tom's activities hung unspoken between them but the need to vent her annoyance far outweighed any qualms she had. It was another item on the list of things that were aggravating her lately that she felt culpable, as if she was in some way responsible for the way Abi's husband behaved. She wasn't the one playing the unfaithful card, although it might as well have been considering how awful she felt about it. Bloody men.

'You're there, I don't believe it. I was beginning to think you'd abandoned your children,' she said when Abi answered. 'I called six times last night but kept getting your babysitter.'

Abi laughed. 'I was out with Tom. We do still go out occasionally.'

God, not another happy, upbeat person. It was very grating. Beca could hear Abi coaxing her youngest to eat more food with aeroplane noises and unintelligible references to Noddy.

'What's Billy having?'

'Sweet potato and mince.' The plane swept in again.

Beca found space on a sun-scorched concrete bench away from the happy people perched around the central fountain. She peeled the lid off her sandwich and was set upon by a pack of aggressive pigeons who sauntered nonchalantly into place and looked ready to mug her. She kicked out her foot and scattered them.

'Aren't you going to ask where we went?' Abi's voice bubbled with enthusiasm.

'Sorry. Where did you go?' Beca stared the pigeons down.

'To this fabulous restaurant called The Ivy. Have you heard of it?'

'Of course I've heard of it. Everyone has.'

'It was great. I saw Richard Gere. Can you imagine? He's much shorter than I thought, but he smiled when I waved at him.'

Beca pictured the moment and cringed. 'You need to get out more. Why the special treat?'

Abi laughed. 'I've got no idea. Tom said we don't spend enough time together. I wasn't about to argue.'

So he was feeling guilty. What Beca couldn't understand was why it was gnawing up her insides. She wasn't the one he was having the bloody affair with.

'Did you have a good time?' she asked with a cheerfulness she didn't feel.

'Fantastic. Just like it used to be before domesticity took the edge off. When we got home,'

'Less detail,' Beca interrupted. 'I don't want to know.'

Abi chuckled. 'Let's just say he must have read a book.' She sounded so pleased with life, so completely unaware. The only book he'd been reading lately was by one Melissa Cartwright. A sour taste developed in Beca's mouth. She threw the remains of her sandwich at the pack of pigeons and scored a direct hit. At least two got splattered with tuna mayonnaise.

'So how about you?' Abi asked her.

'I met Hal last night.'

'Seriously? You kept that quiet. How did it go?'

'Awful. Just horrible.'

'Why?'

Beca checked for waggling ears. Her co-habitees on the bench looked innocent enough. 'His wife was there.'

'Wife!' Abi burst into laughter. Billy thought it was hilarious too apparently because Beca could hear him chortling and bashing his plate in the background.

'It's not funny.'

'No, of course not.' She clearly thought it was though. 'Did you have any idea? Why didn't he say something before you met?'

'My point exactly. It's not the sort of thing you forget. Why wasn't she there at the cinema when I saw him?' Beca unscrewed the lid of her water bottle and warm fizzy water exploded over her. She leapt up shaking the water off her white linen trousers which had become transparent, and swore.

'What's wrong?'

'Nothing, just one of those days. Anyway, why doesn't he wear a wedding ring?'

'A lot of men don't.'

'Well they should.' Beca sat down again and flicked water at the pigeons nearest to her. 'It should be compulsory.'

'What was she like?'

'French. And grubby.'

'She was dirty? That doesn't sound very pleasant.'

'More smutty than grubby, like Bridget Bardot. You know, smouldering in a bad girl way. Except she has this mass of tangled brown hair instead of blonde.'

'Not that you were jealous.' The humour in Abi's voice was annoying.

'Me? Why should I be? I'm just annoyed I've wasted so much time.' Perhaps her pissed-off tone was too subtle.

'Not that it makes much difference,' Abi said.

'What doesn't?'

'If she'd been a Ukrainian shot putter with hairy armpits, she'd still be his wife. I don't suppose it helps that she's beautiful.'

'Did I say beautiful? Smug, definitely. They were all over each other.'

'Married people are allowed to snog.'

'This isn't a joke.'

'Absolutely not. It must have been very embarrassing.'

Abi had clearly misunderstood the purpose of this call. Beca hadn't phoned to brighten up her friend's day with a couple of self-deprecating anecdotes. She wanted support, but instead of pouring out the sympathy, her best friend was playing chocolate pudding trains. She could always hang up and talk to the pigeons instead.

She swallowed her pride. 'What was worse, Hal thought I fancied him. It was ghastly. Her gloating, him preening and me sitting there like a complete pillock.' She put the phone in her lap and waited for Abi to stop laughing. 'Have you finished?' she asked a while later.

'Yes.' Abi blew her nose. 'Sorry, I know I shouldn't laugh.'

'But that doesn't seem to be stopping you. I swear it was the worst night of my life.'

'It must have been,' Abi said, although it was difficult to tell what with her peeing herself with glee.

'Nothing is going according to plan,' Beca complained.

'Life generally doesn't.' Abi was more sober now. 'Don't worry, you'll find someone else.'

She made it sound so easy. 'Who though? I've only got four days.'

'No you haven't. You've got years. Maybe this crazy scheme of yours just wasn't meant to be.'

'Don't start that again.' Beca threw the lid of her bottle of water at a pigeon.

'I know what it's like to want a baby, but you have to be a bit calmer about it. Charging around like a maniac, offering to pay men to get you pregnant is insane. People just don't do that sort of thing.'

'He called me an emotional retard.'

'That's a bit strong,' Abi said.

'A bit? You're kidding me. How about a lot?'

'A lot then.' The spluttering outrage was strangely absent.

'You think he's right, don't you?'

'Not really. Do you want to come over tonight?'

What chance of getting through the evening without letting something slip about Tom? Besides, he could be there. That would be chummy.

'Thanks, but you're in too good a mood for me. I'm going to go home and sulk.'

Beca said goodbye and hung up feeling no better than she had before. She took a battered piece of paper out of her bag and flattened it out on her lap. At the bottom of the page were three names, all the others had been blotted out.

Beca balled the piece of paper and threw it in the bin under her desk. Her last chance had just hung up on her. Perhaps drawing breath between saying hello and asking him if he was married would have been a good idea. The note of hysteria in her voice might have been off-putting as well. The week had slipped past. Tomorrow was Big 'O' Day and she'd blown her chances of conceiving.

Quite how she'd managed to build herself up to such a state was bewildering. Abi was right, as usual; this wasn't the only chance she'd ever have. It wasn't as if tomorrow her sole remaining egg would head south. There were plenty more, she hoped, waiting to pop out next month and for many more months after that. So why the panic? Why the amphetamine-fuelled heart-pounding? Every thought she had, whether it was about work or what to wear that morning, competed with fluffy images of the child she wanted. Now she was to blame for this tiny human being not having life. It was her fault. She'd failed. It was scary how out of control she felt. Harassing ex-boyfriends on the phone was a ridiculous way to spend every free moment she had. Perhaps now was the time to get that therapist's telephone number from Abi before the police came along to section her.

The week had ended in triumph for her team, not that any of them were speaking to her. They'd nearly doubled on their monthly target. Beca couldn't have cared less. The phrase 'emotional retard' kept ricocheting around inside, taking out vital organs and leaving her more damaged than before. Instead of patching things up with her colleagues over a celebratory drink, she headed for the gym. She wasn't often to be found there on a Friday night, but the need to unleash the pent-up aggression was strong and the treadmill presented the only legal option she could think of.

Her body, like her head, had crumbled during the week. A simple matter of running a few miles became a Herculean task. She couldn't get into her stride. There was no spring in her pace, just a flat-footed, knee-crunching struggle. As her legs malfunctioned she could feel her ankles jarring and her muscles tearing with the strain of moving her body. She was all the more aware of this desperate spectacle because the ultra-stylish Mondrian-inspired gym was less than five minutes from the office. This meant that half the bank was sweating and panting around her. Half an hour ago these workers had been in suits, their clothes loose fitting, their bodies covered. Now, given new surroundings, it was deemed acceptable to bare flesh. Life was bad enough without insight into the hairiness of her male colleagues. How could she ever take the head of ITC seriously again knowing he could, given the urge, plait the hair on his back? She particularly did not want to see Sir Conrad's executive secretary bouncing along in jaunty fashion on the treadmill beside her with her bottom bisected by an up-the-bum-crack leotard. Running next to a full-sized Barbie doll complete with bobbing pony-tail and full makeup was not helping Beca see life in a better light.

For once her competitive streak failed her. She just wanted to survive the eight mile run and go home. She focussed on the bank of TV screens high on the wall in front of the exercise machines. Endless sports and news channels dominated, while a boy band was in full swing on one. Beca changed audio channels and listened in on her headphones. She watched as the boys leaped around in front of a burning car. They had some earnest message which she couldn't quite work out and felt too old to bother trying. Instead her eyes wandered over to one of the fitness trainers. She'd noticed him before because his thighs rubbed together when he walked. A smile spread across her face; she'd have to be desperate to consider a man like that. God only knew what all those steroids had done to his sperm count.

The instructor must have sensed her watching him because the next moment he looked up and smiled back. His teeth practically blinded her. It was hard to hold down her laugh as she looked away and tried to pretend she'd just been glancing around the room and not eye-balling his genital region.

At least she could laugh at herself for even considering him. That had to be a good sign; a measure of the return of her sanity. It was time to make a dignified withdrawal. She needed to restock the dwindling Twiglet and gin supplies and get drunk. First she wanted to wipe the floor with Sir Conrad's secretary, an ambitious but necessary task. Her legs were far from spring-like but she cranked up the speed on the treadmill. Moments later the Barbie doll did the same. Beca sensed victory and smiled. At that speed and with those spindly legs, her rival would not last another mile. Three miles later Beca's legs were beginning to buckle, while the competition remained as perky as ever. The smile had gone from her face, replaced by a tortured grimace. Humiliating defeat was beginning to look the likely outcome when the waistband of her shorts began to vibrate. Beca yanked off the headphones and reached for her mobile as a tinny rendition of *Suspicious Minds* filled the gym.

'Hello,' she gasped.

'How much?' Sophie's feline tones were unmistakable.

Beca was so startled she stopped running, shot down the treadmill and crashed in a heap on the floor. The mobile flew out of her hand and scudded off across the gym. Sir Conrad's secretary looked down at her with malicious pleasure. Victory was hers. Muttering obscenities, Beca crawled off and grappled under a rowing machine to retrieve her phone.

'Are you still there?' Her throat was so dry she could barely speak.

'I'm here,' Sophie replied. 'How much will you pay us if my husband gets you pregnant?'

'What? Are you serious?' A laugh escaped Beca's mouth as she limped towards the water cooler.

'Aren't you?' Sophie asked.

Excitement put a strange edge on her voice. 'Of course, I just didn't expect to hear from you again.'

'I don't have all day. Do you want him or not?'

The truthful answer to that was, no not really, but did she want a baby? Oh, yes. She pulled at her hair trying to think of a price while berating herself for not working one out long ago. 'Three thousand.'

'Pah! Ridiculous. We want twenty thousand.'

They obviously put a high value on his stock. Beca leant against the water dispenser. 'For a few minutes work?'

'Hal says that's what you earn.'

He had a point, but then her job involved using her brain and years of training. Hal just had to use his prick. 'How about ten thousand?' Her stomach twisted with nerves as she waited for Sophie to hang up.

'Maybe you don't want a baby that much?'

She'd give up everything to have one, but the idea of handing it all over to Hal and his wife was another thing. 'I'll go as high as twelve thousand.'

'Then we don't have a deal.'

There was a split second's silence, Beca panicked, fearing what would follow. 'Wait. Fifteen thousand.'

There was another long pause. 'I accept.'

Beca slid down the side of the cooler and sat on the floor. She didn't speak for a moment, trying to absorb what she'd just agreed. It had finally happened, albeit in the bizarrest of circumstances, she'd got what she wanted, a chance of getting pregnant. For God's sake, why though. She plucked up courage and asked.

'Why I'll let my husband do this?' Sophie replied.

Beca loved the emphasis on 'my'.

'Because we need the money. We're broke and I need to pay for my acting classes. I don't want always to be working serving tables, getting my arse pinched. Anyway, he doesn't love you. He will not be making love to you. It will be just sex, like they do with horses and cows.'

Beca didn't appreciate the stud farm comparisons.

'If he was having an affair,' Sophie continued, 'I would kill him. And you. But he is not. He is only doing it for me, because I asked him to. He doesn't even like you. You are no threat to our happiness.'

Beca had never doubted it. She did however wonder at Hal and Sophie's sanity. 'It needs to be tomorrow' she said.

'So soon. What about tests? How do we know you're clean?'

Maybe Sophie would like to inspect her teeth as well. 'I had the relevant tests done a few weeks ago. They came back clear. What about Hal?'

'There isn't time if you need him tomorrow. But he is one of those people who give their blood.'

'A donor.'

'That's right. He told me they test his blood to make sure it's clean.'

'That'll have to do then. Shall I call him?'

'At the studio, not at home. Never call us here.'

Beca had thought the studio was their home. The evening was turning out to be full of surprises. After Sophie had hung up Beca sat and stared at her phone as if it would help her unfathom the weirdness of the conversation she'd just had. Sophie's words resonated around her head but they didn't help clarify things.

She'd just bought a man. She'd negotiated over the use of another human being. Surely it was illegal. It certainly felt as though she'd done something criminal. An unfamiliar primness was beginning to surface. Sophie had not only given her permission to sleep with her husband, but had haggled over the price. Was that utterly bizarre or just very French? Beca shook her head with amazement, picked herself up from the floor and headed for the changing rooms. Perhaps this kind of behaviour was common in France. Having the wife's permission was surreal, possibly even a bit kinky. Beca gasped. Was Sophie expecting to join in? She wanted a baby badly, but not enough to let that woman get familiar with her anatomy.

Her fingers trembled as she scrolled through her mobile phone list to One Eyed Jack's. The changing room was practically empty and as she waited for Hal to be fetched from his studio she made certain that the few women there were unknown.

'You've spoken to Sophie?' he asked.

'Yes. We've agreed a price.' Beca's plucky chirp belied her annoyance at Hal's gruffness.

'That's nice.'

'Is it?' She laughed. 'Don't get me wrong, I'm pleased you've agreed but it all feels a bit strange to me, considering you're married.'

'The mistress of understatement. It's not strange, it's completely insane. It's the craziest idea I've ever heard of.'

'I don't want to put you off or anything, but why are you doing it then?' The nervous fawning into the phone had to stop.

'Because your money seems too much for my wife to resist.'

'Perhaps you shouldn't have told her how much I had.' She had to drop that obsequious titter as well.

'Are you complaining?'

'Not at all. I'm actually very grateful.'

'Don't be. I'm not doing this for you.'

Naturally not. Beca trilled merrily in her head to stop the ire that was building. 'But you'll do it?'

'Reluctantly, yes.'

'Sophie has briefed me on how repellent you think I am, but could you make some kind of pretence? This is going to be very difficult with you being so hostile.'

'I'm not very good at acting.'

'For 15 grand you could try.'

'Is that how much she got out of you?' Hal laughed. 'She's a canny woman.'

'Very. I pay you five thousand up front,' Beca scanned the changing room for eavesdroppers, 'the rest when I'm 16 weeks gone.'

'When what?' Hal asked.

'When it works.'

'We have sex and you pay me 15 grand, no strings attached?'

Had the rest of the gym just heard that? The woman nearby rubbing cream over her legs seemed oblivious, but Beca felt sufficiently self-conscious to wonder if her mobile had been rigged up to the public address system. Right now the entire gym could be listening in. That was another one for the therapist's couch.

'You get me pregnant,' she mumbled into the phone, 'and I pay you, yes.'

'When you're what?'

'Are you deaf?' Beca asked.

'Are you ashamed?'

'Sod off. I'll pay you the remaining £10,000 when I'm 16 weeks pregnant. Is that clear enough for you?' Beca asked loudly in case someone in the saunas had missed it. The woman with the cream certainly hadn't.

'You're not going to come back at me with a paternity suit?'

Beca's toes curled with cringing agony. 'I'll have a contract drawn up.'

'Very professional. You've thought of everything.'

She ignored the barbs. 'You understand it might not work first time. This is a flat fee, non-negotiable.'

'Doesn't this conversation give you the creeps?' Hal asked her.

'Should it?' Of course it gave her the bloody creeps. A few weeks back her idea had seemed like a stroke of genius. Now it was all the confirmation, if ever it were needed, that she had gone completely insane. Only a basket case could be forgiven the spooky conversation she was having.

'Wouldn't it be easier, and cheaper, for you to pick up some bloke in a bar?'

'In many respects, yes. I wouldn't be having this excruciating conversation right now. They'd undoubtedly be nicer than you. But then screwing the first man that happened along wouldn't say much for my judgement.'

'It's a shame you don't know any men, or just one in fact, who likes you enough to want to sleep with you.'

Beca drew breath. Her voice would betray her if she spoke, so she kept silent. It gave her head a moment to clear before she responded. She sounded calm when she spoke.

'There's a line which shouldn't be crossed, and you've just jumped over with both feet. I don't understand quite why, but you've tried to hurt my feelings from the start. I've put up with it because I want a baby. But even that isn't worth being trampled on. I wouldn't sleep with you if you were the last man on earth.'

Beca had no idea what Hal's reaction was. She imagined his shrug of indifference when he heard her hang up. She felt sick but oddly relieved. She'd extricated herself from the pit she'd dug. OK, so the plan had turned into a monster of her making, but she'd been brave enough to cut it dead before it grew even worse. Beca peeled off her sweaty clothes and had a shower. She felt numb and disappointed, but oddly proud as well. Nothing was worth putting up with that kind of crap from a man.

Chapter 1

Beca lay in bed and watched the thin white curtains dance in the slight breeze that had found its way through the open sash window. Bright sunlight stretched across the floor and onto the bottom of the bed casting elongated shadows of the curtains and the window frame. Her feet grew warmer where they lay under the sun's rays. It was going to be hot, and why not have glorious weather on such a disastrous day? There was nothing to say it should be pouring with rain just because she'd hit rock bottom; though it would have been nice to think everyone else had a reason to be hacked off as well. She threw back the covers and felt her bare stomach, kneading first her right, then her left side.

Definitely right. She traced an imaginary path from her right ovary, down her fallopian tube and into her uterus. Pop. She could picture an egg being released and wafted gently down by tail-like projections. She had so decidedly failed this life-giving cell, nothing could save it from its ignominious fate. Her gene pool was wending its way ever closer to the lavatory bowl. Beca rolled over and moaned, life was such a disappointment, it was too cruel. She wasn't being selfish or unreasonable, she just wanted a child. What could be more natural than that? She put a pillow over her head. So what if she was being melodramatic, it was Saturday, she could be mawkish in her own time if she wanted. The Victorians had spent nearly a century doing it, so why shouldn't she wail and flail her arms around for half an hour.

It was really bloody unfair, all she needed was a man. It ought to have been as straightforward as any other want: want a pair of shoes – buy them; want a nice holiday – take one, but men were not available off the peg, they required more effort than waving a credit card. Really unfair.

Beca sat up in bed, her big sulk building up to mouth-pouting proportions. Why was it that she was the only one who didn't have a man? Audrey Hepburn stared back at her from the *Breakfast at Tiffany's* poster mounted on the wall opposite, but offered no counsel. Beca didn't need help in finding the answer. There was no mystery. She didn't have a man because she'd never wanted one. While everyone else had been falling over themselves to get hitched, she'd been doing her damnedest not to. Her single status was a positive thing. She actively chose to be on her own. It wasn't as though she hadn't had offers, but life was too much fun to be wasted on just one man. Right?

Right. Beca banged a couple of pillows together. She hated it when her mind got onto an unwelcome train of thought, but she rallied. God, if she ever needed justification for her stance she only had to look towards Mr and Mrs Wedded Bliss to see how things could go wrong. If Tom and Abi had problems, what hope for lesser mortals like her?

There were things that Beca did not want to give brain space to, let alone say out loud, but her pesky head had a nasty way of thinking what it liked and despite humming loudly to herself, the word 'safe' came to mind. Why were there always a few contrary brain cells just waiting to start up a whispering campaign? She got out of bed. There was no point staying there just to be beaten up;

movement, any kind of activity would clear out the demons. She put a CD on in the living room. The mambo beat cha-cha-cha-ed out of speakers in the bathroom and she showered and danced herself into a better mood.

She wiped the steam off the bathroom mirror with a corner of her towel and flashed a smile, but there was nothing like direct eye contact for seeing into the soul and the paper-thin veneer of cheeriness dissolved. She felt hollow inside as she brushed her teeth and even if she wouldn't admit it out loud, somewhere in her head she was telling herself it was because she was scared. She was afraid of getting hurt, that's why she didn't have a man.

Again Beca rallied, was it so unreasonable to be scared? Being single was definitely safer than being in a couple. A single unit couldn't be broken. Two units, stuck together by an odd adhesion of convention, affection and obligation, could and very often did come apart.

She put on a flowery dress hoping it would add to the cheery illusion but there was only one way to turn the day around. It would involve placatory words and no doubt more humiliation. It might not be nice. The thing to do was just get on with it and not think. If she thought about it she wouldn't go, it was like finding an excuse to not go to the gym. So with an empty head she got in the Merc and headed for Camden Town.

There was a different sales assistant behind the counter at One Eyed Jack's. An older, altogether more spaced out version of Seaweed Boy, who must have taken the day off; bleeding eardrums, she supposed. Gregory Isaacs blasted out from the sound system and Beca found it impossible to walk without slipping into the heavy reggae rhythm. She waited for the track to finish then pounded on the door at the back of the shop. By the time the next track was reaching its peak – something about needing a night nurse quick – the door shook in its frame then opened with a jolt. Hal looked down at her. It was an easy call: he wasn't pleased to see her.

Beca smiled, she'd been practising this moment all the way there, she was going to make a supreme effort to be nice.

'So you've changed your mind. I thought you would,' he said.

Beca's smile was fixed rigid like an insurance salesman's. The rest of her was screaming. 'Can I come in?' she asked through gritted teeth.

Evidently he needed a long time to think this one over. Beca waited. Eventually he loosened his grip on the door and pushed it open. She stepped past him, content at least to have survived the first humiliation, and climbed the dark, narrow flight of stairs up to the next floor. The stairwell smelled neglected and damp, it had that sour odour of bedsit land. It didn't look as though it had been decorated, or indeed cleaned since her last visit eight years before and it made her task feel all the more seedy. But she was on familiar territory and she felt a tingle of anticipation as she reached the first floor landing and waited for Hal to open the door to his studio before she went in.

The malodorous pongs vanished as he closed the door behind him. Beca smiled. The room was shaking in time with Mr Isaacs downstairs, even the panes of glass in the windows rattled.

'It still doesn't bother you?'

Hal shrugged. 'I hardly notice it any more, although I've put an absolute ban on anything by Burt Bacharach.'

Beca laughed. 'Look, I don't want to come on like some raving nympho but –' She didn't get a chance to finish her sentence. Hal took her face in his hands and kissed her. When he let her go she stumbled backwards. 'What did you do that for?'

'I usually do before I have sex.'

'Is that what we're doing?'

'I thought that's what you wanted.'

'Well, yes. It is. That's why I came here.' Beca rubbed the back of her neck. This was going exactly the way she wanted, but not at all according to plan. If she could just rewind the moment and play it back slower perhaps she wouldn't feel quite so giddy. She was supposed to be in charge of the situation, but in a few swift, unexpected moves Hal had taken command. She was disarmed and she could feel herself dithering which was never an attractive sight.

'There's a sofa-bed over there. Get undressed. I need to finish off here first.' Beca watched as he walked over to his easel and picked up a brush. 'You can hang your clothes on that chair,' he said waving an arm behind him. Beca turned to see where he meant. She recognised the chair and smiled like an anxious child finding comfort and security in a familiar toy. It was wooden with a rush seat, such a cliché for an artist. They had bought it together in Camden Market and as a joke had checked to see if Cezanne or Van Gogh had carved in their initials.

There wasn't much else she recognised. The studio had changed drastically since her time as Hal's girlfriend. Nearly all the furniture had gone, she presumed it was now jostling for space with Sophie's stuff, wherever they lived. There was nothing to provide cover for her. The smell of coffee coming from the tiny kitchen was familiar though. It mingled with the strong smell of white spirit and oil paint that had permeated every surface. It above anything else in the room took her back. Another time it might have been comforting to conjure up their shared memories, but they only served to emphasise the strangeness of her present situation and so offered her no solace at all.

Hal's easel stood in front of a tall window. It was open, and above the music coming from downstairs Beca could hear the sounds of the busy street. He stood with his back to her surrounded by the tools of his craft. Canvases and stretching frames were propped against the wall. The wooden bench he had made was covered with twisted tubes of oil paint and glass jars of brushes. It was alive with colour, the floor, his easel, even the walls were spattered with paint. Beca looked at the heavily worn floorboards and noticed islands of colour where he had once set up his easel to work. The studio was undeniably his space and she couldn't imagine ever having that effect on her own surroundings.

The double doors were still there. When pulled across they divided the studio from the living quarters. She couldn't remember a time when they had been used. She toyed with the idea of shutting them now, giving herself some privacy as she undressed. It would be an own goal. She had to appear confident even if her stomach and intestines had turned into self-harmers. She looked for a distraction, something that could justify her delay, but there was nothing, just the sofa-bed, the chair and an old trunk which she remembered held the drapes and props he used for his work.

Hal started whistling to himself and for the first time Beca realised the noise from downstairs had stopped.

'What happened to the music?'

'Blew an amp, maybe. You still not undressed?'

Beca cursed herself for pussy-footing around. Nudity was nothing. Nakedness in a bright, exposed room while sober was not a problem. She'd modelled for him enough times. Exactly. She took her shoes off and walking barefoot across the paint-spattered floorboards she put them under the chair. They looked too neat, too prim. She nudged them with a toe into a rakish, kind of nonchalant pose. She unzipped her dress and slipped out of it and resisting the urge to fold it, she draped it over the back of the chair, then rumpled it a bit. There. She could do bohemian, she could be as outré as the next woman. She wasn't a prude. In fact she was so unprudish that, that – Beca couldn't think of anything. God, she was scared. After all she was usually fairly well bladdered by the time she slept with anyone. Sober sex? She wasn't sure she'd ever had it. Relax. Beca tried easing the word out on a long, deep breath. She was in charge, the money was in her pocket, not his. She undid her bra and flung it at the chair. It landed on the back and dangled by one strap, the cups facing outwards, she was pleased with the laid-back effect. She took off her knickers and pinged them by the elastic towards the chair. They missed and landed on her shoes. Excellent. The very picture of casual cool, with a bit of grubby naughtiness thrown in. That all her knickers were neatly halved and quartered in a drawer at home was her secret alone.

Fighting the urge to rush she took the few steps to the sofabed with feigned ease. Should she cover her breasts with the sheet, or not? Timid or brazen? In or out? The debate ended when something became caught around her foot.

'Oh, bloody hell,' she cried holding up a pair of knickers.

Hal turned around and shrugged. 'Sophie's. She popped by on her way to work this morning. She must have forgotten them.'

'How can anyone forget their knickers?' She lifted the sheet and peered under, then settled on the edge of the bed, clasping the sheet to her body.

'She's just that kind of girl, I suppose. Doesn't bother with them most of the time.'

Beca's free-spirit crashed and burned.

Hal stood back from his painting, ran his fingers through his hair then tilted his head and looked at his work. He had paint on the back of his jeans, finger marks where he'd wiped his hands in the fold of denim between his bottom and the top of his thighs. The stripes emphasised the shape of his backside and Beca's eyes were glued to it when he turned towards her and with one well-practised move pulled his T-shirt off over his head. Beca felt herself blushing, and the more conscious she became of her embarrassed state the redder her cheeks got. The more she beat down the rising tide of fear the closer she came to drowning. She was desperate to be in control, she forced herself to make eye contact, but all she could manage when he undid his fly buttons was a simpering grin. Spittle gathered in the corners of her mouth, she felt gauche, it was like being a bloody virgin again.

'So, tell me, how is the art world these days?' she asked with a tremulous laugh.

Hal ignored her and took off his underpants. Beca looked down and studied her hands. She was so not master of this situation. Her head felt thick. Get a grip, she kept telling herself. Get a bloody grip.

'We haven't talked,' she flustered.

Hal stood by the bed, his hands on his hips. 'You want me to chat you up?'

'No, of course not, but we haven't talked about what we're going to do.'

'Have sex?'

'Do we touch?' she asked.

'I think that's inevitable.'

'But any more than the absolutely necessary?'

'For pleasure, you mean?' The thought was clearly an unlikely one. 'I don't mind, I suppose.'

'Nor do I,' Beca added with indifference.

'Breasts?'

'Absolutely not. No breasts. That's too,' Beca struggled for the word.

'Intimate?'

'Exactly. And what about kissing?' she asked

'Tricky. We ought not to. Strictly speaking it is extracurricular, but it's a bit difficult to you know, get going without it.'

'My thoughts exactly,' Beca said with relief.

'But I don't think so.'

'Oh. Neither do I.'

'Feel better? Only I've got a deadline with the painting.'

'Right-ho.' God, did she really just say that? Were they about to play hockey? Hal smiled. So he was a mind-reader as well now. Marvellous.

Despite what he said Hal did kiss her, perhaps out of habit more than anything else. Then he made love to her. He was gentle, detached, a consummate professional, putting in just enough effort without really exerting himself. Beca had been so focussed, obsessed in fact by the end product of a baby, that she'd completely and very stupidly forgotten about the nitty-gritty, panting, noisy reality of making one. As an eleven year old she'd had a very clear idea what sex was. She had learnt about it in biology class, it involved body parts with embarrassing names and that was about all. How had she managed to regress back to such a naïve state? Why hadn't she thought about how she would feel to have his warm chest pressing against hers, or what it would be like to taste coffee in his mouth. What of his smell and the sounds he made, or indeed the token collection of hairs that ringed his nipples which had always made her laugh? Why hadn't she spared a moment to consider how she would feel when he touched her?

Still, it was done. It was a past tense thing, not something that could be undone or taken away. There had been no Hallelujah Chorus moment, nothing even approaching it. If he'd been a boyfriend she'd have kicked him out for his lack of efforts on her behalf, but that wasn't the point. He had delivered the goods, he'd done his part. She wasn't there to have fun and there was no danger of her forgetting that.

Hal lay next to her for a fraction of a second. 'Well I hope that does the trick,' he said as he got out of bed. Beca watched him as he pulled on his jeans and left his T-shirt on the floor as he went back to work. 'You can stay for a while if you like. I've heard lying with your legs in the air helps the sperm find the target.'

'You'd just love to see me look so stupid.'

'Not really.' Hal shrugged. 'If it helps. It's up to you.'

What was one further humiliation when added to the existing pile? She rolled onto her back and hugged her knees to her chest.

'Do you think once is going to be enough?' Hal turned to look at her, thus chasing off any last vestiges of dignity that were clinging to her backside.

Beca untangled herself. 'Once? What do you mean?'

'I just wondered if once was enough. Presumably if we kept at it, you'd stand a better chance.'

Beca considered this. 'Well, no in fact. We should wait another 24 hours before having another go.'

'Tomorrow? Can't do it. I've made plans with Sophie.'

Her name hung in the air.

'It had better be today, if that's all you're offering.' Beca said trying to sound more cheerful than she felt.

'Fine. Come back in a couple of hours. Are you taking folic acid?'

What was he like?

'I'll take your silence as a no, then,' he said. 'For someone who wants a baby, you've not done much homework, have you? There's a chemist in the high street. Go and buy some and come back in a couple of hours.'

Beca was cross at being found wanting. Of course she knew she was supposed to take folic acid, she'd read enough books about conception and pregnancy, but she kept forgetting. She suspected Hal of trying to score points off her, but one look at him dispelled that idea. His face was a picture of casual indifference; he just didn't care enough to bother.

Once dressed she went to see what he was doing. 'Mind if I look?'

He stood back to show her the painting. It was a picture of a little girl, perhaps three years old.

'It's a commission,' he said. 'Not really my sort of thing, but it pays well.'

Beca looked at the painting. It was impressive, in a few simple brush strokes he had captured the energy and character of the child. She glanced around the studio and spotted a portrait of Sophie, the size and detail of which made it stand out from the others. It was beautiful, or rather Sophie was and Beca felt a stab of envy as she looked at her long brown hair snaking around her pale neck. Other paintings around it were half finished, some were just rough sketches, but this was a work of love.

She looked at some of the other works jostling for wall space and noticed to her surprise there was a painting of herself tucked away up near the ceiling.

'You've still got that.'

'I'd forgotten it was there,' Hal said pulling away the painting that was half covering it.

'God, I look so much younger there.'

'And happier.' He turned and looked at her face intently. 'You're much thinner now and you've got frown marks.'

'That's age.'

'No, it's what you do with your face that shows. If you smiled more you'd have lines, here and here.' He drew a line with his finger at either side of her mouth. 'Not here,' he added trying to smooth away the slight furrow that had recently become a feature between her eyebrows. 'It's a shame, you were quite good looking once.'

She spotted the familiar twitching at the corner of his mouth. He was teasing her, just like he used to. 'It took years for my ego to recover from going out with you.'

'You mean to reinflate itself to Zeppelin-sized proportions.'

'I'm going before we fight.'

'Good. Come back in a couple of hours.'

Beca was astonished to find herself doing what she was told. She went to Boots, bought the folic acid, took one, and was ambling around the market for an hour or so when she remembered Luigi's, the café where she used to go with Hal. She was surprised to find it still there, unchanged except for a few more faded postcards of the Amalfi coast. What amazed her more was that Luigi remembered her.

'Hey, Bella,' he shouted from across the café. What happened to your hair? All gone, chop, chop. Never mind, it will grow back.'

Beca smiled at him, delighted at his rudeness and ordering a large cappuccino she went and sat at a table by the window. She lit a cigarette and staring out at the passers-by she replayed the encounter with Hal over in her head. It was his supreme indifference that was bothering her the most. He just didn't give a damn. Sure, he'd been civil, apart from a few jokes at her expense, but he might as well have helped jump start her car for all the impact the experience had had on him. So what was she expecting? A bit more interest perhaps, a bit of conversation. He could have asked how she was, what she'd been doing for the last eight years, but he wasn't in the slightest bit interested. He was friendly, as in not openly hostile. It was the sort of neutral friendliness he might show to a cashier at the supermarket or a teller at the bank, someone who would expect courtesy but not an invite for tea back at his place.

What bothered her the most about it all was that she cared that he didn't care. She cared that he wasn't even pretending. What did it matter? Here and now something amazing was happening inside her. An army of sperm were fighting their way to be first to her egg. As she puffed away on her second cigarette, the battle for life had begun.

At that moment Hal walked in. He was deep in thought and at first he didn't notice her. When he did, he started slightly as if she'd caught him off guard. He recovered quickly. 'I was beginning to think I'd scared you off.' Then he frowned. 'What do you think you're doing?' he asked striding over towards her table.

Beca shrank back in her seat. 'What do you mean?'

'That,' he said grabbing the cigarette from between her fingers and dunking it in her coffee cup. 'You can't smoke while you're trying to get pregnant. You should stop at least one month before you conceive. And you shouldn't be drinking coffee either, not for the first sixteen weeks, it's not good for the embryo.'

'That's all horse shit dreamt up by male doctors to stop women having fun.'

'And you know better than the experts, then?'

'What's your excuse?'

'I must have read a book once. Luigi, get Beca an orange juice will you. Drink this,' he told her once the juice had been delivered. 'I don't want you stunting my spawn.'

Beca laughed and drank it down.

'Good. Now, are you ready for another go?'

Hal helped her off with her clothes the next time. An unnecessary act considering she wasn't going to have any fun at all. Once again, when the business was done, he was off out of bed and back at his easel without even a cursory nod in her direction.

'Should I let you know?' she asked flatly.

'Might as well, I suppose,' he replied without looking around. Beca had been dismissed, the abruptness left her reeling. She took her time getting dressed, lingering for what purpose she couldn't guess, perhaps she was looking for some acknowledgement of what had taken place.

'She's beautiful,' she said looking at Sophie's portrait.

Hal cleaned his brush with an oily rag and wiped his hand on his jeans.

'Where did you meet her?'

'Paris.' He hesitated as if he was going to say something more then thought better of it

'How?'

'Look, you know, I'd really rather not talk about her with you. What we're doing is business, I don't want it getting tangled with my private life.'

'No of course not.' Beca felt chastened and mortified.

'She's due here soon, so – '

'Right. I should get going. I'll leave this here.'

Hal didn't look around. Beca hesitated a moment then left a cheque on the wooden chair and let herself out.

It took her over an hour to get back to her flat. Her concentration levels had been well below legal and she was amazed that she hadn't crashed the Merc. Perhaps the car had a stronger sense of its own self-worth than she did, either way they had both made it back in one piece.

The sun had gone west leaving the living room bathed in a grey, chilly light of early evening. Beca shivered and rubbed her arms. Her sharp-angled furniture was stark and unwelcoming and she couldn't settle. She had knocked for Mrs Butler on her way up, but there had been no reply. She needed company, human contact of some kind, but she'd made no plans for that evening. She pulled up one of the tall sash windows and stepped over the sill onto the balcony. It was warmer outside than in her flat and she leant on the balustrade, still hot from the day's sun, and looked up and down the street hoping to catch sight of somebody. Tinkling laughter could be heard above a low murmur of voices, and the mouth-watering smells of a barbecue filled the air. Next door were having a party in their back garden. Beca tried giving them faces, but she was never very good at neighbourly chat and other than Mrs Butler she didn't really know anyone.

Then Rhett ambled up from the basement and sat down on the pavement in front of the house. She whistled to him and he looked up, stared at her, flicked a paw and turned away. 'Here, Rhett,' she called. His ears twitched but he ignored her.

The laughter coming from next door began to bother her. Why hadn't she been invited? Perhaps Mrs Butler was there enjoying a glass of wine in the evening sun. She should have made plans. It was miserable staying at home on her own on a Saturday night. She'd just had sex with an ex-boyfriend twice before being turfed out by him and now she felt weird. She hadn't expected elation, but something close to it would have been good. Instead she had this flat, depressed feeling; a sense of nothing.

What on earth was wrong with her? She forced herself to smile. Life was good. Life did not get any better than this. She was probably pregnant, no, definitely pregnant.

She looked up the road that swept in a graceful crescent towards the church. She could see the spire above the roofline of expensive stucco houses. Then a gay couple appeared holding hands. They were very animated, smiling at each other, laughing and swinging their locked arms. The black leather and handlebar moustaches looked incongruous next to the obvious affection they felt for each other, and if they weren't in love, then they were in the throes of a big passion. Tears welled up in Beca's eyes. Everyone was so bloody happy except her. She put a cigarette in her mouth and was about to light it when she remembered the tobacco ban. The flood gates opened and shuddering with tears she reached for the telephone.

'Why are you crying?' Abi asked.

'I don't know,' Beca sobbed.

'It's what you wanted.' Abi's tone was sympathetic but preachy.

'I know,' she said toying with her lighter.

'So why are you crying?'

'I don't know. It's just I didn't expect to feel this way.'

'What way?'

'Used.' Beca flicked open the lighter, then shut it.

'But you weren't used, for goodness sake. You paid him to have sex with you.'

'That sounds so awful.' She sniffed the lighter then recoiled from the smell of petrol

'It is awful.'

'Be nice to me,' she said pathetically.

'Do you want to come over? Tom's out. I could cook you supper.'

A big hug and some sympathy was what Beca needed. 'Where is he?' she asked.

'Out with his German clients. They've gone to some swanky restaurant in town.'

'And you weren't asked?'

'Of course, but I hate schmoozing. He's taking a couple of people from work as well.'

Beca wasn't sure whether to feel pity for Abi's gullibility or relief that she didn't suspect a thing. She put the cigarette back in her mouth.

'So, do you fancy coming over then?' Abi asked.

'Thanks, but I can't. I've been invited to a barbecue next door. I said I'd go. He really loves her, you know?'

'Who?'

'Hal. He really loves Sophie.' Beca inhaled air through the unlit cigarette and breathed out again.

'Well, that's a good thing, isn't it? What are you doing?'

'Pretending to smoke.' She threw the cigarette in a plant pot. 'He's got this painting of her in his studio. You should have seen the way he looked at it. He adores her. She doesn't deserve him.'

'But she's got him.'

'I don't think she loves him. She's using him.'

'So he makes a habit of it.'

'Very funny.'

'I get your point though. I don't see how any woman who really loves her husband would let him sleep around.'

God, how had she got onto the subject of infidelity? It was typical, the more she tried not to mention it, the more it came up.

'Then again,' Abi said, 'maybe it shows how completely together they are. They're so sure of their love for each other that this unseemly episode can't threaten what they have.'

'That's what she said, more or less.'

'There you go then.'

'With luck I'll never have to see him again.'

'Let's hope so, for everyone's sake.'

Chapter 8

Beca was alone in the boardroom at the bank. She was having difficulty standing still on account of the jitters that had taken control of her body, although they had nothing to do with this present situation. The imminent meeting with Melissa Cartwright didn't faze her at all; the quaking was from another source. It was over a week, ten days in fact, since she'd slept with Hal. More to the point, it was also ten days since her last cigarette and the army of ants that continuously marched about on her scalp showed no signs of getting battle fatigue. She was in a prickly mood, she yearned for a cigarette and the headaches from giving up coffee were blinding. The idea of abandoning the good life before conception was confirmed seemed obscene, but she was superstitious enough to do as the pregnancy guru, Abi had said.

This little get-together had been in the planning for weeks. In fact the moment Liz had identified Tom's mistress, Beca had been contriving a way of meeting her. She hadn't wanted to leave it to chance. That could have taken months and who knew how many lunch breaks she'd have to spend hovering outside the bank where Melissa Cartwright worked waiting to bump into her. No, this business needed closure, not pussy-footing around.

She had booked the large boardroom rather than one of the less imposing meeting rooms because she fully intended to intimidate Ms Cartwright into an admission. A kid-gloves approach would be wasted on Tom's mistress, who investigation had shown was not the deceived innocent in this mess; Abi still held that crown. Beca was prepared to get tough, or at least give the impression that she would, and to be honest she was in the perfect mood for a fight.

Getting the prey to meet at all had not been easy. In the end Beca had opted for deception which was why Ms Cartwright was coming today to be interviewed for a non-existent job vacancy at the bank. Beca smiled. She felt like a spider waiting in her lair for the gullible fly.

She walked around the table running her hands along the black leather surface. It was absurd but she did still hope that the whole business had been a misunderstanding, that Ms Cartwright and Tom were friendly colleagues and nothing more. She'd ruled out challenging Tom for that very reason. She longed to be proved wrong and could easily have been persuaded that what she'd seen was innocent rough-play. The role of marriage wrecker was not one she'd asked for and the whole tawdry business left her feeling depressed and disillusioned. Life would be so much better if she'd made a whopping great mistake. As she checked the clock on the boardroom wall, she couldn't foresee a happy ending for this particular story. Ms Cartwright was late.

Beca looked at the tray of coffee and buns which lay waiting on the boardroom table. The jam doughnuts were very appealing, particularly to someone so nicotine deprived. She grabbed one and bit into the greasy, jammy sponge hoping Ms Cartwright wouldn't suddenly arrive. It was a delicious consolation for giving up the fags, and besides she deserved a treat, for despite temptation she had not done a pregnancy test yet. There were another four days to wait. Each one could bring with it the start of her period and the end of her hopes. No wonder she was so on edge.

Beca looked at the table laid out for the impending meeting. It was all wrong. The plump buns and coffee suggested cosy goodwill. She was not there to play convivial hostess to Ms Cartwright but to go fifteen rounds with her if necessary. She picked up the tray and put it on a side table setting the two tightly coiled, phallic-shaped lamps off at a wobble. Subtlety had evidently not been on the design brief.

Even the chairs were wrong. Interrogators always had bigger chairs than their victims, it was a known fact. In order to bully Ms Cartwright she needed to be able to stare down at her, not meet her eyes on a level. She pulled the padded black leather chair intended for the suspect away and was in the process of dragging a smaller one into place when the door opened. Despite the fact she'd been expecting it to open for the last twenty minutes, she still started with surprise when Melissa Cartwright walked in. Liz followed behind like a snarling Rottweiler. They clearly hadn't bonded in the lift. Perhaps Beca should have packed the knuckle-dusters after all. Tom's mistress looked expensive. She sashayed her way towards her in a series of fluid, leggy steps that could only have been matched by Jessica Rabbit. She was wearing more clothes today, a dove grey suit, definitely this season. Hers was the kind of figure that would make a nun's habit look x-rated. How the hell had Tom bagged her?

Ms Cartwright shook hands firmly and smiled. She used all the right facial muscles but there was no suggestion of friendliness about it. Predatory more like. And Beca hadn't even told her why she was really there yet. The air around her sizzled with cattiness. Bad Karma.

Beca offered her the designated interrogation chair, but without being obviously rude she eased herself into the bigger one next to it. She was clever. Beca hesitated. Should she insist she move? Perhaps not. Best not to be too confrontational straightaway. The score was 1-0 to Ms Cartwright. Or was that 2-0? She had already lost count. With a fixed smile and a purposeful stride she walked around to her side of the table, picked up the pile of papers she'd laid out in front of her chair and moved them down one so that she was opposite her adversary.

'You've got something around your mouth,' Liz whispered in her ear before heading out the door.

Beca's hand flew to her face. She instantly regretted the apologetic laugh that escaped as she wiped a sugary moustache from her top lip. Command of the situation was so definitely not hers.

She looked at Ms Cartwright over the top of her CV, her eyes narrowing slightly as if spying her through the crosshairs of a sniper's rifle. If the woman had any idea of the danger she was in, she didn't show it. She was confident. She had a hauteur that bordered on the bloody rude. It occurred to Beca as Ms Cartwright looked off to one side that she was giving her permission to be admired. It was obviously a condition she was used to. Her arrogance sparked an anger which swiftly restored Beca's confidence. Bugger the sugar decoration, this woman was screwing Abi's husband.

She leant back in her chair and pressed her fingers together in an arch. 'You've been seen with a man called Tom Goodall.' Her broadside was swift but failed to startle her opponent.

Ms Cartwright arched a well-pencilled eyebrow and sneered. 'I knew this interview was a con. So whose wife are you?' she asked with an arrogance that was very smackable.

'No one's, but Tom Goodall's wife is my best friend.'

'How touching.'

'Not really. Are you having an affair with him?' Beca tapped her index fingers together.

'Yes.'

Beca was shocked by her honesty. Of all the scenarios she'd imagined, a full confession before the thumb screws came out was not one of them. The woman was all co-operation. Perhaps she didn't feel she had anything to hide.

'And you know he's married?'

'Well of course, that's part of the fun.' It was Ms Cartwright's turn to sit back and look relaxed. She expertly twiddled a pen through her fingers like a baton.

'Who for?' Beca asked.

'Me. The married ones try so much harder to impress. It's pathetic really, don't you find?'

Beca didn't like her confiding tone. She and that woman had nothing in common. For a start, she'd never slept with a married man. Fine. There was Hal, but that brief association was an entirely different matter. No comparison could justifiably be made. Could it?

'Are you in love with him?' she asked.

'God, no.'

'Does Tom love you?'

'That's what he tells me, but they always do. I think this one means it though. He keeps offering to leave his wife.'

The doughnut turned to lead in Beca's stomach. This was so much worse than she had imagined. How could Tom even be considering leaving Abi and the kids for that poisonous strumpet? 'Is that what you want?'

Ms Cartwright inspected a highly polished fingernail. 'I haven't decided. I don't really fancy settling down. That's never been my thing, but it might be fun, for a while at least.' She shrugged with lack of interest and Beca shuddered at the familiarity of her words.

'It doesn't bother you that you're destroying a happy family?'

'Who appointed you the moral police?'

'I just wondered if you'd thought about anybody apart from yourself.'

Ms Cartwright sniffed the air and stared at her.

'Why Tom?' Beca continued. 'What can you possibly see in him?'

Her opponent tilted her head back and laughed. 'The fear of getting old. The ones pushing 40 are much more attentive. Besides, he's great in bed.'

Beca's eyebrows hit her hair line. It was too late to delete the information, her head was flooded with images of Tom being virile.

'I don't suppose there's any chance of letting him go?' she asked.

'Why should I?' Ms Cartwright stopped spinning her pen and laid it down at a precise angle in front of her.

'Because he has a wife and two children.'

'His family, his problem, not mine.'

'You don't care if you wreck his marriage?'

'Seems to me he's the one doing that.'

Beca could hardly argue with that.

'I suppose you're going to tell her?' Ms Cartwright asked picking up her pen again.

'I've got no choice.'

'It'll be interesting to see the fireworks.'

The inclination to spring across the boardroom table and take the smug bitch out with a kick Buffy the Vampire Slayer would have been proud of, was strong. Knowing she'd fall flat on her face was a good reason not to. Besides, the steely look in Ms Cartwright's eyes suggested ownership of a black belt or two. Beca stayed seated and stared at the most selfish woman she'd ever met. Clearly Hal had never come across the likes of this one before when he'd had the audacity to call her self-obsessed.

'If he leaves her, will you have him?' she asked calmly.

Ms Cartwright's top lip curled with indecision. 'Maybe. It depends on what he's offering.'

'Fine.' Beca scooped up her papers and stood. 'You know, I was hoping that this was all one big mistake, that you'd never heard of Tom Goodall. I suppose if you had been in love with him, or cared anything about him at all, it might have been worse. I've always thought he was an idiot, meeting you has confirmed that. Why would he risk his marriage for a slut like you?'

Beca at last succeeded in wounding Ms Cartwright. It was a very small triumph in an otherwise disastrous campaign.

By the time she had emerged from Notting Hill Gate tube station it was raining hard, and as was always the case in such circumstances there wasn't a taxi to be had for any amount of wishing. Beca was feeling anxious and twitchy as though she'd been taking caffeine tablets all day. The last thing she wanted was to hang about the station waiting for the rain to stop. She needed to get rid of some of the tension that had turned her shoulders into concrete and so she set off at a half run towards home.

The encounter with Melissa Cartwright had left her reeling. Every answer she needed had been provided and Beca had spent the rest of the day numbly wondering how she was going to tell Abi; for she certainly was going to tell her. She had to. It was inevitable. Abi had the right to know. She also had the right to expect her husband to be faithful, but Tom had turned out to be a selfish bastard, and so it was down to Beca. If nothing else Abi had the right to expect the truth from her friends.

The rain had begun to soak through Beca's jacket to her shoulders and back. She could feel raindrops slithering down her scalp, collecting in the hair at the nape of her neck and then dripping down the inside of her collar.

By the time she reached home she was as wet and uncomfortable as if she'd climbed into a warm shower with her clothes on. She shut the front door behind her, dropped her bag on the floor and kicked off her soaking shoes. Stepping over the junk mail one of her neighbours had shoved under the door, she walked to the kitchen. A bright circle of light shone down on the kitchen counter from an angle-poise lamp she'd forgotten to turn off that morning. The rest of the flat was in darkness and Beca preferred it that way. The last thing she wanted was to catch her reflection in the big mirror which hung between the two sash windows.

Her instinct was to grab the gin bottle and obliterate the world. She looked at it standing on the counter, the most accessible object in her kitchen, but resisted the urge. She stood dumbly waiting for something to happen, anything that might delay her picking up the telephone. Her wet clothes clung to her. She could get changed, that would fill some time, particularly if she had a bath. But what was the point of getting comfortable? Nothing would make the task at hand any easier.

The phone rang six times. Beca was beginning to hope that Abi had gone out, but before the seventh ring it was answered.

'Hello,' Abi said in a breathless laugh. 'Tom, is that you?'

'No, sorry. It's Beca.'

'Hi. I was expecting to hear from Tom. He hasn't called to say when he'll be home.'

That answered Beca's first question.

'Are you alright?' Abi continued. 'You sound very flat. You haven't done a pregnancy test have you?'

'No. Can I come over to see you? There's something I've got to tell you?' She hadn't meant to say that at all. The tone was wrong. Her voice belonged to a man with a hooded cloak and scythe.

'Of course,' Abi replied. There was a silence which Beca couldn't begin to fill. 'Are you going to tell me what's wrong?'

'Not on the phone. I'll be over shortly.'

'You're doing a good job of scaring me,' Abi laughed.

'I'm sorry. Don't – I'll tell you when I get there.' What was the point of saying don't worry? Abi had every reason to. Beca was angry with herself for ladling on the doom, but she hadn't been able to stop herself. Forewarning Abi might have made her ultimate task easier but she'd left her friend waiting anxiously, which wasn't what she'd planned.

She set off in the Merc for Abi's house. Her heart was racing but her foot stayed light on the accelerator. She drove like a model citizen, stopping on amber, waiting for green, anything to drag out the journey for as long as possible. She had to tell Abi, it wasn't for her to decide whether she should know the truth or not. Certainly it would be easier on both of them if she kept her mouth shut, but it wasn't the brave thing to do, nor the right. If only she hadn't gone to the bar that night, if she hadn't seen Tom with that woman then none of this would be happening. Beca suddenly felt a strong sense of injustice, she hadn't asked to be involved. Why did she have to be the harbinger of Abi's pain?

She pulled over to the side of the road. The old windscreen wipers thwacked rhythmically from one side to the other and back again, fighting a losing battle with the rain. Beca switched them off. She sat listening to the drumming of raindrops on the car's soft-top and watched as water poured down the windscreen blotting out the world. She wasn't feeling particularly courageous, every fibre was shrieking at her to turn the car around and go home. She hesitated with her hand on the keys, then turned on the ignition and pulled out into the traffic. She'd decided what to do and there was no point delaying any longer. She pressed her foot down on the accelerator and headed for Kew.

Beca could barely bring herself to make eye contact when Abi answered the door but she could tell from her body language that she was anxious.

'Has something gone wrong? You've done a test haven't you? I told you not to. It was negative wasn't it.'

'No.'

'It's positive?' Abi's excitement bordered on hysterical.

'No, I haven't done one.'

'You're all wet. You're soaking for goodness sake. The last thing you want is to catch a cold.'

Beca stepped into the hallway. 'I'm fine, really. I need to talk to you.'

'Hal hasn't been pestering you, has he? I wondered if he might not be on some vengeance kick, after all you did treat him pretty appallingly.' Her gestures were wild and edgy, her comments clearly off the mark. She'd worked herself up into a state and it was obvious she knew full well this wasn't about Beca or Hal.

'It's Tom. He's having – '

Abi shook her head and turned to walk towards the kitchen holding her hands up as if trying to block out Beca's words. She laughed nervously. 'Could you not say anything until I've had another drink?'

Beca followed behind. Blood pounded in her head, she felt sick, and the little confidence she had was being eroded by a voice that kept telling her to shut up and not make trouble.

'Do you want one?' Abi's voice was high with false cheeriness. 'No, of course, you can't. Don't mind if I go ahead do you?' She tipped the bottle but only dregs came out. Her sham laugh made Beca wince. She pulled another out of the wine rack and set it on the table. The corkscrew slipped as she tried taking the foil off the bottle and jabbed her finger.

'Here, let me,' Beca reached for the bottle.

'I can do it.' Abi took the foil off but her hands were trembling too much to get the corkscrew into the cork. As Beca stepped forward she silently surrendered the bottle.

'I know what you're going to say.' Abi took the glass of wine she was offered.

'How?' Beca watched her drink and wished that she could numb the moment with alcohol.

Abi shrugged. 'I had my suspicions. I'd have to be pretty bloody stupid not to have noticed. When your husband starts staying out later and later you've got to suspect something.'

Wine slopped in her glass as she put it down next to the sink. She picked up a tea towel and started drying saucepans from the draining board. 'All those late client meetings, the overseas phone calls that have to be done at the office. I can smell the wine and cigarette smoke on him when he gets home.'

Saucepans banged and rattled together as she stacked them and slammed the drawer shut. She put the tea towel next to the sink but it slipped onto the floor. 'When he is here he's pre-occupied and distant, then for a day he'll be attentive, I suppose that's when he's feeling guilty.' She reached for her glass, drained and refilled it again.

Beca watched and wondered how long before she'd break.

'Or perhaps he was just worried I'd find out.' As Abi's eyes filled with tears she tilted her head back. Her voice was more strained. 'And he over-compensates with the children. They think all the attention is great, it's a pity he couldn't have been more like that before –.' She looked at Beca. 'I just knew, I suppose, but I've kept my head down like a coward. I was frightened that if I confronted him he'd leave me.' At last she cracked and the tears came in a flood.

Beca put her arms around her and hugged her as she sobbed. Her body shook with convulsions and she clung to her as if her life depended on it. They both sank down to the floor. Beca's eyes filled with tears. It was so unfair. Why was this happening to Abi? She was such a kind person. Why did it have to be her heart that was breaking? Abi clung to her like a child, utterly helpless and Beca felt that it was her strength alone that was keeping her friend going, as if she was breathing for her.

'I wished you'd told me,' Beca said.

'I didn't want to.'

'Why not?'

'I thought if I didn't say anything I could pretend nothing was happening; that it was all in my mind. I was too afraid to face the truth.'

Beca had no idea how long they stayed like that, moulded into one form on the kitchen floor. It could have been an hour, it felt like days, but eventually Abi stopped crying, her sobs quietened and her breathing became more controlled. She untangled herself from Beca's arms and blew her nose.

'What am I going to do?'

Beca looked at her friend. What could she possibly say that would make her feel better, that could make any difference? What words of comfort had any real meaning?

'I suppose he doesn't love me any more,' Abi said.

'Don't say that.'

'He's been sleeping in the spare room a lot these days. He said it's because he gets back so late and doesn't want to disturb me. But that's not the reason.'

'Abi, you don't know what he's thinking. You must talk to him.'

'Is he going to leave me?'

'God, I don't know.'

'He might, if he loves her. Perhaps he'll want to live with her and have more children.' She broke into fresh tears. 'What about Dulcie and Billy. What will they do if he leaves?'

'You don't know that he is going to leave.'

'But supposing he does.'

'You're not on your own. I'll help you, I promise,' Beca said taking Abi's hand.

'How did you find out? Did he say something to you?'

'That's not very likely. I saw them together a few weeks ago.'

'You've known for that long?'

'I wasn't sure. I thought perhaps they were drunk. You know, that it was a one-off mistake.'

'But it wasn't.'

'No. I met her today. I wanted to be sure.'

'What's she like? Does she love him?'

Beca shook her head. 'She's too much in love with herself.'

'She must be very beautiful. Is she young?'

'She's a bitch.'

'Tom obviously likes her though. It's such a cliché, isn't it? Husband gets bored with sagging wife and trades her in for a new model.'

'Abi, don't punish yourself like this. You've done nothing wrong. He's the prat who doesn't know how lucky he is.'

Abi smiled and wiped her eyes

'Come on,' Beca said pulling her to her feet. 'You've got furniture so we might as well use it.' She picked up the bottle of wine and steered Abi towards one of the big sofas in the living room.

'Wouldn't it be great if we were both wrong. If he was completely innocent.' Abi searched Beca's face for signs of hope.

What could she offer her? She couldn't go along with the pretence. There was no point getting her hopes up. Looking at Abi's frightened, tear-stained face Beca knew the real pain hadn't kicked in yet. Her friend was still clutching to an impossible hope. When that was gone there could be no happy ending. Perhaps somewhere down the line there would be rosy smiles again, but not today, not tomorrow, nor next week; not for a very long time.

The sound of a key turning in the lock made both of them start. Abi's hands trembled as she wiped away the smudged mascara from under her eyes.

'Shall I stay?' Beca asked.

'No, I'll be OK.'

'Of course you will. Be strong.' Beca gave her a final hug. 'Call me, any time. I can be here in minutes, or come to me. There's room for you and the kids. You're not alone, remember that.'

'Thanks,' Abi managed a smile.

'I love you. Stand up for yourself.'

She was relieved to be leaving and felt a coward for it. A part of her wanted to stay if only to kill Tom, but her overwhelming urge was to get home and hide.

Tom was surprised to see Beca. He smiled and said hello.

'Bastard.' She pushed past him in the hallway. 'You utter bastard,' she said and slammed the door.

The rain had stopped. Beca drove home wondering why life had turned out so badly. It hadn't started out that way. Nothing bad had ever happened when she was young. Sure, her father had left and her mother had gone off the rails, but she'd been detached from that; it was just older people messing up. Now she and her friends were those older people making all the mistakes. She was paying a married man vast amounts of money to get her pregnant because she was incapable of settling down with someone, and Abi was sitting in her living room getting her heart torn out by the man she loved. A shopping trip and a drunken night out was not going to solve things. Nothing would, except time perhaps and then it would only make it less bad, it would never really get completely better. Abi could never go back to how life was before.

Chapter 9

Beca was having a lie-in. She wasn't feeling too great. She hoped it was morning sickness but rather suspected it was the continuing withdrawal of all the things that she liked most in life, the things that kept her physically and spiritually together. Her body was suffering catastrophic failure as finally the last micrograms of nicotine, caffeine and alcohol sweated their way out of her suffering corpse. Beca was in non-toxic shock. She lay face down sprawled out across her dishevelled bed. Her head felt as if an axe had been hacked into the back of it, and would, she was certain, split in two pieces if she lifted it from the pillow.

Through the pulsing pain she had a vague recollection that today was important for some reason. She couldn't work out why though and if it hadn't been for the annoying urge to pee she might have been able to give it more thought. Had she got up and gone to the loo when a full bladder first woke her, she could have figured out the life-death issue and got several more hours sleep. As it was she had refused to budge and the niggling feeling in her lower abdomen had banished all possibility of sleep.

Beca threw back the sheets and trudged to the bathroom. She put the lid up, sat, began to pee, then in a stomach-churning moment remembered it was pregnancy test day. How the hell had she managed to forget? Desperate now to not pee she sent her pelvic floor muscles into shock as she squeezed to stop the stream of urine. With her knees clamped together she scuttled to the bathroom cupboard, pulled out the pregnancy test box and rushed back. She opened the packet, ripped open the foil wrapper with her teeth and removed the lid. With huge relief she emptied her bladder over the stick. What a complete idiot. She'd waited for this moment for two weeks and had almost peed away the evidence.

There had been occasions in the past to use a pregnancy test, back when the thought of having a baby horrified her. Now she sat on the loo and watched with a sense of excitement bordering on the euphoric as the two little windows on the stick filled up. In her mind she ran through all the ways she was going to tell her friends the brilliant news. The first box took on a blue tinge and Beca's heart quickened as a thin blue line appeared. A millisecond's jubilation was quelled as she remembered this line just confirmed the test had worked. The tension was making her feel queasy as she watched the all-important second window. Nothing happened. A horrible sense of disaster began to rise in her. She picked up the instruction leaflet on the floor which told her to allow five minutes for the results. Beca laughed with relief. There was no point gawping at the damned thing, the result wouldn't come through any sooner. She left the test on top of the loo and went to the kitchen to make breakfast.

She wasn't really hungry. The queasy feeling hadn't left her and the pounding in her head continued. She stroked the top of the cappuccino maker as she walked past to fill the kettle, then made herself a cup of edifying herbal tea, as instructed by her natural conception and pregnancy manual. She sniffed the steamy contents, recoiled and poured the evil brew down the sink. Next she topped a bowl of nut-free muesli with chopped-up banana and soya milk and took the unappealing ensemble to the living room.

She pulled up the big sash windows to let in some air and slumped down on the sofa. God, how she wanted a cigarette. How was she going to cope with nine months of healthy living? She felt panicky at the thought.

'This is a good day,' she told herself, breathing in deeply. She crossed her legs in as near to a lotus position as she was ever likely to get and closed her eyes. 'Om shanti.' She assumed a mystical pose she'd seen in her yoga for pregnancy book. 'Positive energy is,' she breathed in deeply, 'filling every molecule. Negative energy is,' she breathed out, 'disappearing. Om shanti. Small embryo thing needs positive, radiant thoughts. Om shanti. I visualise my headache leaving my body and it will go in – poof – a puff of smoke.' Beca sniffed. She swore she could smell cigarette smoke. Or was it just an olfactory hallucination?

Untangling her limbs she went to a drawer in the kitchen and pulled out a box of matches. She lit one, blew it out and sniffed the sulphurous smoke. Delicious. She lit two together, blew them out then took a long, deep sniff savouring the acrid smell. The doorbell rang.

'It's me, can we come up,' a voice said into the intercom.

Beca pushed the buzzer and opened her front door. She could hear the door below on the ground floor open and then Dulcie and Billy's excited voices as they ran for the stairs. Dulcie bound up ahead shouting hello. Beca watched as Billy tackled the stairs one at a time frustrated by his short legs, and in his irritation he shouted at his big sister to wait. Abi followed behind him, oblivious to the ear piercing noise. She looked awful.

'You look terrible, Beca,' she said with a weak smile.

'Bit of a headache. What's your excuse?'

Abi smiled ruefully.

'You haven't left him, have you?' Beca mouthed once Dulcie had shot past her into the flat.

Abi shook her head. 'Not yet anyway.'

At last Billy reached the top step and thundered off after Dulcie. Beca and Abi hugged.

'You haven't answered any of my calls. I've been worried,' Beca said.

'Sorry. I've lost track of time. I had no idea it was Saturday today. I tried taking Dulcie to school.'

'I wondered why she was wearing her uniform.'

'I've got clothes for her in a bag. I couldn't face hanging around the house any longer to get her changed.'

'How have things been?'

'Awful. Couldn't be worse.'

'Has he left?'

'No. I suppose that would be worse, wouldn't it?'

'I'll make some coffee.'

'Don't bother, it's such a faff with your machine.'

'It's not. Please, I really want to. The smell will cheer me up.'

Beca felt sad as she watched Abi wander into the living room. She had dark rings under her eyes, her cheek bones looked too sharp and her face was pinched as if she hadn't been eating. She looked heartbroken but her hair was clean and so were her clothes, which was more than Beca would have bothered with in similar circumstances.

'It's so lovely and bright here,' Abi said. 'So uncluttered. I've always thought a person's surroundings reflect their state of mind. Our house is never tidy, I spend my whole life clearing up after other people, just trying to keep the levels of chaos down. It's so calm here.'

'Sorry to spoil your theory but this isn't a reflection of my inner state, believe me. It's just that I'm never around long enough to mess it up.' Calm. That was a joke, Beca's heart was doing the Riverdance in her ribcage. The five minutes had long since passed, the test results would be ready, but was she? Not a chance. She ground the coffee beans, welcoming the distraction. She was too afraid to find out if she was pregnant or not. This way she could pretend for a bit longer that she was.

'Mummy, what's this?' Dulcie came skipping downstairs from the bathroom holding up the pregnancy tester for her mother.

'Oh Christ. What does it say?'

'Haven't you looked?' Abi asked.

'No. You tell me.'

'What is it, mummy?'

'It's for cleaning your ears. Now be a good poppet and give it to Beca.'

'I'm not sure I want it.'

'Let's both look together,' Abi said in a tone reserved for sick children. 'You two. Go off and watch television. You know how to switch it on don't you?' she asked Dulcie.

Beca laughed nervously. Why was she afraid? She was pregnant. She felt sure of it.

Abi stood next to her. 'One, two, three.' She removed her hand from over the test stick. They both looked. Beca gripped the edge of the work-top.

'One line. That's not good is it?' she said.

'Not in these circumstances, no. I'm really sorry, Beca.'

'Oh well.' She tried to sound cheerful.

'Are you sure it's not too soon?'

Beca clung to the thought, then had to admit, 'No.'

'I'm sorry.'

'There's always next month.'

Abi rallied. 'Exactly. You'd have been pretty damned lucky to score first time around. The chances weren't very high.'

Beca searched for a child-friendly expletive. 'Poo, arse and wee,' was all she could come up with. It went nowhere near expressing her feelings.

'Come here.' Abi gave her a hug.

After a few moments she pulled away. 'Damn it, I'm cross. I really thought I was pregnant. Bugger.'

Abi looked worried.

'It's alright, I'm not going to cry.'

'What will you do now?'

'I don't know. Yes, I do,' she said firing hot steam into a jug of milk. 'I'll have a coffee and a cigarette. At least there's one upside to this.'

Beca led the way outside onto the terrace and pulled the sash window down behind them. 'Fucking bollocks.' She lit a cigarette. 'I thought it would work.'

'Welcome to the world of disappointment,' Abi said ruefully.

Beca reached over and put an arm around her shoulder. 'Life's pretty crap at the moment, isn't it?'

'Just about as shitty as it can get, in fact.'

'Are you going to tell me what happened?'

'Not here. Let's go out. I told the children they could go to the Diana playground.'

'Great, they can run around while we talk. I'll get dressed.' Beca was surprised how light-headed the cigarette had made her. It would be nothing compared to the bottle of gin she planned on drinking later.

Beca looked up at the clear blue sky as they walked through Notting Hill. It was a brilliant summer's day, the sort that made people smile and put a spring in their step. Sadly the good weather was wasted on her and Abi. Nothing would lift their spirits. Billy seemed to have caught the vibe and he wailed at the indignities of being strapped into his buggy. Dulcie flaunted her freedom with big sister meanness as she skipped alongside, either oblivious or inured to her mother's sad face.

The sun-induced good mood of the various shoppers and tourists was put to the test as Abi cut a swathe through the crowds, the front wheel of the buggy scything a path in front of her. Beca was faintly embarrassed which rather surprised her, being inclined to obtuseness when strangers' feelings were involved. She fell in behind Abi thereby narrowing the column but there was still a lot of tutting and teeth sucking as they made rapid progress towards Kensington Gardens.

Conversation was pointless with the children around, even if they could hear each other above Billy's shouts, they wouldn't have been able to talk freely. Beca was left with her own thoughts. She was so pissed off but at least mature enough, and in some ways grateful, to realise that in comparison to what Abi was going through, not getting pregnant was just a small glitch. It was a minor slump on the great arc of happiness, from which she would make a full recovery. Meanwhile poor Abi had slipped off completely. She had fallen well below the X equals zero line and was scudding along the bottom. By comparison Beca knew that she had nothing to whinge about, but it didn't stop her eyes burning with tears. It would be unforgivable to unburden herself on Abi who had so little strength left in reserve. She could manage a Pollyanna number for the afternoon, until she was alone and could wallow in a churning pit of self-indulgent woe.

She tried remembering what that gruesomely cheerful child always said about good things and adversity, but Monty Python's *Always Look On the Bright Side of Life*, played on a tight loop in her head instead. Anyway, she was buggered if she could think of anything to be cheerful about. True, her headache had gone, it had taken just one coffee and two cigarettes to clear it, and she could always try to get pregnant again. It wasn't a now or never deal.

They reached the entrance to Kensington Gardens and Dulcie shot off ahead as Abi unleashed Billy from the buggy. She sighed as he tottered off after his sister as though relieved from the strain of having to be, if not exactly cheerful, then not the screaming Banshee that her eyes suggested she really was.

'Don't bottle it up,' Beca said. 'It is OK to cry.'

'No, I don't want to. I've done too much of that already. I'm too angry to cry now.'

'What happened?' Beca asked as they followed the children towards the playground.

'Your departure tipped him off, obviously. All he did was look at me and he went completely white. The colour literally drained from his face. Under other circumstances it would have been funny. It's so bizarre to be living a cliché. He just said "I'm sorry, Abi," which was enough to confirm everything. I started crying again. He tried to comfort me. I hit him. It went downhill after that.'

The two women found a bench inside the state-of-the-art playground enclosure and sat down.

'I don't suppose either of us got much sleep. He kept saying he was sorry, which of course is meaningless. What's he sorry about? That he got found out? I don't see how he can be sorry for hurting me, he hadn't given my feelings any thought up until that point, had he?'

'Doesn't look that way.'

'After my initial outburst I was surprised how controlled I was. He was the one doing most of the crying. I just asked him questions. How long? Where? I'd got it into my head that he must have had sex in our bed, which of course was impossible. I've only been out once without him this year.'

Beca lit a cigarette which Abi took as soon as she'd checked her children weren't watching.

'He said all the right things. His act of contrition was sincere enough. He said he would end the affair, that he loved me, his place was at home with me and the children. Blah blah,' she said exhaling smoke. 'It was better than him shrugging his shoulders and packing his bags, I suppose. But he couldn't tell me why he'd done it in the first place.'

Beca wondered if Abi was going to cry now, but she held back. Her backbone must have been made from reinforced steel.

'I was a naïve fool thinking we had such a great marriage.'

'You've put everything into that relationship. How long would it have lasted if you were forever suspecting something?'

'It'll be that way now, if we stay together. It makes me so angry. Life can never be like it was before. He's destroyed it.'

'Do you want to divorce him?'

'No. I don't know, really I don't. I hate him for what he's done and sometimes I don't care if he goes or stays, but other times I'm physically sick just thinking about him leaving me. God, Beca, why did he have to ruin everything? I just don't understand why.'

'I haven't got any answers, I'm afraid. I wish I did.'

'If I did throw him out he'd just go to her. I'd have to kill them both.'

The pair sat in silence for a moment watching all the children tearing around the playground. Dulcie and Billy were in the sandpit burying their feet.

'Shouldn't they take their shoes off?'

Abi shrugged. 'In an ideal world, yes.'

A fat boy, a year or so older than Dulcie was playing nearby. He was digging a hole with a spade and throwing sand behind him. When she complained about being covered he looked at her, stuck his tongue out and then heaped a spade full of sand in her lap. Dulcie looked indignant, Abi rolled her eyes, but Beca was furious.

'Oy, you little bugger,' she shrieked in a gutter accent that always emerged in moments of confrontation. She streaked over to the sandpit and pulled the boy away from Dulcie by his elbow. He looked up at her defiantly but Beca's withering stare set his bottom lip trembling. 'Do that again and you're in deep shit. Got it?' The boy nodded and abandoning his bucket and spade ran to find his mother.

Beca looked down at Dulcie and Billy. 'He gives you any more trouble, you let me know.' The children looked up at her with astonishment and new found respect and as she walked back, smiling to herself, she wondered if she should spit or something to reinforce the hard-woman act.

'What exactly did you say to him?' Abi asked. 'He looked petrified.'

'Just put him straight.'

'Well it looks like his mother's going to put you straight,' Abi replied nodding towards another bench at the opposite end of the playground where a woman was scowling in their direction as she listened to her tearful child.

'Little bugger had it coming.'

'Remind me to lend you some of my child psychology books in the happy event of you getting pregnant.'

'I wouldn't rush to find them.' Beca lit another cigarette which brought further indignant looks from the fat boy's mother. Beca revelled in her disapproval.

'You'll have another go though, won't you.'

A good question. Beca mulled the idea over in her head. Could she go through that gruesome trysting again? What did it matter if Hal didn't like her, if she ended up with a baby at the end of it? It had to be worth a few moments discomposure. Some women went through infinitely more traumatic experiences just for the chance to conceive. There were no syringes, white-coated doctors or examination rooms, just Hal and his gruff manner. She was being a wimp.

'Sure,' she said breezily. 'Might as well call Hal now.' She got her mobile out of her pocket.

'You don't sound convinced.'

'Oh, I want a baby right enough, nothing's changed there. I'd just much rather not sleep with him again.'

'Why not?' Abi laughed. 'I can think of lots of reasons, but why do you think it's a bad idea?'

Beca cut across Abi as the phone at One Eyed Jack's was answered. 'Hi. Can I speak to Hal, if he's there?' A death metal dirge blared out of her mobile as Seaweed Boy went to find him. 'It was just a bit weird, that's all,' she said to Abi.

'You surprise me.'

Beca waited, holding the phone away from her ear.

'Hello?' Hal shouted above the music.

'Hi. It's me.'

Nothing.

'Beca. It didn't work.'

Hal stayed silent. Beca pulled a 'der-stupid' face and Abi smiled.

'I'm not pregnant.'

'Oh. I see. I'm sorry,' Hal replied.

'Me too. I was wondering if,' she hesitated. Having Abi's eyes boring into her didn't ease the embarrassment. 'Look, can we have another go?'

'I suppose so, yes. When were you thinking?'

Had she called her hairdresser by mistake? Surely not. Even he put more emotion into his appointment bookings.

'It would need to be,' Beca did some quick counting with her fingers. 'From the 23rd August. Two weeks today.'

'I'm not sure. I think I'm going to Paris with Sophie that weekend.'

'Can you check?'

'I'll call you back.'

Beca rang off. 'He's got to check with his wife.'

'Is it just me, or is that a bit surreal?' Abi asked.

'Sorry.'

'Forget it.'

A few moments later the phone rang again. It was Hal.

'Sorry, can't make it. We are going to Paris,' he said.

'How about the Monday?'

'Can't. We don't get back 'til Tuesday morning.'

'It'll be too late then.'

'Will you find someone else?'

'Looks like I'll have to.'

'OK. Let me know if you want to try in September.' Hal hung up.

Beca stared at her telephone. His indifference was infuriating, but why did it bother her so much? It had to be hurt pride for she certainly had no feelings for him. She couldn't recall ever having slept with a man who then treated her with such apathy. It wasn't part of the bargain that he should fancy her, but even so, a little smidgen of something might not have been amiss. She needed some space before Abi identified the sure-fire signs of chagrin. 'I feel like a coffee. That place over there looks like it does them. Fancy one?'

'Go on then. Get us a bun while you're at it, I'm finally hungry.'

By the time she returned, Dulcie and Billy were scrambling over the pirate ship. In fact Dulcie had managed to climb to the top of the mast which was pretty impressive for a four-year-old.

'Should she be all the way up there?'

'Probably not,' Abi said taking her coffee. 'But the Good Mother is having a break. Or is that a breakdown?'

'Just let me know when you want me to get her.'

'She'll scream if there's a problem.'

'Is that before, during or after she falls? There are some good looking blokes here,' Beca said casting an eye around the playground. 'Look at him.' She pointed towards a man pushing a young child on a swing. 'Very fanciable.'

'They say that about fathers, don't they? That women fancy men with children. I wonder why that is? Perhaps they look reliable, or like good providers. Maybe it brings out their softer side. Of course it also means they're married or partnered up.'

'Bad choice of subject, but you know that's not what I meant. I wasn't going to throw myself at him. I was just saying he looked nice. Besides, he could be – ,'

'Divorced?'

'Sorry.' Beca winced. 'Where is Tom, anyway?'

'Seeing her.'

'You're kidding me, Abi. Why didn't you stop him?'

'He's gone to tell her it's over.'

'And he couldn't use the phone?'

'Apparently not.'

'I'm not sure I'd have let him if it was me.'

'It's a test, I suppose. He might decide he wants to be with her after all. I'd rather know now than later. If he tells her it's over and walks away, then that's something.'

'And what if he tells you one thing and does another?'

'I'll know this time. Trust me, he won't get away with it again.'

A screech drew their attention towards the top of the pirate ship. Abi wearily got up from the bench.

'I'll get her, don't worry,' Beca said.

She ran towards the ship wondering why on earth she'd volunteered; she was, after all, afraid of heights and was more likely to cling to Dulcie than help her down. Billy was standing on the deck looking up at his sister. They were both crying. Beca patted him on the head.

'It'll be alright,' she said. 'I'll get her down.' She grinned nervously, kicked her shoes off and began climbing the mast with as much casualness as possible.

'Do you want me to help?' an earnest-faced boy of about nine asked.

'Would you?' Beca replied in a tone forever conferring the boy with superhero status. He scampered up like a monkey and after a few protests from his damsel in distress he managed to coax her down.

Before Dulcie could work her way up to full blown hysterics, Beca suggested they get some ice creams.

'Would you like one?' she asked the superhero.

He looked at her sheepishly wanting to say yes, but his upbringing got the better of him. 'Mummy says I mustn't take things from strangers.'

'Good point. Where is she?' Beca asked, thinking she would go and negotiate.

'There,' he replied, pointing at the mother of the fat boy from the sandpit.

'Ah. Well, she's absolutely right. Thanks for your help.'

The boy went off looking more than a little hard done by.

Dulcie's good humour was restored with the aid of a chocolate ice cream and by the time she got back to her mother she was full of her adventure and the tears had been forgotten. Beca handed Abi an ice cream.

'Thanks,' she said. 'You're a good friend.'

All four sat on the bench immersed in the delights of their treat. The sun shone down on them and Abi tilted her head back and closed her eyes.

'Come on,' Beca whispered to the two children. 'Let's go and find some lunch.'

The playground had settled into a lunchtime lull as picnic baskets were opened and hungry children sat down to refuel. Abi's kids had to make do with croissants and crisps from the kiosk, which didn't seem to bother them. For a while, after they had eaten, they had the playground to themselves. Billy had a new trick his father had taught him. While Beca held his hands he climbed up her legs and chest and then did a backward somersault down to the ground. She shrieked the first time he did it thinking she'd dislocated his arms, but he was very bendy and after the fifth turn she was the one in pain. Dulcie wanted equal time with her and insisted she played wheel-around. Beca spun her around until they were both so dizzy they fell over. Then Billy wanted a go. Half an hour later she limped back to the bench for another fag.

'You'll burn yourself out if you keep up that pace.'

'They're exhausting.'

'It's a lot easier to say no when they're your own. So, you're going to Sally's tonight.'

'How did you know?'

'I was talking to her yesterday. She called for some advice.'

'Does she know?'

'About Tom? No. It's a difficult one to bring up on the phone. "How are you?" "Well actually, now you ask, pretty bad. Tom's been screwing a girl in his office."'

'It is a bit of a conversation stopper. But you do need friends at times like this.'

'And I've got you,' Abi said putting her arm around Beca. 'I couldn't tell Sally, she'd be so upset. You know what she's like. And Claire. Well, there are no half measures with her, are there? I'm not sure I could cope with her smothering big mother style. Besides she'd probably insist Eddie hit Tom.'

'The thought had crossed my mind, but I was thinking of something more violent.'

Abi laughed. 'Anyway, you've got to go tonight. It will cheer me up to hear how you got on with Dan's friend.' Her eyebrows flickered just a little.

Friend? Abi might just as well have shouted 'Brace, brace, brace' for the effect it had on her. A quick-fire sequence of excruciating encounters, dating back to the first time one of her friends had tried fixing her up, flashed through her mind. Despite the speed it was a long moment before Beca focussed her eyes on Abi; the number of well-intended fit-ups she'd had to endure were legion.

'Friend?' Beca repeated the word with as much 'son-of-Satan' ominous dread as it deserved.

'Ah, clearly you don't know.'

'So it would seem.'

'Actually I sort of assumed you didn't. I wasn't supposed to tell you, but I know you hate surprises. That's why Sally phoned me up last night, to see how I thought you'd react to meeting another one of Dan's friends. You got incredibly drunk the last time, I seem to remember.'

'I had to. The whole evening was horrendous. It was like being a panda bear in the bloody zoo. Hordes of eager-eyed spectators watching to see if I'd cop off with Ping-Pong or whatever his name was.'

Abi laughed. 'You really do know how to cheer me up.'

'Glad to oblige,' Beca replied with mock indignation.

'According to Sally, he's very nice.'

'And she thinks I should meet him because?'

'He's single.'

'And that's the only criterion?'

'It's a start.'

'But it's always so cringeworthy. Everyone assumes that because I'm 36 and single that I'm frantic to find a mate. Well I'm not. I like being single. I don't know why no one ever believes me.'

'It is just conceivable that you're right.'

'I know I am.'

'Still, now that Hal has blown you out?'

'Are you suggesting I lure this man into bed just to get me pregnant?'

'It is a bit underhand, isn't it?'

'It's inspired. I just can't believe you of all people are suggesting it.'

Abi shrugged. 'Whatever it takes.'

Beca hoped her friend's jaded outlook on life was temporary. It was helpful advice though and a scheme worth giving serious consideration to. The gin binge might have to wait for another night. Then again, by tomorrow it would be unnecessary if she had a new man in tow.

Chapter **10**

Beca felt like asking the taxi driver to wait while she rang Sally's doorbell. She didn't rank cowardice particularly high up on her list of failings, but there was something very down-at-heel about the neighbourhood and when telling the driver her destination was 'just off the Goldhawk Road,' she had instinctively locked the doors. She knew her prejudice was absolutely without foundation. In terms of neighbourly friendliness, Sally and Dan won every time. Their neighbours knew and even seemed to like each other. They held annual street parties with trestle tables in the road to celebrate the fact and Beca, who was invited every year, always left wondering why community spirit was so lacking where she was. Her neighbours, with the sole exception of Mrs Butler, were imperious, money-grabbing ex-pats with gigantic 4x4 vehicles and very little going on in their highlighted heads.

As it was, the taxi driver shot off before Beca could reach the kerb. And she'd given him a decent tip. Bastard.

'You're early,' Sally said as they pressed cheeks. Beca spotted the obvious signs of edginess, the fleeting eye contact, the overly cheerful voice.

She smiled to herself; even as a teenager Sally was pathologically incapable of deceit. The idea that she'd conned her friend into a blind date was probably giving her an ulcer.

'You don't mind do you?' Beca replied between air kisses. 'I wanted to see Tabitha before she went to bed.' She wasn't so squeamish about stretching the truth. Seeing Sally's baby would of course be delightful, but Beca was keener to get herself settled in before he arrived. It would be to her tactical advantage not to be the one entering potentially hostile territory. Not that she planned on declaring war, but there were certain similarities between a successful military campaign and the seduction of a man. It took planning and a fool-proof strategy. She assessed her weaponry. Her dress was long, light and simple but revealed enough décolletage to be interesting. The Indonesian silk shawl added a softness that wasn't quite in keeping with her character but offered a degree of modesty if required. It could easily be discarded if the moment seemed right. The kitten heels were a more practical choice, in case he turned out to be a midget.

Masculine laughter resonated from the floor above.

'Where's Dan?' Beca asked as they passed the open door to the living room.

'He's upstairs with a friend of his. He just popped by to show Dan his new website.'

So he was here already. Beca shrugged it off. It was a setback, but not irreparable. Tabitha's squidgy face rested on her mother's shoulder and Beca smiled at her as she followed Sally into the narrow strip of a kitchen at the back of the house. Every surface was covered with food at various stages of preparation. All the rings on the stove were occupied by a simmering saucepan and Beca could see a large joint roasting in the oven.

'Something smells delicious,' she said.

'We've been cooking all day, haven't we,' she said to her baby.

'You didn't make those as well, did you?' Beca asked, pointing to a mountain of neat ciabatta rolls. Sally nodded and a wave of inadequacy engulfed Beca. How could she ever be a good mother and homemaker? Cooking anything with more than two saucepans needed outside caterers. Sally had old glass jars overflowing with fresh herbs, while Beca had a packet of dried grass cuttings in the back of the cupboard which had to cover for every culinary requirement. It was just as well she wasn't having a baby. Her child wouldn't have any friends, they wouldn't want to come back to play because there'd never be home-made cakes or meringues for tea. What would it take to be more like Sally?

She was completely at ease in her steaming kitchen, she actually appeared to be enjoying the mayhem. The fact that her husband was upstairs playing with his toys hadn't seemed to register any irritation. Beca had no doubt that given the same set of circumstances she would be shouting up the stairs for him to bloody well come down and lend a hand. She would then ruin the meal, sour the atmosphere and take one more irreversible step towards the divorce courts. Sally showed no signs of resentment. She was always so much better balanced than Beca. Just plain nicer, in fact.

'Here, take Tabitha will you?'

Beca held out her arms and took hold of the little bundle. She seemed to have even less hair than when she last saw her in Norfolk. She hoped on this occasion that such close proximity to baby flesh wouldn't have her blubbering out her own desires to have a child.

Beca was no more proficient with baby handling than the time before and Tabitha's head lolled a couple of times on her weak neck before she got a good hold. Sally was gracious enough not to notice as she stood at the sink shelling eggs and then leaning over to stir a bubbling saucepan. A couple of tresses had escaped from the pile on top of her head and were framing her face. She moved around the kitchen with all the grace of a ballet dancer in her against-the-bias Ghost dress. A battery of cooking implements hung from a rack over her head and without looking up she was able to locate the exact tool she wanted. Maybe she just had more female hormones than Beca. Perhaps that was why she seemed to come with her own diffuse light.

'Tabitha smiled at me.' Beca was enchanted.

'Did she? That's nice.' Sally stroked her baby's face. 'You are a friendly little thing, aren't you? You do look stunning tonight, Beca, is that a new dress?

'No. Not too dressy?'

'Absolutely not.'

'You're looking pretty delicious yourself. You'd never know you'd just had a baby.'

'I'm back to my pre-pregnancy weight already. Claire says it's unhealthy, but I've been eating like a horse. I really have.'

'Well you can discount anything she says on the grounds of jealousy. She still insists her lardy arse is maternal fat.'

'But Charlie is over 18 months old.'

'Exactly.' Beca kissed Tabitha's bald head. 'So, do you recommend it then, motherhood?' she asked punishing herself.

'Absolutely. It's the world's best kept secret. By the way,' Sally stepped closer, 'did you ever get anywhere with that idea of yours to get pregnant?' The last word tailed off into a whisper. She always was such a prude.

'No,' Beca whispered back. There didn't seem any point in filling her in on a past-tense event.

'Well, if and when you do, you must let me do your feet. Reflexology is great for balancing the hormones.'

'Right.' Beca was distracted by another pang. Sadness kept catching her unawares and even though she had convinced herself that life wasn't at all bad, reminders of her failure crept over her in hot, panicky flushes. She tried to snap out of it, bringing herself back to the present. 'So, who is this man with Dan?'

'Oh,' Sally said dropping a peeled egg into the sink. 'He was just passing. They're colleagues more than friends, but he's very nice. He's divorced, lives in Chelsea in a fabulous house, has two sons in college – he had them very young apparently.' She caught her breath.

'Just passing?' Beca fixed her with a questioning eye.

'Actually he did call first. He practically invited himself over,' she said with an unconvincing shrug.

'And he's staying for supper?'

'I couldn't not ask him. There's plenty of food. And he really is very good company.'

'I see.' Beca's cruel streak was surfacing. 'So he wouldn't have anything to do with the man you're trying to fix me up with?'

Sally gasped. 'Abi promised not to tell you.'

'Well I'm glad she did.'

'But you're always so anti this kind of thing. I thought if we were subtle perhaps you wouldn't notice.'

Beca laughed. 'Thanks for going to all the effort.'

The men's voices arrived ahead of them.

'You will be nice to him, won't you,' Sally pleaded, chopping some coriander with a heavy hand.

'Of course, unless he's an odious creep.' There was a glint in Beca's eyes, but it was too late for Sally to do anything other than glare at her. He walked into the kitchen ahead of Dan, beer bottle in hand and very much at home. He smiled at Beca, a little too knowingly perhaps, leaving her with the feeling she had no clothes on.

'There you are,' Sally said to them with mock reproach. 'Mitchell, this is my very dear and old friend, Beca.'

Beca shook his hand, managing not to lick it despite the Old Shep introduction. His handshake was firm, his hand big and capable, if a bit better manicured than her own.

'You don't have a drink, Beca. What can I get you?' Dan asked.

'Gin and tonic.'

'Driving?'

'Taxi.'

'Good, I'll make it a sensible one then.'

Sally looked bright-eyed with excitement and Beca could tell by the way she wiped her hands on a tea towel that she was nervous. She needn't have been, not on her account anyway. She was going to be the model guest, she wasn't going to get drunk despite any encouragement from Dan and she would, for the sake of appearances, give up her forays into the garden for a fag. More than that she couldn't do.

'Shall we go and sit down in the living room?' Sally said retrieving Tabitha from Beca's arms so she could take her drink. 'Everything's under control here.'

Mitchell stood aside in an overtly chivalrous manner and Sally led the way. The living room was one of Beca's favourite rooms in the house, done up in a style that she herself couldn't even begin to imitate. It required natural flair to be able to mix knackered old leather sofas and chairs with dainty throws and glittery cushions. Plastic rose fairy lights wrapped around thin hazel branches sparkled in reds and pinks from the fireplace. If Beca attempted anything like that it would be a casebook example of bad taste. She would be more likely to start a fire if she had a mass of little candles twinkling on the mantelpiece and along the floor. She settled into a corner of a sofa, kicked off her kitten heels and pulled her legs up under her. She wasn't quite sure what effect she was trying to create, perhaps she was just letting Mitchell know she wasn't fazed by him. The leather upholstery squeaked against his jeans as he sat down opposite her. Sally launched into a series of questions about his website, Beca feigned interest but was intently studying her prey.

He was undoubtedly good-looking, exceptionally so. He was probably 40, possibly younger, but he had the air of confidence that older men have. His body was well proportioned, he was tall, his hair was thick and brown. He had the square jaw and perfect features of a man in an American disposable razor commercial and Beca could well imagine him stroking his smooth chin on the prow of his yacht. Yep. He was fanciable. He bore more than a passing resemblance to George Clooney, they could in fact have been twins, although perhaps that had more to do with the low lighting. But there was something about him, Beca struggled to put her finger on it, that reminded her of George Hamilton. Next to Dan, whose speciality was cute but crumpled academic, Mitchell did look a little too well groomed. His jeans showed distinct signs of having been ironed. Never mind. She was in the mood for forgiveness, besides, it wasn't those sort of jeans she was interested in.

'So, Beca, how come you know Sally and Dan?' Mitchell had spread one arm across the back of the armchair, his crossed legs stretched out in front of him. His pose made her think of a peacock fanning his feathers in a display of courtly love, and even though he was rather overt, she quite liked this blatant approach.

'That's an easy one. I've known Sally since I was eleven. We were at school together. And I met Dan at the L.S.E.'

'You studied there?' He sounded impressed.

'Economics. The year below Dan. And you?' Beca sipped her drink hoping the tumbler would break his penetrating stare. His eyes were the weirdest pale blue. Weird, but nice.

'Dan and I keep hooking up together for work. And I met Sally when they came out to my centre in Vermont.'

'I thought I detected an accent.'

Dan laughed and shook his head. 'Not guilty. I've just lived there for a number of years. 'My wife's a Yank.'

Wife? Not again. Hadn't Sally and Dan done their homework? 'Where is she now?' Beca asked, counting the number of hours before she could escape home.

'We're divorced. It's been two years now. I don't know why I said "wife", we can't stand each other.'

Beca was relieved, but why make such an obvious mistake? Was he winding her up? Perhaps he was just forgetful.

Sally had disappeared back into the kitchen and returned a few minutes later carrying a big serving dish. 'Shall we eat?' she said gesturing towards the dining table.

Beca wasn't surprised to find Mitchell sitting opposite her. A smile played on her lips. She could tell he fancied her, which was great. Normally she hated such contrived encounters, but she had her own pressing agenda to consider. From what she had seen so far he was interesting, certainly attentive and she could do with being swept off her feet for a little while. She could sense adventure in him, or perhaps that was the Gillette advert again. Nevertheless she could imagine a series of weekends abroad with him, sailing, diving, or perhaps a bit of shopping in New York or Rome. Or both. Why not? Before she had started in on the kedgeree she had lined up a fun-filled summer for herself.

'What business are you in then?' she asked him. Not that it really mattered but she had several hours of conversation ahead of her.

'I'm what's known these days as a life coach.'

'A what?'

'A life coach. I help people reach their true potential.' That sounded grim.

'How do you manage that?' Beca asked, hoping he wouldn't say through Bible classes

'Through motivation.'

'Perhaps you could come and motivate some of my feckless traders.'

'Careful,' Dan said. 'You might find yourself motivated out of a job.'

'Oh, so it's down-sizing on the cheap?' Beca asked.

'Not at all,' Mitchell said with good humour. 'I can find out what's wrong with a team or a whole organisation and put it right.

Occasionally a person just doesn't fit and I can help them find what it is they're really looking for.'

Sally was lapping it up. She sat with her chin resting on her hand looking wistfully at him, all but ignoring the smoked haddock sitting on her plate. Beca wasn't so easily won over. She needed to loosen up a bit and so she gestured to Dan and he refilled her glass. If she needed to be a bit tipsy to see the sun shining out of Mitchell's arse, then so be it. So far she was entirely won over on the looks front, but there was something a tiny bit creepy about his approach to life. She was prepared to put aside her usual sneering judgements because she really wanted to get on with him. On the plus side when she explained about her job he didn't make some guffawing quip about the size of her bonuses.

Tabitha woke up with a gummy yawn and a cross whimper which developed into a monster yell.

'It's time for her feed,' Sally said lifting her out of her Moses basket. 'I'll just take her upstairs.' Had Sally suddenly become breast-shy or was she making a tactical withdrawal? When she asked Dan to clear the plates and put the vegetables on, Beca's suspicions of a ruse were confirmed. They were alone. Excitement bubbled up inside her; she loved flirting. Mitchell leant back in his chair and smiled. Lifting his glass to his lips he drank without breaking eye contact with her. Had someone just put Barry White on? Or was the love stuff going on in her head? It must have been the gin and wine. Her newly de-toxed body wasn't up to the abuse.

'I'm very glad to have met you, Beca.'

'Likewise, Mitchell.' Why did he keep using her name? He already had her rapt attention. There was something too polished about his approach. There was no hesitancy, no hint of self-doubt. This was after all a blind date, yet he showed no signs of embarrassment. Beca put it down to his time spent in America. Anyway, she liked confident men.

'So what about you, Beca? Is there anyone special in your life?'

'There's Rhett.'

Mitchell's face froze for a moment. He clearly hadn't been expecting this.

'But he's a cat, so I don't suppose he counts.'

He laughed. 'But no serious love interest?'

God, this man didn't waste much time.

'No,' she replied. 'And to be honest, there never has been anyone special. I just don't have the knack of finding a good man.'

'I could help you change all that,' he said with what looked like a straight face.

Beca fought the urge to burst out laughing. 'I was hoping you would say that.'

'Sorry I was so long,' Sally said as she slipped into her seat. 'Tabitha kept falling asleep as I was feeding her.' She reached for the wine bottle, but Mitchell beat her to it; she smiled at him as he filled her glass. 'Dan seems to be doing fine on his own in the kitchen, so I'm leaving him to it,' she said raising her glass of wine. 'Mitchell's really into personality typing. Tell Beca what you were saying earlier on.'

Was this some kind of new keyboard skill?

'Sure.' He rested his hands on the table and spread his fingers, then looked up at each woman in turn. 'We each have our own unique character. You, Beca are quite different from Sally, but in important ways are very similar to me. Our likes and dislikes might be vastly different, but the way we see the world, the way we think is in fact close to the same.'

'How can you tell?' Beca asked.

'I can't for sure. I'd need to run some tests.'

'Being pigeon-holed has never appealed to me,' she replied.

'I'm with you on that one.' Dan laid a plate in front of her.

'You're suggesting the system is limiting, but it's not, it's liberating. You need to know yourself before you can achieve your optimum potential. You, for example, are an extrovert, you think on your feet, you are driven to achieve. Sally on the other hand is reflective, she's an introvert, she thinks with her heart not her head. I'm not saying one is better than the other, far from it, just different.

'So, if there's something I want, it's fine for me to go after it, because it's in my nature to be like that?' Beca asked.

'Correct. Going counter to your instincts would be detrimental to your happiness.' This was an excellent philosophy. With that kind of reasoning it would be hard for him to complain about her hidden agenda.

'Where's the morality to such an approach?' Dan asked as he helped himself to grilled courgettes before passing the dish along to Beca.

'The individual has to work within the moral boundaries of the society he finds himself in,' Mitchell replied.

Drat. Still, sperm stealing would only be a minor infringement of his human rights if she made sure he enjoyed being misused. Silence fell as she and the others ate their meal.

Beca was marvelling at Sally's ability to turn a dried up grey lentil into something quite delicious when it suddenly dawned on her. What if he'd had the snip? It wasn't an unreasonable concern. He was certainly older than she was, and there'd been mention of two children. Supposing he didn't want any more and had taken the drastic step of having a vasectomy. Beca scrutinised his face. Was he the sort who could wave goodbye to such a potent symbol of his manhood? There was only one way to find out.

An opportunity presented itself when Mitchell helped Sally to clear the table. He followed her into the kitchen complimenting her on her culinary skills. That left Dan alone with Beca.

'Do you know if Mitchell's had the snip?' Beca asked directly, scissoring her fingers.

Dan spluttered wine across the white tablecloth. 'Jesus, Beca. What kind of question is that?'

'I need to know.'

'You ask him then,' he laughed.

'He's your friend. You're a bloke. It's straightforward enough. If I ask him he's going to think I'm gagging for it.'

'And you're not?'

'Please, Dan, it's really important.'

'Because why? Exactly?'

'Don't ask me to explain,' she said. Dan was unmoved. 'Look, OK, I'll be honest. At my age I'm having to work to a tight agenda. I don't have time to mess about with men who don't want to settle down. I just thought given his age, the fact that he has two kids, that he might, not unreasonably, have had the snip.'

'Could you stop doing that with your fingers every time you say "snip". It's making my eyes water.'

'Sorry. Look, you set me up with him. If this was the 18th century I wouldn't be allowed anywhere near him until his credentials had been checked out. Perhaps not specifically his sperm count, but you know what I mean. You'd be honour-bound to find out.'

'And you'd be on the shelf.'

Beca was unimpressed.

'OK, I'll try and find out somehow.'

She was aware that it wasn't a great performance. She'd lied to her friend, but necessarily so. As a man she expected him to get mardy if he knew what she was really planning. It was another thing to add to the litany of bad behaviour. But then, in Mitchell's own words, she was just responding to type. It was pre-determined; beyond her control.

Beca was, under normal circumstances, a real pudding fan but Sally's delicious lemon and lime tart went down like a cement flan. What would she do if he'd had his tubes tied? She didn't know an awful lot about surgery but guessed that a vasectomy reversal couldn't be completed – and more importantly healed – in a two week timeframe. There was also the small matter of explaining why she wanted it done. Beca had already noticed his fastidiously clean hands. He looked so well scrubbed, so completely erased of any bodily excretion that he was probably the sort of bloke who would insist on wearing a full body condom. It would be hard enough trying to peel him out of that, but insisting on major surgery beforehand? That was perhaps pushing things a bit.

'World leaders are where they are because they're not afraid of success,' Mitchell said to Dan. It annoyed Beca that he had started up a serious conversation. She was pre-occupied with more pressing matters. 'People fail because of the limits they set themselves,' he continued.

'What about outside factors?' Dan asked. 'You can't control everything, particularly where other people are concerned.'

'But you can, especially where other people are concerned.'

He had just pressed Beca's interested button.

'There are simple ways to influence the way a person responds to you,' Mitchell continued.

'That's obvious,' Sally said. 'If I'm rude to someone then they're unlikely to think well of me.'

'It's more subtle than that. Body language, posture, gestures are all studied subconsciously. We all do it all the time. If I sit back like this,' he said leaning back in his chair and folding his arms across his chest, 'what would you think?'

'You're trying to put space between us,' Beca said.

'Correct,' Mitchell said pointing at her. 'By knowing how the mind interprets body language I can control the effect I have on people.'

'Are you doing it now?' Sally asked.

'Of course. We all are. Take Beca. She's leaning forwards, she's relaxed, look, she's running her finger up and down the stem of her glass.' Beca squirmed under the scrutiny and hoped he wasn't a mind-reader as well.

'What does it mean though?' Dan asked.

'That she's comfortable in our company, that perhaps she isn't concentrating on our conversation, that her mind has wandered to more sensual thoughts.'

Beca laughed to cover her embarrassment and as she tried to push a non-existent piece of hair behind an ear she was acutely aware that every move was being analysed by the others. 'What about Dan?' she asked shifting the spotlight.

Mitchell studied Dan's pose. 'Actually, he's quite easy. We can tell he's not in full approval.'

'That's obvious from the scowl,' Sally said.

'Ignore the face. Try reading the body language. His elbows are on the table, his forearms are covering his chest.'

'A classic defensive posture,' Beca said knowledgeably.

'Correct. And his hands are under his chin. He's giving the subject his full attention, but he's sceptical, and feeling outnumbered, he's protecting himself.'

'Presumably you can use this knowledge to your own advantage?' Dan asked, removing his elbows from the table.

'Sure, if you're trying to unnerve someone. It's easy to throw a person by shifting position.'

'Doesn't sound very fair.' Sally was sitting straight in her chair trying to give nothing away.

'That's because it's manipulative,' Dan said.

'It can be, if used the wrong way. But that's not what I teach. It can be of real benefit to people who just don't understand why they can't get on in life. Some people naturally have awkward body language.'

Beca and Sally nodded with approval. Dan's sideways glance suggested he had his doubts.

'Think of the nerd in your class at school. He looked like a loser, didn't he? That's why he was singled out. It had nothing to do with his clothes and geeky haircut, but everything to do with the way he interacted, the way he was perceived.'

'I'm impressed,' Beca said. He smiled at her, so she smiled back.

Sally gathered the pudding bowls up. 'Beca, could you give me a hand with the coffee. You're so much better at making it than me.' Thinly veiled code for a gossip up-date.

'Well?' she asked as she pulled Beca into the kitchen.

'Well what?' Beca asked.

'You like him, I can tell. You haven't done anything to antagonise him all evening.' Sally took a tin of coffee out of the fridge.

'I've only just met him,' Beca said. 'Do you want a hand with these?' she asked, gesturing towards a pile of dirty dishes.

'In the dishwasher, if you don't mind. Yes, but you're usually so quick to decide.'

'He's OK.'

'Only OK? I think he's gorgeous.'

'Don't you think he's a bit too aware of his own charm?' Beca sat down on a kitchen stool and watched as Sally filled the Italian percolator with coffee grounds and put it on the stove.

'I think women just respond well to him.'

'He flirts with them you mean,' Beca said.

'Outrageously, but I don't think it's calculated. He seems quite natural.'

'He's the phoniest guy I've ever met. I don't suppose there's a single gesture in his repertoire that hasn't been rehearsed in front of the mirror.'

'You're very cynical.'

'Maybe.'

'Does that mean you don't fancy him?'

'I wouldn't say that at all. He has certain qualities that I find attractive.'

'Such as?' Sally asked.

'Well, he's good-looking, well-built, capable of serious conversation, and if he's extended his philosophy of excellence into his private life, then I dare say he's a top shag in bed.'

Sally clapped her hands with pleasure. She obviously saw Beca's interest in Mitchell as a personal triumph.

'Need a hand ladies?' He was leaning in the doorway with a massive smirk on his face. Both women screeched with surprise.

'How much of that did you hear?' Beca asked.

'Enough,' Mitchell replied.

Which was how much? The part about him being a fraud? Or the bit about his sexual prowess?

'Catch you in a bit,' Sally said squeezing her way past Mitchell.

'Coffee's ready,' Beca said trying to follow. Mitchell put an arm across the doorway blocking her way. She stepped back and tittered nervously. What did she have to go and do that for? Had there been a blushing virgin blinking back at her in the mirror that morning? No. She wasn't scared of him. Jesus, she'd spent the entire evening working out how to get into bed with him. But he was so frighteningly sure of himself. There was nothing for it but to take the lead. She reached up and kissed him. Fear that she'd misread the signs, that he'd actually just come into the kitchen for a glass of water, were forgotten when he put his arms around her and kissed her back.

Chapter 11

Beca raced through the front door and slammed it behind her. She was still wearing the shorts and baggy T-shirt she had put on first thing that morning. Not that she made a habit of going shopping in her slobbing around the house clothes, but time was tight and she was in the middle of a clothes crisis. In a move Buster Keaton would have been proud of, she skidded to a halt at the bottom of the stairs, then turned and ran back to the shelf by the front door to gather her post. Mrs Butler's door opened and the old lady poked her head out into the hallway.

'Oh, it's you, Beca. I thought we were in the midst of an elephant raid.'

'Sorry, Mrs B. I'm in a bit of a hurry,' she replied in a cheerful sing-song voice.

'Are you up to something special this weekend?'

'I'm going away with my new gentleman friend,' Beca replied with a coy smile.

'And you've bought something new to wear.' Mrs Butler gestured towards the collection of boutique bags hanging from Beca's hand. 'How nice.'

'Just a bit of last minute panic buying. It's so difficult to decide what to take.'

'That rather depends on where you're going, doesn't it?'

'The Cotswolds,' Beca admitted reluctantly.

'Oh.' Mrs Butler seemed to share her own sense of disappointment.

It had been on their second or third date when Beca had suggested to Mitchell that they go away for the weekend. The crucial weekend. The 48-hour period when she would conceive. Of course she'd omitted that particular detail when presenting her idea. Mitchell had jumped at the chance and announced over a clink of wine glasses that he would take care of all the arrangements.

Beca had tried hard not to be miffed by the lack of consultation. Life, she had long-since concluded, worked a lot better when she did the organising, but she'd managed to convince herself it would be nice to let a man make the decisions for once, in a big shoulders and testosterone kind of way. But that was when she had still been fantasising about rugged sailors with stubble-free chins. As it became apparent he wasn't capable of making the right decision, she had tried hard to steer him around to her way of thinking.

Sadly he hadn't budged. She had suggested New York, he had booked them into a Jacobean manor house, converted tastefully into a hotel complete with its own resident minor aristocrat. Beca didn't dislike the countryside, but being city born and bred she wasn't equipped for it. She didn't have an off-road button to press. Her wardrobe was well able to handle a trip to the Guggenheim, supper in the Rainbow Room and a night of bar-crawling, but not open country. She didn't own a pair of wellington boots, and neither did she want to. Her tastes were urban. The last thing she wanted in the morning was warm tea delivered in a floral teapot and the Sunday Telegraph folded beside her hearty English breakfast. But these were small, peevish irritations. It didn't really matter where on the planet they were so long as his sperm and her egg were on intimate terms. A chilled Margarita at the Paramount would have been nice though.

'Archie and I stayed in a lovely B&B in the Cotswolds for our honeymoon,' Mrs Butler said. Beca had expected something more exotic from this ex-Foreign Office globe-trotter. 'It was wartime you see so we didn't have much choice.'

'What was it like?'

'Couldn't say. We only came out of our room at mealtimes.'

Beca's eyes widened with mock surprise and Mrs Butler retreated into her flat with a smile on her face and a wistful look in her eyes. Archie had been dead for over sixty years and she was still in love with him. That was loyalty. Beca didn't reckon she could ever come close to such devotion.

Still, one weekend at a time. She bounded upstairs to her flat and then up to her bedroom. A large suitcase lay open on her bed surrounded by clothes, some neatly folded, others dumped in piles. She emptied her new purchases out of their bags and began tearing at the tissue paper that surrounded them. She was nervous about the coming weekend, not in an anxious, doom-laden manner, but in excited anticipation. It was the thought of getting pregnant, not of spending more time with Mitchell that had her so worked up; indeed for a while now her suitor had been truly marginalised in her thoughts.

She checked her watch. Twenty five minutes to go before he was due. It was time to get dressed. She put on a new blue dress with tiny polka-dots. It had a faint air of the 1930s about it with its deep cut neckline and ruching at the bottom. She smiled at herself in the mirror as she imagined Mitchell trying to fireman-lift her over a stile. Why bother? They could play burning houses in the bedroom.

She dragged her suitcase down the stairs and left it by her front door. Beca had begun going off Mitchell pretty much as soon as she'd asked him to go away for the weekend. She could at least, with her hand on her heart, say she did fancy him when she asked him. And it wasn't as if she didn't fancy him now. Certainly, he was an interesting, dynamic man, if not exactly very funny. But more crucially, he was revealing himself to be a fraud. Beca had presumed his chiselled good looks were part of Mother Nature's blessings. Increasingly, however, she was beginning to suspect they owed more to the skilful workings of a plastic surgeon's knife. It was bizarre to think her child-to-be could be the spitting image of his father and yet bear absolutely no resemblance to the man. She shrugged off the thought and went to close the sash windows in the living room. What did it matter if his nose wasn't his? His tackle was, as Dan had put it, 'firing from both cylinders.'

She checked her watch again. There was time for a cup of coffee, not that her nerves needed any extra stimulation. It should in theory be her last; soon to go, along with the booze and fags, until the next pregnancy test and then on until her baby was born. It was such a depressing thought having to abstain again.

It had been on the same night when Beca had suggested they go away together that she had begun to think perhaps he'd been a bit too economical with the truth about his age. Under closer scrutiny, Gillette man had become Just for Men man, with dark rumbling possibilities of a star appearance in a stairlift or easy-access bath commercial before too long. The image of George

Clooney had begun to fade and in his place stood a surgically rebuilt George Hamilton with orange suntan advertising vari-focal lenses. It was his implausibly bright teeth that had tipped her off. What irritated her most about all this reconstructive activity was that he would have been a whole lot more fanciable with grey hair and frown marks. It was his unseemly struggle against the inevitable that she found so unappealing. It marked him out as vain and perhaps even pathetic.

It was depressing that wishful thinking had so succinctly won over common sense and good eyesight. How exactly had she fallen for the surgically-enhanced charms of this man? Beca put her eagerness to only see heroic qualities in him down to her double set-back, viz. not being pregnant and having no one lined up for a second chance. She had been delighted when he'd opened another door, once Hal had slammed shut the first. Only now did she realise the bright light emanating from beyond was not inspiration or anything approaching it, but his teeth.

She tipped the dregs of her cup down the sink and put it in the dishwasher. She was leaning on the kitchen worktop wondering how to fill the next ten minutes before Mitchell arrived, without raking over the past two weeks, when her eyes settled on the suitcase. At that same moment, the meaty roar of a motorbike pulling up shook the window panes at the front of the house. This seismic action barely registered a blip compared with the explosions going off in Beca's head. What had Mitchell said about his car? It was small. An MGB, or a frog-eyed Sprite? Either way it had a boot big enough for one spare pair of knickers and a hairbrush. He was going to be there at any minute and she had to repack. This wasn't just a blonde moment, this was a platinum blonde with split ends situation. How could she have been so stupid? She flung open her suitcase and stared at the neat layers of clothes. Then the doorbell rang and the lid she had been keeping on her growing unease finally blew off.

He was early. She ran upstairs, tore into the spare bedroom next to hers and opened the wardrobe doors. She pulled suitcases and bags of various sizes out until she settled upon a small sports holdall that was wedged at the bottom under the sleeping bag she'd never used. The doorbell rang again as she hurtled down the stairs.

'Hi,' she said breathlessly. 'Come on up. First floor.' She had about thirty seconds to repack. What an idiot. He'd told her about the car and how much to bring. She really needed to start carrying a notebook around with her to write these details down in; her brain clearly couldn't be trusted to remember. She skimmed off the first three layers of clothes and shoved them into the holdall.

As she flung the suitcase into a cupboard in the hallway where the vacuum cleaner lived, there was a knock at the door. She opened it.

'I'm almost ready, just a few last minute adjustments,' she said scooping up some underwear that had fallen on the floor. She darted into the kitchen and slung them into the nearest drawer.

'Going somewhere?'

It was Hal.

'Christ. What are you doing here?' She watched him put his motorbike helmet down by the door. 'You can't stay. I'm expecting someone.'

'Nice place,' he said ambling into the living room with his hands thrust deep into his jeans pockets.

'It's great. Now leave. He'll be here any minute. I thought you were him. Anyway, why aren't you in Paris?' Beca said now unzipping the holdall and pulling her clothes out.

'We fell out on the way to Waterloo. I said something rude about her mother. She called me a "Cold Inglish Feesh," and threw me out of the taxi.'

'Oh.' Beca examined the clothes from the holdall. Three skirts and a pair of trousers, a bra and a pair of stockings. She pulled the suitcase out of the cupboard and opened it up on the kitchen floor.

Hal shrugged. 'She'll get over it. She's always had a quick temper. It's one of the reasons why I love her.'

'That's nice. Why don't you go and make up with her?' Beca was distracted, her mind was on her clothes, most of which were now scattered on the kitchen floor. Where the hell had she put her knickers?

'Anyway,' Hal began as Beca opened and slammed shut kitchen drawers. 'You seem a little tense.'

'It's nothing. What were you saying?'

'I thought I'd come and offer my services.' Beca stopped still and looked at him, by this time he was casually checking out the sofa for comfort. 'But clearly that's not necessary,' he said. 'Well done for so swiftly replacing me.'

'Anyone would think you were jealous,' Beca said studying him from the safe distance of the kitchen.

He laughed. 'Don't flatter yourself. I was thinking of the money.'

Beca smarted. She found the knickers and selecting four pairs she ostentatiously dropped them into the bag.

'How much are you paying him? Is that original?' he asked, walking over to the *Brief Encounter* film poster framed on the wall.

'Yes it is. And I'm not.'

'Congratulations, for not paying him that is. How did you manage it?

'More to the point, how did you know where I live?'

'Didn't you tell me?'

'No.'

'Then I haven't got a clue.'

Beca stood with her hands on her hips watching him. So he was offering his services, was he? As soon as he found himself free for the weekend. Well too bad. She'd made other plans. What was he expecting? That she'd give up trying to get pregnant just because he wasn't around? The arrogance of the man was galling. Besides, why would she want to get involved in a loveless tryst again, when she had Mitchell champing at the bit? He was the man she'd be going to bed with that weekend. He was clearly desperate to get into her knickers. She felt certain, although she couldn't yet account for his performance, that there would be passion and a damn sight more fun. The thought put a smile on her face.

'You need to get going now,' she said snapping back to reality.

'Aren't you going to offer me a coffee?'

'No. I don't want you around when he gets here.'

Hal showed no signs of being offended. 'Embarrassed by him?'

'Of course not. He's actually a really nice man. I just don't want to have to explain you.'

'Erstwhile inseminator should do it.'

'You're just doing this to wind me up, aren't you?'

His smile was all the confirmation she needed.

'Fine, have it your way. I can't physically throw you out, but I want you to know I think you're a complete prat.'

'Does that mean I get a cup of coffee?'

'Piss off.' Even though she was furious with him a smile played upon her lips. She had always enjoyed sparring with him. If this had been eight years ago, they'd have gone a few more rounds and then jumped into bed.

The doorbell rang again.

Beca stared at the intercom.

'A telepathic door buzzer, very impressive.'

'Shut up,' Beca said with a laugh. She pressed the voice button. 'I'll be down in a minute.'

'Do you need a hand with your bag?' Mitchell's voice was crackly over the intercom.

'Such a gentleman,' Hal taunted.

'No thanks,' she replied, gesturing wildly at him with two fingers. 'Just wait for me there.'

Hoping to get out of the flat before Hal reached the door was a futile aim. As it was he had the holdall out of her hands before she had a chance to dodge past him.

'Allow me, I insist,' he said with a bow and a mischievous grin.

'No,' Beca replied, pulling the bag petulantly. In the tussle she dropped her keys on the floor. Hal brushed past her as he bent to pick them and she caught a whiff of blokiness and oil paint that made her stop. She stood back as if she'd been stung and stared in confusion at him. If he had noticed the effect he'd had on her, he did an excellent job of not showing it.

The knock at the door only added to Beca's panic. Hal looked at her and hesitated with his hand on the door knob and that taunting smile still working its way across his lips.

'Open it,' Beca said, managing to rearrange her features to look less like a dumbstruck fish and more like the savvy chick she wanted to be.

'Hi there, honey,' Mitchell said in a jokey American accent. 'The old dear downstairs let me in. She kept winking at me. Very perturbing. You ready?'

He didn't appear to have noticed Hal.

'Ready.' Why did she feel so embarrassed about him? 'You're wearing gloves,' she said unintentionally, her thoughts escaping through her mouth. She managed to seal the escape hatch before, 'You're wearing natty string gloves with leather patches worn exclusively by old men with sporting pretensions,' got out. Hal chuckled and at last Mitchell acknowledged him, although that could have been the botox between his eyebrows wearing off.

Oh dear. It was no contest really. Next to Hal he really did look so much older, and more serious, and dull. Even if sex was going to be lousy with Hal, and she would be several thousand pounds the poorer, at least she might have a laugh or two. Mitchell just had no sense of humour. He didn't know how to laugh. It wasn't so much that he physically couldn't any longer, what with his various chemical augmentations, it was just that nothing stirred him into laughter. So perhaps the fun she'd been having over the past two weeks was at his expense. She had been laughing at him, rather than with him.

It was all so confusing. Why had Hal turned up to complicate life? She needed to be alone to unscramble her thoughts, but there wasn't much chance of the two men chatting pleasantly while she went off to mull over her options. A decision was needed. Both men were keen to bed her. The single one for lustful reasons, the married one for her money. Why was she even considering the latter option? Was she completely insane? Quite possibly. There couldn't really be any other explanation because she had no feelings for Hal, truly she didn't, it was just that their brains connected in a way that hers and Mitchell's never would.

'Mitchell,' she said clapping her hands together as if that would galvanise her. 'Something really terrible has happened.' She hesitated, not having a clue where she was going. 'This is my brother, Hal, by the way. 'He's,' she looked at him for inspiration. None was forthcoming. 'He's come to take me to see mother. Who is dangerously ill in hospital.'

Hal smiled. 'Nice to meet you, Mitch. Beca's been telling me all about you.'

Mitchell automatically shook his hand. His face was the picture of surprise. 'Your mother?' he asked.

'Yes. She's very ill, isn't she?' Beca said turning to Hal for support.

'Well –' he said dragging the word out as if he wasn't certain.

'She had a stroke last night. The doctors don't think she will last. We're off to see her now. Right now, this minute. So you see you'll have to leave.' She tried skirting around him to open the front door.

'Would you like me to come?' he asked.

'No.' Panic. 'That wouldn't be possible. She's in Edinburgh. Hal has booked the flights.'

'Mitch could go with you. I'm sure there'd be another seat on the plane,' Hal said leaning against the kitchen worktop with his arms folded across his chest.

Beca turned and looked at him with horror, her eyes pleading with him to help. None was offered.

'You wouldn't mind delaying your trip, would you?' he said to Mitchell. You might even make it back by this evening.'

'Unless mother dies, of course,' Beca said through gritted teeth.

'It's not that bad. Anyway, mum would love to meet you. She's so pleased she's finally got herself a boyfriend' Hal said, rolling his eyes in Beca's direction. Mitchell nodded, acknowledging what he had said, but his mind was clearly elsewhere.

'Why don't we try next weekend?' Beca said. 'Or perhaps we could meet up during the week. I'm really sorry about this,' she said steering him towards the door. 'It's just one of those things. And even if she wasn't so seriously ill,' she said glaring at Hal, 'I don't think I could enjoy myself. It's best if you go.' This was no Oscar-winning performance.

She could see Mitchell's jaw clenching as she shut the door behind him. He was clearly not a happy man.

'So, do you think he believed me, then?' Beca asked.

'Not for a second. Not even for a fleeting millisecond. You are the worst liar I have ever come across.'

'Would you say he was pissed off?'

'I think he handled the situation very well.'

Chapter 12

A laugh escaped from Beca's mouth. Not because she found that particular moment in her life especially funny, but the build up of pressure inside her chest needed to be released in some way and rather than throwing herself around the room like a leaking balloon, she laughed.

It was momentary and slightly deranged, and once it had passed she remained still. She stared at the door now that it was firmly closed and listened to the sound of footsteps rapidly descending the stairs. Her eyes narrowed in concentration as she tried to divine Mitchell's state of mind. She waited, then flinched as the main door slammed shut and shock waves resonated throughout the house. Furious was an understatement.

'What the fuck have I done,' she shrieked.

Perhaps it wasn't too late. She could still get him back, explain it was a joke, a bad joke admittedly, but. Damn it. She hadn't just thrown the baby out with the bath water, she had strapped him in his car seat and had sent him zooming off up the road with Daddy. Bugger. She ran across the living room and out onto the balcony. Below a car door slammed and an engine roared into life. She gripped the balustrade for support. Her insides had ruched themselves into a vivid bilious scrunchie. She felt sick and light-headed.

It was all such an horrendous mistake. She had surrendered control and neatly handed it over to Hal. Hal. A bolshy, opinionated, unreliable, pig-headed … God, what had she been thinking of? She watched Mitchell's sports car race off around the crescent and out of sight. His mobile would be on. She could call him, beg him to come back. Why had she dismissed him like that? She'd been pulling his strings for the past two weeks. There was no question that he would have slept with her. He would have been a willing, if unwitting, part of her plan. She'd carefully nurtured him, stroked his ego, built him up for this weekend and now she'd dropped him in favour of bloody Hal.

She heard footsteps and turned. Hal was standing behind her. She had to be some kind of masochist. Was she perverse enough to relish his particular brand of put-down and caustic remark? That must be the case. Why else had she blown out a weekend of flattery and attention, albeit from an ageing baked bean? She could offer up no rational explanation. Certainly she had no intention of falling for Mitchell, but at least the potential for doing so was there. With Hal, there was nothing. Dementia must have set in.

Beca could hardly miss the glint of triumph in his eyes as he stared up the street at the dispersing exhaust fumes. 'Poor bastard.' He shook his head in pity.

'What do you mean "poor bastard"?' She was incredulous.

'Treating him like that. Bet he's gone to a lot of trouble for you. You've got to feel sorry for him. Poor bastard,' he said again.

'That's just bloody typical of you. It was your idea to get rid of him.'

'That's not the way I remember it.'

'You're kidding me.'

'Nope. Seems to me I turned up here to see if I could help you out.'

'That's one way of putting it,' Beca said.

'I didn't know you'd lined yourself up with someone else, did I? I don't recall telling you to do anything.'

'No, perhaps not in so many words, but you encouraged me.'

'Not me.'

'But you did.'

Hal shook his head and frowned. 'Such a bad way to treat a man. You shouldn't have done it.'

Beca cringed. Of course she'd acted appallingly. It was true, she'd not given Mitchell's feelings a single thought since the moment she'd met him. He hadn't seemed the type to have feelings, not vulnerable ones, at least. Clearly Hal was more perceptive than she was. It was just bloody infuriating to have him piously sucking his teeth over it.

'For God's sake, he's not mortally wounded. He'll get over it,' she said.

'I wouldn't know about that.'

'I don't suppose for a minute I was his only option this weekend.'

'If it helps, by all means darken his character.' Hal folded his arms across his chest and sat on the balustrade wall.

'Fuck off.' Beca looked at him. He was smirking, she was nearly certain of it. The irksome bastard.

'If you want me to.' He gave her a formal, curt bow of the head and walked back towards the living room.

'What are you doing?'

'Fucking off.'

'Don't be so annoying. You can't go now, who the hell else am I going to have sex with.' Instinctively she checked for eavesdropping neighbours; the weight of potential opprobrium made her shrink into her shoulders.

Hal shrugged as if it were entirely inconsequential to him. 'You could try calling Mitchell back.'

She looked at him askance and smiled. He'd had her going for a bit, but now his game was sussed. 'You're doing this on purpose, aren't you?'

He feigned innocence but his smile was getting the better of him.

'You're a sadistic sod winding me up like that.'

'I thought it might be a useful exercise for you to have to show some consideration for another person for once.'

'You thought it would be a good laugh to scare me, more like.'

'You need me.'

Beca laughed and punched him on the arm.

Hal cowered. 'Be nice.'

'And break the habit of a lifetime?' she asked, playfully jabbing him again.

'Give it a try,' he said protecting his body.

'Fine. To prove to you what an excellent character I am, I'll do it.'

'And that coffee?'

'My pleasure.' Beca glided gracefully towards the kitchen, her face set with comical superiority. She would be the perfect hostess for the weekend. He wanted a display of good manners, then he'd get it. She could do conviviality. It was her middle name. Graciousness and charm pumped through her veins. The Miss Congeniality crown would have been hers had she been born an American.

Hal sat on one of the stools on the living room side of the kitchen counter and watched as she put the coffee grinder to work. He rested his chin in his hands and she could tell without turning her head to look that he was smiling at her. She found a packet of biscuits and put some on a plate. They were only just past their sell-by date. He'd survive. She offered him one with a smile worthy of a beauty pageant merit badge.

'Anyway, it's probably just as well Mitchell's gone. For him, I mean.' She began to froth the milk.

'How did you figure that out?' It was Hal's turn to look incredulous.

'It's less complicated this way. Chocolate?' she asked holding up the chrome powder shaker. Hal shook his head. He looked annoyed. Was he getting weary of the fawning? 'There's no chance of you and me getting involved, so the situation is ideal. I had no long-term plans for Mitchell, I hadn't really thought beyond this weekend, so it would have been awkward if he'd got too attached.'

'No doubt very inconvenient,' Hal said flatly.

Beca met his eyes. His face was stony. 'I didn't mean it to sound that awful, but it is what I meant.' She'd forgotten he'd always had a way of making her feel bad. She resented it now; he wasn't there to improve her character. She looked at him crossly. He was spoiling her fun.

'Have you got a spoon, to stir the coffee?' he asked

Beca took one out of the cutlery drawer and pushed it across the worktop to him. He stirred his cup and tapped the teaspoon on the edge of his mug like a tuning fork then placed it face down on the counter. His old habits hadn't changed. Funny that.

'I think we should lay down some ground rules,' Beca said watching him.

'Such as?'

'I don't know, I've only just thought of the idea. For example, do we sleep in the same bed?'

'Why not? It's easier. Saves washing more sheets.' He picked up the teaspoon and began tapping it absent-mindedly on the worktop.

'But not very professional. I don't want us forgetting the purpose of our –'

'Liaison?'

'Association.'

'The purpose is to get you pregnant. It's the means we need to tangle with. If it helps, keep reminding yourself that a) I'm a happily married man, b) I love my wife very much, c) I don't fancy you in the slightest, d) until very recently I loathed you, and e) I'm only having sex with you for your money; money my wife will use to further her acting career. All in all, I'm not getting much out of this.'

'You're charm itself.' Could he dig the knife in any deeper? Perhaps a rude comment about her body. That would certainly ice the huge sponge cake of insecurity she was turning into.

'Anyway, I'm a tits man,' he said and continued to tap.

'Excuse me?' The Miss Perfect mask was slipping.

'I like a woman with tits.'

'What are these?' she asked thrusting her chest out. 'I think most reasonable people would consider me well endowed.'

Hal looked at her chest, angling his head to get a different perspective. It would have been difficult to complain considering she'd invited this scrutiny.

'Yeah, I guess so. They're not bad. It's just Sophie's are -'. His hands took over where words left off.

'She could probably eat off hers if she wanted,' she said lunging for the spoon. She jumped as Hal swiped it away. The tapping resumed.

'Your jealousy is touching.'

'I'm not jealous,' Beca laughed. 'Will you give me that bloody spoon.'

Hal held it out, then pulled back as she tried to take it. She drummed her fingers on the counter. He offered it again. This time she grabbed it and flung it in the sink.

'I've thought of some rules. No kissing,' he said.

'We kissed last time.'

'Are you sure?'

'Quite.'

Hal shrugged. 'A lapse, in which case. No kissing this time then. How many times do we have sex?'

'Given what you've said, as few times as possible I'd have thought.'

'OK. Well that was easy enough.'

'You reckon? Let's go out.'

'Shouldn't we have a go first?'

A go? No she did not want a bloody go. She wanted to find the nearest psychiatrist and lie on his couch. This behaviour had to be traced back to her childhood. There could be no other explanation. There was that time she'd peed on a policeman's feet while he'd been trying to help her cross the road. Did it stem from there? Was she stuck in some ghastly cycle of public humiliation? Why was she having this excruciating conversation? She really should have gone to the Cotswolds with Mitchell, at least there would have been some chance of romance.

'Anyway what's the hurry? We've got all weekend,' she said.

'The longer between sex, the better for the boys.' He looked rather pleased with himself. If he thrust his crotch at her she would have to hit him. Instead Hal pulled his T-shirt off. 'Bedroom or here?', he asked pointing at the living room rug.

The self-destruct warning siren went off in Beca's head. She had about five seconds before she liquidised with mortification and seeped between the cracks in the floorboards. Why did he always get in there first? Was he preordained to take charge, while she was just destined to urinate on people's feet?

'Here,' Beca replied trying to outwit him.

From nowhere the theme tune to *The Graduate* popped into her head. Thank you, Anne Bancroft. Surely a role model if ever she needed one. If Mrs Robinson could terrify Benjamin with her cantilevered bra, then so could she. She unzipped her dress and let it slide between her fingers to the floor. She stepped out of it seductively. The effect on Hal was imperceptible. If she'd expected him to break out in a sweat and start jibbering, she was short-changed. The script needed reworking. He looked at the raspberry-coloured ensemble as if she'd just flaunted her new stripy apron. How much of a battering did he think her ego could take?

Beca was flummoxed. What was she supposed to do now? Shake his hand? What was the customary greeting if alluring 'come fuck me' looks had been ruled out of the game? Was she supposed to assume the position with her arms pinned to her sides? She felt awkward and embarrassed. Why was he making it so hard?

'I can't do this. It's impossible,' she bent down and picked her dress up.

'What?' Hal was struggling to pull his jeans off over his left foot.

'I'm not doing it again. It was lousy last time and it's going to be even worse now,' she said clasping her dress to her chest.

'You didn't like it? You should have said.'

'There's a kitchenware shop down the road. They'll have a turkey baster.'

'You're kidding?' Hal finally pulled his foot out of his jeans.

'I'm not. I can't do clinical, unfeeling sex.'

'And I can't wank into a plastic cup.'

'You'll have to.'

'No chance.'

'Then what do you suggest?'

Hal shrugged. 'We could pretend to fancy each other.' It was obvious he didn't relish the idea.

'Please, don't force yourself.' Time had clearly fogged her mind because she didn't remember him being such an insensitive sod when they went out together. It must have been the influence of that wife.

'It's not what we agreed, but if it makes it easier for you, then I suppose we could. How much will you pay me?' he asked.

'What?!' Beca's brain spun like a Catherine wheel.

'You're only paying me to get you pregnant. There was no mention of acting in our contract. So how much?'

'You're serious.'

'No, of course I'm not serious,' he said throwing his jeans on the floor. 'This whole business has gone well beyond weird as it is.'

How dare he be indignant? That was her preserve, her area of expertise. 'I'm not sure how much more of this I can take.'

Hal looked at her for a moment, evidently weighing up her comments. He shrugged an OK and before she realised what was going on he pulled her towards him and unpinged her bra. One moment her breasts were covered, the next they were exposed, a moment later his face was buried in them and she was on her back. Beca screeched with surprise and laughter. The slight against his manhood had obviously fired him up. Maybe it wasn't going to be such a terrible weekend after all.

'I'm starving,' Hal said as he rolled off her onto the floor. Beca's mind was blown away. It would take a while before basic bodily functions like thinking and talking came back again. She couldn't focus on the white ceiling rose above her. Had she stretched her corneas? Perhaps vision would be restored once the spasms went away. She could see now why she hadn't conceived that last time. What foetus would want to be created out of such loveless rutting? This, on the other hand, was going to be a real honey of a child. She sat up slowly, looked at him and smiled. Hal was leaning back to pull his jeans on, the effect on his abs was impressive. He fastened the buttons then sat up and rolled away from her. He didn't smile, he didn't even look at her.

'Have you got anything to eat?' he asked as he walked to the kitchen.

Beca was stung into silence. He deserved an Oscar, for a moment back there she'd thought he was beginning to like her. The last thing she wanted was a declaration of love, but a smile might have been nice. Something to make her feel slightly less like a tart.

'Take a look in the fridge,' she said gathering her clothes. 'I'm going to take a shower. Do you want one?'

He shook his head without looking up. He looked crestfallen and angry, presumably because he was ashamed of what they'd just done. The realisation didn't make her feel great about herself but, if nothing else, it was to his credit. Had he been swaggering about, she'd have hated him.

'It's OK, you know,' she said gently. 'You don't have to feel bad. We mean nothing to each other. Pretending we did just helped things along. You haven't betrayed Sophie. I know you love her.'

He flinched when she said her name but didn't reply. Beca waited looking at him, and after a while, when it was clear he wasn't going to speak, she turned away. Feeling sorry for him was somehow less damaging to her ego. She could cope if his ears were down. If she'd fancied him, it would have been quite another matter.

The spiral staircase did not present her with the most elegant of exits. She was naked, her bottom stung from its violent encounter with the Turkoman rug. It was probably just as well Hal was looking forlornly at the ground, one glance up and he'd have caught a perfect low-angle view of her ascending friction-burnt arse.

Beca dropped her clothes on the bathroom floor. Her skin tingled as she stood under the shower and as she scrubbed, the feelings of tartiness washed away. Right then and there she might be pregnant. That was all that mattered. She dried herself, put away her new spotted dress for another occasion and pulled on her favourite pair of old jeans.

'There's nothing here,' Hal said to her as she came down the stairs. 'Nothing in the cupboards, nothing in the fridge.'

'A slight exaggeration.'

'What do you eat?' He looked up at her as if nothing had happened, like he'd just popped around to borrow some sugar. If her backside wasn't still stinging, she would have believed she'd dreamt up the whole last hour.

'Out mostly,' she said breezily. If that was how he wanted to play it, fine. A bit immature, but she could deal with it, after all she was an expert at denial.

'Let's go out. My treat', she felt like saying, because he'd earned it, just to make him feel worse but she held back. 'A fry-up still your favourite post-shag meal?'

'You've got a good memory.'

'Just similar tastes. Follow me.'

Chapter **13**

Beca felt upbeat as she walked down Portobello Road with Hal. They had stopped at a stall that made fresh fruit smoothies and had bought one each. She found the act of sucking through a straw comforting and the thought of a fresh blast of vitamins made her feel virtuous. She didn't mind the silence between them as they ambled down the hill.

The market was heaving with the usual Saturday mix of tourists and locals. Everyone seemed to have a baby with them. There were so many children in fact that she wondered if their parents were doubling back just so they could walk past her again. Why not be happy and smug? They had every right to be, and so would she. Soon she'd be one of them. Or would she? Perhaps she was being super-sensitive but it seemed to her that every child had both parents with it. And they didn't look like the average harassed parent either. Toned midriffs were on display with no sign of stretch marks or cottage cheese skin. The fathers were managing their three-wheel buggies with dexterity borne only from practice. Was someone holding a family values rally for the beautiful nearby?

Beca searched the crowds for a single parent. There had to be one out there, this was the inner city. Where had they all gone? She looked at Hal and wondered if he'd noticed this perfect family phenomenon, but his smoothie seemed to be taking up all his concentration. Presumably people looking at them would think they were a couple. Was he feeling awkward about that? Did it feel weird sucking smoothies with a woman who wasn't his wife? Not half as weird as screwing her.

'You know, I really appreciate you doing this,' Beca said between slurps on her straw. 'I mean getting me pregnant, not going for a walk,' she added cheerily.

He didn't respond.

'It can't be easy for you. I know you'd much rather be with Sophie. I'm sorry if you're not comfortable.'

'Are you?'

'Of course. I'm trying to make you feel better, not pick a fight.'

'Well, thanks for making the effort.'

'I mean it would be different if we fancied each other. If we were having an affair, that would be quite something else, wouldn't it? But we're just friends and you're helping me out, like a friend does. And I'm thankful.'

Hal smiled at her. 'You're welcome, for now at least.'

'It's actually to your credit that you feel bad about this.' She didn't want to over-egg it, but his ego obviously needed pumping up.

'How did you work that one out?' he asked.

'Because it means you're committed to Sophie. If it was easy for you to jump into bed with me, then it wouldn't bode well for your marriage, would it?'

'I suppose you're right. I hadn't thought of it. It's strange, but you seem to be showing an unprecedented degree of consideration.'

'If I tried really hard, I reckon I could winkle out a compliment from that.'

'You could find one anywhere.'

They both drank their smoothies and continued through the market. Beca smiled at babies as they passed in their buggies. One looked delighted to see her, his smile showing off a pair of brand new teeth and releasing a long slick of dribble down his stripy top. Did his parents want to keep him? The same smile from her induced near hysterics in another child whose mother scolded her with cross looks. There seemed to be a direct correlation between prettiness and a cheery disposition. Those that had inherited their parents' sour faces were definitely more inclined to scream while the sweet ones burbled and clapped at the merest hint of attention.

It made Beca wonder about her and Hal's collective gene pool, what each of them would bring to the mix. When they had been going out together she had refused to meet any of his family. Perhaps in retrospect that had been a mistake. Supposing he was the only good-looking one?

'Are there many ugly people in your family?' she asked.

'Excuse me?'

'I was just wondering. On the surface at least you and I should make a pretty handsome child. Are there any hunchbacks or chinless wonders I should know about?'

'It's a bit late now to start worrying. Anyway, from what I remember, your family doesn't have much to recommend itself. Moral fibre and good character were absent in your upbringing.'

He had a point. A good one in fact. A lecherous, skirt-chasing father, and a pill-popping drunk of a mother. Still, she'd turned out alright. Sort of. All things considered. She shrugged it off.

Hal stopped in front of a shop and peered through the window. Beca knew it only too well, she'd spent half an hour that morning trying to find something to wear for her trip with Mitchell. It felt like a month had passed since then instead of a few hours.

'Mind if we have a look?' he asked.

She shrugged in acquiescence and followed him in. A Cab Calloway song sailed out from speakers cased in old Bakelite radios. The tune fitted in with the vintage style of the clothes and the lush setting. The sales assistant recognised her and smiled a welcome. Beca sat in a faux Louis XV chair and finished her smoothie, sucking noisily to get at the last remnants of juice. She watched as Hal examined the clothes on the rails, taking the occasional dress off, holding it up and looking at the style and finish. He was thorough, she'd give him that.

'What do you think of this sort of thing?' he asked holding up a cinch-waisted frock in a bold 1950s print.

'A bit busy,' Beca replied.

He considered this information and then put it back. 'How about this one?' He held up a black crepe dress with a plunging neck. It was the sort of thing Lana Turner would have worn with sultry eyes and a pearl-handled pistol.

'It's great,' she replied.

'Come here a minute.'

Beca obliged and Hal held the dress up to her and assessed it, tilting his head and squinting his eyes in thought. His nose twisted with disapproval and he put it back. He playfully nudged her back along the line of clothes until he found a moss green shift dress that left no room for physical error. 'What do you think?'

'It's a good cut, very sophisticated, but not really my colour.'

Hal's eyes shot to her face, he looked faintly amused. 'I meant for Sophie. Do you think it will suit her?'

Blood vessels exploded across Beca's face, her body temperature rose by several degrees. She was mortified. Of course the bloody dress was for Sophie, what had she been thinking? Once again reality had slipped enough to expose a chink of complete lunacy. What chance was there of Hal buying her a dress? Zero. A big, fat, round zero. Stupid girl.

'Of course. I was just forgetting … I mean I knew you meant Sophie, I just forgot …' She kept digging herself in deeper.

Hal seemed satisfied enough with the victory to ignore her floundering explanations. 'You're about the same size, if a bit scrawnier. Hold this.' He pushed the hanger into Beca's hands leaving her little choice but to take it. She held it up to her shoulders as he pulled the fabric into shape across her stomach and hips. Her brain raced. Was this the most humiliating experience of her life? She searched her database of cringeworthy moments. Nothing came close, if she discounted the occasion she'd spent an entire evening in a wine bar with lipstick smeared over her face.

'Would you mind?'

Beca looked vacant.

'Trying it on?'

She waited a beat. He was being serious. He actually expected her to try on a dress for his wife. She had misjudged him. He wasn't obtusely insensitive at all, he was perverse, sick-minded. He was a degenerate. The father of her child was a freak of nature. She snatched the dress away from him and stormed into the changing room as the bemused sales assistant held the curtain open for her. It was her father who'd taught her how to swear and now every expletive he'd ever uttered poured out like molten lava. She re-emerged moments later and would have looked stunning if it weren't for the demented fury twisting her face.

'You're right about the colour. I'll take that in the dark blue,' he said to the sales girl while gesturing towards Beca. Bastard. Crass, heartless toe rag. How dare he? She was livid. This was one indignity too many. OK, so some of the others were self-inflicted, but still, there was a limit to how much she could take.

She returned unnoticed to the changing room. The assistant was far too busy taking Hal's money to offer any help, so she struggled alone. The zip was just a fraction too high for her to reach even if she tried rotating her shoulders out of their sockets. How dare he use her like a floor walker, expecting her to model clothes for his bloody wife. It was outrageous. Her fingers stretched for the zip. She caught it and pulled. It wouldn't budge. She tried again, stretching further to reach and ripped the seams under both arms. The tearing fabric made her stop. No one burst in to berate her. She yanked at the zip again and at last it came down, she wrestled the dress off over her hips and trampled out of it when it fell to her feet. It was a tatty cheap rag anyway. Just perfect for Sophie.

She stormed out of the shop and slammed the door behind her. Pulling a pack of cigarettes from her back pocket, she lit one and raced down the road. She hadn't meant to smoke today. It was going to be day one of her new clean-living regime, but this situation required nicotine and some deep inhalation. Bastard. She had every right to be upset. He had been rude. She didn't need any other reason. She certainly wasn't jealous or anything like that. She didn't want Hal, his wife was welcome to him; she didn't even like him that much. Fair enough, they'd had a good shag, but so what? She'd done that plenty of times and felt nothing very much for her trysting partners. It wasn't any different now. So why was she being emotional about it? Hormones. That had to be the answer. A surge of mind-fuddling pregnancy hormones was flooding her body. Nothing else.

She covered a fair bit of Portobello Market by the time Hal caught up with her. He pulled her back by the wrist so that she ended up pressed against a brick wall. It was smothered with posters and she could smell the paste that had been used to stick them up. He was laughing at her.

'You've got a bloody nerve asking me to try on clothes for your wife,' she said.

'You always get so hilariously worked up. It's nothing, just a dress. Don't be so prickly.'

'Me?' Beca scoffed. 'I'm just used to hanging about with men with more finesse.'

Hal smiled, clearly he wasn't convinced. 'Anyway, I'm grateful. She'll love it.'

'And you'll tell her I modelled it for you?'

'Probably not. I don't think she'd appreciate it.'

'Neither did I.'

Hal's eyes flitted over her face. He smiled again.

'What?' she asked rather petulantly.

He said nothing but looked at her until a frown shadowed his face, then he walked away. Beca was left with an unnerving feeling that he had been about to kiss her. She brushed the feeling off as absurd and followed him. Of course he wasn't going to kiss her, was she nuts? But God, how she wished he had. Her body burned for the want of kissing, but she knew absolutely that he wasn't about to. But damn, damn, damn. It would have been nice.

Carlos' Café was the sort of place that only did one type of bread. White, thinly sliced and made from aerated foam. It could be pressed flat between finger and thumb and was guaranteed never to spring back to its original form. Someone somewhere had gone to a lot of effort to make such an unappealing loaf. It came toasted, fried or smeared with an oily slick of yellow marg, not because it was asked for that way, but because that was how Carlos fancied serving it.

Beca put up with the owner's eccentricities because it was her nearest caff, but she'd never understood why the place was so popular. It had nothing to recommend it and Carlos seemed to do his best to dissuade anyone from staying, but instead of a few near-destitute pensioners who couldn't afford anything better, the place was packed with Notting Hill's trendiest, nursing hangovers with full fry-ups and mugs of tea. A lot looked like they hadn't been to bed yet, at least not their own and their party clothes looked well post-modern in this peeling formica and chrome setting.

Beca and Hal hung about at the front door until a table by the window came free. They sat down and waited for a while until eventually one of Carlos's daughters came to take their order. Customer relations had obviously not been a big part of her training. Exposing a large ring of flab, she slouched on one hip and stared blankly at them as they put in their requests. Instead of writing down the order she sniffed and sloped off to the kitchen.

Beca put her cigarette box on the table. She'd already broken her pledge not to smoke, so why not have another one? A few fags surely couldn't have that much impact on conception. Perhaps if she had fertility problems, maybe then it would be worth looking at the issue more seriously. Until that time. A shrug finished the internal conversation and, having absolved herself, she took a cigarette out of the pack, tapped the end on her lighter and put it in her mouth. As she flicked the Zippo open she caught the look on Hal's face. Without thinking she closed the lid, took the cigarette out of her mouth and put it on the table.

She felt faintly sick. A tremor started in her stomach and crept up to her throat. She took a deep breath and laughed it out and then began rolling the cigarette over the surface of the table. She started humming which was a sure sign something was wrong. A few grains of tobacco fell out of the end of the cigarette forming a trail. She couldn't bring herself to look up at Hal and was relieved when he turned to a bloke on the neighbouring table and asked if he could borrow the sports section of his newspaper.

Why hadn't she lit the cigarette? Sure, she knew she shouldn't, but that wasn't usually enough to stop her. What was going on? It was him. He was what was going on. The thought of him kissing her was stuck in her head. She'd not smoked the cigarette because she didn't want to antagonise him. What a complete disaster. It could only mean one thing. She fancied him.

Now that Hal was distracted she peered up at him, scrutinising his features. She stared and waited for some physical sign. When it happened she felt even sicker. The squelching feeling was all the evidence she needed. She'd just entered a new level of nightmare. She had a crush on him which was bad enough on it's own merits to justify a major panic attack. The fact that he was married, therefore unavailable, not to mention totally uninterested made matters infinitely worse. How was she going to climb her way up out of this latest hell pit?

Smoking the cigarette would be a good start. She picked it up and conspicuously flicked open the lighter and lit it. She leant back in her chair and exhaled a plume of smoke. Hal didn't notice which made her feel very childish indeed.

She needed to be matter-of-fact about it all. He was hardly the first bloke she'd ever fancied. She'd just have to work him out of her system quickly before he went back to his wife. Hal need never know. In fact he mustn't know, unless she liked the idea of further humiliation. He would laugh and then leave, or leave and laugh on his way out if she told him. Sophie got back from Paris on Tuesday, she had until then to get over her brief flirtation with insanity. He would be out of her life forever. Which was a good thing. A very, very good thing. Right?

'You've gone very quiet,' he said to her.

'Sorry. I was just thinking.'

'About what?'

'You, as it happens.'

Hal looked at her quizzically. If he was expecting elaboration he was stupid. Thankfully Carlos's hulking great daughter heaved into view with two plates. They had just milliseconds to move their mugs of tea before the food was shunted at them.

She looked at her food. It had come too quickly for it to have been cooked specifically for them. She suspected Carlos had a holding bay for plates of food to sit in and gather fly shit and turn glutinous under the heat lamp. She poked a finger at her fried egg but the skin didn't pucker or drag. It tasted surprisingly good, certainly Hal seemed to be enjoying his which gave her the chance to study him further and, as she did so, unwelcome images of him as the perfect father filled her head. Hal bouncing the baby on his knee. Pushing their child along on his tricycle. Building sandcastles on an idyllic beach. She held that last thought in her head; he did look very good in his skimpy swimming trunks. Perhaps it was a nudist beach.

'Stop.' Beca banged her hands on the table and sent her fork clattering to the floor.

'What's up?' Hal asked.

'Nothing a lobotomy wouldn't sort out,' she said hanging under the table to recover her fork. She picked it up quickly but continued upside-down, trying to buy time as her head filled with blood. It was difficult to erase the images crowding her brain, but by the time she'd counted to ten they'd gone, more or less.

He was trying to spread the marg that had been smeared on his toast as she reappeared. This new image brought memories flooding back. Instinctively she smiled. 'Is it hot enough?'

'Now that you ask, no it isn't,' he replied.

Beca chuckled. 'I'd forgotten how anal you are about your toast. If it wasn't buttered the second it came out of the toaster you'd get in a strop.'

'Perfectly reasonable.'

'And if the crusts weren't buttered as well it would just about ruin your day.'

'Still does,' he replied with a smile.

'It's nice to think you haven't completely changed.'

'I haven't changed at all.'

'Neither have I,' she said.

Hal paused. 'No, I didn't think you had.'

There was something about his tone that made her stop and look at him. He sounded disappointed, and it really bothered her.

They were out of breath when they reached Beca's front door after the climb up Ladbroke Grove. They put down the bags of food that Hal had insisted on buying as she searched for her front door keys. Once inside she put the bag of cat food she'd bought on Mrs Butler's doorstep.

'I'll drop them in later,' she said.

'Why not now. She might fall over them if you leave them there.' Hal knocked on Mrs Butler's door before she had a chance to argue. Beca groaned, the last thing she wanted was to have to explain him to the old lady.

'She's not in,' she said tugging at his arm after a short wait. 'I'll pop by to see her later.'

Hal looked as if he was about to concede defeat when the door opened and Mrs Butler stuck her head around. 'Are you still here,' she said to Beca. 'I thought I heard you leave a while ago. Who's this?' she asked looking up at Hal, her lips pursed with consternation. 'This isn't the man I saw calling for you this morning, is it?'

'No, that was someone else.'

'Hal Carson,' Hal said leaning forward and shaking Mrs Butler's hand. There was a slight nod of deference. Beca would have thought it was charming if she'd let herself.

'Edie Butler.' She might have been eighty but she could still flirt. 'I must say, Beca, I'm so glad the other gentleman left. I thought he was the one you were going away with. Most unsuitable. He looked like a spiv I knew during the war; used to sell chocolate. And he was a rather odd colour. Don't you think? A bit orange. You're much better looking.' Hal repaid her with a boyish grin.

'We ought to get going really, Mrs Butler. I'll pop in to see you tomorrow,' Beca said in a tone she hoped would bring closure to the conversation.

'So you're not going away then?'

Was it a prerogative of the old to be obtuse?

'A change of plans,' Beca replied.

'How confusing. Why don't you come in for tea now that you're here.'

Why? Because she didn't fancy explaining to the old lady her current turnover of men. The small matter of this latest one being a married man was not a topic for polite conversation either. The horror of Hal revealing their arrangement flooded her mind. 'Really, we can't. We need to get this lot into the fridge. Quite urgently in fact.'

'It'll keep for a while,' Hal said. What was the trouble maker playing at?

Mrs Butler smiled at him and held the door open. He stepped into the hallway with his hostess close behind. 'Do you like lemon drizzle cake? I made one this morning,' Beca heard Mrs Butler asking from inside.

'Sounds delicious,' came the reply.

She left the new best friends to get tea in the kitchen. It made her nervous thinking about what Hal might be saying, but she was too much of a coward to listen. The sound of broken crockery would alert her to any inappropriate honesty from him. She went to the living room instead. Rhett was curled up on the sofa. He was saggy and heavier in sleep and as she picked him up his limbs seemed to stay behind. She sat down on the warm patch he'd made on the sofa and moulded him into her lap. He barely stirred, a twitch of the ear was all the recognition she got, that and the occasional purr as she stroked him. A sleeping furry ally was better than none at all.

She was staring blankly at the odd collection of African tribal masks above the fireplace when Mrs Butler came in with Hal following behind. Her attention easily shifted to the new attraction and she found herself scrutinising the way he walked, how straight his back was, the way he held the tea tray. Even when he caught her looking, she found her eyes wandering back to him. It really was time to get a grip.

'I think you've picked a good 'un this time,' Mrs Butler said. 'And about time too. All those other men looked so feckless. Put the tray down there, Hal,' she said moving a glass vase of flowers from the centre of a lace-covered occasional table. Beca found herself agreeing. If nothing else she had chosen him to be the father of her child. Surely that showed some taste and superior judgement. 'It is rather a strange name. Is it short for something?' Mrs Butler asked.

'Henry,' Hal said ignoring Beca's smirks.

'How lovely. Very traditional.' Mrs Butler poured the tea and handed a cup to both of them. 'Cake?'

'Yes, please,' Beca said regretting the enormous lunch.

'Hal, how about you?'

'Thank you,' he said taking a dainty plate.

Mrs Butler picked up her own cup and sat down on the edge of her armchair. 'Now then how did you two meet?'

Beca stared at Hal's profile. He really did have the best nose of any man she'd ever known. 'Sorry? You were talking to me.' She laughed to cover her embarrassment. Hal frowned at her and ran a hand down his left cheek. If he thought she was staring because he had cake on his face he was wrong, but she wasn't about to correct him.

'We've known each other for years,' Beca said as if theirs was just an inconsequential friendship.

'Young people today are so afraid of commitment. It's as though marriage has become a dirty word.'

'Well, actually,' Hal began until Beca's choking fit silenced him. Mrs Butler looked at her as if her manners needed working on.

'So what is it that you do?' she asked him.

'I'm an artist.'

'Are you? How fascinating. Of course you'll know that Beca is quite an art fan.'

He clearly didn't.

'Next Sunday we're going to the National Gallery,' Mrs Butler continued. 'Although we'll have tea next door at the National Portrait Gallery. The cakes are much nicer there.'

'Do you see many exhibitions?' Hal asked while sipping his tea. The china tea cup looked minute in his hand.

'Beca treats me once a month. I get to choose, which is very gracious of her. We make a lovely day of it, don't we?'

Beca nodded and realised that she was the one being scrutinised. She didn't suppose for a minute it was for the same reasons that she found herself unable to take her eyes off him. Still it was better than being completely ignored.

'Last month we went to the Tate Modern, which was very interesting,' Mrs Butler continued. 'It would be lovely if you'd come with us. You could give us your professional view,' she said to him.

'That won't be possible,' Beca replied. Perhaps she'd been a little too quick to reject the idea. A little too screechy. Mrs Butler looked startled. She lowered her voice. 'You have a commission to finish, don't you?' she said nodding to Hal slowly in case he had any doubt what he was doing next Sunday.

He hesitated as if going for a further wind-up. 'You're right. It would be great, but I can't. Next time.'

What next time?

'Well that's a shame,' Mrs Butler said. 'But as you say, there's always next time.'

Beca managed to restrain herself until Mrs Butler closed the door behind them and they were climbing the stairs to her flat.

'I can't believe you did that', she whispered angrily.

'What?'

'Why did you want to meet her? For God's sakes, you'll never see her again after this weekend. Now she thinks I've got a serious boyfriend. What the bloody hell am I going to tell her when you don't show up again?'

'I was intrigued, that's all.'

'By what exactly?'

'You.'

Beca stopped on the stairs to look at him. 'What do you mean?'

'You always present yourself as a hard-nosed, me-first bitch. I was just interested to see another side to you. You're unpredictable. I think that must have been one of the reasons I used to like you. It's difficult to remember now.'

'Don't go overboard, it's just bloody cat food and the odd day out.'

'Whatever. You wouldn't want anyone to think there was a real heart beating in there, would you?'

Chapter **14**

In Beca's experience it was always the feelings she had immediately after sex that determined whether a relationship was going to last a day, a week or indeed a month. During the act, sensibilities were usually turfed out of bed along with unnecessary clothing, but afterwards as the panting and sweating abated, those sensibilities returned, honed to pick up on the slightest self-doubt. A man could make or break a relationship by what he said and did in the seconds after post-coital separation. Right now Mr Hangdog in the bed next to her had cocked his leg and was peeing all over her insecurities, albeit metaphorically.

Hal stared blankly into space. Something big was obviously going on in his head. Either that or he'd had a seizure and was in fact dead. Beca leant closer to him to check but there was no sign of dust on his eyeballs and he seemed to be breathing. It was one hell of a guilt trip then. She presumed the deep furrow between his eyebrows was another outward sign of inner turmoil.

She'd long since given up expecting him to make small talk with her, but his silence hung heavily around her and gave her ample chance to analyse her performance. Had she overdone the sound effects? Was there a link with her quite obvious pleasure and his miserable condition? Perhaps she had been a little too enthusiastic, a little unseemly for a woman whose only interest supposedly was to get pregnant. In another country she might be beaten for such carnal behaviour. She wasn't trying to make him feel guilty at all, but it was difficult not to enjoy herself, now that she had given up pretending to fancy him and was doing the real thing.

It was a pity that his pretence couldn't extend beyond the act of sex. He was behaving like a man who had sinned. Any second now he would start flagellating and that really would be the end. It was getting very wearing. To be honest she could probably have spared him this last session in the torture chamber. Strictly speaking it wasn't an absolute necessity, according that is, to the books she had read. But Beca had little faith in what the fertility experts had to say.

The idea of abstaining in order to conserve sperm supplies made no sense to her at all. She saw the whole business of getting pregnant as a bit like going to war. There was only one window of opportunity every month and as far as she was concerned, the best strategy was to throw everything at it. If that meant bandaging up the injured and hurling them in as cannon fodder, then fine. That would leave the crack troops with a fighting chance of breaking through. She had Hal for a limited time and she was going to get every last one of his plucky little blighters out and onto the beaches. What she really wanted was a video link to her insides so she could watch his heroes surging towards their mission target. Sacrifices had to be made. If he ended up demobilised and walking like John Wayne for the rest of his life, well too bad.

'Shall we watch *The Dam Busters*?' Beca didn't really expect an answer.

Hal laughed. It wasn't a hearty appreciation of her sense of humour, more the sound of air compressing out of his chest cavity in resignation.

'*A Bridge too Far? Ice Cold in Alex?*' she asked.

'You like your war films don't you?'

'I just thought a bit of human resilience and forbearance in the face of adversity might be appropriate seeing as you're having such a miserable time.'

Hal leant up on an elbow. The furrow disappeared and the smile returned. Why had he outlawed kissing? It was so unfair. Surely a good snog would make him feel better.

'Is it that obvious?' he asked.

'Not really, hardly at all.'

'Sorry.'

'So am I,' she said. 'This wasn't supposed to be torture for you.'

'I'll try harder,' he said as he got out of bed.

That wasn't really the bloody point though, was it?

Beca showered and dressed. Having already established that nothing she did would ever turn him on, she put on a faded Guns n' Roses tour T-shirt – a souvenir from an interesting night many years before – and some jogging shorts, and went downstairs.

It took just seconds for her to be demoted to *sous chef* in the kitchen, and even then a very *sous, sous chef*. Having taken the sharp knife away, Hal set her the task of opening a tin of tomatoes.

'How have you managed to stay alive so long and not know how to cut up an onion?' he asked while scraping her endeavour into the bin.

'I can, perhaps not the way you like it, but I was getting there.'

'I said chop, not annihilate.'

'I'm more than happy for you to do it.' Beca put down the tin opener and filled her glass of wine. She was risking the chagrin of the pregnancy police again, but at least she'd steered clear of the gin, which deserved a commendation considering the mounting stress levels. Under such circumstances a glass or two of wine had to be an aid to conception, not a hindrance. She sat down on a stool on the living room side of the kitchen counter and watched Hal. He was wearing surfer shorts which he had produced from a small back-pack. She'd never been a great fan of long baggy shorts because of the stumpy-leg effect they created. That was until she saw Hal in them. Far from making his bottom look six inches away from his feet, it accentuated his slim waist and the rising triangular shape of his broad back and shoulders. He really was the best put together man she'd ever slept with. Such a shame he had to go home to his wife.

'Olives?' he asked.

Beca focussed her eyes.

'Hello. Do you have a jar of olives?' he asked again. 'I forgot to buy some.'

'Should be some cocktail ones up there,' she said pointing to the top cupboard.'

Hal opened the cupboard door and rooted around. As he pulled out a likely looking jar, a tin of chocolate powder tipped out and spilt over the floor. He swore as a cloud rose up from the ground.

'I'll get the vacuum cleaner,' Beca said laughing at him.

She returned with a low level green and grey contraption that she'd bought because the cleaning lady had asked her to. She'd phoned John Lewis, ordered it, signed the delivery note and left it in its box for her to sort out. That was six months ago and Beca hadn't bothered with it since.

'You don't know how to work it,' Hal said laughing at her as she tried to pull the plug out from its neat home.

And why should she? She was a retail analyst. Her core skills lay elsewhere. Why should she know about the vacuum cleaner's operating intricacies? Because she owned it? Not a good enough reason.

'Of course I do.' She pulled too hard, the cable flew out and she banged her elbow on a base unit. Trying her best to look au fait with the machine she plugged it in and shrieked as it leapt into action. At least that solved the problem of how to turn it on.

She picked up the pipe and tried to straighten the sweeper head which was stubbornly wedged at an angle. At last it made contact with the floor, but very little happened in terms of sucking.

'It's on carpet mode,' Hal said watching her with more than a hint of amusement on his face.

'What?' Beca shouted above the drone of the cleaner.

'It's not on the right mode for hard surfaces.'

'How can it not be in the right mood for God's sake, it a vacuum cleaner?' She banged the sweeper on the floor as a means of getting it in a more amenable frame of mind. She tried again, there was still a lot of scraping noises but no suction. Then she tried pulling the sweeper head off in order to use the pipe but again fell foul of the new technology. She was getting incredibly pissed off and belatedly realised Hal was laughing at her, not just chuckling but holding his sides in pain. She threw the over-designed piece of junk at him and let him get on with it. It was just bloody typical of the man that she couldn't get a smile out of him in bed, but as soon as the opportunity to make an arse of herself came up he was practically hysterical. She would need an ego upgrade before the day was out.

'You are going to feed the baby aren't you?' the domestic god asked once he'd resumed cooking.

'Of course.'

'It's just suddenly dawned on me that I should be concerned. After all you're going to be bringing up my kid.'

It had only just occurred to him? Jesus, she'd been thinking of nothing else. 'So come around and do the cooking.' Anyone who volunteered to puree carrots was welcome.

'That's not really part of the deal, is it?' Hal looked apologetic. Worse, he looked cornered by an unwanted obligation. Christ, did he think she was lining up to become a liability once she'd had her child? He couldn't be more wrong, but the mistake was of her making. He was never going to meet the baby. It was in the contract. He had no visitation rights, nothing. His name wouldn't even be on the birth certificate. It was her and the baby, nobody else. A brief infatuation wasn't going to change that.

'I don't remember you being able to cook,' she said breezily as if inviting him to puree vegetables for the baby had been just one on a long list of meaningless subjects.

'Sophie taught me. We cook most evenings. It's a good way to reconnect.'

Beca cringed at the thought of such an open and frank relationship. Being in touch with each other's feelings was way too New Age for her. Keeping things bottled up worked better every time.

'What else has she taught you?' she asked.

'To trust again.'

Brilliant Beca, well done. Straight back into the firing line. 'So is this where you ask me why we split up?'

'No. That's old news.'

What a relief. She took a long drink of wine and looked at him. He had stopped dicing the chicken and was staring down at the chopping board. When he looked up at her his eyes flashed with anger.

'Shouldn't I be at all interested to know why the woman I loved, who I thought loved me, suddenly disappeared? One moment we're talking about moving in together, the next you've fucked off leaving some pathetic note about needing more space.'

'No, you were talking about moving in together, I wasn't.' Beca's hackles were rising.

'And that was it? You didn't want to live with me?'

She nodded slowly, trying to delay the inevitable question.

'Why? Don't say it was because you didn't love me. I know you did.'

What was she supposed to tell him? That she was shit scared? She loved him so much it terrified her? That she had to leave before he left her? No chance. She said nothing and looked at her hands.

'Beca, you are so screwed up.' He threw down the tea towel that was hanging over his shoulder. 'You've got no business becoming a mother. I'm going home.' With that he went upstairs.

She guessed he was getting his things, not that she much cared. She drank her wine and stared at the space where he had been standing. A tear ran down one cheek. Another brimmed over her lower eyelashes and ran down the other cheek, then splashed onto the worktop. It was such a mistake bringing him back into her life. Why hadn't she given more thought to the impact his return might have? Typically she had forgotten how complicated dealing with emotions could be. Why had she been so sure of her strength? Hal had shaken her fortified walls and inside she was crumbling. Her heart was supposed to be impenetrable. What the fuck was going on?

There were footsteps on the stairs. She didn't want to turn around and look at him. Silence charged the atmosphere. It pressed down upon her, slowing down time, dragging out every painful thought. She could sense him behind her, she thought she could hear him breathing. Why didn't he just leave?

He cleared his throat. 'I'm sorry,' he said. 'I was out of order.' There was a pause then his hand touched her shoulder. She turned on the stool to face him. He seemed surprised that she was crying. 'I was cross with you for a very long time, but it doesn't matter now.' He cupped her face with his hands and brushed the tears away with his thumbs. He smiled. 'I've got Sophie, and you'll have your baby. You'll be a good mother, even if you are a crap cook.'

Perhaps it was his kindness that finally made her crack. Or maybe it was yet another reminder of his wife. She began to cry fresh tears and he put his arms around her and gave her a hug. She imagined it was like the hug he'd give his sister or some kid who'd fallen off his bike, but it made her feel better. Right now she'd take whatever she could of him.

The meal was delicious and they did justice to it by eating at the dining table rather than slobbed out in front of the television.

'Why me?' Hal asked. Beca looked at him and eventually he met her eyes. 'Why did you choose me?'

Beca picked off the shrapnel from that bombshell. What were her options? Should she explain? It sounded so mercenary now. It hadn't occurred to her for a minute that contacting him might have an impact on his life. She went to the bottom of the class for consideration and empathy skills, again, but was no nearer deciding what to say.

'I literally don't hear a word from you in eight years then bam! In crashes breezy Beca like nothing had ever happened. I hated you. Did you know that? You broke my heart.'

She was staggered by his honesty. The thought of another emotional display panicked her. Getting drunk quick seemed like a good option. She reached for the wine bottle, it was empty.

'Could you hold that thought while I go for reinforcements,' she said. He was not impressed.

She returned with a fresh bottle and filled her glass. Hal shook his head when she held out the bottle for him. 'You weren't my first choice.'

'Honest, if nothing else. The others rejected you?'

'They weren't available. And those that were.' She sighed. 'Put it this way, you were the best of a very bad bunch. I thought of all the men I could just about bear to see in my child's face and you were the only serious contender.'

'I suppose that's a compliment.'

'I guess so.'

'Have you never had a serious relationship?' he asked.

How deep was he going to dig? 'Depends what you mean by serious.'

'What's the longest you've ever been out with someone?'

'Six months.' She knew it wasn't impressive.

'Is that all?'

'I thought that was pretty good going at the time.'

'It's pathetic.'

'Not really. I just don't want to go out with anyone for longer.'

'Was it me?'

Beca nodded. She got up and cleared the table. If she'd gone to the Cotswolds with Mitchell they'd have spent the evening talking about him again. It would have been boring but a lot less hostile than this interrogation. 'And what about you? What's your track record like?' she asked as if the matter was only faintly interesting to her.

'I didn't go out with anyone for years after we split up. I had a few flings, mindless stuff really. A few of my models, women I met at parties, that sort of thing. But it was too lonely. I need to be with someone.'

'And then you met Sophie.'

Perhaps she'd overdone the twee tone because he hesitated before replying. 'That's right.'

'What I don't understand is why you're here. When I realised you were married, I didn't for a minute think you'd buy into my plan.'

'I didn't, if you remember. It was Sophie's idea, not mine. Even so, I feel like I've betrayed her and it hurts.'

'It's not been that easy for me having you here,' Beca said trying not to feel like a complete pariah.

'What do you mean?'

It would have been pointless and embarrassing to admit to him how all over the place she had been since he'd arrived. And because ritual humiliation had never appealed to her, she saw no need to tell him of the unwelcome feelings his visit had unearthed.

'It's nothing,' she said. 'Having you hanging around like a sick dog is a bit boring.'

Hal studied her face then turned away. 'For a minute there I thought we were going to glimpse behind the armour.'

What would have been the point? Perhaps it would have satisfied his curiosity to know that she'd fallen for him. But how would that help her exactly? Of what benefit would that be to her? Cathartic experiences were best left for those with nothing to hide.

Beca was awake at 7 o'clock the next morning through habit more than choice. Hal slept beside her. He looked faintly Galliano-ish with his messed up blonde tresses and naked chest wrapped in her kitsch 1950s rose print sheets. He would have looked angelic had it not been for the oil paint indelibly marking his finger nails. She really had been such a fool letting him get away, or more accurately throwing him away. She wanted to reach over and kiss him but didn't dare. What would be the point? He was asleep in her bed because she was paying him to be there. Even so, the very small girl in her thought that if she closed her eyes she could wish Sophie away, that if she was very good maybe he'd fall in love with her again.

Once, the idea of waking up next to the same man day in day out would have appalled her. Now, this morning, she understood. For the first time in her life she could imagine a future stretching beyond the next weekend to the years ahead. At last she could see the point of being with a man for life. It was just such a pity she'd left this discovery until it was far too late.

Hal rolled over, bumped into her and woke up. At first his face was the picture of bleary-eyed confusion. He tried to focus, then succeeded. Horror, bewilderment and recognition followed in quick succession. He crowned it all off with a very weak smile. Apparently she hadn't yet reached her pain threshold, there was room for more before she passed out.

'I wondered where the bloody hell I was,' he said with a feeble laugh.

'I'm so glad this isn't the start of a relationship. I'd be crying by now,' Beca joked.

'Sorry. I thought for a minute Sophie had cut off all her hair.'

'Sleep OK?' Beca asked, deliberately trying to steer away from the subject of his wife.

'Sure.'

The phone next to the bed rang. It was nearest to Hal so he picked up the receiver and passed it over. Beca would have happily ignored it. The voice on the other end of the line was unintelligible. It was female, probably French and blubbering badly.

'This could well be your wife.'

Hal didn't miss the disdain in her voice. 'Hi babe. Is that you?' he said. Beca could feel her lip curling. 'Calm down. Of course I love you. What's wrong?' This was delivered in a coochie-coo loved-up tone. 'No of course I don't. Not at all. It's just to pay for your classes. This is for you. I thought it's what you wanted.' There was a pause, presumably so she could drivel on a bit more. 'Babe, you're the best. I swear.' The way he said 'babe' was nauseating. 'You know what English women are like.' Beca watched him. She had no intention of discreetly leaving the room, she wanted to know what else he thought about English women. 'I promise, no one is as good as you.' This last fawning remark seemed to calm Sophie down. Hal smiled into the receiver. 'That's fantastic,' he said a moment later. 'What time does it get in?' He looked around the bedroom and barked at Beca, 'What time is it?'

Not responding very well to his tone she merely pointed at the clock.

'OK my love, I'll be there. Wait for me at the exit if I'm late. I'm setting off now.' He hung up and jumped out of bed. 'She's coming back early. She'll be at Waterloo in an hour.' He was ecstatic, over the moon. He was literally bouncing about with glee. Beca felt sick to her stomach.

'Fine, that's great for you. You'd better get off and meet her,' she said.

As if he was waiting for her permission.

Beca wandered around her flat in a daze. Everywhere she looked there were reminders of him. She could smell him on the sheets on her bed. There was an imprint of his body on the sofa where he'd sat the night before. He had managed to leave a T-shirt in his haste to get out and she held it out in front of her and sniffed it. Was she pathetic enough to put it on? Not quite. She threw it towards the rubbish bin in the kitchen and cursed herself for even considering it. The radio was still tuned to the music station he'd listened to and she kept it there hoping to hear a particular song he'd liked until she berated herself for being so foolish.

She couldn't quite work out what she was supposed to be feeling. She should have been blissfully happy, anticipating the sound of her baby's laugh.

She should have been snuggled up with her Penelope Leach learning about good parenting. Instead she was pacing the room like a trapped animal, frustrated and cross with herself. Why did she care that he'd gone? It wasn't supposed to be like this. He was with Sophie now, kissing and holding his wife in a way that he'd point blank refused to do with her. She didn't want to feel jealous, but she did.

How the hell had she managed to fall for a married man? She sat down heavily on the sofa. Such a brilliantly executed plan. Getting an ex-boyfriend to get her pregnant had just metamorphosed into falling in love with a completely unavailable man. It was a stunning example of ineptitude. She should fire herself for gross incompetency. Without realising it she had managed to entirely circumvent the being in love and happy bit and had plumped straight for the broken heart. It was comical in its precision. What a total blithering idiot. She'd thought every eventuality had been covered in her plan, but never in her darkest dreams had she envisioned such a farcical outcome.

Beca laughed ruefully at herself and raised an imaginary glass of champagne to toast her brilliance.

Chapter 15

Two weeks later the sheets on Beca's bed were still unchanged. She kept meaning to put out fresh ones for the cleaner but somehow, when it came to it, she dithered, berated her folly, then left the ones Hal had slept in for a bit longer. She could offer up no excuse; time, economy, lack of alternative bedding didn't come close to cloaking the fact that she missed him.

She rolled over and looked at her alarm clock. It was set to go off at 5:30am. She had another twenty minutes to wait. At a guess she reckoned she'd been lying awake for an hour, maybe longer. It didn't matter. Under normal circumstances sleeplessness was sure to guarantee a mind-spinning, sweaty panic. The more desperate for sleep she was, the less likely it would come, leading to even greater agitation and teeth grinding. But there was nothing normal about life at the moment, which perhaps helped explain the smelly sheets she lay wrapped in. It was odd to be at once depressed and excited about life. She yearned to be with Hal, but couldn't have him. The depression this caused came a close second to the smarting humiliation of falling for someone she thought she had no feelings for. In love with Hal? Derisory, but sadly true.

In between the daily bouts of self-flagellation, she soared on the anticipation of motherhood. Each day brought more excitement and today was the climax of that wait. Her period was two days late. A good sign. Instead of leaping at the first chance of doing a test, she'd held back and waited, uncharacteristically and most painfully. Now the selected moment had come and the pregnancy tester kit was laid out waiting for her in the bathroom. Euphoria bubbled. She could feel her insides rubbing together with glee, effervescing as if she'd swallowed a bagful of sherbet bombs. She smiled and rolled onto her side, hugging herself into a foetal position.

There was nothing to stop her getting up and doing the test now. Nothing except the private agreement she'd made; that and the fact she wanted to relish every moment. All of it was being recorded in her mind, every thought, every sensation. In the future she would be able to recall perfectly how she'd felt just before her pregnancy was confirmed. So, she would get up at 5:30 and no sooner.

Besides, it was so much nicer to think of the possibilities the future held rather than what the last two weeks had offered. She felt as though she had completed the Lee Strasberg method acting curriculum since Hal had raced off to meet his true love. 'Head thrown back with delight at the world' had lasted all of 24 hours, and for most of those she'd been asleep. The notion that Hal would take one look at Sophie and do a rapid u-turn back to her arms was a waste of mental energy. It wasn't going to happen. Ever. No amount of wishful thinking would change that.

'Hope springs eternal' had been next on the syllabus. To keep in this frame of mind she'd carried an image of herself, Hal and the baby happy together somewhere perennially sunny. The small fact that he didn't want her kept marring this fantasy. If there'd been even a smidgen of sadness as he'd run off to collect

Sophie from the station, then perhaps it might have worked. The truth was, like the death-row prisoner whose reprieve had come, he hadn't even stopped to say goodbye.

'Stoical, brave little woman' had lasted fifteen minutes. Pining pitifully held no appeal. Next up was 'triumph.' For this Beca had struck a 'Liberty leading the people' kind of pose. She, loosely clad in flowing robes, strode forward, facing the future with her baby clasped to her naked bosom. Under foot was Hal, crushed by the weight of his mistakes. A broken man who in the last gasp of life realised the error of his ways. This had mollified Beca's pride. A degree of comfort could be found from thinking he'd regret his choices in the long run.

But if she couldn't have the man, at least she would have his child. A whole new adventure was about to begin. A new life was starting, not just for the embryo growing inside her, but for her as well. Her world was going to be so different from that morning on, and it would be brilliant, shiny and exciting. She unballed her legs and stretched, smiling with contentment until the alarm clock sounded. She lay listening to it getting louder and more urgent then smacked it off with a well-practised swipe. She rolled up to a sitting position and dangled her legs over the edge of the bed.

A cautious note sounded somewhere in her head; the bit that controlled self-preservation. Inflating her pregnancy out of all realistic proportion was gratuitous and irresponsible. It was plain stupid. She had to stop, but the temptation to lie back and dream for a little bit longer was strong.

She pulled herself together and bounced off to the bathroom. It was a working day and there was no time for dallying. Perkiness didn't come naturally, particularly at that time of the morning, but it was a good way of beating down the nerves, that and the deep breathing exercises. She exhaled as if being breathalysed and picked up the tester. The moment of truth. She tore off the wrapper, peed on the stick, waited for the two windows to fill, put the cover back on and propped it up on top of the cistern. As simple as that. She hummed an inane tune and turned the shower on. Given the choice she'd have whistled but her facial muscles had tightened with fear and she couldn't pucker up sufficient to blow. Nervous? God, yes.

The soap slipped through her fingers and thudded onto the shower tray. She retrieved it, all the while keeping her back to the loo. Water streamed down her face. She could barely make out her own hands through the clouds of steam, let alone two blue lines on the other side of the room, but still she diligently avoided that corner. Her fizzing innards weren't so much fun any more. The bubbles felt more like an Andrew's liver salts purge. Panic pulled at her. What was plan B? She couldn't remember.

She could feel the pregnancy stick behind her lurking malevolently and felt cowered by the power it held over her. So this was what it was like to go mad.

Bugger that. She pushed open the shower door, crossed the room in a couple of strides, grabbed the tester and stared at the two boxes. Her eyes were bleary with water making it hard to focus. She rubbed them with her free hand but the water returned as tears. There was only one blue line. Dripping wet she sank down onto the bathroom floor, her legs offering little alternative. Only one blue line when there should have been two. It meant she'd failed again and no amount of angling or tipping the stick towards the lights in the ceiling would change that. She tried though, because searching for the second blue line was easier than accepting the truth.

The stick slipped from her fingers and fell to the floor. She wasn't pregnant. It had all been for nothing. The energy that had driven her to this point abandoned her now, leaving her with a cruel montage of wasted hope and optimism. Even the anguish of falling for Hal would have been worth it, if only she was pregnant. His barbed wit, the endless jibes, the obvious love for his wife which left her feeling worthless and hollow would seem like mere nicks, if she was pregnant. The drubbing her ego suffered would have been nothing, if only there were two blue lines. But there weren't. Now that her failure was starkly apparent those slights and injuries came back as fresh wounds and she cried pitifully, all the more so because there was no one else to cry with her.

She'd never imagined that disappointment could manifest itself into physical form. Now she knew better. She hurt. Her heart felt twisted and cramped, her whole body ached. An iron corset was clamped around her chest. Each time she tried to breathe it tightened, crushing the air out of her. She shook with the effort of trying to fill her lungs. She put her hands on the floor to steady herself, then sank back down again.

An hour and a half later Becca was at her desk. The mascara Liz had lent her had turned her eyelashes into spider's legs and they crawled and scratched across her bloodshot eyeballs. She looked a mess. The bank buzzed with activity around her and she watched, distanced by the numbness that enveloped her. It took a while to realise one of the phones on her desk was ringing. Eventually she picked up the receiver, took a deep breath and connected the call.

'Beca Morley.' Breezy Beca was back on the job. Problems? Not her. Life was just perfect.

'Hi, it's me,' Abi said. 'I need to go out and get very drunk. Will you come with me?' She obviously wasn't pretending as hard as Beca.

'Can it wait until after work?'

There was a pause loaded with disappointment. 'I suppose so.' She sounded impatient. 'What time will you finish?'

'I could get out of here by eight.'

'Meet me at Zigi's, half past.'

'Are you alright?' Beca asked, but Abi had already hung up. Stupid question really. Abi rarely needed to get drunk. She often got pissed unintentionally, trying to keep up with her. But actually needing to get drunk? That was different. Still, she rather fancied getting shit-faced herself. Even a chronic hangover was better than struggling for breath all the time. If the combination killed her, she didn't particularly mind.

Zigi's was practically deserted which suited Beca just fine. It had become a victim in the cut-throat business of cool places in Soho to be seen in. Once it had been the place, now with a décor that was so last year, its glory days were gone.

A few of the white plastic egg seats were occupied, but Beca had the bar to herself. She sat in the middle nursing a gin. A fluorescent light glowed from somewhere behind the bar, edging her glass and its clear contents with a blue tinge. The gin rippled suddenly. Once and then again. She'd seen the effect in a film as an ominous portent of danger. She swivelled on her stool in time to see Abi lurching towards her. It was unsettling to see her friend looking quite so demented. Her eyes were fiery and cross, her face strained and her curly hair stood out behind her in its own private wind. She looked like an aerodynamic hood emblem off the front of a 1930s car.

Abi reached for Beca's cigarettes and before she'd climbed up onto a bar stool she was inhaling like a 60-a-day professional.

'Wine?' Beca asked while catching the barman's eye.

'Gin,' she said taking a swig of Beca's as if the wait for her own would be way too long.

'That bad?' Beca asked. Abi's rare use of violent red lipstick was answer enough. 'Tom?'

'He has the unmitigating gall, the unforgivable fucking cheek to mope around the house feeling sorry for himself,' she said through a cloud of smoke. 'You know he actually asked me to hug him this morning. He pulled a pathetic droopy face and held out his arms like Dulcie does. It was revolting. A grown man blubbering to his wife because he's had to give up his favourite whore.' Spittle was gathering at the corners of her mouth. 'I hate him.'

Beca needed her drink but Abi didn't look like she was going to give it up without a fight. 'He's stopped seeing her?' Beca asked.

'Oh yes. Apparently he's given her up for my sake. He's martyred himself for me and the children. I can't tell you how infuriating it is. He thinks he's made a noble sacrifice.'

'I can see how that would piss you off.'

Abi passed back the remains of Beca's drink as her own arrived. Beca ordered another one for herself while she had the barman's attention. Abi took a swig from the fresh glass, smacked her lips then wiped them on the back of her hand. She was clearly determined to get very pissed.

Beca passed her a small square of napkin that had come with a free bowl of nibbles. 'You've smeared.'

Abi took it and wiped. 'I never knew how to wear lipstick anyway. Gone?'

Beca nodded.

'I've given him his space.' Abi picked up her drink and gulped again. 'I thought, "We're going through a healing process here, we need to respect each other, talk without shouting." I told him there was nothing he couldn't tell me. I wanted him to be frank. That didn't mean he could cling onto me like an oversized baby. I wasn't planning on mothering him through this crisis.'

'What a wanker,' Beca said supportively. There was a lot more besides she could have said about his character, or lack of it, if she could get a word in.

'He keeps apologising with varying degrees of self pity. I thought he might feel guilty for what he's done to me. I stupidly expected some kind of contrition, some display of remorse that went beyond the pouting bottom lip. But nothing. I tell you, Beca, I'm sick of him. I'm fed up with being the solid, together one. He has destroyed me and the family and yet he's looking for sympathy.' She stubbed out her cigarette furiously and lit another one. She was going to feel horrible tomorrow morning. 'Not once over the past month has he asked how I'm feeling. He's a,' she spluttered trying to find the word.

'Dick-driven, self-serving, arrogant fucker? Banana-faced fuck pig?' Beca suggested.

'Exactly,' Abi said gesturing frantically at the barman for a refill. 'A hollow-chested, flabby-arsed banana-faced fuck pig.'

They nodded emphatically and clinked glasses.

'It's amazing you've lasted a month.'

'I deserve a bloody medal.'

'What are you going to do now?'

'Divorce him. Burn his clothes, trash his car and kick him out.'

Jesus, she was serious. 'Don't you think it might scare the kids a bit seeing you torch his suits at the bottom of the garden.'

'I'll send them out for the day.'

'Where are they now?' The mood Abi was in, they were probably waiting in the car outside, hungry and unwashed.

'Babysitter. You don't know any good lawyers do you?'

'Plenty. They'll serve his balls up on a plate.'

'Perfect,' Abi said draining the remains of her drink through icecubes and lime.

'Do you want a contract taken out on him?' Beca asked. 'I could probably stretch to breaking his legs myself.'

Abi smiled. The first wave of self-destruction seemed to have passed. She looked at her cigarette with revulsion then stubbed it out. Beca could see her brain engaging. She glanced at the cigarette in Beca's hand then frowned.

'I thought you'd given them up.'

'Not much point now,' Beca replied.

Abi's eyes widened with realisation. 'God, I've been ranting on and I didn't think once to ask. I'm so sorry. You poor thing. When did you find out?'

'This morning.'

'Are you very miserable?'

Beca nodded.

'Poor darling. It's such a shame.'

Beca shrugged. 'It doesn't matter really. Maybe I like my fags and booze too much to be a mother anyway.'

'It hasn't stopped me.' Abi leant over to give Beca a hug. She misjudged the distance between bar stools and toppled. Her embrace became a struggle to stay vertical. Beca gripped the side of the bar with one hand while trying to support her own weight, Abi's and that of her bar stool which was tipping away from her. The barman looked too startled to help. Abi's face was buried in Beca's chest. She could tell she was laughing from the gusts of hot air in her cleavage. Beca laughed too. Her stomach muscles ached with the double exertion but eventually Abi managed to find the ground and pulled herself off Beca. With a heave Beca righted herself and her stool. Both women laughed loudly and uncontrollably, wiping tears from their eyes. For a moment Beca thought she was going to wet herself.

Eventually the laughter simmered down and Abi smiled at her. 'It's bad luck, really it is, but you can try again.'

'We'll see.'

'Have you seen much of Mitchell since? You never know, if you really hit it off you could end up with him as well as a child. Had you thought about that?'

Funny, that one hadn't occurred to her. She looked in her drink for moral support but the slice of lime was offering none. She needed to steer the conversation onto safer ground. 'Want another one?' she asked gesturing towards Abi's glass.

Abi nodded. 'So how are you getting on with Mitchell?'

Beca wondered how long she could string out the silence before answering. It wasn't anywhere near as long as she wanted. 'I'm not,' she said eventually.

'Why not? I thought you liked him.'

'The thing is we didn't actually spend that weekend together.'

'What? I don't understand. You told me you did.'

'I know,' Beca mumbled through a mouthful of pistachios. 'You didn't seem in the right frame of mind for me to explain.'

'I am now.' The demented look was returning to Abi's face.

'No. I don't think you are,' Beca replied.

'Try me.'

'Do I have to?'

'You slept with someone, right? Otherwise there wouldn't have been any need for a pregnancy test.'

Beca nodded.

'But it wasn't Mitchell?'

'No.'

'You met someone else?'

'Not exactly no. Where are those drinks?' Beca drummed her fingers on the bar. Abi was waiting for an answer. 'I didn't meet anyone else.'

It took only the briefest time for her friend to figure it out. 'You had sex with Hal.' She could hear the anger hissing out between Abi's teeth. The drinks arrived and she grabbed at hers.

'Yes. Sort of.'

'How can you sort of have sex with someone?' Abi asked.

'You can't, I suppose.' Smart arse.

'Are you mad? Are you completely insane?'

Beca found herself nodding. She wasn't sure if it was because she agreed with Abi or if she was just trying to defuse her rage.

'Let me see if I've got this one right,' Abi continued. 'You blew out Mitchell, the single, eligible, interested one, so you could screw Hal? He being the married one. The one with the wife at home.' Abi dragged out her words to emphasise the point. She needn't have bothered, Beca would have got a more subtle version.

'OK, I know it sounds bad. But you've got to remember we're not having an affair. He was trying to get me pregnant. His wife knows all about it.' Beca noticed the barman had edged his way closer.

'It must be a comfort knowing you have her approval.'

'It's nothing like that. You know it isn't,' Beca said, but Abi didn't look interested in the finer detail.

'You're sleeping with a married man.'

'I know.'

'He's not available.'

'I know that too. I don't want him.'

Abi's eyes narrowed. The concentration of anger into two narrow slits made her even more frightening. Beca could feel the next phase of the interrogation coming on and reached for her cigarettes.

'What happened?' Abi asked.

'Nothing,' Beca said shaking her head as if it was a ridiculous question. What could possibly have happened? They'd had sex, he'd left. End of story. Tra-la-la.

'Beca?'

'Bloody hell, Abi, leave me alone.'

'You've fallen in love with him?' she said banging her open hand on the bar.

Beca flinched but remained silent. Her eyes began to burn.

'How did it happen?' Abi asked.

'I'm not feeling proud of myself. I'm pissed off in fact, for being so stupid.'

'What happened?'

Beca shrugged. 'We had such a great time together.'

'He did?'

'Yes.' Beca leant further away from Abi.

'Bastard.'

'What do you mean?'

'He's married. He wasn't supposed to have a good time, was he?' Abi spat the words out like burning shrapnel.

'No. To be honest he hated having sex with me.'

'That's something I suppose.' Abi looked cross but a bit more satisfied. 'At least he didn't enjoy being unfaithful to his wife.'

'He wasn't being unfaithful.'

'Of course he was.'

'Well, if it makes you feel better, he was practically sick with revulsion every time we did it.'

'Good.' Abi sneered.

'He didn't even say goodbye when he left. He just ran off to meet her.'

'Even better.'

Beca was horrified. Tears filled her eyes.

'You broke his heart once, now he's broken yours. Call it natural justice.'

'You're such a cow,' Beca said and promptly burst into tears. Deep down she knew Abi was right. She also knew her friend wouldn't be saying any of those things if her bastard husband wasn't trampelling her life into the ground. She hated him more than ever.

Abi looked contrite. She reached over more adeptly this time and gave her a hug, not that Beca would have cared if she had landed up on the floor with Abi on top of her.

'I'm sorry, I didn't mean what I said.' Abi started sniffing loudly and the barman scuttled away. 'I'm just so angry with everyone. I even shouted at Billy the other day. Then I spent the night in his room crying as he slept. I've never felt such fury before.'

'Maybe you could channel it a bit more towards Tom.' Beca took the scrunched up napkin Abi had used to wipe lipstick off her face, and blew her nose.

'You mustn't see him again.' Abi's sudden vehemence startled Beca, but just one look told her she wasn't joking. 'You've got to promise me you won't ever see him.'

Beca was silent. She couldn't make such a promise. It didn't matter that she'd already decided never to sleep with him. If she was going to try for a baby, it wouldn't be with Hal. A brief liaison with a vial of frozen sperm would be the way. She wasn't going through the last two weeks again. But promising was so, so final.

'Promise me. You have to Beca. You know it's for the best.' Alcohol and rage were making a frightening cocktail.

'I don't think I can.'

'You're making a fool of yourself. He's married. He doesn't want you. Can't you see that?'

Now that her friend had so gently pointed it out, yes she could.

'OK.'

'Say it,' Abi insisted.

'I promise. I won't ever see Hal again.' She felt sick. She felt cast adrift and frightened, just when she didn't think it was possible to feel any worse.

'Good. You've got no business mooning over another woman's man.'

'Are you sure it's me you should be having this conversation with?'

'If you were that whoring bitch Tom's been screwing, I'd have had your eyes out by now.'

Fair point.

Beca weaved her way to the loo. When she returned Abi had got another round in. She was being out-paced by an amateur, although she noticed Abi was slouching over the bar more than she had before and her face looked like it had melted slightly.

'Let's get the bill. I don't think I can cope with another one after this,' Beca said waving a hand at the barman.

They tripped up the stairs to street level. Beca had no idea how much the bar tab had come to. Her signature on the credit card slip hadn't borne much resemblance to the sober version and her surname had ended up scratched into the surface of the bar. She had been trying to finish her last drink at the same time which might have had something to do with it. She figured the people at Visa would make allowances bearing in mind the time of the transaction.

'How about some chips? Large, greasy, thigh-building chips.' She was too pissed to wait for a meal in a restaurant, her hunger needed instant carbohydrate gratification, but when they got to the chip shop around the corner from Zigi's, the window ledge where customers sat was full. They ended up walking the streets with their bags of chips until they found a doorway to sit in that didn't reek of bodily emissions.

'So was Mitchell really that bad?' Abi asked taking a bite out of her deep-fried, shiny saveloy sausage.

'I don't know, I never shagged him,' Beca said through a mouthful of chips.

'I meant as a person.'

Beca smirked at her error. 'He was alright.'

'Why don't you give him a ring?'

'Because he's an arsehole. I've got no respect for him. Hal might have made me feel inadequate and unlovable but at least he's got a sense of humour. Anyway, it's him I'm in love with.'

'Are you sure that's not because you can't have him?' Abi asked giving Beca a probing stare.

That was deep. A record-breaking dive into murky, chilly depths kind of deep. Beca was happier just snorkeling around on the surface. She didn't like the lack of oxygen down where Abi was lurking.

'What the fuck's that supposed to mean?'

Abi wasn't picking up on the dive-buddy signals to back off. 'I mean that perhaps you feel so strongly about him because it's safe to. There's no chance of him returning your feelings, is there? There's nothing to unsettle you.'

'I feel pretty flat on my arse at the moment, as it happens.' What was it about pissed best friends that made them think they could be as bloody rude as they liked? 'You reckon the only reason I'm in love with Hal is because he's not in love with me?'

'Not in love with you and more importantly not available. You can pine away all you like but he's never going to be yours.'

'So you think I enjoy feeling miserable?'

'Not exactly, but you're allowing yourself to be in love.'

'And you think I'd be scared if he loved me back?' Beca was conjuring up places where Abi could shove her saveloy.

'Remember what happened last time.' Abi missed her nose as she tried to tap it knowingly.

'But I didn't love him then.'

'Exactly.'

'Exactly what? What are you talking about.' What the hell did Abi know anyway? If she was so bloody clever why hadn't she seen her own marriage breakdown coming? Beca's chips were turning cold and stiff.

'I think it's possible that the reason why you didn't love him the first time around was because you were afraid to. Now there's no chance of him wanting you, it's safe to love him.'

'You're mad.' Or was she mad for putting up with her friend's cod pyschobabble bullshit?

'You've always made a big deal about never getting into relationships because your father showed you what pigs men are. I'm just wondering if sub-consciously you made that decision because you were scared of being loved.'

Beca laughed. It was ridiculous. 'Of course I'm not scared of being loved. I want to be loved, by Hal.'

'So you say,' Abi said really getting into her stride. 'And maybe the pregnancy business was a ruse to get in touch with him. I think deep down you've known all along that he was the man for you and you've been regretting it ever since you dumped him.'

'I have not.'

'Not consciously, that would be too dangerous.'

'You're crediting my sub-conscious with too much cunning which just shows how wrong you are. If it was that clever how do you explain the obvious fact that I don't have either a baby or Hal? Where's the brilliance in that?'

'You've got a point.'

'So shut up and let's go home.'

The first two taxis they stopped refused to take them and their chips which was a great opportunity for both Beca and Abi to hurl abuse at some men. Beca for one felt better for getting some of her stronger feelings off her chest, but by the time they'd hailed down a third taxi she was beginning to regret the extra fish cake.

The taxi driver grumbled when they told him his second drop was out in Kew and they laughed when he slammed the connecting window shut. On the drive home they tried to work out how much they'd drunk. By their best guess work it was four gins each, although Beca reckoned she'd had one extra while waiting for Abi, but she wasn't sure, it could have been two. Considering each drink had been vast, they calculated they must have drunk a whole bottle between them. This was important information to have should it become necessary for either of them to seek emergency treatment during the night.

Beca spun with the effort of slamming the taxi door as she got out in front of the house and laughed at Abi's exaggerated shushing. That was about as funny as the rest of the night got. She laboured her way up to her flat, her legs feeling heavy and each stair vastly bigger than she remembered it being.

As she opened the door, evidence that the cleaner had visited singed her nostrils. She looked around the pristine and shining rooms. Every cushion was plumped and exactly positioned. Even though it had been scrubbed clean of human life, she still got a strong sense of Hal. His spirit had been hanging around in the flat since he'd last left. Occasionally he would cross her path. As she climbed the spiral staircase she could picture him down below in the living room sprawled out on a sofa. When she was in the kitchen she would remember his culinary prowess. Tonight as she drank a glass of water in front of the sink, she wished she could have come home for supper with him, instead of sitting in a doorway eating chips. But he wasn't there, he was with her, his wife. Perhaps Abi had been right. Maybe she was wallowing in impossibilities, but fantasies were always so much easier to control. They were brighter than reality.

It had been a long day but the possibility of sleep seemed far off. Beca stumbled upstairs to the bedroom and searched in a drawer until she found the T-shirt Hal had left behind. She hadn't the courage to throw it away then, and despite the shame, she'd folded and put it away. As she pulled it on she could smell him. The cotton was a poor substitute for the real man and feeling it against her skin just made things worse. What a pathetic fifth rate compromise. She didn't have him so she'd wear his cast-offs instead. That didn't stop her holding the front to her face and breathing in hard. Amongst the familiar smells there was a hint of rosemary. It was her shampoo. He must have used it, and from this fact she dredged up a feeble amount of satisfaction knowing he'd have gone back to Sophie smelling of her.

Downstairs she curled up on the sofa. Tucking her feet up under her, she hugged a cushion to her chest. There was only one film to watch when on the point of a drunken crying jag. She pointed the remote control at the DVD player and it whirred into action. Moments later as the soaring chords of *Gone With the Wind* burst into the room, Beca's bottom lip gave way to the pressure and her face screwed up as frustrated, unhappy tears rolled down her cheeks. Even when sober the music made her throat tighten and the back of her neck tingle. When drunk it was a guarantee that she'd cry and for once she had a really good reason.

How had she got into this position? Until a couple of months ago she'd not given Hal a moment's thought, not since she'd last seen him. Yet now he was even more important than having a child. A few weeks back it would have been inconceivable, ridiculous in fact to think that she'd have wanted any man, let alone Hal, more than a baby of her own. But that was the present reality. She deserved to be pilloried.

She tried to clear her head, to arrange her mind and open it up to the possibility of sleep. She focussed on the film but couldn't get the comparisons out of her head. If Sophie died like Melanie did, then she, Scarlett could have Ashley. But if Hal was Ashley, who was Rhett? He was the man Scarlett really loved, although she only realised that when he walked out on her. Had she always loved Rhett, or rather Hal, but never known it? It was all so very confusing.

As the film ended Beca reminded herself that tomorrow was another day, and that unlike those pale-skinned Southern belles, she had to be at work by 7 am. She trudged up to bed with Mammy telling her that Hal loved Sophie, that he was a married man, while she was just white trash. Beca wanted to spit. She hated Sophie. She hated Hal, and anyway that bloody Scarlett O'Hara was a pain in the pampered derrière.

Chapter 16

It was after 10 o'clock in the evening by the time Beca and Liz packed up work. Beca shrugged off the darkness and the loss of another Sunday as they emerged through the swing doors of the bank. Work for her was the cure-all she needed, and she needed it most at the weekends when there was too much time to sit around and feel lonely, too many hours to wade through before Monday morning came to relieve her. It was three months since she'd last seen Hal, ten weeks give-or-take since she'd found out she wasn't pregnant and she still didn't feel safe on her own. She didn't trust herself to keep up the bluff of not caring. Whistling cheery tunes and constantly telling herself that life was so much better and more straightforward this way was wearing. Men. Babies. Who needed them?

The morning after her gin binge with Abi, Sir Conrad had ridden to her rescue. Her boss wasn't renowned for his altruism and it was mere coincidence that his plans for world domination had kicked off at the same time Beca had discovered she had very little besides work to live for. Sir Conrad's ambitions to take over the bank's biggest rival were audacious, requiring absolute commitment from his staff and with her he'd got it, without question and in double measure. It'd had been a full-blown Technicolor, cast-of-thousands deliverance. Such was the relief of having a distraction that Beca could have fallen on her knees and kissed his feet. She'd probably have bathed them for him if he'd asked. She'd have been Spartacus for him any day.

The streets outside were deserted. Autumnal leaves whirled and eddied, scooping up rubbish and scudding across the empty plaza, then falling lifeless to the ground again. It felt as though the world had been wiped clean of people except for the pair of them, or perhaps the mere fact it was a Sunday explained the bleakness. Beca pulled her coat closer to her. She hadn't noticed the weather for weeks. The last time she'd really taken a good look around her it had been summer and everything had been so bright and promising. Her hopes seemed now to be as fleeting as those long-gone sun-baked days.

Liz offered her a cigarette. She took one and leant forward for a light. She inhaled anticipating the smoke curling into her lungs, her head becoming light and fluffy after a day's abstinence. Instead she lost a layer of tissue from her trachea.

'Jesus,' she spluttered. 'I'd forgotten you like throat peelers.'

Liz laughed at her and exhaled a cloud of smoke into the cold evening air. Beca tried again, happy to risk more pain than forego her nicotine. The burning was less intense the second time and by the time she took a third puff her lungs had been anaesthetised.

'Want a drink?' she asked Liz.

'It's a bit late. You need to look your best for tomorrow's press announcement.'

'True.'

'Don't fancy dropping me off though, do you?'

'Sure.' It was an odd request considering Liz lived at least ten miles in the opposite direction, but it would delay her return home for another hour which had to be a good thing. Besides, she owed her a few favours. Despite Beca's off behaviour over the past few weeks, Liz had held back from quizzing her and she was grateful.

It wasn't hard finding her Merc in the car park; it was the only vehicle there. She climbed into the driver's seat and slammed the door shut behind her.

'You alright?' Liz asked as she clambered in beside her.

'Fine.' Even now, thinking about Hal sent her shoulder muscles into spasms. Wanting a baby, falling in love with him, it was absurd and so unlike her. It had been a momentary derailment from the course she'd chosen for herself. But she was over all that now. She was back on track and focussing on what really mattered. Work.

The engine chewed and spat as she turned the starter motor. After two attempts it came to life and Beca backed out, swung a hard left and headed for the exit ramp.

Liz swore as she banged into the arm rest. 'I can easily get a cab,' she said.

'No problem,' Beca replied spinning the car into a sharp right and out into the night. Then without warning she pulled over to the kerb and slammed on the brakes.

'Let's have the roof down,' she said and began to unclip the catches above the windscreen.

'It's bloody freezing,' Liz complained.

'Sink down in your seat if you get cold.'

Liz grumbled as her neck disappeared into her coat. Beca rammed the car into first and screeched off up the road again. She didn't give a bugger about being cold, if anything it helped to calm her down. Nothing was guaranteed to piss her off more than thinking about what she'd been through. She'd not heard a word from Hal since he'd left, but then again, why should she? Why should he be interested to know if she was pregnant or not? It was down to her to call him if she needed his services. But she didn't and she wouldn't.

Logic had had a tough time battling it out with her own special brand of madness. She knew Hal wouldn't call her, but that hadn't stopped her from obsessively checking her mobile for texts or missed calls. She'd even up-graded her answering machine at home so she could pick up her messages wherever she happened to be. Likewise she'd kept a vigil going by the letter box hoping for a note from him. Nothing. Why was she perpetually surprised by his lack of correspondence? They weren't friends, they had nothing in common. What exactly did she expect him to say to her?

Beca wildly two-fingered a driver who'd hit his horn in protest when she cut him up. Anger had a way of giving her tunnel vision and she hadn't noticed him. She headed for Dalston and tried to ease her foot off the accelerator. Weaning herself off her obsessive behaviour was proving more difficult. She was now on the carrot phase of recovery, the stick method having failed completely. Inspired by Dulcie's good behaviour star chart, Beca was rewarding herself points for not thinking about Hal. Self-enforcement was proving less rigorous than Abi's application and so half points and lesser fractions could be earned for thinking of him only fleetingly. Semi-conscious thoughts did not count, nor did any triggered by some sort of physical reminder. Hence Beca pretty much had carte blanche to moon about him anywhere she liked in the flat. Which meant about the only time she wasn't thinking about him was when she had her head down at work or was redeeming her points in the shops. Recovery was proving lengthy and extremely expensive.

As she hurtled along towards Dalston she was aware of Liz beside her, perfumed, tired and pissed off. Beca had pumped the air with relief when Sir Conrad had told them they'd be working the weekend, again. Liz, who had better things to do with her life, had been in a quiet strop all day about it. It was obvious she wanted to talk, so Beca loosened her white-knuckle grip of the steering wheel and tried to relax in her seat. A manic face with a forehead bisected by a frown scowled back at her from the rear view mirror but there wasn't much she could do about that.

Liz put two cigarettes in her mouth, lit them, then passed one to Beca. Deep in her lungs her bronchioles were screaming.

'The thing is,' Liz said through a plume of smoke. 'I've been thinking.'

'What about?' Beca asked, too tired to crack any jokes.

'I've decided to hand my notice in. I've had enough of working at the bank.'

Beca hoped she'd heard Liz wrong. She was momentarily distracted by an articulated lorry that was throwing its weight around. Once she'd caught up, over-taken and swapped a few obscenities with the driver she asked, 'Sorry, what was that again?'

'I'm quitting.'

'That's what I thought you said. Yeah, you too arsehole. Save it for your boyfriend,' she shouted when the artic man came back for more.

'Maybe I should wait until you've stopped driving.'

'Will you have changed your mind?'

Liz laughed. 'No.'

'Then go on. I'm listening.'

'That's it really.'

'You know I'll have to chain you to your desk. I can't possibly cope without you. It'll be horrible on my own.' She was being selfish and knew it, but the bank without Liz? It was unthinkable.

'You'll manage.'

'I won't. I thought you enjoyed working there.'

'You're kidding. Slaving late every night and weekend, never getting any time off. That's no way to live, is it?'

Beca couldn't argue that point, but she kept quiet about how much she'd needed it. It was her fix, her rush of oblivion. A panacea to the debilitating ailment called misguided love. The more she worked the better as far as she was concerned.

'What about your pay cheque? You won't earn half as much out of the City,' she said.

'I know, and so what? What's the point of all the money if there's never any time to enjoy it?'

Beca could think of plenty of reasons, like the fact she had it in large quantities.

The wheels of the Merc and Liz did a duet as Beca tried to beat the set of lights ahead. The car sped across the junction leaving a trail of angry horns blaring in its wake.

'Jesus fucking Christ,' Liz screamed. 'Are you trying to kill us?'

Beca laughed.

'You need to take it easy.' Liz's voice was shrill with fright. 'You need to take some tranquilizers or something because at this rate you're going to wind up dead. And me with you.'

'There was no real danger.'

'Pull over.'

Beca was struck by her fierce tone and did as requested.

'You've probably been too busy to notice,' Liz continued in full rant mode, 'but you're getting close to cracking up. Do you know how many cups of coffee you've have today?'

'No.'

'Well I do. I counted. Sixteen. Not including whatever you had before you got to work. Sixteen is about fifteen too many. And you're drinking too much booze. I can tell. Your eyes are all puffy, your skin's crap. You need to sort yourself out.'

Was it possible to fire someone who'd already handed their notice in. 'I'm not in that much of a state,' Beca said testily.

'You reckon? I checked your file and you haven't taken any time off since Christmas.'

'I have.'

'You haven't. You need a holiday.'

Was it really that long? It just showed how preoccupied she'd been. 'I'll take one once things quieten down at work.'

'Why does the bank always have to come first? They won't miss you when you drop down dead. You need to look after yourself, because nobody else is going to.'

'Isn't that the truth.'

Liz's voice was calmer now. 'I've been planning my escape for months. Why don't you come with me?'

'Where to?'

'Everywhere, starting in South Africa. I'm going for three months, longer maybe.'

'It sounds great.'

'Come with me then.'

'It's tempting,' Beca said with a smile. 'But the last thing I need is more time to think.'

Beca dropped Liz off and managed to stay within the speed limit as she drove home. Her stalwart secretary had given her plenty to think about, not least what she would do without her. She had always been there, from the first day Beca had started as a wet-behind-the-ears graduate. Going it alone was becoming a recurring theme and it was hard not to consider the possibility that she was getting something drastically wrong.

When she eventually got home she had difficulty parking because of the large motorbike in front of her house. It looked vaguely familiar but she was tired and all it meant was added irritation as she struggled to get her car into the only parking space in the street. She managed it in the end with only one minor bang.

The porch light came on automatically as she put the key in the lock. As the heavy front door closed behind her she leant against it and looked up the stairs towards her own door. She dreaded this moment every night when there was no longer any excuse to stay away from the flat. She felt desolate and longed for a reason to run away, something she could use to explain her cowardice, for it was when she was alone at home that she missed him the most.

She could hear laughter coming from Mrs Butler's flat. There was more than one voice and Beca strained to separate the different tones. She could make out the old lady's high ringing laugh; the other belonged to a man. Either her neighbour was talking to the television or keeping company well past midnight. Under other circumstances she would have cheered at the idea of Mrs Butler entertaining a man, tonight she was too ashamed of the envy she felt.

She checked the post. Even though it was a Sunday and she knew there'd be nothing new for her she had a hard fight beating down the tremor of expectation. There was nothing but junk from the day before. Why did she have to put herself through the same torture every time? He was never going to write to her. She had been hoping to see Rhett, to lure him upstairs with the promise of tuna fish and a cuddle, but apparently he was in on the soiree. She picked up the Sunday papers that had arrived long after she'd set off for work and because she could put it off no longer she headed towards the stairs. Her heart jumped when Mrs Butler's door opened and the old lady popped her head around.

'There you are dear. I've been listening out for you.'

'Is everything alright? What are you doing up so late?' Beca asked.

'Come on in,' she said tapping the side of her nose. Beca could have hugged her.

He was there, in the sitting room, relaxing in Mrs Butler's best armchair. He'd made himself right at home with his legs stretched out before him, crossed at the ankle. Rhett was sitting on his lap enjoying a back scratch. A smile played on Hal's lips when he looked up at her.

Beca's gasp was one of raw, unprotected feeling and once it had escaped her mouth it couldn't be coaxed back in. She was stunned, rooted to the spot. This moment had lived in her head for weeks, now that it was happening the much-practised responses left her ill-equipped. She'd only rehearsed the part where he made his declaration of love. Judging by his expression, words of such high emotion were not imminent.

'What are you doing here?' Her voice trembled in her ears.

'I was just passing,' he said as he scratched around Rhett's ears. Beads of saliva gathered on the cat's whiskers. 'It seemed rude not to stop for a chat. I've been wondering how you are.'

This did not mean he cared. In a parallel universe somewhere it might, but on planet Earth, it didn't. Had not this married man on numerous occasions made his feelings for her starkly clear? Precisely. Grinding her keys into the palm of her hand helped drive the message home. He was here because he was curious. Which was fine. On that she could accommodate him.

'It didn't work,' she said.

Mrs Butler tilted her head slightly inviting an explanation.

'I'm sorry,' Hal replied. It was hard to tell if he actually meant it.

'Don't be. I'm not. I still owe you some money, don't I?'

'That's not what I came for.'

'Of course not.' Beca's tone suggested that was exactly what she did think. 'My cheque book's upstairs.'

Mrs Butler pursed her lips.

Hal shook his head and tipped Rhett off his lap. 'I'm sorry to have taken up so much of your time,' he said to his host. 'You should think about writing your memoirs.'

'Come and see me again and I'll tell you more,' she said holding his hand between hers.

Beca stood watching as the pair said goodbye. She felt awkward and close to tears. All she really wanted was a hug from him. Perhaps being rude was a defence mechanism. There was no chance of getting a cuddle from him, not the sort she wanted anyway, and being unpleasant made the impossible even more unlikely.

Mrs Butler closed her door behind them and Beca stood looking at Hal. He'd been smiling when she'd walked into her neighbour's flat. His face had been open and free of lines. Now he looked bad-tempered and pre-occupied. It was horrible having that kind of effect.

'I'm sorry. Why don't you come up for a coffee. It's been a long day.'

He hesitated then nodded. As they climbed the stairs to her flat she could feel him behind her. Here now was the body of the spirit that had been occupying her home and heart. And all the hard work of the last three months vanished. The hundreds of times she'd told herself she was better off without him, the thousands of pounds she'd spent reassuring herself that a high-earning career was all that she really cared about, all of it melted away with one look at him.

It was a serious blow to realise she did still have such strong feelings for him, but at the same time she felt wildly happy. She so wanted to shout out that she loved him. But the moment was brief and in an instant it was swallowed up by green bile. She climbed the stairs with lead in her boots. What was the point of telling him? So he could laugh at her? Or worse still, pity her. Happy endings belonged in dreams. She knew there could be only one possible outcome, it was just a matter of preserving as much dignity as she could.

Beca felt jittery and self-conscious. A silence had fallen between them that had gone beyond embarrassing into the excruciating. She put the coffee grinder to work, thankful that the noise covered the lack of conversation. She held her finger down on the button pulverising the beans into powder so to avoid the inevitable silence that would follow.

'I'm sorry I was rude,' she blurted out once she'd atomised the coffee grounds. 'It's been a while and seeing you brought back some unwelcome memories.'

Hal looked surprised.

'The point is this,' she continued. 'I didn't get pregnant and I've given up trying. It was a mistake. I'm not cut out for motherhood.'

'You seemed pretty sure before.'

'I was deluding myself. Anyway it didn't work and I'm not going through that again.'

'It takes some couples years.'

'But we're not a couple. Besides, I've got my career to think about. This whole baby business has been a distraction and it was beginning to show.'

'You don't think that might have been a good thing?'

'Don't start on the work-life balance lecture, Hal. I don't need it from you as well.'

'I think you'd have made a good mother.'

So did she, but wishing wasn't getting. 'I don't agree.'

'I could sue you, of course.'

Beca knew he was joking. Or rather she knew he wasn't being serious. He'd need to review his material if he was actually trying to make her laugh. She wasn't in the mood either way.

'There's an opt-out clause,' she said. 'Page 3. You'll get a 50% settlement on the remaining fees. Not bad all things considered.' She hadn't quite dared to question his manliness but the implication was there.

She could sense his anger even without looking at him and she kept her head down as she searched in the kitchen drawers for her cheque book. She found it and leaning on the counter she wrote out a cheque. She held the pen tightly trying to stop it from shaking, even so her writing scratched across the paper. Hal remained silent. She was afraid to look at him and avoided his eyes when she held out the cheque. He didn't take it. She waved it at him, as if that would sway him.

'Have it,' she said in a more up-beat tone. 'You've earned it. Hopefully it will win Sophie her Oscar. I think it's best we don't see each other again, so thank you.' With that she held out her other hand and waited for him to shake it.

Hal shrugged as if on consideration he couldn't have cared less. 'Fine.' He took the cheque but refused her out-held hand. 'Sophie's taking a break from acting. The summer was quite tough on her. I hadn't realised how much all this had got to her,' he said looking at the cheque as if it were the sum total of what they had been doing together. 'Anyway, we've decided to start trying for a baby.'

It was hunger and tiredness, nothing else, that made her giddy. She wasn't in the habit of fainting over a bit of devastating news. She should have eaten something at work. Hal held her arms to steady her. She felt so light-headed and sick.

'I'm fine, really,' she said pulling away from him. She could have sworn he was smiling. What was the bastard playing at?

'When did you last eat?' he asked.

Beca struggled to remember. 'I had a banana for breakfast, and sixteen cups of coffee apparently.'

'Fool. Frankly it's no wonder you didn't get pregnant if you treat your body like that.' Hal led her to the sofa and made her sit down, then he began rummaging in the kitchen cupboards but could find nothing edible.

'For Christ's sake, Beca, when are you going to grow up. You have to eat. I'll see if Mrs B's got anything.'

'Just go away, will you.' Beca got to her feet. 'I'm fine. Besides it's none of your business, now.' Not that it ever was.

'Shut up and sit down.' Hal found a tin of soup hidden by a stash of cough remedies and headache pills.

Beca was furious at him. Furious for seeing her in such a mess, for taking charge when he had no bloody right to, for caring enough so that it hurt, but not enough for it to have any meaning. God, how had she got herself in such a state? She was the same as her mother. She'd spent her whole life trying not to be anything like the door mat she had been, yet just like her she'd allowed her happiness to hinge around a man who didn't care. Such stupidity had to be genetic.

While Hal was stirring the soup in a saucepan the telephone rang. By then it was nearly one o'clock and Beca didn't bother answering. She assumed it must be Sophie checking up on her husband. Hal waited for her to pick up the receiver but, when it was clear she wasn't going to, he did so himself.

Beca watched him. She wanted him to look at her so he could see just how much she didn't care that his wife was on the phone. She couldn't quite make out what he was saying but from his tone, from the way his head dipped down, she could tell he wasn't making small talk. He looked up at her and she knew instinctively that something was wrong. The hairs on her neck stood up and she became uncomfortable sitting, as though her body was getting ready for what was about to follow.

'I'll just get her, she's right here,' Hal said.

What is it?' she whispered.

'It's Abi.'

She took the telephone from him and tried to read his face, to get some clue as to what was wrong. He stood close to her and she reached out and held his arm.

'Abi, what's wrong? Is it the children? Has something happened to them.'

'No. It's Tom.' Fear was making Abi's voice quaver. 'I think he's had a heart attack. He's lying on the floor. I don't know what to do, I think he might be dead.'

'Have you called an ambulance?' Beca asked.

'They said they'd be here soon.'

'Dulcie and Billy are safe?'

'They're asleep,' Abi laughed bitterly. 'They have no idea what's going on.'

'That's good. I'm on my way. I'll be there as soon as I can. Everything will be OK, trust me. I'm coming.'

She hung up and looked at the telephone. 'Tom's had a heart attack.'

'I know. We should get going.'

'I have to get to Abi.'

'We'll go on my bike. It'll be quicker.'

'Are you sure?' Beca didn't understand why he wanted to help.

Hal put his hands on her shoulders and steered her towards the door. 'Don't be an idiot, of course I'm sure.'

Beca clung to Hal on the back of his motorbike as he broke every rule in the book. She'd never been through roundabouts in a virtual straight line before and after the first one she kept her eyes shut for the rest of the way, her head bent down between his shoulder blades. Even though she knew a crisis was waiting for them, even though she knew she shouldn't be feeling good about anything, her whole body glowed where it pressed against him and she wished the bike ride could go on forever. It was the closest she'd felt to happiness in a long while.

Ten minutes later they were several miles across London and tearing into Abi's street. The noise of the motorbike could barely be heard above the din of radios and running engines. Blue lights flashed and bounced off the houses, windows were lit up with an unnatural electric blue, and trees and hedges cast terrible deep shadows. A paramedic's motorbike stood on the road in front of Abi's house. Next to it was an ambulance with its doors wide open, the interior shining out brightly into the night. Beca saw a stretcher being wheeled out of the house. Tiny amongst the team of medics was Abi. Beca called out and ran to her. Abi turned and searched the sea of neighbours' faces, fear making her movements jerky and unsure.

'We were arguing,' she said when Beca reached her. Her face was pale and tight. 'He was so angry. I finally told him I'd seen a solicitor, that I wanted a divorce. He went mad. God, Beca, I've killed him.'

'Don't say that,' Beca replied. 'It's not your fault. He'll be OK.' She looked at the paramedic for confirmation but she was giving nothing away. 'He's strong. He's a tough bugger. He'll pull through.'

Beca continued with reassuring inanities and led Abi towards the ambulance which was ready to leave. She stepped inside then turned back to Beca.

'Will you look after the children?' she asked. 'Please don't leave them.'

'Of course, but don't you want me to come with you?'

'I don't want them to get frightened if they wake up and I'm not there. Especially Billy. You won't leave him if he cries will you? Sometimes he loses his dummy and he cries.' Tears choked Abi's last words.

The ambulance driver began closing the doors, Hal pulled Beca out of the way. 'I promise, Abi. They'll be fine with me. I won't leave them for a second.'

Then the ambulance was gone. With sirens wailing it peeled off into the night, and as it disappeared from view the neighbours in their dressing gowns turned and went back to their homes. Lights went out at bedroom windows, barking dogs were silenced and people went back to sleep. The drama was over for them, but not so for Beca as she stood with Hal in the empty road.

The evening had been so simple when it had begun. She was going to go home, pick out something to wear for the next day and go to bed. That was all. First Hal, now this. What a mess. She hated Tom with a passion but she didn't want him dead.

Beca was expecting a scene of devastation in the house and was surprised to see what little impact a heart attack could have on physical surroundings. Unlike fire or a bomb, the failing of a heart was apparently quite neat. There was silence from the children's rooms upstairs, the living room looked untouched by events. In the kitchen the washing up waited in the sink and in the corner the washing machine was building up for its final spin. And there it was, the only sign that something was wrong, an overturned glass and a pool of red wine soaking into the wooden table. Beca righted the glass and hoped that Tom could be fixed as easily.

The tension of a few moments earlier had vanished but the house felt eerily quiet and Beca found herself tiptoeing around. She emptied the sink of dirty pans and filled it with hot water. It was the only practical thing she could do to help and after she'd finished that she wiped the surfaces clean with a thoroughness that Abi would have laughed at in happier times.

Hal came in from the living room and looked in the fridge. 'Are you still hungry?'

'Not really.'

'You should eat anyway if you're going to be of any use.'

'I suppose so.'

'See if you can find a plate and some glasses.' He took an opened bottle of white wine out of the fridge and looked at the label.

'Do you think we should?' Beca asked. It seemed wrong to relax while Tom was on the point of dying.

'Will Abi mind?'

'No. Not at all,' she replied. It wasn't like they were having a party. She took a couple of glasses out of the cupboard above the dishwasher and filled them, then watched as Hal cut up some cold chicken and made a salad for her.

'Why don't you go and sit down in the living room?' Hal asked.

Beca did as he suggested taking her glass of wine with her, but she would much rather have stayed looking at him. She didn't have long to wait for a few minutes later he joined her.

'Eat up,' he said putting a plate in front of her on the coffee table.

'Thanks.' She wasn't really hungry but she picked up a fork and began to slowly eat. Hal watched from the sofa opposite taking the occasional drink of wine. They didn't speak and Beca was grateful for it, she felt numb and frightened and over again in her head she kept thinking that this was not supposed to happen.

'He's only 39,' she said eventually. 'What the hell's gone wrong? We were all going to be so happy.'

Hal leant forward with his elbows on his knees so that his face was level with hers. She looked at him then down again at her plate. She was embarrassed and wondered if he'd noticed. Even now when such terrible things were happening her heart glooped like a lava lamp. What kind of friend did that make her?

'Why is Abi divorcing Tom? She didn't look like a woman who wants to be shot of her husband.'

'He had an affair.'

'But he didn't leave her?'

'No. He finished with the other woman. He wanted to give his marriage another chance, but from what Abi's said he's been moping around feeling sorry for himself. He blames her for making him unhappy. She saw a lawyer weeks ago, I suppose she reached her limit this evening and told him.'

'That's very sad.' Hal watched the wine in his glass swill as he turned it between his hands.

'I never thought it would happen to them. Abi deserves so much better.'

'She's a good woman.'

'What he did is unforgivable. I think she belittled herself not throwing him out in the first place.'

'Presumably she wanted to stay married to him.'

'But why? I don't understand how she could forgive him.'

'Because she loved him?' Hal looked at Beca over the rim of his glass.

'He betrayed her. He doesn't deserve her love.'

'Maybe not, but she loved him anyway.'

'I'm glad she's getting a divorce. I don't want him to die, but he should pay for what he's done. If it was me, I'd never forgive him.'

'That's why you'll never be truly happy, Beca.' Hal sat back on his sofa and studied her face.

'What do you mean? I am happy.'

'No you're not. You make a good show of it, but you're not. No one can be who stands so isolated from the world. You can't understand Abi's love for Tom because you've never been in love yourself.'

Beca shoved the plate away from her. 'You've got no right to say such things to me?'

'Someone's got to.'

'I have been in love.'

'With who? Name one man you've come close to loving like Abi loves Tom.'

'You've got no idea,' she whispered burying her answer in her wine glass.

'I pity any man who ever falls in love with you. He'd be an idiot,' Hal said bitterly. 'He'd be doomed to fail because you expect perfection.'

'Because I expect a man to stay faithful to me?'

'It's not that. It's because you can't conceive of forgiving a man who made a mistake.'

'I wonder if you've got any idea how much I hate you.'

Hal picked up his wine glass, took it to the kitchen and a moment later Beca heard the front door quietly close. He wasn't even angry enough to slam it. She began to cry, for herself, for Abi and even for Tom, for the children sleeping upstairs and the whole damned mess. If her heart wasn't broken before, it surely was now.

Chapter 17

Beca lay motionless on the sofa, too afraid to open her eyes. She felt like a child again cowering in the dark, frightened of looking in case the monster that stalked her room was lurking. She willed herself to go back to sleep but the rough cushion which was imprinting a tight weave pattern into her face and the lumps and springs of the sofa digging into her, made pretence a futile exercise.

Her watery eyes focussed on the sofa opposite her. It was an innocuous enough piece of furniture, something she'd sat on plenty of times in the past, but the sagging red cover and cushions confirmed everything she'd suspected. There was little point trying to make believe her way back home to her own bed. Tom's heart attack, Abi's horror, Hal and all the rude things he'd said were real. The images and words came rushing back at her, jumbled and loud enough to make granny knots of her insides.

Her mouth felt lived in and she ached all over. It was so bloody typical of Tom to inconvenience everybody. It wouldn't be surprising if the mean-spirited sod upped and died leaving Abi a widow just because he could. Beca groaned and lifted her head, bringing the cushion that was stuck to her face along as well. It tested the elasticity of her skin for a moment then fell off. Her legs became entwined in her coat as she struggled to sit up. She rubbed her eyes with the heel of her hands and tried to remember how it had got there. She was certain she'd left it on a hook in the hallway like she always did. She brushed the matter off; there were more important things to think of.

She was surprised to find how worried she was for Tom. She'd never liked him and his departure would be no great loss to humanity, but to think of him not being around was shocking and it didn't give her cause to celebrate. The children would be devastated if he died. Then there was Abi's face last night. She hadn't been the picture of the merry widow as she'd climbed into the ambulance. Far from it in fact. Indeed from where Beca had been standing she'd looked like a woman who cared desperately what happened to her adulterous husband. In which case it might be just as well if he didn't peg it. So, if there was anyone up there floating on clouds, which frankly she doubted, perhaps they could see their way clear to letting him live. She for one wouldn't object. She didn't place much value on alternative spiritual stuff either but she found herself willing him to stay alive just in case her positive thoughts could get as far as the hospital.

The smell of freshly-made coffee drifted across from the kitchen. She smiled, inhaled deeply and relished the aroma. Wanting him to live didn't change the way she felt about him, she wasn't going to become a hypocrite in a crisis. He was still an odious man even if he was on the edge of death and she wasn't about to pretend to like him. She stretched her arms and laughed off the self-consciousness of appealing to a higher body. Once again the rich scent of Javanese roast wafted in her direction, this time it caught her attention as well as her senses. Abi must have come back which could only mean Tom was alright. Or did it?

Beca felt sick to the pit of her stomach. 'Abi? Is that you?' She fought the coat off her and struggled to her feet.

'I figured you might need this.' Hal stood in the doorway to the kitchen holding two mugs. 'You must be parched what with all the snoring.'

Surprise knocked Beca back on the sofa. 'You frightened the crap out of me,' she said at the same time as her heart jumped with delight at seeing him.

'Sorry.'

'No, don't be. I thought you were Abi. I had this horrible feeling that Tom was dead and she'd been sent home.' Tears welled up in her eyes. How was it possible to feel devastated and yet so pleased at the same time? To have such conflicting emotions converging on her at once was too much to bear. Why couldn't these things happen one at time in an orderly fashion instead of pummelling her from all sides?

'The phone hasn't rung all night. Here,' he said holding out a mug.

'Thanks.' She roughly wiped away a tear that had escaped and took the coffee. 'I thought I heard you leave.'

'I did. You won't believe the struggle I had trying to get over the back fence.'

So he'd come back. She chided herself for thinking it was romantic. Of course it wasn't, but even so. Her mug hid her smile as she fought the urge to put added meaning into his actions.

'I shouldn't have left you in such a state. It wasn't fair,' he said knocking the air out of any illusions she was building. He looked tired as he sat down opposite her and cupped his mug in his hands.

It had been a nice feeling for the two milliseconds it had lasted, but now it was time to return to planet Earth.

'I'm glad you're here,' she said.

'Truce?'

'Truce,' she replied clinking his cup.

'You haven't spoken to Abi either?' he asked.

'No. And she managed to leave both her mobile and purse behind. I guess she'll call when she can.'

'So we'll just wait,' Hal said.

We? That was fine by her, but didn't he have a wife to be getting home to? Beca held her cup close to her face and inhaled the steam. Occasionally she glanced up at him when she thought he wasn't looking and wondered at her depravity for being so pleased to be with him. Still, it wouldn't be for long and then maybe she'd never see him again. So what was wrong with storing up a few nice feelings?

'Mummy, where are you?' an angry voice demanded from upstairs. 'I need you, mummy.'

The children. In her excitement at seeing Hal, Beca had forgotten about Dulcie and Billy. The reason why she'd spent the night on Abi's sofa had slipped her mind, now one of them was screaming the house down. There was another protracted complaining stream of words. Hal smiled. She appreciated the support.

'You might want to do something about …', he said leaning forward and running his finger under her eye.

Beca needed only a moment to interpret the gesture. Her heart sank. No wonder he'd had such a broad grin on his face. He wasn't smiling with benign encouragement, he was pissing himself with laughter. She looked in the mirror above the fireplace. What an utter nightmare. Mascara had turned the bags under her eyes into coal sacks and her skin was the texture of a dried-up face pack. Meanwhile the entire right side of her hair where she'd slept was lying flat against her head, except at the top where it had bouffanted overnight. She could patent the look as the best turn-off ever and make a fortune. Want to get shot of a man? Try the Beca Morley dead cat experience. Success guaranteed. Was it any surprise that Hal had no feelings for her? Other than revulsion and amusement, of course. A bitter image of him laughing with Sophie as he described how hilariously dishevelled and unattractive she'd been soured her stomach.

'Here,' Hal said passing her a screwed-up paint-stained bandana from his pocket. Did he practise that belittling grin? Beca wanted to stamp her feet with frustration.

Looking a little less menacing she followed the indignant shouts coming from upstairs. 'OK, Dulcie, I'm coming, it's OK.' In fact it was anything but.

Explanations whirred in her head. How was she going to break the news to a four-year-old that her dad was probably dead? Despite all the blue lights and drama of last night, she'd been expecting Abi and Tom to be home by now. A bad case of indigestion brought on by red wine and shouting. The remedy? Take three chalk pills and get a divorce. It was only now that the seriousness of what she was dealing with sank onto her shoulders. This wasn't play-acting. She had to keep her head and take care of two children. The occasional game and ice-cream in the park was not much of a practise run.

She took the turn on the stairs with a smile any children's television presenter would have been proud of. Dulcie stood above her on the next landing in her flowery nightdress rattling a stair gate with one hand.

'It's Beca, sweetheart. Your lovely Godmother.'

Dulcie looked at her crossly and took her thumb out of her mouth long enough to ask, 'What are you doing here?' Her tone was pure adult.

'Well.' Keeping it simple. 'Mummy took daddy to see the doctor and she asked me to look after you,' Beca replied trying to break through the security cordon.

'What's wrong with him?'

Fair enough question.

'Nothing very much,' Beca said through gritted teeth as she tried to wrench the gate off its hinges. 'He ate too much pudding last night and he felt a bit sicky.' Dulcie's lips pursed tighter around her thumb. She wasn't convinced.

'There was lots of cream and sugar in it,' Beca added.

Dulcie nodded knowingly. 'Poor daddy.'

The gate was impenetrable. Beca couldn't figure out how to get the damned thing open. She lifted, lowered, and then pushed anything that might conceivably have been a release button, but it wouldn't budge. Dulcie looked wary. Beca could tell she was wondering what kind of idiot adult her mother had left her with. And who could blame her?

A furious voice shouting, 'Mama here,' announced to the street that Billy had woken up as well.

'He's lost his dummy,' Dulcie said.

'Let's find it for him.' Beca gave the stair gate one final heft before she surrendered and clambered over it.

'His bedroom's back here.' Dulcie led the way. 'I've got a bigger room because I'm oldest. It's pink, I'll show you later.

Billy's room is blue, that's because he's a boy. I think blue's boring, don't you?'

Beca's head whirred. 'Blue's a lovely colour.'

Dulcie's eyes widened with incredulity. 'But all girls like pink.'

Beca quickly bolstered Dulcie's crumbling world. 'Well of course and pink is my absolute favourite.'

Dulcie looked relieved. Clearly not liking pink was infinitely more serious than a sick father.

Billy was trying to escape from his cot. He had one leg tantalisingly close to the top of the bars and was teetering between falling back onto the mattress or, with one last push, hurtling head first onto the floor. If his spaceman pyjamas weren't hanging about his knees he might have made it to freedom. As it was he remained red-faced, cross and in his cot.

'He's always doing that,' Dulcie said with an exasperated sigh. With her hands on her hips she looked exactly like her mother.

Beca picked him up out of the cot and smiled at him. 'You remember me don't you. I'm your mummy's best friend.' She felt sick with anxiety. She didn't have a clue how to handle a crying child.

His round anxious eyes examined Beca's face. She kept grinning and nodding as if looking like a lunatic would win him over. It didn't. She didn't belong in his bedroom and she definitely wasn't his mother. His bottom lip began to tremble. Beca's heart flapped. They looked at each other. She didn't know whether to cuddle him or put him down. Instinct told her to run, but she knew Abi would take a dim view. It was like facing down a mad dog. She had to maintain eye contact and show she wasn't scared. She went one step further and hugged him. Bad mistake.

He must have sensed the tension in her shoulders because he pushed her away and let out a wail.

'Here,' Dulcie said holding up his dummy.

Billy threw himself out of Beca's arms, open mouth first and connected with the rubber stopper. The wail was replaced with contented sucking noises and he sat on the floor stroking his hair.

Thank God for Dulcie. Beca's heart rate slowly began to sink back into the safe range and when she felt in control of herself again she took Billy's hand and led the way downstairs.

'Aren't you going to change his nappy first?' Dulcie asked.

'He wears nappies?' Beca asked as she swung him over the stair gate.

Dulcie rolled her eyes. 'Of course he does, silly, he's only a baby.'

Billy protested this fact through a mouthful of rubber while Beca followed Miss Smarty Pants to the bathroom.

Just to show how grown-up she was, Dulcie got herself dressed while Beca struggled with the intricacies of a disposable nappy. What seemed like hours later they headed downstairs.

'What's that noise?' Dulcie asked as their descent brought them nearer to the kitchen.

It was a good question. 'That's my friend, Hal. He's come to help me take care of you. I think he's singing.'

They entered the kitchen and found him dancing to a James Brown track and howling whenever the occasion presented itself. In between all this he was laying the table. Both children giggled and pressed themselves close to Beca's legs as he spun around and pretended to be surprised to see them.

'Teddy bear or star toast?' he asked, holding out a couple of pastry cutters in their direction.

Dulcie's face lit up as she pointed to the teddy bear. 'Can we have honey too?' she asked him. Beca had just been demoted for which she was hugely relieved.

Feeling the strain of the day already she refilled her coffee cup and sank down on a chair. Abi would be back soon, very soon. With any luck. Her eyes wandered to the telephone mounted on the wall next to the fridge and she willed it to ring. She smiled at her stupidity. Dulcie and Billy were her best friend's children. She saw them practically every weekend. Taking care of them couldn't be that difficult. Really. She looked at the telephone and counted to ten. It didn't ring but something familiar on the fridge caught her eye. It was one of her business cards stuck to the door by a magnet.

'Shit!' She slammed her cup down on the table and choked on the coffee in her mouth. 'I'm supposed to be at frigging work.'

She raced into the living room to find her mobile and in the background she could hear Dulcie explaining, 'She uses rude words a lot. Mummy says it's because she doesn't have children of her own and we shouldn't take any notice.'

'Very wise,' Hal replied in a serious tone.

Beca thought she'd been pretty moderate considering the huge quantities of crap she was in. Her heart pounded in her ear as she pressed the mobile to it. Her chest rose and fell quickly as her lungs tried to cope with cigarette damage and this new catastrophe. She checked her watch. It wasn't 7 o'clock yet, but perhaps stricken by guilt for leaving her, Liz was at her desk already. Beca waited. Apparently the remorse hadn't been that overwhelming.

She tried to control her breathing. How had she managed to forget all about work? If she ordered a taxi she could make it there in less than an hour. She could stop off at her flat, pick up a clean suit and get changed on the way in. The press conference was in, she checked her watch again, two hours time. Had she suffered a stroke in the night? Perhaps Hal had performed a lobotomy while she was sleeping. Never in her adult life had she forgotten about work. It was like forgetting to breathe.

While waiting for Liz to answer the phone she tried to sort her hair out. She licked her fingers and patted it down but the springy tufts kept bouncing back. She rushed into the kitchen past Hal and the children, turned on the tap and stuck her head in the sink. With hair dripping water over her mobile she grabbed a tea towel and ran back to the living room.

Why wasn't Liz at work yet? She needed to get going. She needed a cab. Hal could order one on the landline. She grabbed the yellow pages from under the coffee table and flipped until she found the taxi section.

'Can you call this number for me?' she asked stumbling into the kitchen dragging one foot behind her as she tried to wedge it in her shoe. The shoe fell off, she tripped and dropped the directory and her mobile on the floor. Water dripped onto her shoulders.

'Bugger.'

Hal and Dulcie exchanged exasperated looks and shook their heads.

'What's the problem?' he asked.

Beca stared at the trio. The breakfast things had been pushed to one side and he was sitting with Billy on his lap and Dulcie pressed up as close as she could get without pushing him off the chair. In front of him was a large wad of paper on which he was drawing. The children were mesmerised. And so was Beca. The little group looked like an advert for washing powder or breakfast cereal. The attentive father-figure, the curly-haired adoring children. Except it wasn't nauseating, it was real.

'Nothing,' she replied in answer to his question and kicked off her other shoe.

She stepped closer and watched as a picture of Dulcie the mermaid appeared. Soon she was surrounded by starfish and seashells. The real Dulcie's eyes were wide with admiration and when Hal presented the finished drawing to her she stretched up and kissed him on the cheek.

Beca returned to the living room and tried to call Liz again. This time her secretary answered on the second ring.

'He'll kill you,' she said after a lengthy explanation.

'I don't care.'

'What do you mean?' Liz sounded horrified.

'I mean I don't care. You're right, there's more to life than the bank. My friend's asked me to look after her children. She chose me. Not someone else. Me. I tell you I feel a hell of a lot more important here, than I will in front of those TV cameras this morning.'

'Blimey.'

'My thoughts entirely.' Being necessary to her friend was beyond value, it was even more important than counting the zeros on her bonus cheque. As she waited for Liz to put her through to her boss she planned what she'd do with the children for the day.

'Morley,' Sir Conrad bellowed. 'Why in God's name aren't you here?'

His tone shook Beca's new found resolve. She could feel herself backing away from her shiny halo. She hadn't asked for it anyway. She could still make it to the bank. Hal could look after the kids. He'd probably do a better job anyway.

'There's been a family crisis.' What chance was there of a little understanding from her boss?

'So what?' Sir Conrad snapped. Not much then.

'I'm looking after my friend's children.'

'You?' It was that tone again. Why did everyone always sound like that when kids and her were mentioned in the same breath?

'I can't leave them.'

'Why not?'

'They're too young.'

'And?' There was a fine line between being taciturn and plain rude.

'It's illegal for one thing.'

'Piffle. My mother used to pin me to my cot and go out to work.'

That explained a lot, but Beca couldn't take the chance Billy would grow up to be like Sir Conrad.

'It really can't be helped,' she said.

'I'll give you thirty minutes to get here.'

'I can't, not today.'

'You realise what this means?' Sir Conrad's voice was rising to a screech. 'This is gross insubordination. A firing matter. Today is the most important day in this bank's history. I insist you get here.'

It was nice to be wanted.

'I'm sorry, but I can't oblige.'

Beca held the mobile away from her ear in case shockwaves from exploding megalomaniacs could be digitally transmitted through the air. She pressed the off button on her phone and wished she could have been there to see him hit the ceiling.

She couldn't be absolutely sure she wouldn't explode herself. She'd never been fired before, never without a job, even at school there'd been the paper round and Saturdays at Jean Machine. She sat on the sofa and waited for a reaction, a *petit mal*, perhaps a bit of raving and foaming at the mouth. Nothing happened. Sure, her heart picked up pace a little but apart from that she felt fine. Just great in fact. She didn't want to cry, she wasn't shaking. She felt elated, skittish even. As she walked back into the kitchen she remained wary of a delayed catastrophic meltdown.

'Aren't I going to school?' Dulcie asked as Beca retrieved her coffee cup.

'You go to school?' she asked.

'Of course I do, silly, this is my uniform.' Dulcie pulled at her red sweatshirt.

'What about Billy?' Beca asked.

Both children guffawed behind their hands. 'He's only two.'

'Silly,' Hal added.

'Isn't it time you went home?' she asked with mock irritation.

'I could hang around. Look after Billy if you're going to see Abi. If you wanted me to.'

If she wanted him to? Of course she did. She couldn't think of anything nicer but he had a wife to get pregnant and she had the real world to rediscover. Too much hanging around with him would just make the inevitable more painful. It was time he left.

'Thanks. You've been great, but I can handle it from here,' she said reluctantly.

'You're right, I should be getting back.'

Beca watched as he put away the drawing things, pulled on his jacket and headed for the front door. With his hand on the lock he turned around to look at her, then changed his mind about whatever he was going to say and, after waving at the children, he left. Beca stared at the space he'd occupied and realised she still didn't know why he'd come to her flat the night before.

She shook the thought out of her head. There'd be plenty of time to think about it later.

'Right then,' she said holding coats out for the children. With Dulcie kitted out she heaved Billy into his buggy then negotiated the obstacle course in the hallway and only half tipped him out of his three-wheeler as she took on the steps to the front path. She stood on the pavement in front of Abi's house and looked first one way up the street, then the other. Billy strained against the buggy restraints while Dulcie hopscotched up and down the pavement. There was just one problem.

'Where exactly is your school?' she asked.

'Oh, Beca,' both children replied.

'It's this way,' Dulcie said pulling Beca by her coat pocket.

'I knew, I was just testing you. Really.'

Chapter 18

A sense of calm filled the kitchen. Dulcie and Billy were eating their supper. It was nutritious, had arrived at the table hot, and most remarkably of all, had been cooked by Beca on her own without help from anyone; if the detailed conversation with Abi from the hospital didn't count. Beca sat back, sipped her tea and watched the children wolf down their food. The gin and tonic which she so richly deserved would have to wait until they were in bed on account of the tale Claire had told her once about the mother who got drunk and left her children to drown in the bath.

It had been an exhausting day but a smile of satisfaction softened Beca's face and helped smooth out some of the fret lines. Not only had she coped brilliantly, but she'd also discovered a whole new set of skills. The children were both still alive, the house was in one piece, more or less, and she'd turned out to be a dab hand at making play-dough dinosaurs. Likewise on the happy news front, the children's father was off the critical list and in a stable condition, and Abi was due home for a brief stop-off that evening. All things considered the day was rounding off nicely. The entire house might need reassembling before Abi got back, but there was plenty of time for that. Beca had earned her present breather; she'd never worked this hard at the bank.

The bank. Now there was a thought to turn her stomach into a squelching mess again. Throughout the day, the cold realisation that she wouldn't be going back there set her insides palpitating. She was fairly certain she could, with a vast amount of grovelling, get her job back, but now that she'd been ousted she wasn't at all sure she wanted back in. It was exhilarating to have broken free. That didn't stop the sporadic fit of nerves from rattling through her.

Instead of making deals worth millions she'd built a train track for Billy that covered most of the living room floor, complete with bridges, sidings and stations. They'd done bubble painting, played in the garden, fed the goldfish and made fairy cakes with purple icing. It had been delightful, except when she remembered hers was only a caretaker role, that once the real mother was back she'd be out again. But where to? The gates to one world had been shut on her, and she didn't know the magic password to get her permanent entry into the new world. She was in limbo. In such circumstances it was better not to think, but to do.

She poured herself another cup of tea and watched the children ploughing through their mashed potato. It was amazing the volume they were putting away. They couldn't have been that hungry considering the huge quantities of raw cake mix and icing they'd eaten. A knock at the front door distracted her away from the new fear of salmonella poisoning. Both children leapt down and ran screaming with excitement towards the front door. Beca crashed into them as they suddenly stopped in the hallway. The person silhouetted in the stained glass panels of the front door was too big to be their mother and with moans of disappointment the pair retreated back to the kitchen. Beca opened the front door.

On the doorstep stood a smartly turned out woman in astonishingly bright clothes with make-up and hair to match. She was as well co-ordinated as an air stewardess.

'Holy Christ, Claire. What have you done to yourself?' Beca asked the apparition before her.

Claire smiled and fluffed her hair back with one hand. 'It's nothing, darling. Just a little self improvement.' With that she swept into the house leaving Beca slack jawed in an orange slipstream. By the time she caught up with her in the kitchen she was trying to maul the children.

'You poor, poor darlings.' Claire reached for Dulcie but kissed air as she slipped under her arms and ran to Beca. Billy wasn't as nimble and got caught in Claire's embrace. He emerged moments later indignant, red-faced and sporting an orange mouth-shaped oil slick on one cheek.

Beca squeezed her lips together trying to smother her amusement. She should perhaps be defending Billy in some way but frankly nothing was more pressing than Claire's metamorphosed state. The last time they'd met, which was only four months ago in Norfolk, she'd been her usual enormous, dowdy self, proud to wear Eddie's old shirts with baby sick and snot epaulettes. That woman was gone, instead there stood a vastly reduced version. That's wasn't to say she was slim, rather that she was the size of a small barn as opposed to an enormous one. Even more surprising were her clothes. She was wearing a neat cream silk shirt tucked into floaty silk trousers of the most astonishing dried apricot colour. Perhaps on its own the outfit wouldn't have been so startling, even on Claire, but with the co-ordinating scarf twisted neatly around her neck, the gold brooch and all that make-up. It was terrifying. She looked like the sort of woman who bought limited-edition porcelain ornaments as advertised in *The Lady*.

The sound of whimpering snapped Beca back to attention. Billy had taken the assault more seriously than she'd suspected and only the enticement of two more fairy cakes could persuade him back to the table to finish his supper. Claire hadn't noticed the damage she'd inflicted, she was too busy assessing the state of the kitchen.

'I spoke to Abi,' she said as she looked around. 'Tom's in a stable condition.'

'I know.' Beca could feel her hackles rising. Why did Claire assume she knew nothing?

'She'll be back later.'

'I know.'

'And Sally's coming around to lend moral support.'

'I know.' What she didn't know was why Claire was there. Evidently Abi had been too preoccupied, or plain scared, to tell her she was coming.

Claire cut across her thoughts. 'I went to the supermarket on my way here to get some basic things. It's all in the car. Could you go and bring it in while I start on this lot?' She gestured towards the washing-up with a look of weary self-sacrifice, then unbuttoning her cuffs, she rolled up her sleeves and found an apron to put on. With that Beca gathered she'd been dismissed. She didn't mind being excused the chore of washing-up, far from it, but to have bossy Claire barging in and taking over when she'd been doing just fine was bloody annoying.

Five trips to Claire's estate car later and she'd done as she'd been told.

'Just leave it there', Claire said without turning from the sink. 'I'll put it away later.' Because naturally Beca wouldn't have a clue where to begin. It was easy to see how Eddie got away with doing sod all.

'So what's with the new look?' Beca asked, sitting down with the children.

Claire gave a nonchalant shrug. 'It was nothing. I had a few pounds to shift. Not much more than that.'

Beca chuckled inwardly at her under statement and was ready to dig deeper when she was distracted by a new smell. It had the strong odour of cooked mince and she presumed it must have wafted in from outside because the sausages for supper hadn't smelled anything quite so meaty. Billy's red straining face brought the source of the smell closer to home.

'Billy's having a poo,' Dulcie said with a large grin. Her brother gave her a Judas look.

'Yes, I'd come to that conclusion myself,' Beca replied.

'Right, off we go then,' Claire said drying her hands on a tea towel and heading for Billy like a Soviet health spa matron with a colonic hose.

The two-year-old screamed, abandoned the remains of his fairy cake and threw himself off his chair. "Eca do it. 'Eca do it,' he wailed and attached himself to Beca's legs.

Her eyes stung with tears, her throat tightened. Fanfares rang out in her head. What a glorious moment. What a magnificent smack in the face for Supermother Claire. Billy knew what a complete incompetent Beca was. He'd spent the day trying to put his own nappies on because she just couldn't get to grips with the sticky tabs. Yet he wanted her to wipe his bottom. Glory be. Beca did little to tone down her satisfaction as she led Billy in a slow, knock-kneed shuffle upstairs to the bathroom.

'Dulcie, would you like your bath now?' she asked.

'OK,' Dulcie cheerily replied. Another victory. Beca punched the air.

As she climbed the stairs she swallowed hard and hoped her courage wouldn't fail her. She'd never done a crapped-in nappy before.

Maybe it was the tiddly mosaic tiles that made it feel as though the bathroom walls were crowding in. The room could have been the size of a 25-metre swimming pool and would still have been too small for the task at hand. Dulcie pulled down the lid of the loo and hauled herself onto it for a prime view. Billy very self-sufficiently got the changing mat out from behind the sink. He rolled awkwardly onto it trying to keep his bottom from making contact with the mat and watched Beca as though waiting for the first sign of cowardice.

It wasn't long in coming. She looked at his sagging trousers with trepidation. Despite the layers of clothing and bulky nappy, the smell was close to unbearable. She breathed through her mouth and gingerly pulled his trousers down. Then began to unfasten the tabs.

'You haven't got the wipes ready,' Dulcie said. 'And you need a bag.'

'Of course I do.' Beca's laugh was hollow. What she really wanted was to shout for help.

Dulcie slid off the seat and fetched the necessary tools. Beca took a deep breath and undid Billy's nappy. Her recoil was involuntary. 'Holy fudge. What the hell have you been eating? Rancid hippo flesh? This is disgusting.'

Dulcie giggled. 'It's even worse when he's had sweetcorn.'

'Are you still here? You must be nuts. Can you fetch me a gas mask.'

Dulcie's giggle grew into a laugh.

'Don't breathe so deeply, you'll scar your lungs,' Beca instructed.

Billy began to laugh as well. It was a spluttering, cheeky little chortle and Beca knew as soon as it began that she was in trouble. He rolled over onto his front to share the big poo joke with his sister. The unfastened nappy followed him then slid away as he stood.

'No. For the love of God, lie down.'

For a millisecond she considered catching the falling nappy, but self-preservation won over and she let it fall crap side down onto the floor. She watched as gravity played its part, pulling the runnier bits between the cracks in the floorboards. Never had she seen such a volume of shit before, certainly not spread over such a wide area. It would be easier to move house, to simply abandon everything and start up again somewhere uncontaminated than to attempt to clean up this dung heap. Beca picked Billy up, stood him in the bath, pulled his remaining clothes off and turned the shower on.

Minutes stretched into hours. Beca was certain it had taken the entire evening and half the night to clear up after Billy, then bath and put them to bed. Neither child had been sympathetic to her exhausted condition and had insisted on the full bedtime ritual.

Beca staggered downstairs expecting it to be well past midnight. Instead only an hour had passed in which time Sally had arrived and put away the children's toys. The camp leader was cooking supper. The smell of Billy's crap stuck to the lining of Beca's throat like tar. She could taste it. It would be a long while before she could eat again. She kissed Sally hello despite fears of contamination. After exchanging some boggle-eyed looks about Claire, she fixed a round of gin and tonics and, like a leper, she took hers out to the front step to purge herself with cigarette smoke.

She knew watching the end of the road wouldn't bring Abi back any sooner, but time and again her eyes wandered towards the corner where the ambulance had disappeared the night before. Each time she held her gaze longer than was sensible.

She smoked one cigarette, then lit another. The gin settled nicely in her stomach and with each sip the blanket of numbness got heavier. She took a long last drag on her second cigarette and exhaled smoke into the cold evening air. Her fingers opened slightly to let the butt drop and she ground it out on the tiled path. She walked to the edge of the kerb and dropped it down a drain, then turning back to the house took one final glance towards the end of the road. As she looked away a pair of headlights swooped around the corner spotlighting the houses opposite.

The car pulled up in front of her and Abi climbed out. They smiled and hugged each other. Abi's shoulders and back were stiff and Beca could feel her body trembling beneath her coat.

'Let's go in,' she said steering Abi towards the front door. 'They're both asleep; went out like lights. It must have been the vodka I put in their milk.'

'That's good. I hope they won't have hangovers in the morning. Have they been much trouble?'

'Not at all. Although you might want to consider putting Billy on a vegetarian diet.'

'Oh dear.'

'Indeed.'

Abi hesitated at the front door. 'Do you have your cigarettes on you?'

'Naturally.'

'Good. I feel the need for one.'

'A whole one?'

'After the day I've had, absolutely.'

'You can have the whole pack if you want, only don't be sick.'

'Just one. I don't want to start anything habit forming.'

The two friends sat on the low wall that bordered the front garden and stretched their legs out across the pavement. Abi bent over the lighter that Beca held cupped in her hands. When her cigarette was lit she straightened up and watched the cloud of smoke from her lungs dissolve into the night.

'Funny. Don't usually see so many stars,' she said.

'Not much cloud cover.'

'I suppose that's what it is.'

'So how was it?' Beca asked.

'Oh, you know, just the average day. Tom hovered between life and death for most of it. Having to phone his mother was the worst part.'

'He's stable now though, isn't he?'

'Amazingly, given the state of his heart. The doctors say he should make a full recovery in time, although the cigars and booze are off the menu from now on.'

'How do you feel?'

'Like crap.'

'I'm not surprised. Did you get any rest?'

Abi shook her head. 'There was a chair in his room, but I was too frightened to sleep.'

Beca put her arm around Abi's shoulder and gave her a squeeze. They both looked up at the stars again.

'It's funny how unimportant things can play on your mind in a crisis, but you know I spent much of the time wondering what Hal was doing with you last night. You promised you wouldn't see him.'

Beca smiled. 'Not guilty. He turned up to collect the money I owe him. At least I think that's why. The funny thing is, he never really said.'

'And that was that?'

'More or less. He told me I was incapable of love, and,' Beca took a deep breath to ward off any tears, 'then he said he and Sophie are trying for a baby.'

'What was the point of telling you?'

'I don't know. It just slipped into the conversation.'

'And it hurt?'

'Oh yes.'

'Is that why he did it?'

Beca looked confused.

'I just wondered what made him say such a thing.'

'Presumably because he didn't realise it would mean anything to me.'

'Which makes him bloody obtuse. It must be obvious how you feel about him.'

'Not really. I'm a good actress.'

'If you say so.'

'What are you hinting at?'

Abi shrugged. 'Nothing. I don't know. Something's not right about his behaviour. If he just wanted the cheque why didn't he pick up the phone?'

Beca couldn't answer that one, but no doubt she'd spend plenty of time trying to work it out.

Abi bypassed the kitchen and went straight upstairs to see her children. Beca fixed herself and the others a fresh round of drinks then sat and watched Claire busy herself in front of Abi's stove. Her arse really was considerably smaller than the last time she'd seen it swathed so unforgivably in floral leggings. Perhaps it was an optical illusion. The brightness of her trousers contrasting so sharply with her pale shirt to create an effect a bit like those ziggurat camouflaged boats in the First World War. Confuse the eye and see nothing. Beca pondered this as she drank.

Light footsteps sounded on the stairs and Beca turned to see Abi coming down. She was moving slowly, her mind somewhere else entirely. As she reached the bottom step, the hallway light fell upon her face and Beca was surprised to see how fragile she looked. The departing daylight had snatched the aura of invincibility away from her. She looked young and old, vulnerable and weary at the same time.

Her face changed with a smile as she entered the kitchen. Beca could see her mouth shaping up to say hello.

'Fuck me, Claire. What have you done to yourself,' she said instead.

Claire spun around from the stove. 'You look dreadful, poor darling.' With arms spread she rushed forward and Abi braced herself for impact. 'Have a hug,' Claire cooed.

'But your clothes,' Abi managed as the air was pressed out of her lungs. 'They're so, so amazing.'

Sally stopped laying the table and gave Abi a more gentle hug. 'She's had her colours done.'

'She's an Autumn.' Beca held out a glass of wine.

'Sounds intriguing,' Abi said as she took the drink and sat down.

'How's Tom?' Sally asked.

'Not dead.' Abi's laugh was strained, it wasn't the sort that had Beca clamouring to join in. 'It's been one hell of a day,' she added and rubbed her forehead with the heel of her hand.

'You don't have to talk about it if you don't want to,' Sally said.

'There's not much to tell.' She drained her glass. 'Only to say I don't ever want to go through it again.'

Beca poured her some more wine.

'More importantly,' Abi said between gulps, 'What's all this colours business?' Her voice was shrill and louder than usual. She was overdoing things in an effort to sound up-beat and Beca didn't know whether it was best to let her change the subject or steer her back to Tom again. What did she know about letting out pent-up feelings? She was a graduate of the keep-it-bottled-up school.

Typically, Claire grabbed the opportunity to talk about herself. 'It's very simple,' she said while serving up the large slabs of meat she'd been cooking. 'There are four seasons, each representing a different palette of colours. I happen to be an Autumn.'

Beca wasn't paying attention; the incident of Billy's bottom was fresh in her mind as she edged her steak away from under her nose.

'There's more,' Claire said. 'I've gone into business.'

The others looked at her expectantly.

'Claire's Colours and Makeovers.'

One involuntary guffaw might have passed unnoticed, but three simultaneously were hard to ignore. Even for thick-skinned Claire.

'Mock if you wish,' she said, 'but I'll show you after supper.'

'You've brought your kit?' Sally's enthusiasm was clear to see.

'How do we know you're any good?' Beca asked cynically.

'My trainer says I'm naturally gifted. I have a good eye.'

'For what?' Sally asked.

'Judging which colours and shades of make-up suit a person best.' This from the woman who'd struggled with black eye liner at school. 'Laugh all you want,' she said pointing her finger at Beca, 'but I personally know of one woman who met her future husband the day after having her colours done.'

'Well, clearly any advice you can give me on the advancement of my marriage prospects will be gratefully received.'

Claire did that cat's arse thing with her mouth that Beca loved so much. It was turning out to be quite a good evening all things considered. She had no job, no man and no baby, but there was plenty of gin and wine, and Claire was always good for a laugh.

'It'll take more than a few new clothes and an eye shadow to turn my life around,' Abi said. She was right, which left Beca with no grounds for complaint whatsoever.

The others looked like they were considering their luck in the silence that followed. Abi looked up. 'Sorry,' she said with a weak smile. 'I didn't mean to sound so miss-ish.'

'You didn't,' Beca said putting her hand on top of Abi's.

Sally put her hand on Beca's, then Claire did the same to Sally's. They smiled at each other and looked at the hand stack. It had been their gesture of solidarity back in the days when a box of ten fags lasted a week and a big bottle of cider was enough to cure even the worst of their troubles. If only life were still so simple.

'I'm going to call my lawyer and get her to cancel the divorce papers,' Abi said after a while.

'Are you sure that's what you want?' Sally asked.

Abi shrugged. 'It's very difficult to stop loving someone. Tom says he's sorry and I believe him.'

'Is that a good enough reason?' Beca chose her words with care.

'It's good enough,' Abi said. 'The children love him. I can't bear the idea of them missing him.'

'What's in it for you?' Claire asked.

'I think he means to change,' Abi replied. 'He's keen to try again. The doctors have given him a second chance, it seems unfair not to do the same.'

Claire broke the long silence that followed. 'I think you're doing the right thing. He's paid a hefty price. Not that I'm suggesting his heart attack was punishment for his infidelity, although there is an element of natural justice to it. Perhaps now is the time to let him off the hook.'

'What if he has another affair?' Beca asked.

'He'll be straight out.'

'You're sure about that?' Beca pressed.

'Positive.'

'In which case I agree with Claire.' Beca took credit for this softening of attitude; it had nothing to do with Hal.

'He's a lucky man,' Sally said.

'Damned right he is,' Abi said. 'Enough of all this serious talk.' She pulled her hand out of the stack, 'I need a makeover.'

By the time the others had cleared away the supper things, Claire had set up business in the living room. Cases were opened to display an array of cosmetics and a free-standing mirror with light bulbs wired to the frame was waiting in the middle of the room.

'Who's going to be first?' Claire asked, eyeing them each in turn.

Beca counted to three before she felt the first nudge in her back from Sally.

'Who do you think?' Beca replied.

'Sit here.' Claire held out a chair for her in front of the 1000 watt mirror. 'Are you wearing any make-up?'

Beca squinted at her reflection. 'Not so you'd notice in this light.' Claire waited for confirmation. 'Just whatever's left from yesterday and the mascara borrowed from Abi.'

Sally and Abi groaned with distaste.

'I've been busy,' Beca said to justify her slovenliness.

'It'll need to come off.'

'All of it?'

'Completely.'

There was giggling now from the safety of the sofa where the other two were ensconced with a bottle of wine. Beca took a cleansing pad from Claire and wiped off what little make-up still clung to her face.

'Put this on, please.' Claire passed Beca a white towelling hair band. It was pointless fighting. She looked at herself in the mirror again and rather wished she hadn't.

'What we're doing here is trying to find Beca's palette of colours,' Claire said, addressing her audience. 'Seasons represent different shades and tones of the same colours.' At this point she held up a board with four spectrums of colours fanned out into quarter circles. Abi and Sally nodded and sucked their cheeks intently. 'We can all wear blues, reds and greens, it's just a matter of finding the tone that suits our complexion best.' Beca was sceptical.

It was a well-polished performance. Claire had the other two hooked judging by the way they hovered on the edge of the sofa.

'As an Autumn,' Claire continued, 'I should wear russet and moss colours, deep oranges and dark reds. In other words, tones that are warm and earthy with a dark yellow hue, rather than blue.'

Beca was prepared to pay large amounts of money not to be an Autumn. But then she wasn't taking any of this triviality seriously so what would it matter if she was one? It was puerile rubbish, but at least it was keeping Abi smiling which counted for something.

Claire then swathed Beca's neck and shoulders with large pieces of shiny coloured nylon. Sludge green was followed by a blinding lime. White vied with vanilla. Claire flicked between competing colours pursing her lips and scrutinising Beca's face. Next she tried two blue scarves. To Beca's eyes they were identical, but apparently they brought about remarkable changes when held close to her face.

'It makes you look so old,' Sally said of the darker shade.

'It's incredible. The bags under your eyes completely vanish with the lighter one,' Abi chipped in.

The mention of bags persuaded Beca to take matters a little more seriously. Claire stood back and chewed her bottom lip. She angled her head to the right, then the left, all the while concentrating on Beca's face. With a flourish she whisked away the lighter of the blue scarves to show the darker one underneath. Then she flicked it back. She nodded to herself with satisfaction.

'You're a Spring,' she announced.

A Spring? Beca did not brim with confidence at this pronouncement. 'That sounds rather insipid to me,' she said.

'Not at all. Apple green, dove grey, all the pastels.'

'Pastels?' Beca spat the word out. 'You mean peach, yellow and cream?'

'They'll work wonderfully with your complexion.'

'Bugger that. They're loo roll colours. I want to wear black.'

'Sorry. Black is for Winters only.'

'Then make me a Winter.'

'You're a Spring.'

'I don't want to be.'

Claire folded her arms across her chest. 'Wearing black just heaps years onto your skin. It makes you look sallow and old.'

'Practically everything I own is black.'

'Indeed,' Claire said with a flick of her eyebrows.

'Meaning?'

'I can only give you my opinion,' Claire said with slighted professional pride. 'I can't make you take my advice and act on it.'

Too bloody right she couldn't.

'But I promise you, it'll transform your life,' Claire continued. 'I've known people to get job promotions purely from changing the colours they wear.'

That could be tricky given the current circumstances but there seemed little point in updating the others now. 'In which case I'm completely sold. Out with the black, in with the beige. If I'm not chairman of the bank in a year, I'll sue.'

'Speaking of work, were they OK about you missing the conference?' Abi asked.

'Sure.'

'Your boss didn't mind?' Sally sounded surprised.

'Sir Conrad? Not in the least. Said I could have as much time as I needed. So in fact, I could look after Dulcie and Billy tomorrow, if you wanted.'

'Christ, he fired you,' Abi said.

'No, he didn't. Really,' Beca said shaking her head.

'You're telling me Sir Conrad let you prioritise him out of first place?' Abi asked.

'Sounds unlikely, doesn't it.'

'Very,' Claire put in.

'So he did fire you?' Abi looked horrified.

'Yes, but,'

Abi cut across. 'I don't know what to say. I'm so sorry. What if I called him and explained.'

'See, that's why I wasn't going to tell you, yet. You don't need to apologise. In fact I should be thanking you.'

The looks on their faces made it clear she wasn't convincing any of them.

'Seriously, I'm fine about it. I've been there way too long. This is a good thing. I'm feeling very positive about it.' She failed to add, only between bouts of gut-churning fear.

Chapter **19**

As a woman of leisure there was no reason whatsoever why Beca shouldn't be doing what she was. There was nothing to be embarrassed about, women did such things all the time. But she wasn't one of them, which perhaps explained why the curtains were still drawn. She felt self-conscious and what made the whole distasteful business even more unpleasant was the certain knowledge that if her mother caught her at it, she would approve.

Beca came away from Abi's house knowing she had three great friends. More importantly she knew thanks to Claire's Colours and Makeovers, which had been endorsed by none other than the American Association of Beauty Technicians, that she was a Spring. Never in her life would she have considered giving such a concept brain space. Women had chained themselves to railings so she could break free of such mindless thoughts and there she was, letting them all down. She was appalled with herself. The whole idea of wearing the 'right colours' belonged in the pages of a 1950s *Woman's Own.* Outside the sun was shining, the air was cold and clear. There were any number of more interesting, intellectually challenging things she could be getting on with. Instead she was sitting on her bedroom floor surrounded by every item of clothing she owned. Her big wardrobe and the ones in both spare rooms had been emptied. All the chests of drawers and cupboards had come under similar attack. When pulled together in a tangled mess, it was astonishing just how many clothes she owned and now each and every one of them was undergoing rigorous comparison with a nasty little plastic wallet of Spring colours that Claire had sent her home with. Unemployed for only one day and already she'd sunk so low.

According to the makeover guru, peach was a 'good' colour for her to wear. It was one of her '100% colours', which meant if she was certifiably insane she could wear it from head to toe. No doubt such an eye-catching outfit would go nicely with the multi-coloured Spring silk scarf that she had found herself parting with good cash for. And she really hadn't drunk that much. Memories of Princess Diana's trousseau stuck in her mind. What little there was left of it.

A question that had run through the hollow spaces in her head since first light when she started on this epic task was, why? Why had she taken Claire, whose opinion regarding anything sartorial was worth bugger all, seriously? And why, despite knowing this, was she prepared to consign nearly ninety-five percent of all her clothes to the nearest charity shop? It was small comfort to know that Abi and Sally had been equally drawn in and at least she hadn't signed up for the scarf tying evening class.

Perhaps she was doing her colours precisely because it was so mindless and she needed something to keep her from thinking too much about Hal, or rather what Abi had said about him. It was either jangled nerves from a hangover or paranoia that kept bringing her back to Abi's comments and the possibility that he was playing games with her. Could he really be on some kind of revenge kick after all these years? It didn't seem feasible, but then she'd never made any pretence of understanding him, or any man come to that.

She had decided to allow herself the morning to complete the facile exercise of colour checking her clothes and, therefore, was not unreasonably annoyed to find herself checking the Springness of her shoes at 5 o'clock in the afternoon. Exactly how close were they going to get to her face anyway? And why, for God's sake, was it so important to know if her pink Jimmy Choo slingbacks fell into the Spring camp or not? She'd been right to keep those curtains closed. Dementia was a private thing.

The sound of the doorbell brought her back to the real world with a jolt and it dawned on her that she hadn't spoken to anyone all day, except Mrs Butler and only then because she'd run out of milk. But she was far too shoe-colour focussed to be cordial and didn't want to talk to anyone. The person ringing the bell got ignored.

The doorbell rang again. She blew the tannin film off the top of her cold tea and drank it. Resisting the urge to see whether the mug colour conformed, she looked at the sparse collection of clothes she was now compelled to wear in order to look her best. Why did the colours remind her of bridge and sherry? Why did setting lotion and rollers spring to mind? And the smell of Deep Heat and Bluebird coffee? She tried to force all the pieces together into a temporal jigsaw puzzle. She looked at the wallet of shiny nylon colours and then it clicked. Her grandmother. The only person who had ever consciously worn violet and then dyed her hair to match.

It was a relief to have finally worked out what had been causing that unsettled feeling. Perhaps Claire was right about wearing lilac, maybe she would look less haggard, but she would also look like her grandmother. Skipping a generation and plunging straight into old age had not been her plan.

The doorbell rang again. This time it was more insistent. It couldn't be Abi, she was certain of that. They'd spoken first thing in the morning and Beca had been keeping an ear out for the phone. Besides, Abi had most likely abandoned Tom's bedside to assess her clothes for their Summer worthiness. Beca really ought to tell her not to bother.

The next time the doorbell rang, the person doing the ringing forgot to remove their finger which meant that Beca now hated them. She got up from the only bare piece of sisal carpet in the bedroom and waded through clothes to get to the door. As she ran downstairs to the ground floor, the person on the other side of the door had taken to playing a frantic tune with the buzzer. Beca was ready for bare knuckle fighting.

'What?!' she screamed once she'd flung open the door. Hal remained impassive. Possibly that smile of his grew a little wider. Beca bounced back as if she'd run into a pane of glass.

'Oh,' she said when she'd gathered her thoughts. It wasn't an aloof sort of 'Oh' accompanied by an arched eyebrow, it was rather more of a gormless, round-eyed, spittle-dribbling 'Oh.'

'I called you at the bank but they said you didn't work there. In fact the first receptionist I spoke to had never heard of you,' he said.

'Fast turn around. She must have started yesterday.' God Almighty, hadn't he got the message last time? She didn't want to see him again.

'And?' Hal asked.

'What?' Aftershocks were addling her brain.

'Don't you work there any more?' He spoke slowly for her benefit.

'No.' Did he really have to angle his head in such a provocative way?

'Why not? Can I come in by the way?' Hal asked.

'No. I got fired. It's no big deal. How did you know I was in?'

'Intuition.'

'You mean Mrs Butler?' Beca asked, trying to block his path with a casually outstretched arm. She was too late and had to guess what Hal said next because he'd already walked past her into the hall and was on his way upstairs.

'Hey!' she said. Full marks once again for such brilliant erudition. It was almost as classy as her first monosyllabic offering. Beca followed him in, her heart clattering around her ribcage with delight. She hated herself for being so pleased to see him. She hated him for coming, so why was she bubbling with excitement? Her mind raced. Get him out. Make him stay. Be horrid. Be nice. She wanted to scream. It was so taxing being at such odds all the time. She needed a break.

Hal walked into the living room and looked around. Now that he was inside he didn't look quite his usual calm self. 'You making coffee?' he asked as he fiddled with the label at the back of his jumper.

'No.' She had to be emphatic. He was married, he couldn't stay.

Hal rubbed the back of his head. 'How is Tom?'

Now she felt like a mean-spirited bitch. 'He's much better. I'll let Abi know you asked.'

'How's she doing?'

'Fine. She's at the hospital again today. Claire's with the children. I'm looking after them tomorrow, and Dan and Sally are going to do a couple of days together. Everyone's doing their bit.'

'That's nice. Abi's lucky to have such good friends.' His pacing was putting her on edge.

'Yes.' She hesitated and took a deep breath. 'Look, I meant what I said before. I know things got a bit blurred what with Tom's heart attack and the way you helped me so brilliantly.' Didn't he just? His fitness for fatherhood was undeniable. Focus. 'But the deal really is off. I don't want to have sex with you any more. Besides, I'm not ovulating so there's no point.' Phew. It was out. She'd done it. Abi would have been proud.

She was fixing him with a steely-eyed stare to show she meant business when it suddenly dawned on her that perhaps he wasn't there for that reason. Maybe he'd come for something which had nothing to do with sex at all. Her heart took a white-knuckle ride down to her anti-slip socks. Was it likely she'd ever recover from the mortification? Her body stiffened with shock and she squeezed her eyes shut in the vain hope that when she opened them again he'd be gone.

Truth was she didn't have to open them for quite some time because she'd never been big on kissing with her eyes open.

Hal kissed her hard, like a man who wanted to, not because he was being paid. He held her so tightly she wasn't sure she could have stopped him, even if she'd wanted him to; which she most certainly did not. She kissed him back and considered whether to faint with delight. Wretched, wanton hussy her puritanical side shrieked. Beca didn't care. Hal wanted her right then and there. She wanted him just as bad. They tore at each other's clothes, pulling at all obstacles and made love on the living room floor. Thank God she'd kept her Spring-conforming knickers on.

Beca had never abandoned herself in such a way before. Even during the act of sex she always stayed in control. That was the way she operated. She might pretend to give way to wild passion, to let all her animal urges out, but she'd never actually really done it. Not like this. Not until now. Her body hadn't asked for permission, it hadn't given her any warning of what to expect. The force of her feelings was like nothing she'd ever experienced before, it was very close to being frightening.

Hal didn't say a word, neither during, nor after, except for 'Oh God' a few times and then finally, after they'd finished, he said, 'Let's go to the bedroom,' although she might have imagined that. Anyway, she didn't have a lot to say about the matter because next he picked her up and carried her. Moments later he stood in the doorway to her bedroom, swaying from the exertion of carrying her upstairs but valiantly holding on.

'Jesus, have you been burgled?' he asked, awestruck by the chaos in her room.

Holy shit, she'd forgotten about the mess. She jumped out of his arms and landed awkwardly. Banging her shoulder on the door frame was all that stopped her from falling head first into the mountain of clothing that was engulfing her room. If the municipal dump relocated there it couldn't be much worse. This was very definitely not the impression she wanted to create.

'You could do with a bit of a clear out.'

'That's what I was doing before you showed up,' Beca replied. 'It won't take a minute to sort,' she said as she scrambled over the foothills.

There was little she could do to make the moment more alluring, a stark naked woman hurling piles of clothes off her unmade bed and onto the floor was unlikely to be a turn-on. She straightened the sheets, plumped up the pillows and then shrieked as she turned to find him practically on top of her already. She hadn't been expecting to hand out an invitation first, but even so. Still, there seemed little point getting formal now. They fell back onto the bed with their lips locked and their bodies clamped tightly together.

They made love as though they'd been starved of each other, at least that was how Beca felt. She was hungry for him, she wanted to touch and lick his body as if feeling him was her only means of survival. She couldn't be sure about Hal. She didn't understand what was driving him to make love so voraciously. It seemed like he was trying to work a longstanding irritation out of his system.

Then it was over and they lay loosely in each other's arms. Still Hal didn't speak because exhausted, flushed and sweating he had fallen asleep. Beca choked on the urge to wake him up and shout how much she loved him. Every inch of her tingled. She felt utterly alive, properly awake for the first time. She'd never felt so exhilarated in her life.

She forced herself to lie still and listen to his quietening heart, but her brain re-asserted itself. She didn't want it to. She didn't want to be brought back down to earth. If only the moment could be kept, preserved forever, but even as she wished it, she could feel the warmth from their love-making leave her body. She moved closer into his arms and pulled the sheets up over them both. He was so hot and yet she grew colder. The coldness of reality. Her throat tightened and she felt as though great weights were being laid across her chest. Her eyes burned and she knew she was going to cry. The moment had been spoilt, from here on in she was back in the real world with all the hurt and unanswered questions. She needed to know why. Why he'd come to her flat, why he'd wanted to make love so passionately. If she woke him up she could find out, but it didn't matter why he had come. The truth remained the same. He was a married man and she and his wife deserved better.

Beca padded downstairs in her dressing gown and made herself a drink. She went to the living room and scanned the rows of videos and DVDs searching for a film that fitted her mood. *Fatal Attraction* was an obvious choice, right now she and Glenn Close had a lot in common. But she didn't want to align herself with a psychotic bunny-boiler, besides there was something creepy about Michael Douglas. Beca wanted clean love, no tongues, just smouldering looks and passion with clothes on. A 1950s weepy with a broad shouldered hero and a small-waisted blonde. It had to be *All That Heaven Allows*, and even though she knew Rock Hudson was only ever pretending, she didn't care. She wanted to believe Jane Wyman was the only woman he'd ever need.

The director spared none of the corn. The strings in the orchestra did their stuff and Beca cried. A shower of pink apple blossom blew from the trees as the camera zoomed in and she cried a bit more. She tried to focus on Jane and Rock but real life wouldn't let her. It kept pulling her out. She loved Hal. A married man. A happily married man who fancied a shag with someone who wasn't his wife. It was bad enough being in love with an unavailable man, but to be in love with an unavailable arsehole was too awful. What gave him the right to come crashing into her flat and expect sex?

At least she had an excuse, not a very good one perhaps, but nonetheless, in her defence, she did happen to be in love with him. It was all his fault, every sweaty moment of it. He should have known better. He was the one with a wife. God, he was no better than Abi's husband. No, in fact he was worse, at least Tom wasn't trying to get his wife pregnant at the same time. When it came down to it, she was no better than that trollop he was screwing.

Beca flicked the off button on the remote control and stared at the black screen. Evening had crept up on her and daylight had stolen from the room. She could see the mound of his clothes silhouetted in the gloom. Draining her glass, she picked up his things and ran up the stairs.

Tears were streaming down her face before she'd even started.

'Wake up. Get up and get out of my home.' She threw his clothes at him harder than she'd meant to and the buckle on his belt clipped his mouth. She flinched when she saw blood. Her resolve drained away but she stamped on the urge to nurse him better; his wife could do that for him.

'What's going on?' Hal fingered the cut on his lip. He looked so bewildered. If he'd been angry she could have handled it all much better. If she'd been able to fight with him then she wouldn't have felt so bad.

She kept going. She had to now that she'd started. 'You're a bastard. This was never supposed to happen. This,' she said waving her arms at her mutilated bed, 'was not part of the deal. Sex was supposed to be business.'

'God, Beca listen.'

Tears tightened her voice into a strained squeak. 'You said you wanted to have a baby with her but you're here screwing me.'

Hal sat on the edge of the bed and rubbed his eyes. 'I wish you'd let me explain.' There was no fight in his voice, just tiredness.

'Why? Because you think I'll buy any of your lies.'

'Beca would you shut up for a minute.'

'No I won't. None of this is fair on me.'

'I want to talk to you. I've been trying for ages. Will you please listen to me.' He was beginning to sound cross.

Beca sniffed and waited.

He ran his fingers through his hair. 'I don't know where to begin. Come here a minute,' he said patting the bed next to him.

Beca stayed put. He wasn't going to get cosy with her now. 'I'm not going to be your mistress, if that's what you're wondering.' Frankly she would, but that was her sordid secret.

'Tell me how you feel.'

'About what?'

'Christ, Beca. Us.'

'There isn't any "us".'

'I need to know.' He was angry now.

'Isn't one woman enough for you?' Beca fell over a bag of clothes. When she got back up he had moved across the room and was only inches away from her.

'That's not the point.' He was so close she could feel his hot breath on her face.

'Look,' she said. 'You're a good shag, but that's as far as it goes. I'm not in love with you.' She turned away then added a little laugh to sound more convincing. 'Nor am I ever likely to be.' She didn't have to do this. No one was making her do the sensible thing. He could come and visit whenever he wanted. 'If you're trying to wreck your marriage, don't use me to do it.' She couldn't get much breezier than that.

The lines on Hal's face hardened. 'I'm not,' he said.

'Then why are you here?'

'It's probably just as well you're never going to give me the chance to explain.'

'Explain what?'

'It doesn't matter. It was a bad idea from the start.'

Beca was glad she was pressed up against the wall. She watched Hal gather up his clothes and put them on. He didn't seem in any hurry. Beca tried breathing deeply to plug the molten fury building up in her chest. If he left within the next thirty seconds he'd be out before she screamed. Inside her head a clock was ticking. The door slammed after twenty-five.

The valve finally blew on her sanity and the flat filled with Beca's shouts. The need to do damage, to tear at things, to destroy them was unstoppable. She wanted to rip, bite and smash, but above all she wanted to yell out her indignation. Her clothes lying around her bore the brunt. She kicked and grabbed, randomly pulling at seams and buttons. She sank down onto the shredded remains of her clothes, rubbed her elbow where she'd banged it and looked around her. She was too angry for tears now. She caught her reflection in the tall mirror that had survived the onslaught. Her instinct was to throw something at it but she hesitated. Instead she stared at the wild-eyed red face. Her dressing gown had fallen open at the waist, her hair was poking up where she'd tugged at it. She looked like a raving inmate of Bedlam. Mrs Butler could do a fair trade selling tickets for a public viewing of her lunatic neighbour.

Had she bothered washing that morning? It was something she'd meant to do but kept putting off along with brushing her teeth. She'd been so engrossed with Claire's bloody colours. Still, it showed Hal couldn't be that particular about who he went to bed with. The air in her flat was stale, the smell of sweat and sex hung heavily around her. It clung to her skin and she could feel it within her, growing with every breath. She was coarse and unkempt, a gin swilling tart that could be screwed and thrown aside, no better than one of Hogarth's scabby trollops. It was downhill to the sewers for her from now on. Panic burned in her empty stomach. She rubbed her arms and legs to wipe away the self-loathing, but it was too deep within her. She had to get out.

The T-shirt she pulled over her head was inside out but she was beyond caring. She found tracksuit bottoms under the bed where she'd flung them earlier. Her fingers shook as she pulled the laces on her trainers. She yanked at them, snapping a nail, but they had to be tight. Then she fled her flat as if her life depended on it.

Street lights lit up the pavement, pointing out with deep shadows the jutting paving slabs that were poised to trip her up as she ran. She flew over them, ignoring her jarring ankles and shins which ached with each foot fall. There was no time for warm-up stretches, she wasn't out for a run, she was escaping. Pure white anger drove her on. Her mind burnt like magnesium wire, incapable of rational thought, empty except for the screaming.

She ran so fast that she struggled to keep from stumbling over her feet. Her arms worked like pistons pumping backwards and forwards, driving her on. Icy air bit into her hot cheeks and dried her mouth, its frosty tendrils caught in her throat and reached down into her lungs, stealing her breath away. She wanted to be cold, it helped blot out the pain. One mile, then another and still she ran.

She reached the edge of Holland Park and turned sharply into a steep, narrow path that edged the park all the way to Kensington. High garden walls rose up either side hiding the enormous stucco houses beyond. The path was badly lit and eerie, but right now Beca was frightened of nothing or no one. She looked up at the dark path rising into the distance, put her head down and carried on. Her speed slowed, she tried to fight the gradient but her calf muscles rebelled. A laugh exploded into the air. How ironic. Hal had turned out to be just like her father after all, just another man who couldn't keep his dick in his trousers. Disappointment always followed idolisation, she should have learnt that by now. Were all men the same? First Tom, now Hal. Who would be next? Would Dan and Eddie follow their example?

She gasped for breath, air escaped from her lungs in wheezing screams. At least she'd get over him now. There was no reason to be in love any more. Indignation was a far more powerful weapon than infatuation. She was better armed. Now she stood a fighting chance of getting on with her life. The steep incline tore into her thigh muscles and then a stitch stabbed at her side. She jammed her fingers into the pain but couldn't reach, it was too deep. She tried to stretch the agony away and keep running but her body would not allow her to self-destruct. Despite instructions, her legs slowed to a stagger and then she stopped.

She pushed against a mossy garden wall, her head hanging down on her chest, and considered the likelihood of being sick. Her trainers went in and out of focus keeping rhythm with her heart. Hal was different from other men, she'd been so certain of it. The love for his wife had made her bitterly jealous, but she had respected him for it. It had marked him out as special. Was it her own fault? God, how would she tell Abi she'd broken her promise? Beca felt faint. She squatted down and leant back against the wall.

She was convinced her body was metamorphosing, she could feel her internal organs liquefying, the bones in her legs had turned to jelly. After a minute she tried them again, putting one foot gingerly in front of the other. They seemed able to support her weight. Perhaps she'd become an invertebrate while no one was looking. She pulled herself up to the top of the hill and looked down the other side. It was darker than before with the park emerging from beyond the houses on her right, but off in the distance she could see the glow of shop lights and civilisation. She jumped as a man emerged from the shadows with his dog. They smiled at each other in recognition of their mutual fear and the man hurried away. The trees rustled in the wind making unfamiliar sounds and as Beca began to run, white, frost-tipped leaves crunched under her feet. She picked up the pace to get quickly through the woods and into the world of tarmac and concrete again.

As she ran, solidity returned to her legs. They felt warm and limbered up now and, as endorphins flooded her system, the pain washed away. Now her strides were measured, her heart beat strongly and a smile began to replace the death-throes grimace. She reached the bottom of the hill and emerged into the high street. The contrast was startling, the dark shadowy park had gone, now noise and commotion surrounded her. Enormous sparkling snow flakes and bells hung across the street. It was the beginning of November and people were out buying Christmas presents already. A man wearing a hat with foam reindeer antlers sticking out of the top shook a collection box at her as she ran past. Yuletide tunes rang out through shop doorways trying to lure in customers. The tactic was working. People were actually being drawn in, and Christmas was still weeks away. The world had gone mad. Then again, perhaps she was the crazy one. There weren't many other women, or men for that matter, running with sweat-soaked clothes on inside out.

Beca left the Christmas shoppers behind her as she turned towards Notting Hill. The big bookshop on the corner was still open and jogging past she peered in. Smartly dressed people were sipping wine and laughing. It looked warm and highbrow inside. Further down a queue shuffled along in the cold in front of the cinema, huddled together for warmth and mutual anticipation. Next door, through the steamed-up windows of a small restaurant, Beca could see couples chatting over plates of spaghetti. Watching people enjoying life lifted her spirits. She wasn't one of them yet, but she was part of the crowd and, in their company, she knew she'd get over Hal. A broken heart wasn't going to kill her; it wouldn't last forever. The run was just what she'd needed. Psychologically she'd cleared the air. Her brain felt fresher now, although there was the danger she'd no longer have a body to house it in.

There would be no baby, not for now at least. When she'd licked her wounds there would be time to try again. But not in the same way, she couldn't do that. She'd grown up, she'd learnt too much about life and relationships to go back to that clinical approach.

What to do now though? Beca couldn't come up with an answer as she ran home. She didn't want to rush into another job. Liz was right, she hadn't taken a holiday for ages. She needed a break. A change of scene. Something to take her mind of Hal. Why not New York? She ran with the idea for a while. It would be fun. There were enough distractions to keep her going for weeks. She knew people, friends she'd made when living out there. As she opened her front door the irony dawned on her. Of course, she'd gone to New York to get away from Hal eight years before. Life was repeating itself. Although this time she doubted he would notice she was gone.

Chapter **20**

Beca tried to tear the plastic wrapper off with her teeth. She'd bought the CD in New York, and like all the others she'd picked up there, the cellophane was welded tight. It was impenetrable. The tab was supposed to unpeel along the top side. In theory. In practise it came off in her mouth and stuck to her lips. She blew and tugged at it until it flew off and caught on her coat.

Driving with the heels of both hands on the steering wheel she negotiated the traffic on the A10 and ran a nail along one of the hermetically sealed seams. The most developed country in the world and they couldn't design a pull tab that worked. Ever. Beca knew this was displaced anger. The CD wrapper wasn't the villain of the piece, life was, starting with the fact she'd managed to leave the bloody map behind. What really grated was that she'd put it out by the front door but somehow had managed to step over the damned thing in order to get out of her flat. She hadn't forgotten the presents. Although much use they'd be once she'd abandoned all hope of finding Eddie and Claire's place and was stuck on her own in a Welcome Inn for Christmas. It did occur to her repeatedly that she should stop and buy a map, but the fear of missing Christmas altogether was continuously overruled by a perverse confidence that she'd know how to get there once she'd spotted a familiar landmark. It wasn't as though this was her first trip to Norfolk. It also wasn't the first time she'd got lost.

Through a combined effort of nails and incisors she penetrated the outer shield of the CD wrapper. Eventually her efforts were rewarded and Elvis's *Blue Christmas* exploded into the car. There was something about his husky, snarling voice that sounded like a randy wolf. Beca's top lip curled and she joined in. She couldn't understand a word he was saying so she just howled along with the backing singers.

She'd been on the go for 16 hours since boarding the plane at JFK. Back in London she'd taken Mrs Butler out for brunch, endured some last minute Christmas shopping in the West End and then set off to meet up with her friends. Her head buzzed, she felt wired, stoked up with caffeine and the excitement of Christmas, but she knew herself well enough to know that it wasn't a healthy *joie de vivre* that was pushing her on.

It was a lonely business driving amidst the Christmas mass exodus, particularly now that darkness was descending. Every car she passed was packed to the roof with presents and children heading off for the holidays. Perhaps she should have brought an inflatable Santa along to keep her company. Still, she wouldn't dwell, she had promised herself there'd be no Yuletide mawkishness. Life was good. Fantastic in fact. She put on her newly acquired American smile. Brenda Lee began *Rocking Around the Christmas Tree* in a high-pitched wail and Beca was astonished she knew the words. It must have been the non-stop seasonal medleys that got played in every public place in the States.

New York had been fun, undeniably, but it had been a distraction rather than the cure she'd been looking for and the undercurrent of sadness and loneliness never quite went away.

Sure she'd got chatting in bars; New Yorkers were never slow when it came to picking up single women. She'd met a lawyer from Queens who had tried to explain the rules of American football, and a carpenter, originally from Ohio, who was hoping to make it big on the stage but had severe allergies to deal with. Then there had been the professor from Columbia University who kept going on about Napoleon's penis. He had been particularly weird. None of them had come close to her picture of the ideal man.

Stupid girl. Beca rapped the side of her head with her knuckles in annoyance. Hal had got in, again. She'd promised herself not to think of him and yet he'd slipped in obliquely when she hadn't been concentrating. She gripped the steering wheel and sang loudly. It was too late. Her mind was already filled with soft-focussed, slow-motion home movies of Hal and Sophie's perfect Christmas together. Whether they were giving each other presents, concocting some wonderful meal side by side in the kitchen, or throwing snowballs, they always wore matching snowflake jumpers and self-satisfied, white-toothed smiles. It was clear to anyone who saw them that they were blissfully happy, so perfectly matched. Beca squirmed with jealousy.

The heater in the car had packed up somewhere near Enfield and she was relying on chain smoking to keep herself warm, except her lighter was two fags away from empty. At least the windows had stopped steaming up now that the inside and outside air temperatures had reached an equilibrium. The fake fur puff ball hat she'd bought in New York on impulse because the sales assistant said she looked like Julie Christie in it, was pulled down over her forehead. A fringe of synthetic hair hung in front of her eyes. The collar from her matching coat was pulled up under her nose in a vain bid to keep it and the rest of her face warm. She could see steam filtering through the soggy nylon tufts and each time she breathed in, strands clung to her lips and pressed cold against her skin.

The journey to the house should have taken three, perhaps four hours at the most, at least that was how Beca imagined it. In this flight of fancy she would cruise along the main road, come off at the right junction, then skip along the narrow lanes until her tyres screeched pertly to a halt outside Claire and Eddie's front door. Why did reality have to be that much more complicated? She had been driving for five hours already, was no closer to her rendezvous and the brightly lit main road had given way to dark, uncharted lanes. None of which looked remotely familiar.

Beca pulled up at a junction. There was nothing to tell her which way to turn. She didn't have a clue where she was. All she could say with any conviction was that this was the countryside. This much was obvious from the field-to-people ratio. There was one person – herself – and then there were the endless, ironing-board flat fields as far as she could see. Which wasn't very far because it was now black outside and the weak lights of the Merc were doing little to expand her shortened horizon. Her car was not meant for this kind of rough terrain. It had been designed to wend its way along the Amalfi Coast or to cruise along the Croisette in Cannes with a blonde starlet behind the wheel, not tackle ruts and hassocks, let alone have headlights bright enough to point out anything useful like a road sign.

It was also freezing cold as her bone-chilled fingers kept reminding her. At least conditions were so unpleasant that there was no real danger of her falling asleep at the wheel. And even if she did, the car was bound to stay on the road because it felt as though her fingers had long since frozen to the steering wheel. Not only had the tips turned a deathly wax colour but her nails had gone purple. It would take a hot kettle and some pliers to prise them off. Assuming anybody found her frozen corpse before next spring.

In New York the endless musical reminders that Christmas was coming had seemed asinine and intrusive, now the same tunes were a comfort. How demeaning to find succour in a Bing Crosby song, but as Beca pelted up and down in the Norfolk wilderness she crooned along. Scouring the road ahead for signs of humanity she noticed a gate hanging off its hinges. She'd passed one like that not long before and did so again shortly after. She was going in bloody circles. Throwing the car into reverse she swerved blindly into a clearing in the hedgerow in order to turn around. The wheels spun on frozen mud as she tried to accelerate away. She was stuck. Damn, shit, bugger. She banged the steering wheel with her hands then winced as pain shot up her cold fingers. Why couldn't things go right just once?

'Shut up.' She hit the stop button on the CD player and cut Dean Martin off mid-song. It was a mistake. The silence that followed stripped her bare. The tune echoed in her head then faded away leaving her with nothing to bolster the false jollity, nothing to cover up the fraud. She'd been caught pretending. One slight mishap and the carefully nurtured veneer was crumbling. She wasn't happy at all. In fact she'd never felt so bloody miserable. It didn't help that she was completely alone. That precise moment summed up everything that was shitty about her life.

'Merry Christmas to you too,' she shouted to no one in particular. She sat in the darkness listening to the sound of the engine. She tried the accelerator but once again the wheels spun on the frozen ground. A slow painful death seemed inevitable.

She was resigned to it. No one would miss her anyway. She wouldn't mind dying so much if she could have a drink but there wasn't any to be had.

Beca thought wistfully of a final last glass as the chill spread up from her toes to her feet. Perhaps she should get out and try lighting a distress signal. It seemed like too much effort, but at the very least she should die with her Manolos on. It would be a fitting end. She got out of the car, opened the boot and rummaged for her precious new shoes. It was then that she discovered the bottle of whisky she'd bought for Eddie.

Back in the car she took the bottle out of its box, ripped the metal cover off with her teeth and pulled out the cork. The whisky ripped through her like molten lava. It splashed down into her empty stomach and shot into her bloodstream. She could feel the ripple effect all the way down to her toes. What a delightful way to die.

Peace was momentary. Her stomach rebelled. In fast rewind the cosy warm glow was beaten back by an angry mob of viscose matter. Her stomach imploded and the contents shot up her throat. Beca wrestled with the door and pushed it open and by milliseconds avoided vomiting all over her Bergdorf Goodman coat. Of the low moments in life that she could immediately recall, this one got top prize.

She sat back in her seat waiting for the next wave. Her hands shook with the surprise of such a violent attack. What had caused it? She was never normally sick. Sally and Abi were the barf queens, not her. In truth she had been overdoing things a bit lately. New York tended to have that effect on her, that and trying to obliterate all memory. Perhaps the whisky had been one assault too many for her body to take.

Such an extreme occasion merited the use of her precious lighter fuel reserves. Besides, she needed something to smother the taste of bile in her mouth; she could feel her teeth corroding. The lighter sparked worryingly a few times until a tiny flame appeared. She lit her cigarette and inhaled deeply. She would light the next one with the butt of the first. It was cheering to think there were enough duty free fags in the boot to keep her going for weeks. Well, days at least.

Beca's hands had stopped shaking by the time she lit her second cigarette. Deep in the folds of her coat her mobile phone began to ring. After the fifth ring she found it.

'Hello, Beca, is that you?' a distant voice asked.

'Eddie.' Thank Christ and all the saints in Heaven. 'I'm lost.'

'Thought you might be. We've been trying to reach you for ages.' It was then that Beca noticed all the missed calls. So much for the cheery Christmas tunes, they had nearly cost her her life. 'Why don't you drive to the next sign post, then we'll know where you are.'

'I can't. The car's stuck.'

'Has it broken down?'

'No. It's on ice. I can't get any traction.'

'Have you tried starting in second gear?'

Of course not, she lived in a city. 'I'll give it a go.'

It worked and Beca gingerly drove off the ice and back on the road. Using every opportunity to berate her driving skills, Eddie guided her back along the several miles of mud-ridden lanes that separated her from her friends. It turned out she'd passed the gates up to the house once before, but when she'd seen the flashing reindeer on top of the gate posts she'd assumed it was a roadside steak house and not an astonishing lapse in good taste.

The tyres of Beca's car crunched along the gravel drive and came to a stop at the front of the house. She sat for a moment staring at her numb fingers and marvelling at her survival. Women and children had set off in wagons across America and survived. She'd driven from London to Norfolk and had come close to perishing. If she'd been a pioneer, the West would have stayed with the Native Americans until the invention of the aeroplane.

Eddie pulled hard on the car door to get it open. 'Bloody cold, isn't it,' he said when he finally managed. 'Very nice to see you.' His voice was booming and as Beca climbed out of the car he enveloped her in his big bear arms. She was willingly smothered and fought hard not to weep with relief. 'Come on into the warmth,' he said leading her in.

The hallway glowed with Christmas lights, and the smell of pine cones from the abundant decorations saturated the air. Perhaps she had died after all for this was the closest she'd ever come to Heaven.

'Haven't got a hanky, have you?' Beca asked Eddie through a long sniff.

'Of course, old girl. Not the cleanest,' he said passing over a balled up specimen from his pocket. His faced reddened as Beca thanked him and wiped her eyes.

'It's just the contrast in temperatures,' she said blowing her nose.

'Exactly. Quite so.' Eddie dabbed his eyes with a shirt cuff lending action to the lie. The poor man looked anxious but clearing his throat loudly several times didn't conjure up any moral support.

'Good God,' Beca said once her eyes had demisted. 'Have you taken Holy Orders?'

'What? Oh, very funny. You mean the black.' Eddie looked visibly relieved to have been spared an emotional scene. He held out his arms and turned around for full effect. 'It's Claire's fault. She says black is one of my optimum colours.'

'She got to you as well.' The poor bastard looked really crestfallen. 'You know, thinking about it you look more like an ageing rock star.'

'Do I?' Eddie preened. The thought seemed to comfort him. 'She's dyed all my clothes.'

'Even your mustard moleskins?'

'Those as well. And she hasn't done a particularly good job. Everywhere I sit I leave a greyish stain. It can be very embarrassing.'

'I can see how it could be.'

'You should see my underpants.'

'I'd rather not.'

'Quite,' Eddie replied blushing again. Beca reached up and kissed him on the cheek; she was so pleased to see him.

When her name was called she looked up and saw Sally coming towards her.

'You're so cold,' Sally said as she kissed her. 'Here, take this.' She pressed a glass of mulled wine into Beca's rigid fingers. 'We've been tracking your progress on a local map.'

Such kindness made her eyes smart again. She sat down on a window seat in the hall and sipped cautiously. The spicy concoction licked and curled its way through her and settled in her stomach. Why was she so tearful all of a sudden? No wonder Eddie was alarmed. She'd have to get a grip if she hoped to survive Christmas with any dignity left at all.

'Do you want all your bags in your room?' Having escaped at the first sign of reinforcements, Eddie had unloaded her car and brought in all her bags.

'If you wouldn't mind,' she replied. What a sweet, jovial man. Not easy to fancy, but dependable. He was what a woman wanted. If Claire hadn't snaffled him up, she'd have had him. God, what was she thinking? Of course she wouldn't. Live in the middle of bloody nowhere with lard-arse Eddie? No chance. She had to stop sizing up men for their mate-for-life potential and imagining herself ecstatically happy with them. It had started in a cinema in New York. She'd been watching *The Quiet Man*. Instead of cringing at the brutal, misogynistic way John Wayne dragged Maureen O'Hara around the Irish landscape, Beca had rather fancied someone being so manly and assertive herself. Pitiful.

Tom appeared at the top of the stairs. Now there was someone she'd be hard pressed to fancy. It was odd to find herself smiling at him. Even before his affair had been exposed she'd always tensed up around the shoulders whenever he approached. It had only been six weeks since his heart attack and yet he looked better than he had for years. She was genuinely pleased to see him so healthy, although the kiss he planted on her cheek diminished the pleasure factor. She resisted the urge to rub her face.

'You're freezing,' he said. 'I'm looking for Billy's snookie.'

Beca and Sally waited for clarification.

'No snookie, no sleep for anyone. I've got a sickening feeling we left it at home.' With that he dashed off to the kitchen.

Beca stared into the space he had vacated. 'For a fleeting moment I thought that was Tom. Then he opened his mouth and spoke a whole sentence without mentioning himself once.'

'Eerie, isn't it?' Sally replied. 'He's been like that since he got here. He even played with Tabitha.'

'That must have been scary.'

'Maybe it's the side effects of his medication,' Sally suggested.

'I suppose we ought to be grateful he's alive.'

'Well of course,' Sally said suddenly chastened by the merest hint of bitchiness.

Beca laughed at her. 'I'm only kidding. I didn't think I ever would be, but I'm pleased to see him still walking around.'

'Me too. You could probably come into the sitting room now. Abi should have finished wrapping your present.'

'So you were a decoy.' Excitement tickled Beca's insides and memories of the ghastly journey began to fade. What would she get this year? Something big? Small? Expensive? Not that the price tag mattered at all. Absolutely not. Bad girl.

'You've made it.' Abi uncrossed her legs and lifted herself out from a sea of wrapped presents. 'Are you alright?' she asked when Beca hugged her.

'Oh, I'm fine.' Beca laughed and rubbed away the tears. 'I'm just tired and overly emotional. It's good to see everyone. New York can get a bit wearing.'

'Come here,' Abi said giving her another hug. 'We missed you.'

Beca found herself an armchair by the fire and as she sank into its comfortable embrace she looked around. It was amazing how the change of seasons could alter a room. The last time she'd been there, the French windows had been thrown open for dogs and children to hurtle in and out of. Now heavy curtains had been pulled across to shut out the cold and the room felt smaller and introverted. A vast Christmas tree sparkled with white fairy lights and apart from the flickering flames of the fire and a few lamps, there wasn't much else to light the room. But it wasn't just the change of seasons. Claire had removed the lurid chintz print that had dominated the room and instead all the sofas and chairs had been swathed in purple velvet. Beca felt like she had been swallowed by a plum.

She took a walnut from a bowl beside her and cracked it open. The warmth from the fire made her ears throb as they thawed and she could feel herself melting. Nothing was going to get her out of that chair, not even an empty glass.

The door swung open and Claire strode in with a tray. Beca was amazed to see she'd lost even more weight. No longer the size of a small barn she was now reduced down to an average sized potting shed.

'You've always had an appalling sense of direction. I'll never forget how you got us lost on that school trip to Dartmoor.' Claire was joking, after her own fashion.

'If I recall rightly, it was you who ate all the emergency supplies,' Abi said.

Claire harrumphed at this reminder. 'Anyway, it's lovely to see you,' she said pressing her cheek against Beca's. 'I've brought you supper. We ate earlier.'

Beca looked at the tray Claire had put on her lap assessing each item for its potential to make her sick again. The ham and baked potato were pretty innocuous albeit shrivelled from being kept warm in the Aga.

Eddie made a welcome return with a pan of mulled wine which he placed in front of the fire and ladled into everyone's glasses as if he were Father Christmas dishing out good cheer. Beca's levels of cheeriness were quite low so she felt justified in holding out her glass on a near continuous basis. It was even less likely that she'd be persuaded out of her plum. She sat in a mulled wine fug and watched her friends. Their voices sounded distant and echoey as she shrank further into herself.

Dan came in, gave Beca a friendly peck on the cheek and sat next to Sally. He was immediately engrossed in a whispered conversation with his wife. Their heads were practically touching and it was hard not to feel a pang of envy at their intimacy. The source of their concern seemed to be the baby monitor he had brought in with him. There was a lot of fizzing and crackling coming from the device but no signs of a crying Tabitha. Surely a good thing.

'How do you know it's working?' Sally asked him.

'Because of the noise.'

'But does that mean we'll hear her if she cries?'

'It must do. The volume's turned right up.'

He was right on that point. The monitor was making a distinctive and increasingly irritating sound.

'You can get them with video cameras,' Beca said. 'I've heard you can, anyway. Not that I've seen them myself. Someone must have told me.' Because she had never spent hours flicking through baby catalogues.

'Can you?' Concern swept over Sally's face. 'Perhaps we should have got one of those. Then we'd be able to see if she was alright.'

'Don't worry, the dogs are locked away in the kitchen so they can't possibly get to her,' Claire pointed out.

This did little to allay Sally's fears.

Beca sat and listened to her body as the no baby tragedy played out inside her again. The sickening panic was there, so too the scratching of her insides as her future tried clambering out of the deep, dank pit she'd fallen into. The best thing to do was get drunk. She held out her glass again which Eddie obligingly began to fill for her until a sudden explosion of baby screaming caused him and the rest of the room to leap with fright. Sally shot out of the room while Beca tried to reassure Eddie that she didn't mind wearing a ladleful of mulled wine.

It took awhile for her heart to settle on a healthy beat and, as it did, her thoughts returned to her; she rather wished they wouldn't. It had begun to dawn on her in New York that she'd spent her adult life in a two-dimensional world. The quantity of living had been there, no one could fault her enthusiasm, but what was missing was the quality. What made it even more ironic was that she'd never even noticed. Until Hal. With him she'd briefly touched on a three-dimensional world, the real one her married friends were living in. Or had she? Perhaps that was part of the myth she'd built up. There hadn't been a single message or letter from him when she'd got back. He'd had six weeks to get her out of his system and clearly he'd done just that. No doubt he'd been so busy trying to get his wife pregnant that he'd forgotten all about her. Which of course was as it should be.

The fairy lights on the Christmas tree went into soft focus and each one sparkled in a hazy aura. Someone had smeared Vaseline over her corneas. No, in fact she was crying. The shame. She didn't know whether to sit tight or bolt for the door. Tom unwittingly presented the solution when he walked into the room and cleared his throat.

The effect was immediate; he had the room's attention and as he stood rocking back on his heels, Beca knew he was about to say something embarrassing. The others seemed to have come to the same conclusion judging by the dread on their faces. Abi's expression was unique amongst the group. She looked thunderous as she tied a ribbon around another present.

'This won't take a minute,' his apologetic tone was so significantly out of character to be alarming. 'As you all know, Abi and I have had our own *annus horribilis*, to borrow from the Queen.'

Beca cringed into her plum and hummed a manic tune in her head to block out what he was saying. The chair was narrow enough for her to put both elbows on the arms and then a finger in each ear. Sadly Tom's legal training had included voice projection.

'If it wasn't for this beautiful lady here, I'd be dead.'

Eddie interjected with some supportive braying.

'I've made a fool of myself this year. I came close to wrecking my marriage. I've broken Abi's heart and made my children unhappy.'

No one looked set to argue the point with him. Would he dare say 'affair'?

'My.' He hesitated. Beca unplugged her ears. 'My behaviour was unforgivable.'

Coward.

'I am deeply ashamed of myself. Abi has stood by me. She nursed me through my illness and I am hugely grateful.' His wife didn't look like she wanted his thanks. In fact the muscles clenching in her jaw suggested she'd rather like to hit him.

'I owe her everything.' Tom's voice faltered and for one dreadful moment Beca thought he was going to cry. Being the recipient of such contrition made her fidget in her chair. She looked around the room at the others. Dan was venting his masculine embarrassment by crushing walnuts and Claire was closely examining the contents of a box of chocolates, but then she had her own dietary demons to deal with. It fell to Eddie to shoulder Tom's public act of atonement.

Tom was oblivious to his wife's anger. He held out his hand to her. She hesitated. Then faced with little choice she took it and he pulled her to her feet.

'Abi. I love you. I want to tell you, in front of all our friends how sorry I am. Can you forgive me?'

She looked at him then replied icily, 'Of course.'

'Bravo,' Eddie roared. The others clapped lightly and tried to laugh. Beca stayed absolutely still just in case she was sick again.

Chapter **21**

Beca lay in bed and gazed up into the darkness. She'd forgotten to draw the curtains but that didn't make much difference, except to the temperature of the room. She was glad she'd kept her socks on. In London the pale glow from the street lights meant that at night it was never really dark. Never absolutely black like it was now, here, in the middle of the countryside. She could see the eiderdown moving as she rubbed her feet together, but beyond the end of the bed board was utter darkness.

Christmas Day had arrived before they'd all gone to bed. With the help of the carriage clock on the landing she'd been counting the hours since then, reflecting on things that were best left alone. Her brain was in full throttle and showed no signs of running out of fuel. Why was it always like that? She could barely speak when she'd dragged herself upstairs to her room. She hadn't even bothered cleaning her teeth she was so knackered. Then as soon as she was in a horizontal position, ping, she was wide awake.

She'd long since abandoned any attempt to keep Hal out of her mind. Indeed she'd set aside the stories of Sophie and him, and had allowed herself unrestricted access to the large supply of Hal and Beca fantasies; the happy-ever-after secret thoughts which no amount of torture would ever get her to reveal to a living soul.

Beca rolled over onto her other side. The mincing, brassy chime of the clock told her it was five in the morning. So considerate. Then she heard giggles. She thought it was her mind going until she heard them again, more clearly this time. It was Harriet and Dulcie, who were sharing a room. Beca smiled as their footsteps approached. There was an odd crunching sound like the crushing of tissue paper and Beca guessed they were carrying their Christmas stockings. Bare feet padded past her door and on to the next room where another fit of giggles announced their arrival in Oscar's room. Billy was billeted there for the holidays and once he was awake the whole house would be as well. Beca leant over the side of her bed to see if there was a stocking for her. Just a pile of clothes.

Her sticky eyes cried out for sleep. It was barely bedtime in New York and her body wasn't going to slip into oblivion without a fight. Why couldn't she shut her jabbering, whirling brain down? If it wasn't Hal it was mindless inanities, stupid things that daylight thankfully banished. What was the name of the person who dubbed Lauren Bacall's voice when she sang in *To Have and Have Not*? Was it really Andy Williams, or was that just a Hollywood myth? And who cared anyway? How many frames were there in a 90 minute film? Would that depend on the speed it was shot at? Shut up! Beca pulled a pillow over her head and sank under the eiderdown.

An anti-suffocation reflex must have kicked in while she was asleep because the pillow had gone when she woke up. Sharp sunlight forced its way between her eyelashes. So it was morning at last. It had been a damned long time coming. With the pillow gone, there was nothing to shield her eyes when she eventually opened them fully, and her optic nerves could have done with the help. How had she managed to get to bed the night before and not notice the colour of the walls? She'd spent hours dissecting the minutiae of life but hadn't once noticed the paint job. Claire had said something about redecorating but had failed to mention the need for sunglasses. It was a blessing she hadn't turned the light on when she came to her room. What a criminal combination. And so much of it. Grass green all around the room below the dado rail and pale yellow above. She was in a huge primrose. It was enough to make a person sick. And she was.

In the split second between thinking and knowing she was going to vomit, she grabbed the nearest container which happened to be a wicker wastepaper basket. Fortunately it too had been painted with a thick layer of yellow paint which made the gaps between the weaves smaller, although not entirely absent. Beca stared at what her stomach had produced with disbelief. It took a moment to realise the level was dropping. Before too much had leaked onto the floor she rushed to the bathroom and tipped the contents down the loo.

She pulled the handle, put the seat down and sat with her head in her hands. She felt vile. Not as vile as that time in Calcutta, but then that had been something else entirely. What was causing all this throwing up? Drink couldn't have been the reason this time; she hadn't exactly partied the night away. Perhaps she'd picked up a bug on the aeroplane home, one of those lethal chicken flu viruses that would kill her before New Year.

She was going to be sick again. She lifted the lid and waited, hovering above the bilious smell that still clung to the bowl. Nothing happened. She sat down again and noticed for the first time that the connecting door which led from the bathroom to Abi's room next door was wide open. Had she or Tom heard anything? Beca poked her head around the door and looked into the gloom. She could make out Tom in the bed, but no Abi. Carefully she shut the door and stumbled back to her own room.

She flopped down onto the bed and groaned. Her face prickled with sweat and her legs ached with cramp. It was hard to imagine feeling more terrible and the room wasn't helping. She had to get out of there before she started hallucinating. She dumped layers of clothes from her suitcase onto the floor until she found her dressing gown. She shoved her cigarettes into the pocket and with her eyes shut she evacuated the room, bashing her right hip on the door frame as she left.

The corridor and stairs rocked gently as she made her way downstairs clasping to the banister tightly. She edged along beside the wall until she reached the kitchen. Already the room smelled of roasting turkey flesh. Groaning in response to the high decibel greetings she slumped down into a chair.

'I'm not feeling very well.'

'Coffee?' Abi asked.

'Christ, no.' The thought made her want to be sick again.

Claire tutted as she peeled a parsnip and threw it into the growing pile on the table.

Dan took time out from the saucepan he was stirring to explain the sudden piety. 'Taking the Lord's name in vain on this of all days. Shame on you.' He even looked like one of the Disciples in his stripy dressing gown.

'I'm suitably chastened.'

'Rightly so,' Claire said hacking into another root vegetable without mercy.

Sanctimonious old bint. Beca took a piece of cold toast from the toast rack and chewed the corner, throwing Claire death-ray stares which she failed to wither under.

'There's butter here if you want it,' Sally said holding out the dish. Tabitha was clamped to her breast and as Beca declined the offer she watched the baby. She was kneading her mother's chest and wriggling gently with ecstasy. Sally absentmindedly stroked her soft head but seemed unaware of her daughter's delight. Perhaps it didn't seem so miraculous after a while.

'Is breakfast ready yet?' Dulcie shouted as she burst into the room with Oscar pushing her from behind. Why did they have to shout so bloody loudly?

'Almost. Where's your brother?' Abi was standing next to Dan turning bacon in a frying pan with a fork.

'Outside. He won't keep his hat on,' Dulcie replied.

'Go and get him and the others,' her mother told her.

'Where did all the snow come from? They're covered in it,' Beca asked as the two children shot out again. It seemed a reasonable question. The others stopped mid-action and stared at her.

'There's about a foot of it outside. Hadn't you noticed?' Dan asked.

'I was too enraptured with the colour of my room.'

Claire beamed at her. 'Marvellous isn't it? I am glad you like it. They're Spring colours, of course. I chose them specially for you.'

Despite the need for new retinas Beca was touched. Claire's heart was in the right place and she was a good friend, even if she was a staggeringly large pain in the arse sometimes.

'Fried or scrambled?' Abi asked.

Beca swallowed hard trying to get rid of the eggy film that had sprung out of her saliva glands. 'Maybe I'll just stick with the toast.'

'Nonsense,' Claire said. 'You're too thin as it is.'

'I'll have something in a bit.' She should have stayed in bed.

Billy was the first child in for breakfast. His ears and cheeks were red bordering on purple from the cold, and his eyes sparkled with excitement. When he saw Beca he ran over and climbed onto her lap. Memories of his crappy nappy brought on a fresh wave of nausea.

'Have you got me a big present?' Dulcie asked after she'd been enticed to kiss Beca hello.

'It's so big I couldn't fit it in my car,' she said with a jollity she was far from feeling.

Dulcie looked crushed until Beca winked to reassure her.

'Big isn't always best,' Abi said putting a plate in front of her daughter. Beca looked at the brown frilly edges of the fried egg and started shallow breathing.

'Yes it is.' Harriet might as well have added 'stupid.'

Claire's cheeks doubled in sized and turned crimson. 'Say sorry immediately or there will be no presents for you, miss.'

Harriet visibly shrank under her mother's tirade and her features slipped from superior older sister to embarrassed child.

Her bottom lip quivered as she apologised and she then ate her breakfast in silence save for the hard-done-by sniffing.

Billy plunged into his breakfast as soon as it was put in front of him. It was a struggle for Beca to keep her nose elevated above the rising smells. She breathed through her mouth, sipped her tea and only when essential, helped Billy scoop fried egg up with his spoon. He ate slowly but got bored quickly and just when Beca began to feel overwhelmed he jumped down and ran out with the others.

As the adults ate their breakfast in peace Beca waited for the sick feeling to subside. When it got stronger instead she knew it was the prelude to more puking. She pushed Billy's plate of congealing food further away from her. The effort seemed to drain the blood from her face.

'You look lousy. What's wrong?' Dan's words were laced between half-chewed sausage.

'Jet lag. I need a cigarette,' Beca pushed her chair back in the rush to be gone. In the hall she put on her coat and hat, borrowed a pair of wellington boots and went outside with her cup of tea. The air was sharp and crisp upon her face. It cooled her clammy cheeks making her feel instantly better. She took a deep breath and smiled gratefully. The world was white as far as she could see. Looking harder as her eyes adjusted to the brightness, she could distinguish the different shades, the pale, watery greys of the fields spreading towards the horizon. Black hedgerows cut across the landscape and skeletal trees loomed up into the sky.

Eddie shouted and waved hello to her from the front garden which was vastly bigger than anything to be found in London. He was marshalling the children into snowman-building duty; an ink-black blob surrounded by little people in bright hats and scarves. Beca leant against the cold brick wall and sipped her tea. She couldn't remember it ever having snowed on Christmas Day before. It was such a fantastic cliché. Filled with the joys of Christmas she lit a cigarette, inhaled and promptly threw up over the neat ornamental shrub next to the front door. She looked at her meagre breakfast as it steamed on the snow covered leaves and then dripped to the ground.

'Beca's been sick,' Harriet shrieked with accompanying sound effects to mark her revulsion. This prompted similar expressions of disgust from the others. Perfect. Just what she needed. An audience of vomit-phobic children. Having alerted the neighbourhood, Harriet rushed past her into the house to do the same inside, shouting gruesome details for anyone who wanted, or indeed didn't want, to know.

Eddie ran over. 'Are you alright there, Beca? You look a bit peaky. Do you want me to carry you to your room?' he asked positioning himself for an affirmative response.

'No. Get off.' Beca batted his arm away and tried sounding more cheerful than she felt. 'It's just jet lag. I haven't got the vapours. Sorry about your plant though.'

'Don't worry. Probably good fertiliser. Bit acidic mind you.'

Abi, Sally and Claire collected joint first prize for the five metre dash from the kitchen.

'I'm fine, really.' Beca feebly laughed off their enquiries. In fact she felt disorientated and seasick. The close inspection of the contents of her stomach by the shorter members of the group wasn't helping to steady her.

'You should go to bed,' Abi said.

'What a shame,' Sally said.

'She'll miss church,' Beca heard Claire say as she staggered through the Bad Ship Vomit up to her bedroom. It had turned gale force 9 and the crew were manning the bilge pumps when she flopped onto her bed and closed her eyes. After five minutes of waiting to die a gentle tap at the door heralded nurse Abi.

'Good God, no wonder you're sick,' Abi said taking in the full glories of Beca's room. 'Drink this, it's got lots of sugar in it. She put a cup of tea on the green bedside table. 'How are you feeling?'

'Hideous. I hate throwing up.'

'Do you know what's causing it?'

'Not really. I must have picked something up on the plane. It could be food poisoning I suppose.'

'How many times is it now?'

'Three. Once yesterday and twice this morning.'

'And today of all days. Can I get in?' Abi asked climbing into bed next to Beca. 'Your room's a bit chilly. If you're going to be sick try giving me some warning.'

'Don't get much notice myself.'

'I'll chance it.'

'It could be catching,' Beca said sounding a warning tone.

'Then I've probably got it already.'

'In which case, cheer me up by telling me all about the new Tom.' Beca took the tiniest sip of her tea and waited for a response from her insides.

'Don't. It's really grim.' Abi settled back on a propped-up pillow. 'He's become so irritating. It's because he's trying too hard.'

'That'll wear off,' Beca said.

'Maybe so, but the problem is I don't think I love him any more.'

Beca looked to see if she was being as serious as she sounded. She was. 'That has its drawbacks.'

'When I look at him I just see a dull middle-aged man.'

'Which of course he is. But that's nothing new. He's always been old.'

'I used to value the stability. That's gone now of course, and the relief of him not dying just isn't enough to sustain a relationship.'

'Doesn't sound to me like you've forgiven him.'

'Deep down I haven't. It still hurts too much. Maybe in time'

Beca gave Abi's hand a squeeze. 'You have to stay married, I've been trying so hard to get on with him.'

There was another scratch at the door and Sally popped her head around.

'Do you want to climb in as well?' Beca asked her. 'There's plenty of room. We're just dissecting Abi's marriage.'

'Oh dear. I did wonder if that's what you'd be doing. Are you alright?' Abi nodded. 'I came to see if you wanted your feet doing,' Sally said to Beca. 'Reflexology is very good for detoxing the body.'

'Are you back in business then?' Beca asked.

'She did mine yesterday,' Abi said.

'I've been getting as much practise in as possible, I'm going back to work after Christmas,' Sally said.

Beca pulled the eiderdown up to uncover her feet. 'Help yourself. Nothing could make me feel worse.' Sally perched on the edge of the bed and opened a drawstring bag. She took out a little bottle and poured some oil into her hands and rubbed them together. Then she began to gently knead the sole of Beca's right foot, working her way up into the arch. Her cool fingers probed between Beca's toes, pushing at the fleshy undersides. It was deliciously masochistic and Beca could feel her eyes rolling to the back of her head with delight.

'How about you?' Abi asked her. 'What are you going to do with the rest of your life?'

'I've been giving serious though to pottery,' Beca said with a wry smile.

'Professionally?' Sally asked joining in the joke. 'Your whole system is very blocked.'

Wait until she found her liver. 'It could take a while to get up to scratch. What do you think?'

'If memory serves me, you were a liability with a potter's wheel,' Abi pointed out.

'I thought that was with a bunsen burner,' Sally said.

'That as well,' Abi said.

Beca flinched as Sally touched her heel. 'God, that hurt.'

'Sorry. It's incredibly gritty. Your uterus is very busy.'

'I still can't decide what to do. I thought about opening my own cinema.'

'What are you good at?' Abi asked reaching over to the bedside table and taking Beca's cup of tea.

'Smoking and drinking.' Which was the truth, if not very elevating. She watched Abi eat the ginger biscuit that had been resting in the saucer.

'I don't see how you could turn that into making a living,' Abi said.

'What else are you good at?' Sally asked.

'Sex.'

'That presents some obvious possibilities, but not recommended ones,' Abi said.

'Jesus! Are you trying to amputate my foot?' Beca pulled away from Sally's sadistic hands.

'Sorry.'

'Maybe you need a bit more practise before you start on the general public,' Beca said warily returning her foot for more torture.

Sally ignored the dig. 'Are you having a heavy period?'

'No. I haven't had one for a while.' Beca now felt even tenser than she had before. She gripped the edge of the mattress waiting for another wave of pain.

'How long has it been?' Abi asked washing the biscuit down with a sip of tea.

Beca shrugged. 'It's hardly important.'

'One month? Two?' Abi was getting into her stride.

'Could be.'

'Well which?'

'I don't know. Just one. I'm due on any day now.' What did it matter?

'Have you seen a doctor?' Sally asked.

'No of course not.'

'Christ, you're not pregnant are you?' Abi sat bolt upright tipping the cup over in its saucer. It teetered, rattled, then settled back again.

'That would explain what I'm feeling here,' Sally said calmly.

'Piffle. You're touching my foot. What the hell's that going to tell you except I've got ten toes.' It made as much sense as asking a foot spa. All that New Age hokum was fogging up Sally's head. Pregnant? It was a ridiculous idea.

'Well could you be?' Abi asked.

Not her as well. 'Of course not. Don't you think I'd know if I was.'

'Not necessarily. It doesn't always work like that,' Sally said.

'Well, I'm not. It's quite impossible.'

Abi's eyes narrowed. 'Who have you been sleeping with?'

'No one. God Almighty, who made you my mother?'

'What about Hal?' Abi the Inquisitor asked.

'That was ages ago and definitely at the wrong time of the month.'

'Are you sure?'

'Absolutely. And no I haven't slept with him since.' It was very difficult arguing her case lying down with Abi's scowl and pursed lips looming over her. 'I really haven't.'

'Have you had a period since you slept with him?' Abi pressed.

'I really don't remember. I probably did, I just wasn't concentrating.'

'You should do a pregnancy test.' Abi was now beyond reason.

'What for?' Beca was incredulous. 'I am not pregnant. Just because Sally says my heels are a bit gritty doesn't mean that I am. Maybe my new Manolos are rubbing.' Even as she said it she knew that was impossible. About as likely as being pregnant. Or being 25 again. Or being left alone in peace.

So if being pregnant was impossible why did Beca waste the whole day thinking about it? Clearly because she wanted to drive herself insane. If it wasn't bad enough to spend Christmas Day fleeing from one culinary stomach churner to another, the thought of a miraculous pregnancy followed her everywhere. It exploded into her consciousness like the bubbles in a bottle of tonic water, effervescing up and spilling everywhere when the lid came off. It took the greatest will power she could muster to get it back on. But when her guard was down the lid would untwist and she'd be off again. In the middle of *My Fair Lady* she was gripped by a euphoria the film barely merited. She sat grinning moronically on the sofa picking the icing off a slice of Christmas cake and making a mental list of names for her baby.

Even at lunch time when her full faculties were needed to negotiate the minefield on the table, the bubbles erupted leaving an air pocket where her brain should have been. Beca's nose gained heightened sensory powers. She could smell the acidic vapours rising from the stewed red cabbage ten feet away. She had to hold her breath until the Brussels sprouts were out of range. In the end all she could eat was bread sauce, roast potatoes and lots of gravy. This odd combination was a sensible choice, considering the state of her digestive tract, and did not merit that knowing grin from Abi. Did she have any idea how unkind she was being stoking up all the excitement again? It was a stomach virus, nothing more. It would take more than Abi's worldly experience to convince her otherwise.

But bread sauce, potatoes and gravy were an odd choice. Perhaps it was a craving. Maybe there was a hidden layer of significance which she had failed to detect. Abi was a perceptive person. Could she be right? Did that last time with Hal really do the business? Beca never wanted to see another bottle of tonic water again in her life.

The next morning, Beca urgently needed to pee. It was so cold in her room that she could see her breath in the air. She pulled the eiderdown closer up to her ears and ate another piece of the chocolate orange Eddie had given her the day before. Right now it seemed a worthy trade for the Tiffany cufflinks she'd given him; she felt sure the sugary confection was all that was keeping her alive. Peeing in her bed would warm things up for a while, but it would almost certainly only be temporary and the shame that followed would be far greater than any comfort she might have derived.

The urge wasn't going away. Delaying action was making an accident more likely. There was nothing for it but to hunker down and charge to the bathroom, which she did. Beca sat down on the freezing loo seat and peed. The relief was worth all the effort and if she was able to empty her bladder in less than 10 seconds she might yet avoid frostbite. It was while in mid-stream that she became aware of the ominous quivering in her throat and gut. A bad sign like the sucking away of the sea before a tsunami arrived.

Time, she discovered, was elastic in such a situation. Bizarrely she found herself with ample time to contemplate her next move. She could a) stand up, turn to be sick in the loo and hope her pelvic floor muscles were up to scratch, b) continue peeing and attempt to vomit between her legs into the lavatory bowl, or c) abandon the loo, leap into the bath and complete all bodily expulsions in one inelegant fell swoop. Her stomach and bladder co-opted for the first option.

'God. Christ. Sorry.'

Beca knew her inner voice wasn't male, which meant whoever had spoken was real. Sniggers and a door slamming confirmed the magnitude of her horror as the owner of the slightly too pleased voice disappeared into the connecting bedroom. Either Abi had taken steroids, was having an affair, or Tom had just seen her hanging over the loo with her pyjama bottoms around her ankles and her backside on display to the world. Fuck. The pain in her stomach and wretched indignity made Beca burst into tears.

Tom's guffaws were no less audible when rapid tapping announced another intruder.

'Beca, are you alright? Bloody Hell. Come and lie down.' Abi assumed the strength of ten men and hauled Beca back to her bedroom. Her tears burned her cheeks and were unstoppable. The humiliation was complete, she wanted to die.

'You're pregnant,' Abi said emphatically. The layers of jumpers she had on made folding her arms over her chest difficult, but the point was made.

'I am not. I'd love to be, but I'm not.' Beca cried even more and stared at her lap. 'Have you any idea how awful this is for me? I haven't been able to think about anything else.'

'You have to do a test.'

'I don't have one.' Beca felt the bed dip as Abi sat down next to her and took her hand. 'I wish you'd leave me alone. You're being so cruel.'

'Perhaps you're right,' Abi said softly. 'But there's only one way to find out. Go back to bed, the central heating's broken down. I'll be back in a minute.'

When Abi left, Beca considered barricading her door, although the worst demons were in her head. A shrill squeal like a pig going for slaughter came from Claire's room and the thud of heavy feet announced Beca's fate. The bedroom door burst open before she had the chance to pull the wardrobe across it.

'I've got one darling. Isn't this exciting. It's a bit old but not past its use-by date. Pop off to the loo and put us all out of our misery.' Under other circumstances Beca would have said something rude about the quilt she had belted around her coat.

'I can't. I don't need to pee.'

'Tea,' Claire shouted as if she'd invented the damned stuff and hurried off to the kitchen.

'This is all a waste of time,' Beca said.

'We'll see. I've got a strange feeling about this one. This morning is prophetic,' Abi said.

'Pathetic more like.'

'Humiliating scenes are a feature of pregnancy and childbirth. All those check-ups, the nudity, bodily functions, all that screaming, and of course an audience. You're off to a good start.'

'Just as well I wasn't taking a dump,' Beca said grudgingly. She looked at the pregnancy test kit on the bedside table, next to the debris of her chocolate orange. She was hardly a stranger to them having kept the manufacturers in business over the summer.

Supposing she was pregnant. What then? Having given up entirely on the idea, how would it feel to have Hal's child after all? But she wasn't, she couldn't be. It was hopeless, wishful thinking and Abi, Claire and Sally would be sorry they'd ever put the idea into her head. Beca wished she'd never started on the whole stupid business of trying to get pregnant. She particularly regretted telling her so called friends about it.

Abi fidgeted as they waited for the tea. Beca stared gravely into her lap feeling more wretched by the minute. She would cry if the result was negative. She knew it would be, but she'd still cry. Claire returned and Beca dutifully took the tea and drank it.

'I put lots of milk in so you can get it down you quickly,' Claire said.

Good thinking. Beca took her time, she was in no hurry to confirm what she knew already. Besides there was a sliver of pleasure to be got out of watching Abi and Claire squirm.

Without a word Beca put down the empty cup, picked up the tester kit and went to the bathroom. She made certain both doors were locked, then tore the wrapper off like an old pro and peed as nonchalantly as it was possible to onto the tip. It was a struggle mustering up any urine but once done she put the cover back on, propped the stick in front of the mirror, unlocked the door and walked away.

She hoped her shrug showed Claire and Abi how little she cared then, putting on every item of clothing she had, she went downstairs. The children were playing at full volume in the sitting room and with an empty kitchen Beca got the chance to do something she'd wanted to do since first arriving. She opened the fridge. The white ramekin she was looking for was there in the door. For a moment her heart sank. She had expected it to be heavy, full of brandy butter but it lifted too lightly to be anything but empty. Then she saw another one pushed to the back of the fridge. It was brimful and untouched. Cupping it in one hand she picked up a teaspoon from the draining board and sat down at the table. She peeled away the clingfilm, then began to shave slices off with the edge of the spoon. The butter dissolved marooning gritty almonds and sugar on her tongue while the brandy made her legs and head heavy. She ate some more relishing each mouthful and waited for her friends apologetic faces to appear around the door.

Until that moment she had always thought the sound of five children shouting was enough to drown out everything including a small nuclear explosion. She'd been wrong. The moose mating call coming from her bathroom triggered a stampede that silenced even the children. Beca watched the kitchen door. As the noise grew closer she took the spoon out of her mouth and braced herself. Abi and Claire burst in, shoulder to shoulder, displacing air and making the curtains at the window flutter.

'You're pregnant. Look, look.' They were both holding the tester stick between them like eager children.

Beca took the stick. They were right. Two blue lines.

'Blimey.' She couldn't think what else to say.

Chapter **22**

Beca entered the waiting room of her local health centre. She stood in the middle of the floor looking at the other patients and assessed the nature and level of their contagion. On the whole a sick lot, but sick enough to damage the tiny embryo growing inside her? How could she tell? A safer alternative would be to wait outside on the access ramp and hope she'd be able to lip-read the receptionist calling out her name. It was a toss up between catching a communicable disease or hypothermia. She pulled her scarf over her mouth and nose and took shallow breaths. The weight of responsibility was making her head spin. Her feet were frozen into ice blocks and chilblains were a certainty if she went back outside. Surely a drop in body temperature had to be detrimental to mother and child. She looked around the room again and the fear of throbbing, burning toes won out.

She chose the seat between the magazine table and a woman who looked more sad than ill. Beca looked out of the window at the cold, grey world outside. She'd done three more pregnancy tests since getting back to London the day after Boxing Day. Despite the weighty evidence of near constant nausea she was convinced it was all a mistake; she still needed bona fide medical confirmation to set her mind at ease, even if that meant mingling with ill people.

The doctor was running late which made Beca regret the decision to by-pass the coffee shop on her way there. Instead of breathing in germs, she could be nursing a decaf latte while inhaling other people's cigarette smoke. Compared to the risks she was taking in the bug-infested waiting room, wilfully breathing in a few micrograms of nicotine could hardly be called reckless. She hadn't had a cigarette in the eight days since Claire had confiscated her duty free stash, which was clear evidence of how seriously she was taking this pregnancy. She had however discovered the pleasures of a secondary hit of smoke, whether a coiling trail from a cigarette or a regurgitated cloud from someone's lungs. Anyone's lungs; she wasn't a snob when it came to smoking.

The rain and sleet that had been falling all morning hadn't stopped and as new patients arrived, the overheated waiting room filled with a stronger smell of steaming unwashed winter coats. Beca tilted her head back, breathed through her scarf and shut her eyes. As seemed to happen every time she closed them, her mind set to thinking about what the father of her child was doing that day. A poisonous voice mocked her with the obvious news that he was with his wife, stupid. She had long since forgotten that she'd planned her life as a single mother. What was that saying about not wishing too hard? Beca smiled ruefully. It served her right. She'd got exactly what she'd asked for out of life, only that strident, over-confident woman who'd drawn up the game plan had gone. The irony of her situation wasn't lost on her. It had all seemed so easy, back then. A baby was something else to tick off on the check list of successful living. Motherhood was another thing to excel at. On reflection, Beca wasn't entirely certain she liked the woman she had been.

How her feelings had changed and precisely when was a mystery. She couldn't pinpoint the start of the metamorphosis, nor could she be sure that it had finished. Somewhere between now and her first encounter with Hal, her outlook on life had undergone a drastic about-face. Had it really been Hal who'd brought about the renaissance?

Before she handed him any accolades, it was worth remembering that she had never been so miserable in all her life. Thanks to him she had been in love, unloved and completely lost. True, since she'd found out she was pregnant she'd been in a dizzying state of happiness. In between bouts of sickness she glided on air.

While shaming, she had to admit that there was a perverse side to her that liked the torture. It appealed to her masochistic streak to wonder what Mr and Mrs Ecstatically Happy were doing. She had convinced herself that Sophie was having a baby too. Ever since Hal had told her they were trying, she'd assumed they'd succeeded, and first time. Needless to say, the only signs of Sophie's pregnancy would be an even larger set of breasts than usual; hard and self-supporting. Sophie would have no need for Rich Tea biscuits to stave off nausea. A quick root around her bag wouldn't turn up a toothbrush, toothpaste, or an economy pack of travel tissues to mop up after each incident.

Grumbling to herself about the inequities of life, Beca pulled a tupperware box out of her bag. The effect was an excellent study in air movement and circulation as the sad woman next to her, followed moments later by most of the other patients interrupted their own musings to frown at her. Fish paste sandwiches were not the most sociable of cravings. No doubt Sophie's were altogether more sophisticated, buttered asparagus and carrot juice perhaps. On the bread, Beca was very particular; it had to be thin and very white. The origins of the paste didn't matter. Scraped off the bottom of a trawlerman's boot and thrown in with the bits left over after they'd finished pressing out fish-shaped nuggets was just fine. Mid-mouthful her name was called and to the evident relief of everyone else there, she went into the doctor's consulting room.

The doctor's brow wrinkled as she pointed Beca towards a chair. She sat down herself, folded her hands in her lap and encouraged Beca to speak with an almost imperceptible nod.

'I think I'm pregnant,' Beca said speaking from the corner of her mouth.

'I see. And is that good news?' The doctor asked mildly.

Beca forgot the fishy breath as she gushed forth with enthusiasm. 'Yes. Very. I've been trying for a while. It's really exciting. I'd just about given up on it ever happening.'

The doctor was less enraptured. 'Have you done a test?'

'Four.'

'One wasn't enough?'

Beca shook her head. 'Can you do another one? I can't help feeling it's all a big mistake. I hadn't expected to get pregnant you see, not that time.' Far too much detail, but she wanted to talk.

'Home kits are usually very reliable,' the taciturn doctor said.

'Even so,' Beca started.

'We can find out quick enough. Hop on the couch and I'll examine you.'

A few moments of silent probing and kneading was sufficient to satisfy the doctor. 'You're pregnant, without doubt.'

'It's true then.' A warm comforting glow spread throughout Beca's body.

'Are you taking folic acid?'

Beca confirmed that with a nod.

'Good. I'll write to the local antenatal clinic. They'll make an appointment for you to see the midwife.'

And that was it. Beca shrugged off the doctor's lack of interest. All that mattered was that she was definitely pregnant, and on that basis life couldn't be any better.

Beca was bursting with excitement as she returned to her flat. It was as much as she could do not to laugh out loud, and the broad smile that accompanied her home was returned by passing strangers in the street. She was barely back in her flat two minutes when there was a knock at her door. She went to open it.

'Thought I heard you come in,' Mrs Butler said as she followed her into the flat. 'You're looking very cheerful.'

'I've had some good news, but I've got to keep it secret, just for a few more weeks.'

'Aren't we the mysterious one.' Mrs Butler smiled. 'Might it have something to do with this?' she said handing Beca a package of crudely wrapped brown paper and string. 'That young man of yours left it for you.'

Beca took it and turned it over in her hands. There was evidence of previous use and a liberal smear of yellow paint in one corner as if fingers had been wiped on it. The man in question could only have been Hal, but while 'young man' was debatable, 'hers' was not.

She hesitated before opening it, hoping Mrs Butler would excuse herself, but the old lady was rooted to the spot, as keen as she was to find out what lay within. Beca put the package on the kitchen top and cut the string with scissors. Beneath the crumpled brown paper was another layer, this time of pink tissue. It looked familiar. She'd seen it somewhere before, but couldn't recollect where as she separated the layers. Inside, to her astonishment, was a blue dress; she recognised the label instantly. A note fell to the floor as she shook out the folds but she was too mesmerised by the dress to pick it up.

It was the one she had tried on for Hal. The one that had brought new meaning to the word mortification when she'd made the mistake of thinking he was going to buy it for her. The amusement on his face when he'd explained he wanted her to model it for his wife burnt hot on Beca's cheeks.

Why was he giving it to her now? Perhaps Sophie hadn't liked it, although it had taken long enough for her to make up her mind. Maybe, burgeoning with his progeny, she could no longer fit into it.

Beca sighed.

Mrs Butler looked puzzled. 'Might the note explain?'

Beca tossed aside the dress and picked the piece of paper up from the floor. Faint streaks of paint were smudged along the folds and, as she opened it, Hal's large, flowing handwriting leaped out at her. His words filled the whole page, although the message was brief: 'This was always meant to be for you. Call me, we need to talk.'

Beca read and reread the note again. The words were simple but unfathomable. 'He wants me to call him,' she said showing it to Mrs Butler.

'Did you fall out dear? Is that why he hasn't been around for so long?'

Beca smiled weakly. If only it was that simple.

Mrs Butler took Beca's forlorn silence as her cue. 'Well, I shan't keep you. You've got a phone call to make.' She left with a smile brightening her face.

Beca looked at the telephone number. Perhaps it was for the flat that he and Sophie shared; the hallowed ground to which she had never been allowed to venture. The urge to call was undeniable. Her heart had been pounding inside her chest the minute she'd seen the package. It had reached a dangerous peak of activity when she'd read the note but she knew, strictly speaking, she shouldn't call. She'd promised Abi. This, on reflection, was a small detail. She'd promised herself, which was more important, but even so, what wouldn't she do just to hear his voice again? He hadn't left her thoughts once that morning, or indeed really ever since their last encounter, and now he wanted her to call. It was too much of a coincidence to ignore. Even so, she wouldn't tell him she was pregnant. He didn't need to know. Why? Because his response could never match her expectations. He was never going to be delighted, jump for joy, shake the hands of strangers in the street, was he? He might smile and say he was pleased, or perhaps shrug and ask for the balance of payment; he was, after all, due the remainder of his fee for getting her pregnant. Whatever he did, it wouldn't be enough. So, no, she wasn't going to tell him.

It took a while to rehearse what she was going to say, and how. As she dialled, the voice in her head sounded in control and professional. She listened to the phone ringing, confident that she'd achieved the right tone.

'Hello,' Hal said. Beca's vital organs broke into a freestyle dance routine. She sat down in the nearest chair with a thud. She tried to say hello but the squeak that passed for her voice was inaudible. 'Hello? Who is this?' he repeated.

'Beca.' The word squeezed out of her throat. Jesus, he'd just said hello and she could barely breathe. 'Sorry,' she laughed in a high-octave gasp. 'Got something stuck in my throat.' A passable recovery. 'How are you?'

'Fine,' Hal replied. 'You?'

'Fine.' Her nervous laugh broke. Of course she wasn't bloody alright, she was in the middle of making a complete arse of herself. 'Have a good Christmas?' Keeping it light was important. A bit of chit-chat until she'd learnt to breathe again.

'As far as these things go. You?'

'Fine.' She had to stop using the same word. There was a long silence. 'New Year?' she said to fill the gap.

'Yeah, it was alright. You?'

'Fi- Great.' Again, that pregnant silence. God, she mustn't use that word; not even think it. But supposing it came tumbling out? It might spill from her mouth before she could stop herself. She had to focus. 'You asked me to call. I got the package you left with Mrs Butler.'

'That's right.' He seemed nervous although it was hard to judge, what with him using so few words. Beca heard him take a deep breath. 'Could we meet? There are some things I need to tell you.'

What things? Why was he being so mysterious? Already the possibilities of what he wanted to say were whirring around in her head. Wild, irrational, implausible things. Why couldn't she keep her feet on the ground where he was concerned?

'You could come here,' she said.

'No. I think somewhere public.'

Another pause. Beca waited.

'I get the feeling you might be a little cross with me,' Hal finally added.

More mystery. Who needed it for God's sake? Why couldn't he just tell her over the phone.

'How about a pub near you? This evening?' he continued.

'I'd rather not.' She could explain that the smell of beer made her feel sick. That watching other people indulge their vices, while she couldn't, made her feel sicker. Besides, shoving a pillow up her jumper would be less obvious than her in a pub without a drink. 'There's a small café attached to the organic grocers. We could meet there for tea this afternoon.'

It took a while for Hal to answer. 'If that's what you want.' There was a note of hesitancy in his voice. Why? What was he not saying? What was going on inside his head? If only she could see. She wanted to scream it was so frustrating.

'The dress, by the way. Do you still like it?' he asked.

'Not if it's Sophie's cast-off, I don't.'

'It isn't. I never meant it for her.'

He had been pretty convincing at the time. She'd already searched the playlist for that particular searing memory, but she selected the track and put it on again just to be sure. It was still as she remembered, every cringe-worthy moment, but now a new possibility appeared.

'You bought it for me, but decided to humiliate me instead,' she said.

'Something like that.' Was that humour in his voice?

'I'm confused.'

'Hopefully you won't be. I'll see you later on.'

The phone clicked. Beca listened to the silence and then screamed. He had sounded positive, in fact maybe even keen to see her. She threw the phone down and ran around the flat screaming with excitement. She flapped her hands like an hysterical teenager and jumped up and down on the sofa. Even as she relished the moment of complete idiocy, the perpetual nay-sayer kept reminding her, he was never going to say he loved her. Maybe he wanted to collect the T-shirt he'd left behind. It would need washing if he did. But lost clothing didn't come close to explaining what he'd said, or how he'd said it. She looked at her watch. Three hours to wait before finding out. How was she going to survive that long? She caught her reflection in a window pane. Her hair needed washing, she was a mess. Three hours were never going to be enough to repair the weeks of neglect. The nay-sayer warned her to calm down. The picky voice told her to get the armour-plated barriers ready, but Beca wasn't listening. Even if he did just want his T-shirt back, there was nothing wrong with looking her best.

Three hours later Beca was pacing up and down in front of the little café. She had spotted the father of her child on her first swing by but chickened out at the door. Tears had sprung from nowhere and hovered dangerously. Was she really so pleased to see him that she wanted to cry? Apparently so. She walked off before he saw her and stood berating herself in front of the Post Office a few doors down.

She shook her head violently, then her shoulders, then the rest of her body. It was a curious sight but enough to psyche herself up. She walked back to the café. Her hand was on the door knob when once again she lost her nerve. This time she half-ran, half-skidded to the end of the road, avoiding the worst muddy puddles and pumping herself up like a tennis star brat. She was hot and out of breath when eventually she went in, but at least her eyes had stopped burning.

The sudden burst of cold air made the occupants of the café look up. The place was crowded but strangely quiet with lone customers sipping organic coffee or fresh wheatgrass while they read their books and newspapers. Hal looked at home amongst the Left-leaning, eco-conscious high-brows, although Beca suspected his chunky jumper didn't have a designer label inside it. He stood up when he saw her and as she climbed the steps to the raised platform at the back of the shop, he pulled out a chair for her.

'Thanks for coming,' he said. 'Shall I get you something?'

Beca waved her hand in front of her face in a 'give me a minute' gesture. Hal's eyebrows fused together as she mutely shot out of her seat and went to look at the cakes on display. By the time she'd studied the random arrangement of crushed nuts on the walnut cake she'd pulled herself together enough to return to the fray. She set her banana smoothie and slab of carrot cake on the table and sat down.

'Not your usual kind of hangout,' Hal suggested.

She wasn't about to explain why an organic soya drink was better than a gin and tonic. 'It makes a change.' She met his eyes and his smile rendered her limbs useless.

'You're looking well.' His words dripped like honey. Clearly they couldn't. She was hallucinating, or worse, infatuation had pushed her beyond reason. What did it matter anyway? She was so happy. She'd willingly trade sanity for this. A small but persistent voice at last made her take heed. Her tongue needed to go back in her mouth and the drooling had to stop, now, or she would forever hang her head in shame. It took Amazonian strength to reel herself in from planet Beca.

'You don't look too bad yourself.' She rubbed the back of her neck, curling her hair around her fingers. As the rose-tinted mists finally separated she realised that he was not his usual nonchalant self. He kept casting an anxious eye around the shop, particularly at the customers nearest to them.

'I suppose an obvious question is, why did you buy that dress for me?' The words came out just as she'd rehearsed them. The slight shrug of her shoulders was pleasing too.

'I thought it suited you.' Hal stared into his coffee. He probably hadn't seen the shrug.

'Is that a good enough reason? I'd imagine your wife would be furious if she found out.'

There was a pause as he took the teaspoon next to his mug and started tapping it on the table. The effect was far from calming. He looked at her then back down at the teaspoon. 'I don't have one.'

Beca's eyebrows arched in anticipation and she leant forward urging him to find the key word. 'One?' Still she waited.

'Wife.'

She laughed. 'I thought you said,' she stopped mid-sentence. 'What?'

'Sophie and I aren't married.'

'Oh.' To outward appearances Beca might have seemed phlegmatic to the point of being simple-minded as she crushed cake crumbs with her fork. Inwardly there was a riot going on. Petrol bombs were exploding. Somewhere inside she was screaming and laughing at the same time. It was certainly cheaper than acid. Her nemesis in all her forms had vanished in a great puff of smoke. All the home-movies she'd made of the blissfully happy couple melted in the projector. Mr and Mrs Ecstatically Happy were gone, in their place was utter confusion.

The teaspoon was now keeping perfect time with the jig his left leg was dancing. 'We don't live together either.'

'I see.' Like fuck she did. What was he talking about? She understood the words but the meaning seemed so implausible. He'd turned everything on its head. How could he not be married when he'd spent so much time telling her that he was?

Hal pulled his chair closer and leant across the table towards her. His fingers were inches from hers and she saw the oil paint tattooed into his knuckles. She remembered what those hands had done to her the last time they were together and it made her feel queasy. He'd lied to her. Why had he wanted her to feel so dejected every time they'd had sex? He'd made her so miserable. Was it because he hated her? How would she explain that one to their child when it was older. The carrot cake turned to rock in her stomach. Her top lip was cold with sweat.

'Can I have some water?' she asked.

Hal was quick off his feet and returned with a glass. 'I'm sorry I didn't realise this would be such a shock to you.'

She sipped in silence until her stomach released its fearful hold. Of all the things she'd thought he might have said, not being married wasn't one of them. It had never entered her head. And why should it? She'd believed him; he'd been utterly convincing. She knew she should pretend to laugh it off. It could be of no interest to her whether he was married or not. But it was too late to treat it all as a mild diversion. Her face was easy to read, besides she was too bloody angry to pretend otherwise.

'So, all that bollocks about being so together and in touch as a couple was a lie ?' The sourness was unmistakable.

Hal survived the withering look. 'The sanctimonious speeches playing on your weaknesses? Yes, I'm afraid so. I don't feel very proud.'

'But you should, you were very believable. You certainly had me going.'

Hal frowned at her. 'Don't turn this into a fight before you've given me the chance to explain.'

'What's to explain? You came to my flat, had sex with me, under sufferance, waxed lyrical about your devoted Sophie, ridiculed me for my selfish lifestyle, for what? A joke? Was she in on it as well?' Beca challenged a man who was peering at them above his newspaper.

'Could you calm down long enough for me to explain,' Hal said in an angry whisper.

If he thought she would lower her voice because they were in public he was wrong. 'Go ahead. I'm listening. Why did you lie to me?'

He wasn't going to find the bloody answer in the magazine rack he was looking at. Her teeth ground with impatience.

'Protection,' he eventually said.

'Against what?'

'You.' The fierce look in his eyes made her flinch. His eyes narrowed as he studied her. Perhaps he was weighing up how much to tell her, but Beca didn't reckon it was through concern for her feelings so much as his own. Nothing he could say would make her cry; she was too angry for tears now.

'Am I that dreadful a person?' Her laugh sounded hard.

He didn't answer her. He'd also given up trying to be quiet. 'When you left your business card I knew it wasn't to catch up. You hadn't woken up one morning and decided to find out what happened to me. I had something you wanted and whatever it was, you weren't going to get it.'

'I didn't realise you were still angry with me.'

Hal shrugged her comment off. 'Having a wife was the perfect opt-out. I could just walk away.'

'But you didn't.'

'At first I did. But the temptation was too great. I was curious, I suppose.'

'To think I actually felt sorry for you because you were such a tortured soul. You were playing games with me.'

The customers nearest to them were gripped. One or two pretended to be otherwise occupied but the rest blatantly stared.

'To begin with,' Hal replied.

'Then what?'

Hal gave a helpless shrug. 'I fell in love with you. I tried bloody hard not to, but I couldn't stop myself.'

Beca was struck dumb.

'It's a sad irony, don't you think?' Hal continued. 'I lied because I didn't want to fall in love with you again, but I did anyway. That makes me more of an idiot than even you must have thought possible.'

Beca shrank away from him. 'Is it such a bad thing to be in love with me?'

'That rather depends on you.'

Beca's tears were not of the glycerine sort that roll down the cheeks of film stars. Hers were the face-distorting, shuddering type of tears which took her breath away and made her incapable of further speech. He'd lied to her, humiliated her with his fictitious wife and now he'd said he hated himself for being in love with her. Since when was it decided that her life should be such a mess?

Hal ran both hands through his hair and looked at her. 'This hasn't gone according to plan.' His laugh was unconvincing. 'About now you were supposed to say you love me too.'

Beca blew hard on a napkin. 'Did you really think I would after what you told me?'

'I hoped you'd be adult enough to forgive me.'

'You lie not just once but continuously for six and a half months and I'm supposed to declare undying love?'

'Not exactly.'

'Then what, exactly, because I've got to tell you I'm very confused.'

'Do you think this is easy for me?'

'I don't much care. You can't pretend to have had my feelings uppermost in your mind. After all, you were trying to get me to fall in love, weren't you? For revenge.' She was sounding miss-ish.

'A bit melodramatic, but in essence you're right.'

'Why, for God's sakes. What did I ever do to you?' Beca regretted the words as soon as they'd escaped.

'Do you really need that bit explaining?'

Beca looked at him. 'I get it. You wanted to break my heart.'

'No. Yes, at first perhaps.' Again his fingers combed back his hair. 'You're not the same woman you were eight years ago. The one I wanted to get back at doesn't exist any more. You've changed. Ever since the summer, it's like a new you has emerged.'

Beca looked at him bitterly. 'And I suppose I've got you to thank for my transformation. You must be very pleased with the way you've tamed me.'

'I hadn't thought about it like that.' A wry smile tugged at the corners of his mouth.

His smile was just as Beca had imagined it would be and she didn't like it. She picked up her tall smoothie glass and chucked the contents in his face. 'The problem is your plan backfired. I don't love you. I never did.' With that lie branding itself on her heart she fled the shop. Why had she said that? She didn't mean it. He always had to provoke her into saying the wrong things. She just wanted to say she loved him, instead she was spitting and swearing blind she hated him. How had it gone so disastrously wrong?

Hal was not far behind her. He was seething. 'I know you love me.' He gripped her arms and pulled her towards him. She could feel his fingers hard through the padding of her coat. 'I've seen the way you look at me when you think I'm not watching.'

'You're wrong.' Beca wrenched herself free and turned away.

Hal pulled her round by her shoulder and held her arms again. 'You can't deny it. That last time we made love, don't tell me it meant nothing to you.'

'Just leave me alone.' Beca's voice broke into a sob. 'I thought you were different. How did you learn to lie so well? It was a faultless performance. Even better than my father. You must have spent years practising to come up to his standards.'

Hal slowly loosened his hold of her. 'I'm not a saint, just a man. Perhaps you expect too much.'

'Just honesty. That's all.'

Hal's face softened as he brushed a tear from her cheek with his thumb. She turned and walked away from him past his motorbike parked at the kerb and in a moment of madness she ran towards it. Hal did nothing to stop her as she flipped up the stand bar and with great effort pushed the bike over into the snow. It scraped and crashed to the ground. She would have kicked it as well, but her anger didn't blind her to the fact she'd hurt her foot a damned sight more than his precious motorbike.

She might not be able to dent his ego, but she'd certainly dented his pride. Sadly she felt no satisfaction as she hurried home.

'I hate him,' Beca snivelled. Mrs Butler patted her knee and offered another tissue. When she failed to respond she took one out of the box and wedged it into Beca's hand. Beca blew her nose and Mrs Butler stood by with another. 'He did it on purpose. He made me fall in love with him. And he was only doing it to get his own back.'

'That can't be true. He's such a nice man.'

'Oh, he'd like you to think so. But did you know, while he was sleeping with me, he pretended he had a wife.'

'Usually they pretend not to.'

Beca peered over her tissue. She couldn't help but smile at Mrs Butler's confusion. 'It wasn't like that. We weren't having an affair. He was trying to get me pregnant. I was paying him. His so-called wife knew all about it. In fact she was more than keen, which now doesn't seem at all surprising. Does it?'

'Doesn't it? I'm not sure. There's quite a lot to take in.'

Beca wiped the streaked tears from her blotchy cheeks as she looked at Mrs Butler. 'I'm sorry, I've shocked you haven't I? I hadn't meant to tell you, I knew you wouldn't approve.'

'Did it work? Are you pregnant?'

'Yes,' Beca sobbed. 'I should be so happy, but I'm not. I'm such a fool.'

'Quite possibly. I really don't think knocking over his motorbike like that was a good idea in your condition,' Mrs Butler said with disapproval. As she refilled Beca's tea cup, the roar of an engine drew her attention towards the window. 'It's not broken though.'

'How do you know?'

'He's just pulled up outside on it,' Mrs Butler said with a smile.

Beca choked on her tea. 'Don't let him in. For God's sake, I can't take any more.' The tea spilled into the saucer as she put the cup down hard on the table.

'Given the fact that you're pregnant, I won't. However you must promise to sort things out with him.'

'I promise, just make him go away.'

When Mrs Butler's doorbell rang, Beca's heart leapt. She followed Mrs Butler to her door and then peered through the crack as she crossed the hall and opened the main door. Beca could hear Mrs Butler's light voice interchanging with Hal's gruff, angry tones, but the words were inaudible.

Moments later Beca fled back to the sitting room as Mrs Butler closed the door and returned. 'What did he say?' She stayed pressed against the wall and edged her way towards the window. The last she saw of Hal was his back as he sped off on his bike.

'That young man's face was not the picture of sated revenge, I can assure you,' Mrs Butler said. 'If anything I'd say he was more upset than you. I do hope he doesn't fall off his motorbike, the roads are so treacherous at the moment.'

Beca's eyes widened with horror. 'What have I done. Supposing he kills himself.'

'I don't think that's very likely. He doesn't strike me as the silly kind. You on the other hand.'

Beca looked chastened. 'What would you have done?'

'Good Lord, I can't even begin to imagine. If I'd done half the things you have I'd have been locked away in an asylum. As for getting pregnant, intentionally, out of wedlock; my father would have had me flogged. And rightly so.'

The old lady's lecture wasn't helping to lift Beca's spirits. Mrs Butler relented. 'Do you love him?'

'Yes.'

'And he loves you?'

'So he says, but,'

Mrs Butler cut across her whinge. 'No buts. It's as simple as that. Now why don't you clean yourself up and give him a call.'

Chapter 23

Beca returned to her flat with Mrs Butler's sensible words ringing in her ears. It was as simple as the old lady had said. She loved Hal. Hal loved her. So why didn't this feel like a happy ever after situation? Why was she feeling so shocked and oddly flat? He loved her. She'd dreamt of him saying those words an absurd number of times. She'd drift off into pink, fluffy fairy princess land at night imagining her hero professing his love. And he'd done it; the father of her child had said the magic words. But instead of welcoming him with open arms, she'd assaulted him and done her best to trash his bike. All was not well in the enchanted kingdom.

Beca flopped down on the sofa and stared at her hands. They were no longer trembling as much, but the joints ached as she tried to unball and straighten her fingers. He'd said he loved her. That was a good thing, or at least it might have been if his confession hadn't sounded so begrudging, if the resentment and self-mockery hadn't been quite so evident in his voice. If he'd acted like a man in love then perhaps she wouldn't have thrown her drink all over him. Instead his behaviour had been more akin to some poor sod going off to the gallows. It was hardly surprising that someone as cautious about love as she was had turned and fled. It would take nerves of steel to accept that he'd set out to get his revenge, that he'd lied to her, manipulated her into falling in love with him, and then forgive him.

Of course, if she was Abi, the self-aware, confident-about-relationships sort of woman, then forgiveness would be easy. Her husband had screwed around and she'd given him another chance. Was Beca capable of such magnanimity? All she had to do was pick up the phone. He could be at his flat now. It was just a matter of dialling his number, if she dared.

She grabbed the telephone with a decisive swipe, dialled Hal's number and hummed to drown out the wailing protestations inside her head. Things would work out fine. She was a mature, adult woman. It was within her skill-set to forgive, probably. Her breathing and tuneless drone were amplified by the receiver as the phone rang and kept ringing until an answering machine clicked in. Beca listened to Hal's voice, rapidly composed a message, then hung up instead. Not a sign of cowardice at all, she just needed to reconsider her tactics.

It was only as she tried to glean some hidden meaning or significance from Hal's note that she realised evening had descended. A minute ago it had been tea time, now it was time for supper. She walked around the flat switching on lights and as she passed the CD player she flicked it into life. Billie Holliday's plaintive tones cut into the silence. She was singing about her man not loving her and, as Beca went to the kitchen to make another salmon paste sandwich, Billie's man was treating her awful mean. That made two of them.

Beca sat up at the counter and ate her food. Three tracks later she tried Hal's number again and hung up once more when the answering machine cut in. Doubtless he was off screwing another woman. No, that was Billie's mate, not her own. But Hal wasn't hers, not yet at least and maybe he never would be. The thought made her feel sick.

If only he was there now. Perhaps then she wouldn't need to argue with herself over and over again. At least if he was with her, she could ask him questions instead of tearing herself to pieces trying to figure out the answers on her own. Alone she was left to defend the precious potential of happiness against the demons that told her not to take the chance with him. She turned up the music and punched a few cushions into shape.

Where the hell was he anyway? Perhaps his studio. She found the phone number for One Eyed Jack's on her mobile and called it. As the phone rang and rang it became obvious the record shop was shut; not surprisingly given that it was past 8 o'clock. There was the possibility that the staff couldn't hear the phone above the usual brain-melting volume of the sound system. Even if the shop was shut that didn't mean that Hal wasn't working upstairs. It was a long shot but worth a try, if nothing else a drive might shut her head up for a while. She grabbed her car keys and left, making a mental note to buy him a mobile phone when they got it together.

The pavements were still treacherous but the roads looked as though they'd missed the snow altogether. There was just the occasional mushy sound under the wheels to remind Beca to take it easy. She could tell from fifty yards that Hal's studio was as dark and shut as the record shop below. Even so she kept on hoping until she pulled up in front, then faced with obvious failure she came close to crying. She tried to consider her options rationally. The mental blinkers she'd put on were working to a degree but they weren't enough to repel all the negative images that kept lurching into her consciousness. Looking up at the black windows of his studio she remembered the pair of knickers she'd found in the sofa-bed. Sophie's knickers.

A new light glimmered on the horizon. Sophie worked in a restaurant somewhere in town. Beca wracked her brains. It was French, Frère Jacques, Soeur something. Oncle, no, Tante Elizabeth. That was it. Directory Enquiries came up with the number and one call later she was armed with the address.

She drove and battled hard with the memory of Hal extolling Sophie's physical charms. He'd called Beca scrawny in comparison to his curvaceous wife. She couldn't remember if that was just before or after he'd suffered so terribly in bed. Bastard. No. Negative thoughts weren't allowed. He just happened to have a unique sense of humour. Something to be valued. God, she could do with a cigarette. Beca continued humming to keep the nay-sayers at bay as she headed towards Soho. Tante Elizabeth's was easy to find but it took another half an hour of snailing through narrow streets to confirm there wasn't a single parking space to be had. Reluctantly she headed for an extortionate multi-storey garage and left the car there. Pregnancy had brought with it a heightened sense of smell and Beca retraced her route dodging the endless extractor fans pumping out hot, greasy cooking smells from restaurant kitchens. The stench condensed in her throat leaving it lined with saturated fat. She felt the outline of her Rich Tea packet in her bag which left her marginally reassured. Anyway, it would be the perfect revenge if she threw up all over Sophie.

She hovered just inside the entrance of Tante Elizabeth's and assessed the olfactory dangers. The Maitre d' frowned when she confirmed she was alone and led her to a small table at the back, next to the kitchen doors. Beca followed in his wake feeling every bit the valued customer. His frown grew deeper when she asked to speak to Sophie. He gesticulated and sucked air as if to say he might get around to finding her if he had the time.

Beca chewed a biscuit. She'd reached the middle of her second when she noticed Sophie observing her suspiciously. It was a relief to see her there and not playing nursey to Hal's broken heart

'What is it you want to speak to me about?' Sophie's pose was distinctly combative.

'Hal. I've got a few questions for you.' Beca resisted the temptation to spring from her chair and attack the woman.

'Such as?' Sophie folded her arms tightly across her middle and stood in front of Beca.

'Such as I know you're not married to him. He came to see me today. He told me it was all a big joke. You can imagine I didn't see the funny side.'

'So why come to me?'

'Because I need to find him.'

'To kill him?'

'It's tempting, but no.' Beca took another biscuit out of her bag and breathed through her mouth.

'So?'

'He said some things and now I need to say a few back.'

Beca bit her lip as a knowing smile spread over Sophie's face. 'He told you he loves you, didn't he?'

'Yes.'

'And you had a fight.'

Beca shrugged. 'It's what we do best.'

'You love him?'

'I do as it happens.' There didn't seem any point in lying now.

'But instead of telling him, you got angry, threw something at him and ran off.'

'He told you?' The paranoia antennae was up and scanning.

'No, but I can guess. It's easy to work it out, he talks about you and nothing else.'

Beca smiled at the irony. 'I know the feeling.'

Sophie smiled back and sat down. The whites of her knuckles weren't showing quite so much now. 'It was a good performance, no? You believed I was his wife.'

'Absolutely.'

'And you never guessed he was in love with you.'

'No.'

'You must be blind.'

'I got the feeling he hated me,' Beca confessed.

'He did, but I think he loves you more now. Love can be complicated.' This piece of wisdom was dished out with a hazy-eyed look.

'So I'm finding,' Beca replied. She didn't want to break up the special bonding moment, but she had to know. 'If you're not his wife, what are you?' Her throat tightened as she waited for a reply.

'I'm one of his models. He uses me regularly. He likes my face.'

And saying that was supposed to help in what way?

Sophie continued. 'We're old friends, we've had some good laughs together over the years.'

Jealousy squeezed Beca's insides even tighter and left her mouth dry. What did 'old friends' mean precisely when delivered with a slight lift of the eyebrow? Beca wanted specifics.

'When he asked me to pretend to be married to him, I thought it would be fun. Besides, he told me what a terrible person you are, so I could hardly refuse. Do you want a drink?' she added, getting up.

'Water, please.'

'No wine?'

'I'm off booze for now.'

Sophie's inquisitive eyes lingered on Beca's face for a moment before she went to get the water. 'Here,' she said sitting down again. 'You are not well?'

'I'm fine.'

'You look pale,' Sophie said.

'Lack of sleep.' Did Sophie really think she would let on that she was pregnant? 'You do know where he lives, don't you?'

'Of course, I've been there many times.'

Not what Beca wanted to hear. Her eyes narrowed.

Sophie shook her head and laughed. 'Not like that. I don't sleep with him. You're jealous.' Yes, but why point out the screaming bloody obvious. 'We had sex a few times years ago, but it was nothing. I offered to again when he told me he was falling in love with you. I was trying to divert him, but he wasn't interested.' Her Gallic shrug suggested she wasn't that bothered by the snub.

Sophie took an order pad from her apron and wrote down an address. 'I wasn't trying to spoil things for you, you understand, but he was very certain, at the beginning, that he didn't want to love you again.'

'He just couldn't help himself,' Beca said. The man deserved a bravery medal.

'Exactly.' Sophie hadn't noticed the sarcasm. She hesitated before handing over the address. 'You're not so much the bitch any more?'

'How encouraging'

'You're OK, I think,' Sophie said. It was pleasing to know she felt so. 'I went for an audition last week. The part was for a football club director, you know, tight suit, no bullshit, tough cookie.' Sophie clenched her fists for emphasis. 'Anyhow, I pretended to be you.'

Her charm was overwhelming. 'Did you get the part?'

'No, next time maybe.' She shook off the failure with ease.

'Next time.' Now that she was no longer a rival, Beca could afford a genuine smile. Sophie wasn't so bad after all, even if a bit mad. Pregnancy was making Beca feel expansive so she thanked her with more warmth than was strictly necessary.

Beca handed over the ransom demanded to get her car out of the underground car park, and headed north. The A-Z was spread out on the passenger seat, but she had a pretty good idea where she was going and it had to be a mistake.

Not long after, she pulled into an empty space at the kerb in a gracious, tree-lined residential street. Across the road was the house she was looking for. She compared the address to the one Sophie had written down and then looked up again. It was the right place but surely way out of Hal's league. Her assumption had always been that he would be lucky to find the rent for a flat with a bathroom of its own. The embarrassment creeping over her cheeks was justified; she'd misjudged him, on a large scale. The neat stucco house in Primrose Hill that she was gawping at was sufficient evidence of that. She still had him in the same pigeonhole she'd left him in eight years before. Then he'd been a hard-up, happy-go-lucky artist who thought nothing of under selling his pictures to people he liked. So long as he had beer money he was happy. Genuinely happy. Why had he kept his success a secret?

There was a light on in the front room of the house and she could see one of his paintings hanging above the fireplace. She couldn't tell if there was anybody at home. It ought to be easy enough to find out. She just had to get out of the car, cross the road and ring his doorbell. Simple, although more simple in a few minutes time. She looked at the distance to his house and guessed at the number of paces; not an insurmountable length to cover.

A bit of stage fright was to be expected; she'd never said she loved someone before in her life, unless a hamster counted. She tried to bolster her fragile confidence. It would be easy, after all, she wasn't doing this alone. Wherever she went she had company, albeit in the form of a shrimp-like foetus. She'd give Hal a good snog, then stumble upstairs for some wild, unbridled sex. This time he would take his horsehair shirt off and enjoy himself. It would be then that she could express mild consternation at his underhand behaviour, graciously forgive him, get hot and passionate again, then break the news that he was going to be a father. No problem.

Supposing he didn't see things her way? What if her outburst in the organic café was the *nil plus ultra* of their relationship?

While scrubbing the banana smoothie off his jumper he might have decided she was too volatile to make a good mate. What would she do if he shut the door in her face? Beca's heart broke into a gallop.

She got out of her car and strode across the road to the house. Fear and excitement propelled her up the front steps. She rang the doorbell and hammered away with the knocker. The sound resonated around the house but drew no one to the door. She paced on the porch as she waited, gearing herself up to pour out her heart and take the consequences. She wouldn't run away, she was going to be mature about the whole business. It didn't matter what he'd done, she loved him and was going to tell him so.

The chance didn't present itself for the door stayed well and truly shut. She rang the doorbell again out of frustration rather than any real hope. Again silence.

Tears burned her eyes as she gave up and trudged down the steps. Only then did she realise his motorbike wasn't there. Her stupidity merited the small laugh that escaped her. It should have been the first thing to look for. No bike, no Hal. Of course he wasn't at home.

Beca returned to the car and put the key in the ignition, then hesitated. Perhaps she should wait. He could be back at any moment and she would much rather get what she had to say over and done with before she talked herself out of it. She didn't want a whole night to dwell. It had been a hard fought struggle to get this far already. So she waited. The car inside was as cold as the world beyond. As Beca stared blankly at the windscreen, the spots of melted snow below the wipers turned white and froze. It was past midnight by her watch, although the internal mechanism might have frozen and stopped functioning hours back. Her biscuit supply was dwindling, her stomach was groaning for something more substantial and the foetus needed feeding. Cold and hunger decided the matter. It was time to go home.

DVD cases and discs lay strewn across the floor in front of Beca's vast wide-screen television. On the screen Meg Ryan and Tom Hanks were getting syrupy but Beca was paying them little attention. Night-time had given way to dawn although it was still dark. A single anglepoise lamp lit the pad of paper in Beca's lap. The soft padded leather of the Eames chair cushioned her like a womb and her feet, dwarfed in thick wool socks, were splayed out on the foot stool. A layer of scrunched up white paper balls covered the rug in the immediate area. Another joined its comrades and Beca began scrawling on a fresh sheet. A wildly drawn flowchart emerged from her pen. Two different lines swirled off in opposite directions and at the ends she wrote: Stay single and bring up baby; Get together with Hal and bring up baby.

She reached down into the biscuit tin on the floor next to her chair and extracted a fig roll. Turning her nose up at it, she swapped it for a digestive and bit into it as she stared at her creation. Then she gouged the pen into the paper, drawing thick circles around and around the latter option until the nib snapped. She threw the pen on the floor. All night she'd kept coming back to the same answer: Hal was her happy ever after. Why did that news keep sending her off into a panic? And why couldn't she resolve to just let herself be happy? It was those teeth-sucking nags again telling her to be cautious, to pull up the drawbridge and stay clear of commitment and love. Best not to think about it. She pointed the remote control at the TV and turned up the volume. Brainwashing was the answer. *Sleepless in Seattle* was on its third viewing, it being the only unapologetically saccharine film she'd found in her collection, but she was becoming inured to the effect. Anyway, it was stupid thinking a film could do what it would take years of therapy to achieve. She focussed on the screen. Being in a relationship was a good thing. Everyone loved a person who was in love. People who didn't love were sad.

Beca tore the sheet from the pad, screwed it up and hurled it away from her. Hal was the right man for her. Despite the major deception, the calculated lies, he was, what? What exactly was he? The repeating loop of thoughts in her head was getting tighter and more incoherent. Her eyes strained to focus on the DVD player. Its digital clock told her it was 6:30 in the morning. Her eyelids felt heavy, her brain had burnt out. She rested back and the chair pivoted backwards taking her to a cocooned recumbent position. Her lips parted and closed as though fitfully seeking out a thumb and then she was asleep.

The telephone broke in on Beca's peace jerking her awake and setting her heart off on a sprint. She listened to the shrill ringing, frozen for a moment before she lurched towards the phone and answered it.

'Hello?' She looked at the kitchen sink measuring the distance between her and the nearest thing to be sick in.

'Beca, it's me. We need to talk.' Abi sounded serious.

Beca slumped back down in her chair. For one glorious moment she'd thought it was Hal. 'What time is it?' she asked reaching down for the biscuit tin and pulling out a Rich Tea.

'After 11 o'clock. I'd have called sooner but I couldn't off-load the kids.

The dry biscuit stuck in a thick layer to Beca's tongue. Her stomach heaved and turned over. 'Oh God, hold on a minute.' She threw the phone down and ran to the sink to be sick. Clammy with cold sweat she waited for a second wave but her stomach settled back down. She took some deep breaths and splashed cold water over her face before returning to the phone.

'Bad?' Abi asked.

'Sick as a dog.'

'Have you tried the ginger tea?' Abi asked.

'Made me want to throw up.'

'Never mind. It won't last. You've been a busy girl, haven't you?'

'How do you mean?' Beca asked.

'Hal came to see me last night.'

'You? Why?'

'Because he was hoping I could shed some light on how your mind works. He's desperate to make things up with you.'

'Did he tell you what a pathological liar he is?'

'No. But he did admit Sophie wasn't his wife.'

'Did he mention his twisted scheme to get me to fall in love with him by being a complete bastard?' Beca held the phone to her ear with her shoulder as she picked up the balls of paper from the floor and threw them into the bin. She didn't know if her staccato movements came from sleep deprivation or anger.

'It's ironic that it worked.'

'You're laughing.' Indignation halted Beca in her tracks.

'Come off it. It's hilarious. How many men have you been out with and dumped because they were so nice, and dull?'

'Too many,' Beca admitted begrudgingly.

'But the cavalier one has you falling head over heels. I think he's quite clever.'

'Then you've misjudged him.'

'His tactic worked at least.'

'But it didn't. Sure, I did fall in love with him, but he's fallen in love with me too and that was never part of the plan. He wasn't doing it to be nice. He wanted to make me as miserable as possible and then dump me.'

'In fairness to him, that was at the beginning of your crazy plan. From what he told me he's been trying to tell you the truth for months, except you never listen.'

'And you believed him?' Her voice was building into a screech. She picked a copy of *Time Out* off the floor and flicked through it to give her jittery fingers something to do.

'Why not?'

'You're laughing.'

'Beca this is the best thing that's ever happened to you. Why can't you see it? You love each other. Be happy.'

'You're too trusting.' Beca's eyes homed in on the travel section and she started scanning through the ads.

'I told him, by the way.'

'What?' Kerala? The Maldives? Madagascar?

'That you're pregnant.'

'Please be joking.'

'Sorry. The man loves you. Why shouldn't he know?'

'What did he say? Was he pleased?'

'For God's sake, ask him yourself.'

'Maybe I will.' Her eyes dropped back to the page. Seychelles? Sri Lanka?

'What are you up to?' Abi's voice was heavy with suspicion.

'Nothing.' Beca quickly flicked on past the travel section as though Abi was watching her.

'You're running away again.'

'I am not.'

'Don't lie'

Perhaps she had overdone the incredulity. 'You want the truth? OK. I'm scared. I've never done this love business before. I'm nearly 37 and I've never said "I love you", not even in pretence.

'You know Hal loves you.'

'Yes, but is that enough?'

'What more do you want for goodness sake?'

'Cast-iron guarantees. Water-tight, unbreakable, certified promises that everything will work out alright.'

'Life's not like that. Look at me and Tom.

'But you're working it out. Ma and Pa Walton are back together again.'

Abi laughed. 'You've got as good a chance as anybody to make it work.'

'Maybe, but I'm not sure.' Her voice trailed off as her eyes scanned the film listings. She stopped at the Prince of Wales.

There was an all-day screening of 1940s 'women's films', including her all-time favourite.

'Don't you think it's time to stop using your parents' disaster of a marriage as an excuse to hide from life?' Abi asked tersely.

'I'm not. But it is the reason why I make a hopeless double act.'

'How do you know that if you've never even tried?'

'Gut instinct.'

Abi sighed with defeat. 'What are you going to do?'

'Think about it.'

'You haven't done enough of that already?'

Beca did up the top button of her coat and wrapped a scarf around her neck. With her bag replenished with anti-vomit supplies she pulled the door closed behind her and went downstairs. She felt dejected and lonely after Abi's barrage and before leaving the house she knocked for Mrs Butler. A heavy, bittersweet smell accompanied the old lady as she answered the door.

'How are you, dear?' Mrs Butler asked. 'You're looking tired. Did you call that man of yours?'

'I tried, but he wasn't in. Do you want to come to the cinema with me. *Brief Encounter* is on at the Prince of Wales.' There was a lift in Beca's voice as she tried to tempt her neighbour out with her.

'That would be lovely, but I'm making marmalade. I ought to be stirring it now.'

'I shouldn't keep you then.'

'Why don't you come in for a cup of tea? You look like you could do with some cheering up.'

Beca smiled. 'That's kind of you, but I'd better get going.'

She caught a taxi at the end of the road and stared out of the window counting the number of couples she could see with babies. There weren't that many as it turned out; just the occasional cluster of mothers heading to Kensington Gardens together. No doubt the fathers would be rushing home after work for a bedtime story and a kiss goodnight. It wasn't hard to imagine Hal doing the same thing. Perhaps he'd want to be a stay-at-home dad, which would be fine by her. There was so much to talk about, if they ever got the chance.

The taxi pulled up in front of the cinema and she realised with a wry smile that she hadn't been back there since the night she'd gone in search of Hal. Then she had ended up confirming what every right-minded person thought of brash idiots with more money than sense. It seemed like such a long time ago now.

With her collar turned up she bought a ticket and glided past the imperious manager who was hovering by the entrance. Not a glimmer of recognition passed over his face. She stopped at the snack counter and assessed her options. The thought of a mechanically-retrieved hot dog smothered in luminous yellow mustard set her taste buds working. She ordered one along with a drink, and an armful of chocolate. Thus fortified she headed for the auditorium; her spirits lifting with each step she took.

The cinema was surprisingly full for an afternoon's screening of old black and white films. Then again the impenetrable greyness outside was enough to drive anybody off the streets. Beca stood at the top of the long shallow steps that divided the seats into two sections and led down the auditorium to the front row. An involuntary shudder accompanied the flashback of falling flat on her face. Echoes of the audience's applause bounced around in her head as she chose a seat half way in from the aisle.

Once settled in she studied her surroundings. Three rows forward from her were two bicycle couriers, their lycra clad, burgeoning legs dangling over the seats in front of them. Surely in the wrong cinema, or perhaps there at the wrong time; the Russ Meyer double bill wasn't on until much later. One of the couriers had a particularly bad cold. Clearly there was no room under the lycra to squeeze a hanky because the man emptied his nasal passages onto the floor by blocking one nostril with a finger and then blowing hard out of the other. His companion seemed unbothered by this primitive approach but the Sumo-sized man who had sat down behind Beca grumbled loudly and cracked his knuckles.

The hairs on the back of Beca's neck had alerted her to this new arrival. She could sense him without looking and her trouble radar was working at full tilt. Without craning around in an obvious manner she could just make out his huge pig-carcass forearms wrapped around a vast stomach and chest. Odd people went to the cinema during the day as she'd discovered over the years, and what with Sumo man behind her and the courier boys in front she began to wonder if she was the one in for a surprise once the curtains went back.

At last the house lights dimmed and a wave of exaggerated shushing from a group of pensioners brought silence as the film cranked up to speed in the projector. Beca settled back with what was left of her hot dog and watched *Mrs Miniver.*

The last scene in the film of the mourning congregation looking up through the bomb-shattered roof of their church as Spitfires flew past overhead made Beca's heart swell. As the end credits rolled, the house lights came up again and the magic faded leaving her with a smile on her face and the urge for another hot dog. She made her way to the foyer and was back in her seat with fresh supplies when the impromptu intermission entertainment arrived, heralded by a wailing child. Beca turned and gawped as a procession of mothers paraded down the aisle to the front row. There were five of them, each with a child, and all of them oblivious to the code of cinema-going which required that they talk quietly.

'Oh bugger. Lucien's done a boo-boo, again,' one of the mothers announced having stuck her nose in her baby's bottom. Sympathetic clucks came from her friends. 'I'll just have to change him here. Sod's law the film will start if I take him off to the loo.'

Beca hung on her every word and watched as the woman spread out a mat in front of her seat and stripped off her child. The courier boys' revulsion was audible. The mother with the wailing child showed no hesitation as she rummaged under layers of baggy clothes, produced a large, solid breast and stuck her child on it. Peace was restored. Briefly.

'That's disgusting,' the snotty courier said. A frisson of anger swept the front row.

'Not as disgusting as you,' someone said. God, it was her. Beca resisted the urge to hide under her seat.

The courier boys and the mothers turned to stare at her.

'Lesbo,' snotty's friend jeered.

Was that the best he could do? She gave a contemptuous grunt.

'Very clever,' the breastfeeding mother said.

'Remarkably articulate. Should we ask which school?' another asked.

Beca sealed her new friendship with a cheery smile. She felt tempted to tell them she was pregnant too, but the house lights dimmed and Rachmaninov's score exploded over the sound system to herald the beginning of *Brief Encounter* which put paid to that idea.

Beca was already sniffing by the time Trevor Howard had that bit of grit out of Celia Johnson's eye. Such a tragic love story. No high drama, just austerity clothes, stiff upper lips and being terribly brave. When Celia and Trevor were having a paltry lamb chop in the Lyons tea house, Beca was in such a tear-soaked, chocolate-saturated delirium that at first she didn't notice the commotion that had broken out in the auditorium.

She snapped back into the real world to hear snotty courier shout, 'What's your problem, mate,' in a very un-matey tone.

A wave of shushes descended from the pensioners.

'Beca.' The voice was loud and insistent.

'Oi, mate. I thought I told you to shut it.'

'Drop dead arsehole.' God, it was Hal and not in an especially good mood by the sound of it. An uncontrollable giggle blurted out of Beca's mouth. She sank down into her seat fizzing with excitement.

'Beca, I know you're here.'

It was Hal again. Beca hunkered down further in her seat. She was in raptures. He'd come searching for her which had to be the most romantic thing anybody had ever done. She wanted him to come and claim her, so why was she hiding? Her mental processing had clearly packed in because the logical thing to do would be to sit up and wave at him. But that would be too easy. She wanted to be found, not to throw herself in his way. Excitement bubbled up as she wedged some more chocolates in her mouth and watched him being assertive.

'I'm looking for a woman called Beca. Has anyone here seen her?' He was standing in front of the screen unconcerned by the fact that he was blocking the screen. Beca bit her lips together but another bubble escaped from her mouth. 'She's tall, about so high,' he said holding his hand out flat near his shoulder.

'Look, sonny, we're here to watch the film.' Beca craned to her right to see one of the pensioners looking indignantly at Hal.

The lady next to him slapped him on his knee and asked Hal, 'Is she beautiful?'

'Very. At least I think so,' he replied.

So he thought she was good looking. He'd kept that news quiet. Beca cosied up with her Malteser box and watched the performance.

'Why's she hiding from you?' the breastfeeding mother asked.

'Denial,' Hal replied. Such twaddle.

'Of what?' another mother wanted to know. Good question. Exactly what Beca would have asked if her bottom wasn't practically on the floor.

'Love.'

Oh that. Beca rammed another Malteser in her mouth while a ripple of gushing sentiment made its way back from the front row.

'Excuse me.' Sumo man's voice was surprisingly high pitched. 'Sorry, could be wrong. But is that who you're looking for?'

Beca turned and looked up to see him pointing a sausage-sized finger down at her. Her eyes narrowed to give him the concentrated version of her ire. And then the embarrassment of her situation was all too apparent. In a few moments she was looking at Hal's feet ankle-deep in hotdog boxes and cups.

'Found it,' she said holding up a Malteser that she was pretending to have dropped on the floor. Then, unsure how to proceed with the ruse, she ate it. The fact that Hal was laughing at her made her suspect her plan to save face had backfired. She scrambled to her feet with some dignity, sat down in her seat and ate some more.

Hal sat down next to her and stared at the screen. 'Thought you'd be here,' he said. From the corner of her eye she could see his profile. He was still smiling.

'Clever you.' Beca struggled to get the words out. It was difficult to speak, grin and keep all the chocolate in at the same time.

'I just wanted a chat before you run away.'

Beca's words slurred around a cheek full of Maltesers. 'As if I'd do something as stupid as that.'

'Your best friend thinks you might.'

'So she called you to tell you so?'

'Yes.'

'But she didn't know I was here.'

'No, but Mrs Butler did, and,'

'She phoned to tell you,' Beca finished for him.

'Exactly.' Hal settled back comfortably in his seat. 'I had a pretty good idea you'd be here anyway, although I've never understood why you like this film so much.'

'It's about love, stupid. Hopeless, frustrated love.'

'And you're a bit of an expert on that.'

Touché. Beca stared resolutely at the screen and ignored the large tear that had rolled down her cheek. It splashed into the Malteser box that was now resting on her chest not many inches from her chin. Hal slumped down so that their heads were level. He leant over and helped himself to a chocolate.

'So, Beca,' he said. 'It seems to me your choices are these.' He counted them off on his fingers. 'One. You can spend the rest of your life wondering what might have happened if you weren't so chicken. Two. You can have a go at being a grown-up and see what comes of it. Or three,' he hesitated. 'No, I can't think of a number three.'

'What's he saying?' Lucien's mother shouted from the front.

Snotty courier shrugged. 'Dunno.'

'He's just told her to make her mind up,' Sumo man said.

'What did she say to that?' one of the pensioners asked.

'Nothing. Just keeps sniffing a lot.'

'Do you mind,' Beca turned and screeched at the man. He held his arms up and sat back in his seat.

Hal did not appear to be sharing her chagrin, by the look of things he was enjoying himself too much. 'I love you, despite your cock-eyed behaviour and I think life will be just about as good as it can get if we're together,' he said.

'You lied to me.' Beca sniffed again.

'Forget all that. You love me.'

'No I don't.'

'Now who's lying?'

Sumo man began his report.

'Would you shut up,' Beca said with added emphasis in case she'd been too subtle before.

'Beca, we were made for each other. You're an idiot if you can't see that.'

'You gave the impression you felt that way about Sophie.'

Hal laughed at her. 'You're jealous.'

'Of course I was bloody jealous, you idiot. I –,' she stumbled, 'I love you.' There. She'd done it. She waited for spontaneous combustion to engulf her. Nothing happened except a warm, happy tingling feeling spread out from a small knot in her stomach. As it reached her toes a hallelujah chorus began to sing and bells started ringing somewhere. The flock of doves didn't materialise nor the fireworks but she was pretty damned pleased with herself nonetheless. She glanced at Hal and took it from the shit-eating grin on his face that he was happy too.

'If it's a boy, I thought we could call it Steve. After Steve McQueen,' he said.

'Never. By the way, I might not have mentioned this before, but I love you.'

'I know you do. How about Clint?'

'Now you're being stupid.'

Somehow Hal's arm found its way around her shoulder. It felt heavy and comforting and Beca nestled towards him.

'How about Otis?' Beca suggested.

'Poor kid. Anyway, it's going to be a girl.'

'Is that right? Have I told you that I love you?'

'You have. Britney's got a certain ring to it.'

'Only to the insane. If it's a girl she'll be called Saskia.'

'Saskia Carson. It has a nice ring to it,' Hal said.

'Saskia Morley, in fact.'

'Doesn't sound as good. You'll have to marry me.'

'Is that a proposal?' Beca squeaked with delight.

'I don't know. Sounded like one didn't it. I'll try again.' Hal slid off the seat and got onto one knee. Beca laughed with glee and tried to pull him up. He was far too heavy for her and she fell back in her seat.

Hal gave up on the gallantry and sat down. He gently took Beca's face between his hands. 'Look, I'm not promising a Technicolor happy ever after, but I know you inside out. Marry me. There's nothing to be frightened about.'

'Promise?'

'Promise.' Hal kissed her. It was the best, deepest, hardest snog she'd ever had.

When they broke for air, Beca noticed the big screen lovers had parted ways and Celia was standing on the station platform contemplating suicide. She felt sorry for her, but shrugged it off; it was only a film. She offered Hal one of her Maltesers, instead he took the whole box at which she protested loudly.

'You shouldn't be eating these,' he told her.

'Why not?' She snatched a handful and rammed them belligerently in her mouth.

'The caffeine content in chocolate is bad for the baby.'

'That was a detail I was prepared to overlook.' She tried grabbing the box back from him without success.

'Here,' he said dipping a hand into his coat pocket. 'Drink this.'

Beca looked at the pint of milk, then at him and laughed. For the first time ever she did as she was told. Not because she had to, but because she couldn't think of anything nicer, and together they watched the rest of the film.